Fancies and Goodnights

John Collier

Fancies and Goodnights

With an Introduction by Fred Hoyle

TIME Reading Program Special Edition

Time-Life Books Inc., Alexandria, Virginia

Time-Life Books Inc.
is a wholly owned subsidiary of
TIME INCORPORATED

TIME Reading Program: *Editor,* Max Gissen

For information about any Time-Life book, please write:
Reader Information, Time-Life Books,
541 North Fairbanks Court, Chicago, Illinois 60611.

for Gus Lobrano

Contents

Editors' Preface

It is no mere coincidence that John Collier is a practiced poet as well as an eminently successful writer of short stories, for the one draws upon the same fountain of talent that feeds the other. In his hands the poem and the short story both are distilled through fine-screen filters of language and experience until, in the end, each has become a lean, limber gem of impressionism that communicates much more than the sum of its words.

That is not to say that Collier's stories are squeezed clean of vital juices in the distillation process. He is not one of those slice-of-life writers, whose stories are often so bereft of beginning and end that they leave the reader teetering and unfulfilled. On the contrary, in form if not in content, Collier follows the old-fashioned, aged-in-the-wood method in which development follows the natural line of storytelling. There is no mistaking the poet's polished prose—as deft, as precise as any found in the 20th Century.

But Collier's bow to tradition ends with form. He is a

man to whom the bizarre, the weird and the surrealistic
are as tangible—and as tasty—as a chocolate soda. In the
genealogy of short-story masters, he is a direct descendant
of Edgar Allan Poe, O. Henry and Saki, but he has marked
out a field that in some respects stretches far beyond any
one of them.

Collier inhabits two worlds. Only one of them is decorated
with the familiar trappings; here he roams among the lives
of ordinary people, telling ordinary tales that spin out
quietly until—as in "De Mortuis" or "Back for Christmas"
—he suddenly and surprisingly reverses gear and provides
a switch ending that might have been written by O. Henry.

It is when he is in the other world, however, when he
deals in jinns and angels, big and little devils, potions and
witches, that Collier is at his most distinctive. Most of his
predecessors in the art of the short story, and many of his
contemporaries, remain practitioners of the "once-upon-a-
time" method. But Collier's tour de force is the "what
if . . .?" kind of story, in which he fashions a recognizable
setting and superimposes on it a wildly unrecognizable
notion.

What if, for example, a hothouse orchid suddenly developed a bud that looked curiously like the face of Cousin
Jane's missing cat? That is the "what if" that also strikes
Mr. Mannering in the story "Green Thoughts"; it strikes
him even more forcefully in view of the fact that Cousin
Jane herself has mysteriously disappeared. As Mr. Mannering stares in stupefaction at another bud that has a
strangely familiar look, he makes to draw his robe about
him; but, alas, it is too late:

> He could not move. The new lusty foliage had closed in
> unperceived; the too lightly dismissed tendrils were every-
> where upon him; he gave a few weak cries and sank to the
> ground, and there, as the Mr. Mannering of ordinary life,
> he passes out of this story.

The story, of course, does not end there, for John Collier is not simply a teller of horror tales; he has just begun to warm up to his chilling, sardonic best. In him, one critic has written, may be found "a cruelty, a savagery of humor and cold-brained irony. . . . Yet beneath this glacial consideration of the human situation, there lies very often a shy and genuine tenderness which, if it ever got good hold of one of Mr. Collier's stories, could quite demoralize it. But," the critic adds, "Mr. Collier's art lies in his knowledge of this peril, and his stories are never destroyed by tenderness."

Far from it. There is, however, another quality that occasionally is allowed free rein. Though he never moralizes while he entertains, Collier often wraps his hallucinations within a highly respectable point of view. In many of his most successful stories, it is a richly deserved disaster that befalls the selfish. Greed, Collier tells us, is not so simply an evil as it is a folly, and fate will deal with it according to the quality, as well as the measure, of man's stupidity.

That is why Collier's readers may sense something wonderfully correct, something eminently fair about the inevitability of destiny in his stories. For example, what better end could be devised for the jaded hedonist of "Bottle Party," or for his similarly insatiable counterpart in "The Lady on the Grey"? In "Thus I Refute Beelzy," it is not greed but an all-too-familiar pompousness that is the target, but what boy would argue that Small Simon's father did not deserve his picturesque denouement? When we impose our own unreasoned conditions upon the natural order of things, Collier tells us (scarcely hiding a whimsical wink), we ignite the fires of our own personal hell.

Though he finds hellfire dancing in the light of his oddly cut prism, Collier does not always view it with geniality. One of the most successful stories in this collection, in fact, is anything but genial. "Evening Primrose" leads us (we do not go willingly) into the society of a haunted people who come to life in the city's big department stores after the doors have been locked for the night. These are not your ordinary bed-sheet ghosts; they are, rather, half-dead humans, estranged from the real world, who find wraith-like solace amid the darkened counters. Their rituals are reminiscent of the initiation ceremonies of some of our popular service organizations, but they are considerably more fascinating. And these night people have an ingenious method for protecting the sanctity of their civilization, as the narrator of the story discovers. No more of this story should be divulged, but it is worth noting perhaps that readers of "Evening Primrose" have been observed at various large emporiums staring uneasily at certain mannequins.

John Collier himself describes the style of these stories as "a continuing blunder toward an arbitrary, surrealist way of expressing things." The way, of course, has not really been blundering, though it has meandered some-what. Collier was born in London in 1901, and received his only formal education at the hands of a novelist uncle, Vincent Collier. When, at the age of 18 or 19, Collier was asked by his father what he had chosen as a vocation, the young man simply replied, "I want to be a poet." It may be that at this point John Collier learned the uses of the surprise ending. For his father, instead of making the great scene demanded by tradition, merely allotted the boy two pounds a week and left him alone. Collier spent the next 10 years living on that stipend plus what he could pick up by writing book reviews and acting as a cultural corre-spondent for a Japanese newspaper.

All the while, Collier was also working on his poetry, according to plan—and on short stories as well. But it was not until he published a novel, *His Monkey Wife*, in 1930, that his career began to take shape. The novel was not very remarkable except that it dealt, as the title suggests, with the kind of offbeat fantasy that has since become Collier's specialty, but it enjoyed a certain small popularity and critical approval that helped to sell his short stories. Further help came with invitations to write screenplays. In succeeding years, Collier traveled between England, France and Hollywood, meanwhile creating the best of his short stories (and, as it happens, one of the most memorable screenplays ever to come out of Hollywood, *I Am a Camera*). He still works at screenwriting, for it provides a dimension for his themes that the short story no longer satisfies.

Sir Osbert Sitwell has said of Collier (in an introduction to a reprint of *His Monkey Wife)* that he "welds the strongest force with the strangest subtlety. . . . The author is also a poet . . . and thus poetry lends to his prose a quality which enables whole sentences, their words invested with an indefinable but radiant glow, to linger on in corners of the mind long after the last page is finished. . . . The lethal gentleness of Mr. Collier's pen grows out of real strength and is a delight that only genius can afford us—a delight occurring, where a living author is concerned, alas! but once or twice in a lifetime."

Sitwell added that it is Collier's special genius that makes his bizarre material "sound not only probable but real." Other writers have succeeded in entertaining us; Collier, holding that peculiar prism up to our eyes, has produced unsuspected images within ourselves that we might feel were best left undiscovered. But in the end, having savored his stories, and talked it over with ourselves, we are the gladder for it.

—THE EDITORS

ℝℙ Introduction

What makes a good writer? A readable book? Some years ago John Collier, then a young poet, offered his own prescription. "The interbreeding of satirical consciousness and the dumb and angry instinct," he wrote, "is as powerful a source of poetic feeling today as ever it was." As for himself, he felt that in his book of poems, *Gemini*, he had not been able to make his two selves— he described them as the "archaic, uncouth, and even barbarous" Orson and the "hysterically self-conscious dandy" Valentine—speak with one voice.

He was a disciple of James Joyce, and it was Joyce who led him to a solution. "On going for my next lesson to *Ulysses*, that city of modern prose," he wrote, "I was struck by the great number of magnificent passages in which words are used as they are used in poetry, and in which the emotion which is originally aesthetic, and the emotion which has its origin in intellect, are fused in higher proportions of extreme forms than I had believed was possible." So poet John Collier became a teller of tales.

He had had an unusual preparation for this profession. He was born in 1901 into a secure world. Privately educated, he never attended the university. This is not the disaster that status seekers of today might count it. The main value of education is to be taught to think—to be driven, coaxed and stimulated into absorbing and assessing ideas. I myself am very much opposed to the system of stuffing supine young people with facts which they can disgorge at examination time without making any effort in the meantime to digest them. I feel very strongly that a person should be aware of what he knows, and should use what knowledge he has acquired at every stage of his development in life.

John Collier was taught to think for himself. He read widely, kept his eyes open, became familiar with the world of literature and the world of ideas. This shows in his work. He absorbed and evaluated the writings of others and subjected what he had learned, along with his own experiences and observations, to the discipline of poetic form in his projection into prose of his own thoughts and beliefs.

The results are evident in *Fancies and Goodnights*. Each short story in this collection holds the eyes and ears to the end. In each case, against the sharply drawn setting, the freshly evoked atmosphere, his puppets gyrate, effortlessly controlled, while he spins round them his subtle, intricate satires and lights the scene with vivid shafts of wit.

Subtlety is a rarity today. Today we have the obvious, baldly stated in print, or in sound on the radio, or in pictures on TV, or neon-lighted in advertising. We are conditioned to economy. Long, rounded, flowing passages are not welcomed by our dime-novel minds. We have time only for headlines. Yet reading John Collier now, one is amazed by the freshness and contemporary quality of his work. In *Fancies and Goodnights* the subtlety is succinct and the pace is to our taste. We swallow the obvious and familiar along with the wit, and are left to digest the satire. We are also conditioned to fantasy and scientific horror by the ceaseless flow that has poured from pens of postwar writers. Yet many of Collier's more fantastic stories produce a world so startling and weird that they imprint on the mind a memorable impression, as do the stories of Edgar Allan Poe.

Collier's savage satire puts him alongside Swift, his gentle satire alongside the sophisticated irony of Saki. And occasionally there is a mordant waft of haunting humor that calls to mind the two-sided coin of the '20s and '30s. That was an era of grays and golds, of rags and riches, of Noel Coward and John Steinbeck, of the Charleston, champagne, short skirts and breadlines—and yet it was a secure world, familiar, unchanging, the unquestioned center of the universe. Macabre stories in that time could still be polished literary essays.

The devil and his kin provide Collier with one entire sphere of his world of fantasy. He builds for himself and his readers a complex looking-glass world of make-believe when, with a diabolical chuckle, he describes a possible realm called "Hell." Intoxicated by the devil, he sketches in his writings a whimsical fiend whose machinations usually fail dismally. There is no real force of evil veiled behind the humorous excursions into Hell; good flourishes (particularly in the shape of well-rounded young women).

If the stories of the devil are whimsical and warmhearted, those dealing with man are often tales of malice and meanness. In such stories as "Green Thoughts" and "The Steel Cat," man is shown up for his savagery and ugly narrow-mindedness. Yet, to Collier, mankind is neither universally evil nor good but has a many-sided, hence more interesting, personality. Beauty may or may not be a cloak for evil but he usually maintains that true goodness rises above malevolence.

John Collier knows the countryside, the deep country where a man must still live an essentially earth-rooted existence. There is a completeness, a full-rounded wholesomeness about his rural scenes, which have the nostalgic tang of peat smoke and the seductive languor of warm hay.

Collier's exposure of familiar types in strange situations or backgrounds, or of eerie creatures in our normal world, shows up incongruities in relationships, imperfections, inconsistencies. Speculation is aroused, as refreshing as a shower after a ball game, and the iced Martini comes with the caustic wit. Do we in fact possess an inner spirit level that holds most of us in balance between overindulgence that leads to degradation and despair on the one hand, and self-denial that slides into smugness on the other? What gives us our sense of proportion? Is it a sense of purpose in life that makes for stability, or is it conditioning over the ages for survival? How much of our behavior pattern is inherited over the few centuries of man as a writing animal and how much is deeply embedded in our subconscious? Are the peak achievements of a man —or a decade, or an age—chance fluctuations, or is there a deeper reason?

Collier's stories point up a modern dilemma. The old tortoise of mankind seems to lumber laboriously nowadays in pursuit of the elusive electric hare of scientific progress. To add to his difficulties, he has lost his protective blinkers. In the old days the path was straight and narrow, to be followed with confidence and no questions needed. There was always a higher order, social or mystic, giving instructions. Now the collapsing of his secure world has given him peripheral vision, and in the bewilderment of so much more light he blunders blindly, looking for the way. The growing inner struggles of man have been complicated by the speed of the changing world.

Perhaps we should ask ourselves if the human race is really in command of its own destiny. Or are we caught up by chance in the unfolding of a master plan? If we are, we must learn to use our peripheral vision and not become obsessed by a "touch of nutmeg." The most important factor is the state of our own minds. It is not enough to say we believe in freedom of speech, for all our so-called dangerous thoughts are products of our own limited society. What we must be willing to consider are disturbing ideas from outside, from an alien culture. Collier's "Green Thoughts," dominated by the sinister orchid, suggests that it might be wise to steer clear of conventions.

—FRED HOYLE

Bottle Party

Franklin Fletcher dreamed of luxury in the form of tiger-skins and beautiful women. He was prepared, at a pinch, to forgo the tiger-skins. Unfortunately the beautiful women seemed equally rare and inaccessible. At his office and at his boarding-house the girls were mere mice, or cattish, or kittenish, or had insufficiently read the advertisements. He met no others. At thirty-five he gave up, and decided he must console himself with a hobby, which is a very miserable second-best.

He prowled about in odd corners of the town, looking in at the windows of antique dealers and junk-shops, wondering what on earth he might collect. He came upon a poor shop, in a poor alley, in whose dusty window stood a single object: it was a full-rigged ship in a bottle. Feeling rather like that himself, he decided to go in and ask the price.

The shop was small and bare. Some shabby racks were

ranged about the walls, and these racks bore a large number of bottles, of every shape and size, containing a variety
of objects which were interesting only because they were
in bottles. While Franklin still looked about, a little door
opened, and out shuffled the proprietor, a wizened old
man in a smoking-cap, who seemed mildly surprised and
mildly pleased to have a customer.

He showed Franklin bouquets, and birds of paradise,
and the Battle of Gettysburg, and miniature Japanese gardens, and even a shrunken human head, all stoppered up
in bottles. "And what," said Frank, "are those, down
there on the bottom shelf?"

"They are not much to look at," said the old man. "A
lot of people think they are all nonsense. Personally, I
like them."

He lugged out a few specimens from their dusty obscu-
rity. One seemed to have nothing but a little dried-up fly
in it, others contained what might have been horse-hairs
or straws, or mere wisps of heaven knows what; some appeared to be filled with grey or opalescent smoke. "They
are," said the old man, "various sorts of genii, jinns, sybils,
demons, and such things. Some of them, I believe, are
much harder, even than a full-rigged ship, to get into a
bottle."

"Oh, but come! This is New York," said Frank.

"All the more reason," said the old man, "to expect the
most extraordinary jinns in bottles. I'll show you. Wait a
moment. The stopper is a little stiff."

"You mean there's one in there?" said Frank. "And
you're going to let it out?"

"Why not?" replied the old man, desisting in his efforts,
and holding the bottle up to the light. "This one——Good
heavens! *Why not*, indeed! My eyes are getting weak. I very
nearly undid the wrong bottle. A very ugly customer, that
one! Dear me! It's just as well I didn't get that stopper un-

done. I'd better put him right back in the rack. I must remember he's in the lower right-hand corner. I'll stick a label on him one of these days. Here's something more harmless."

"What's in that?" said Frank.

"Supposed to be the most beautiful girl in the world," said the old man. "All right, if you like that sort of thing. Myself, I've never troubled to undo her. I'll find something more interesting."

"Well, from a scientific point of view," said Frank, "I——"

"Science isn't everything," said the old man. "Look at this." He held up one which contained a tiny, mummified, insect-looking object, just visible through the grime. "Put your ear to it," he said.

Frank did so. He heard, in a sort of whistling nothing of a voice, the words, "Louisiana Lad, Saratoga, four-fifteen. Louisiana Lad, Saratoga, four-fifteen," repeated over and over again.

"What on earth is that?" said he.

"That," said the old man, "is the original Cumaean Sibyl. Very interesting. She's taken up racing."

"Very interesting," said Frank. "All the same, I'd just like to see that other. I adore beauty."

"A bit of an artist, eh?" said the old man. "Believe me, what you really want is a good, all-around, serviceable type. Here's one, for example. I recommend this little fellow from personal experience. He's practical. He can fix you anything."

"Well, if that's so," said Frank, "why haven't you got a palace, tiger-skins, and all that?"

"I had all that," said the old man. "And he fixed it. Yes, this was my first bottle. All the rest came from him. First of all I had a palace, pictures, marbles, slaves. And, as you say, tiger-skins. I had him put Cleopatra on one of them."

"What was she like?" cried Frank.

"All right," said old man, "if you like that sort of thing. I got bored with it. I thought to myself, 'What I'd like, really, is a little shop, with all sorts of things in bottles.' So I had him fix it. He got me the sibyl. He got me the ferocious fellow there. In fact, he got me all of them."

"And now he's in there?" said Frank.

"Yes. He's in there," said the old man. "Listen to him."

Frank put his ear to the bottle. He heard, uttered in the most plaintive tones, "Let me out. Do let me out. Please let me out. I'll do anything. Let me out. I'm harmless. Please let me out. Just for a little while. Do let me out. I'll do anything. Please——"

Frank looked at the old man. "He's there all right," he said. "He's there."

"Of course he's there," said the old man. "I wouldn't sell you an empty bottle. What do you take me for? In fact, I wouldn't sell this one at all, for sentimental reasons, only I've had the shop a good many years now, and you're my first customer."

Frank put his ear to the bottle again. "Let me out. Let me out. Oh, please let me out. I'll——"

"My God!" said Frank uneasily. "Does he go on like that *all* the time?"

"Very probably," said the old man. "I can't say I listen. I prefer the radio."

"It seems rather tough on him," said Frank sympathetically.

"Maybe," said the old man. "They don't seem to like bottles. Personally, I do. They fascinate me. For example, I——"

"Tell me," said Frank. "Is he really harmless?"

"Oh, yes," said the old man. "Bless you, yes. Some say they're tricky—eastern blood and all that—I never found him so. I used to let him out; he'd do his stuff, then back he'd go again. I must say, he's very efficient."

"He could get me anything?"

"Absolutely anything."

"And how much do you want for him?" said Frank.

"Oh, I don't know," said the old man. "Ten million dollars, perhaps."

"I say! I haven't got that. Still, if he's as good as you say, maybe I could work it off on the hire purchase system."

"Don't worry. We'll say five dollars instead. I've got all I want, really. Shall I wrap him up for you?"

Frank paid over his five dollars, and hurried home with the precious bottle, terrified of breaking it. As soon as he was in his room he pulled out the stopper. Out flowed a prodigious quantity of greasy smoke, which immediately solidified into the figure of a gross and fleshy Oriental, six feet six in height, with rolls of fat, a hook nose, a wicked white to his eye, vast double chins, altogether like a film-producer, only larger. Frank, striving desperately for something to say, ordered shashlik, kebabs, and Turkish delight. These were immediately forthcoming.

Frank, having recovered his balance, noted that these modest offerings were of surpassing quality, and set upon dishes of solid gold, superbly engraved, and polished to a dazzling brightness. It is by little details of this description that one may recognize a really first-rate servant. Frank was delighted, but restrained his enthusiasm. "Gold plates," said he, "are all very well. Let us, however, get down to brass tacks. I should like a palace."

"To hear," said his dusky henchman, "is to obey."

"It should," said Frank, "be of suitable size, suitably situated, suitably furnished, suitable pictures, suitable marbles, hangings, and all that. I should like there to be a large number of tiger-skins. I am very fond of tiger-skins."

"They shall be there," said his slave.

"I am," said Frank, "a bit of an artist, as your late owner remarked. My art, so to speak, demands the presence, upon these tiger-skins, of a number of young women, some blonde, some brunette, some petite, some Junoesque, some languorous, some vivacious, all beautiful, and they need not be over-dressed. I hate over-dressing. It is vulgar. Have you got that?"

"I have," said the jinn.

"Then," said Frank, "let *me* have it."

"Condescend only," said his servant, "to close your eyes for the space of a single minute, and opening them you shall find yourself surrounded by the agreeable objects you have described."

"O.K.," said Frank. "But no tricks, mind!"

He closed his eyes as requested. A low, musical humming, whooshing sound rose and fell about him. At the end of the minute he looked around. There were the arches, pillars, marbles, hangings, etc. of the most exquisite palace imaginable, and wherever he looked he saw a tiger-skin, and on every tiger-skin there reclined a young woman of surpassing beauty who was certainly not vulgarly over-dressed.

Our good Frank was, to put it mildly, in an ecstasy. He darted to and fro like a honey-bee in a florist's shop. He was received everywhere with smiles sweet beyond description, and with glances of an open or a veiled responsiveness. Here were blushes and lowered lids. Here was the flaming face of ardour. Here was a shoulder turned, but by no means a cold shoulder. Here were open arms, and such arms! Here was love dissembled, but vainly dissembled. Here was love triumphant. "I must say," said Frank at a later hour, "I have spent a really delightful afternoon. I have enjoyed it thoroughly."

"Then may I crave," said the jinn, who was at that moment serving him his supper, "may I crave the boon of being allowed to act as your butler, and as general minister to your pleasures, instead of being returned to that abominable bottle?"

"I don't see why not," said Frank. "It certainly seems rather tough that, after having fixed all this up, you should be crammed back into the bottle again. Very well, act as my butler, but understand, whatever the convention may be, I wish you never to enter a room without knocking. And above all—no tricks."

The jinn, with a soapy smile of gratitude, withdrew, and Frank shortly retired to his harem, where he passed the evening as pleasantly as he had passed the afternoon.

Some weeks went by entirely filled with these agreeable pastimes, till Frank, in obedience to law which not even the most efficient jinns can set aside, found himself growing a little over-particular, a little blasé, a little inclined to criticize and find fault.

"These," said he to his jinn, "are very pretty young creatures, if you like that sort of thing, but I imagine they can hardly be first-rate, or I should feel more interest in them. I am, after all, a connoisseur; nothing can please me but the very best. Take them away. Roll up all the tiger-skins but one."

"It shall be done," said the jinn. "Behold, it is accomplished."

"And on that remaining tiger-skin," said Frank, "put me Cleopatra herself."

The next moment, Cleopatra was there, looking, it must be admitted, absolutely superb. "Hullo!" she said. "Here I am, on a tiger-skin again!"

"*Again?*" cried Frank, suddenly reminded of the old man in the shop. "Here! Take her back. Bring me Helen of Troy."

Next moment, Helen of Troy was there. "Hullo!" she said. "Here I am, on a tiger-skin again!"

"*Again?*" cried Frank. "Damn that old man! Take her away. Bring me Queen Guinevere."

Guinevere said exactly the same thing; so did Madame

la Pompadour, Lady Hamilton, and every other famous
beauty that Frank could think of. "No wonder," said he,
"that that old man was such an extremely wizened old
man! The old fiend! The old devil! He has properly taken
the gilt off all the gingerbread. Call me jealous if you like;
I will not play second fiddle to that ugly old rascal. Where
shall I find a perfect creature, worthy of the embraces of
such a connoisseur as I am?"

"If you are deigning to address that question to me,"
said the jinn, "let me remind you that there was, in that
shop, a little bottle which my late master had never unstoppered, because I supplied him with it after he had lost
interest in matters of this sort. Nevertheless it has the
reputation of containing the most beautiful girl in the
whole world."

"You are right," cried Frank. "Get me that bottle without delay."

In a few seconds the bottle lay before him. "You may
have the afternoon off," said Frank to the jinn.

"Thank you," said the jinn. "I will go and see my family in Arabia. I have not seen them for a long time." With
that he bowed and withdrew. Frank turned his attention
to the bottle, which he was not long in unstoppering.

Out came the most beautiful girl you can possibly imagine. Cleopatra and all that lot were hags and frumps
compared with her. "Where am I?" said she. "What is
this beautiful palace? What am I doing on a tiger-skin?
Who is this handsome young prince?"

"It's me!" cried Frank, in a rapture. "It's me!"

The afternoon passed like a moment in Paradise. Before
Frank knew it the jinn was back, ready to serve up supper.
Frank must sup with his charmer, for this time it was love,
the real thing. The jinn, entering with the viands, rolled
up his wicked eyes at the sight of so much beauty.

It happened that Frank, all love and restlessness, darted

out into the garden between two mouthfuls, to pluck his beloved a rose. The jinn, on the pretence of serving her wine, edged up very closely. "I don't know if you remember me," said he in a whisper. "I used to be in the next bottle to you. I have often admired you through the glass."

"Oh, yes," said she. "I remember you quite well."

At that moment Frank returned. The jinn could say no more, but he stood about the room, inflating his monstrous chest, and showing off his plump and dusky muscles. "You need not be afraid of him," said Frank. "He is only a jinn. Pay no attention to him. Tell me if you really love me."

"Of course I do," said she.

"Well, say so," said he. "Why don't you say so?"

"I have said so," said she. "Of course I do. Isn't that saying so?"

This vague, evasive reply dimmed all Frank's happiness, as if a cloud had come over the sun. Doubt sprang up in his mind, and entirely ruined moments of exquisite bliss.

"What are you thinking of?" he would say.

"I don't know," she would reply.

"Well, you ought to know," he would say, and then a quarrel would begin.

Once or twice he even ordered her back into her bottle. She obeyed with a malicious and secretive smile.

"Why should she give that sort of smile?" said Frank to the jinn, to whom he confided his distress.

"I cannot tell," replied the jinn. "Unless she has a lover concealed in there."

"Is it possible?" cried Frank in consternation.

"It is surprising," said the jinn, "how much room there is in one of these bottles."

"Come out!" cried Frank. "Come out at once!"

His charmer obediently emerged. "Is there anyone else in that bottle?" cried Frank.

"How could there be?" she asked, with a look of rather overdone innocence.

"Give me a straight answer," said he. "Answer me yes or no."

"Yes or no," she replied maddeningly.

"You double-talking, two-timing little bitch!" cried Frank. "I'll go in and find out for myself. If I find anybody, God help him and you!"

With that, and with an intense effort of the will, he flowed himself into the bottle. He looked all around: there was no one. Suddenly he heard a sound above him. He looked up, and there was the stopper being thrust in.

"What are you doing?" cried he.

"We are putting in the stopper," said the jinn.

Frank cursed, begged, prayed, and implored. "Let me out!" he cried. "Let me out. Please let me out. Do let me out. I'll do anything. Let me out, do."

The jinn, however, had other matters to attend to. Frank had the infinite mortification of beholding these other matters through the glassy walls of his prison. Next day he was picked up, whisked through the air, and deposited in the dirty little shop, among the other bottles, from which this one had never been missed.

There he remained for an interminable period, covered all over with dust, and frantic with rage at the thought of what was going on in his exquisite palace, between his jinn and his faithless charmer. In the end some sailors happened to drift into the shop, and, hearing this bottle contained the most beautiful girl in the world, they bought it up by general subscription of the fo'c'sle. When they unstoppered him at sea, and found it was only poor Frank, their disappointment knew no bounds, and they used him with the utmost barbarity.

De Mortuis

r. Rankin was a large and rawboned man on whom the newest suit at once appeared outdated, like a suit in a photograph of twenty years ago. This was due to the squareness and flatness of his torso, which might have been put together by a manufacturer of packing cases. His face also had a wooden and a roughly constructed look; his hair was wiglike and resentful of the comb. He had those huge and clumsy hands which can be an asset to a doctor in a small upstate town where people still retain a rural relish for paradox, thinking that the more apelike the paw, the more precise it can be in the delicate business of a tonsillectomy.

This conclusion was perfectly justified in the case of Dr. Rankin. For example, on this particular fine morning, though his task was nothing more ticklish than the cementing over of a large patch on his cellar floor, he managed those large and clumsy hands with all the unflurried certainty of one who would never leave a sponge within or create an unsightly scar without.

The doctor surveyed his handiwork from all angles. He added a touch here and a touch there till he had achieved a smoothness altogether professional. He swept up a few last crumbs of soil and dropped them into the furnace. He paused before putting away the pick and shovel he had been using, and found occasion for yet another artistic sweep of his trowel, which made the new surface precisely flush with the surrounding floor. At this moment of supreme concentration the porch door upstairs slammed with the report of a minor piece of artillery, which, appropriately enough, caused Dr. Rankin to jump as if he had been shot.

The Doctor lifted a frowning face and an attentive ear. He heard two pairs of heavy feet clump across the resonant floor of the porch. He heard the house door opened and the visitors enter the hall, with which his cellar communicated by a short flight of steps. He heard whistling and then the voices of Buck and Bud crying, "Doc! Hi, Doc! They're biting!"

Whether the Doctor was not inclined for fishing that day, or whether, like others of his large and heavy type, he experienced an especially sharp, unsociable reaction on being suddenly startled, or whether he was merely anxious to finish undisturbed the job in hand and proceed to more important duties, he did not respond immediately to the inviting outcry of his friends. Instead, he listened while it ran its natural course, dying down at last into a puzzled and fretful dialogue.

"I guess he's out."

"I'll write a note—say we're at the creek, to come on down."

"We could tell Irene."

"But she's not here, either. You'd think *she'd* be around."

"Ought to be, by the look of the place."

"You said it, Bud. Just look at this table. You could write your name—"

"Sh-h-h! Look!"

Evidently the last speaker had noticed that the cellar door was ajar and that a light was shining below. Next moment the door was pushed wide open and Bud and Buck looked down.

"Why, Doc! There you are!"

"Didn't you hear us yelling?"

The Doctor, not too pleased at what he had overheard, nevertheless smiled his rather wooden smile as his two friends made their way down the steps. "I thought I heard someone," he said.

"We were bawling our heads off," Buck said. "Thought nobody was home. Where's Irene?"

"Visiting," said the Doctor. "She's gone visiting."

"Hey, what goes on?" said Bud. "What are you doing? Burying one of your patients, or what?"

"Oh, there's been water seeping up through the floor," said the Doctor. "I figured it might be some spring opened up or something."

"You don't say!" said Bud, assuming instantly the high ethical standpoint of the realtor. "Gee, Doc, I sold you this property. Don't say I fixed you up with a dump where there's an underground spring."

"There was water," said the Doctor.

"Yes, but, Doc, you can look on that geological map the Kiwanis Club got up. There's not a better section of sub-soil in the town."

"Looks like he sold you a pup," said Buck, grinning.

"No," said Bud. "Look. When the Doc came here he was green. You'll admit he was green. The things he didn't know!"

"He bought Ted Webber's jalopy," said Buck.

"He'd have bought the Jessop place if I'd let him," said Bud. "But I wouldn't give him a bum steer."

"Not the poor, simple city slicker from Poughkeepsie," said Buck.

"Some people would have taken him," said Bud. "Maybe some people did. Not me. I recommended this property. He and Irene moved straight in as soon as they were married. I wouldn't have put the Doc on to a dump where there'd be a spring under the foundations."

"Oh, forget it," said the Doctor, embarrassed by this conscientiousness. "I guess it was just the heavy rains."

"By gosh!" Buck said, glancing at the besmeared point of the pickaxe. "You certainly went deep enough. Right down into the clay, huh?"

"That's four feet down, the clay," Bud said.

"Eighteen inches," said the Doctor.

"Four feet," said Bud. "I can show you the map."

"Come on. No arguments," said Buck. "How's about it, Doc? An hour or two at the creek, eh? They're biting."

"Can't do it, boys," said the Doctor. "I've got to see a patient or two."

"Aw, live and let live, Doc," Bud said. "Give 'em a chance to get better. Are you going to depopulate the whole darn town?"

The Doctor looked down, smiled, and muttered, as he always did when this particular jest was trotted out. "Sorry, boys," he said. "I can't make it."

"Well," said Bud, disappointed, "I suppose we'd better get along. How's Irene?"

"Irene?" said the Doctor. "Never better. She's gone visiting. Albany. Got the eleven-o'clock train."

"Eleven o'clock?" said Buck. "For Albany?"

"Did I say Albany?" said the Doctor. "Watertown, I meant."

"Friends in Watertown?" Buck asked.

"Mrs. Slater," said the Doctor. "Mr. and Mrs. Slater. Lived next door to 'em when she was a kid, Irene said, over on Sycamore Street."

"Slater?" said Bud. "Next door to Irene. Not in *this* town."

"Oh, yes," said the Doctor. "She was telling me all about them last night. She got a letter. Seems this Mrs. Slater looked after her when her mother was in the hospital one time."

"No," said Bud.

"That's what she told me," said the Doctor. "Of course, it was a good many years ago."

"Look, Doc," said Buck. "Bud and I were raised in this town. We've known Irene's folks all our lives. We were in and out of their house all the time. There was never anybody next door called Slater."

"Perhaps," said the Doctor, "she married again, this woman. Perhaps it was a different name."

Bud shook his head.

"What time did Irene go to the station?" Buck asked.

"Oh, about a quarter of an hour ago," said the Doctor.

"You didn't drive her?" said Buck.

"She walked," said the Doctor.

"We came down Main Street," Buck said. "We didn't meet her."

"Maybe she walked across the pasture," said the Doctor.

"That's a tough walk with a suitcase," said Buck.

"She just had a couple of things in a little bag," said the Doctor.

Bud was still shaking his head.

Buck looked at Bud and then at the pick, at the new, damp cement on the floor. "Jesus Christ!" he said.

"Oh, God, Doc!" Bud said. "A guy like you!"

"What in the name of heaven are you two bloody fools thinking?" asked the Doctor. "What are you trying to say?"

"A spring!" said Bud. "I ought to have known right away it wasn't any spring."

The Doctor looked at his cement-work, at the pick, at the large worried faces of his two friends. His own face turned livid. "Am I crazy?" he said. "Or are you? You suggest that I've—that Irene—my wife—oh, go on! Get out! Yes, go and get the sheriff. Tell him to come here and start digging. You—get out!"

Bud and Buck looked at each other, shifted their feet, and stood still again.

"Go on," said the Doctor.

"I don't know," said Bud.

"It's not as if he didn't have the provocation," Buck said.

"God knows," Bud said.

"God knows," Buck said. "You know. I know. The whole town knows. But try telling it to a jury."

The Doctor put his hand to his head. "What's that?" he said. "What is it? Now what are you saying? What do you mean?"

"If this ain't being on the spot!" said Buck. "Doc, you can see how it is. It takes some thinking. We've been friends right from the start. Damn good friends."

"But we've got to think," said Bud. "It's serious. Provocation or not, there's a law in the land. There's such a thing as being an accomplice."

"You were talking provocation," said the Doctor.

"You're right," said Buck. "And you're our friend. And if ever it could be called justified——"

"We've got to fix this somehow," said Bud.

"Justified?" said the Doctor.

"You were bound to get wised up sooner or later," said Buck.

"We could have told you," said Bud. "Only—what the hell?"

"We could," said Buck. "And we nearly did. Five years ago. Before ever you married her. You hadn't been here six months, but we sort of cottoned to you. Thought of giving you a hint. Spoke about it. Remember, Bud?"

Bud nodded. "Funny," he said. "I came right out in the open about that Jessop property. I wouldn't let you buy that, Doc. But getting married, that's something else again. We could have told you."

"We're that much responsible," Buck said.

"I'm fifty," said the Doctor. "I suppose it's pretty old for Irene."

"If you was Johnny Weissmuller at the age of twenty-one, it wouldn't make any difference," said Buck.

"I know a lot of people think she's not exactly a perfect wife," said the Doctor. "Maybe she's not. She's young. She's full of life."

"Oh, skip it!" said Buck sharply, looking at the raw cement. "Skip it, Doc, for God's sake."

The Doctor brushed his hand across his face. "Not everybody wants the same thing," he said. "I'm a sort of dry fellow. I don't open up very easily. Irene—you'd call her gay."

"You said it," said Buck.

"She's no housekeeper," said the Doctor. "I know it. But that's not the only thing a man wants. She's enjoyed herself."

"Yeah," said Buck. "She did."

"That's what I love," said the Doctor. "Because I'm not that way myself. She's not very deep, mentally. All right. Say she's stupid. I don't care. Lazy. No system. Well, I've got plenty of system. She's enjoyed herself. It's beautiful. It's innocent. Like a child."

"Yes. If that was all," Buck said.

"But," said the Doctor, turning his eyes full on him, "you seem to know there was more."

"Everybody knows it," said Buck.

"A decent, straightforward guy comes to a place like this and marries the town floozy," Bud said bitterly. "And nobody'll tell him. Everybody just watches."

"And laughs," said Buck. "You and me, Bud, as well as the rest."

"We told her to watch her step," said Bud. "We warned her."

"Everybody warned her," said Buck. "But people get fed up. When it got to truck-drivers——"

"It was never us, Doc," said Bud, earnestly. "Not after you came along, anyway."

"The town'll be on your side," said Buck.

"That won't mean much when the case comes to trial in the county seat," said Bud.

"Oh!" cried the Doctor, suddenly. "What shall I do? What shall I do?"

"It's up to you, Bud," said Buck. "I can't turn him in."

"Take it easy, Doc," said Bud. "Calm down. Look, Buck. When we came in here the street was empty, wasn't it?"

"I guess so," said Buck. "Anyway, nobody saw us come down cellar."

"And we haven't been down," Bud said, addressing himself forcefully to the Doctor. "Get that, Doc? We shouted upstairs, hung around a minute or two, and cleared out. But we never came down into this cellar."

"I wish you hadn't," the Doctor said heavily.

"All you have to do is say Irene went out for a walk and never came back," said Buck. "Bud and I can swear we saw her headed out of town with a fellow in a—well, say in a Buick sedan. Everybody'll believe that, all right. We'll fix it. But later. Now we'd better scram."

"And remember, now. Stick to it. We never came down here and we haven't seen you today," said Bud. "So long!"

Buck and Bud ascended the steps, moving with a rather absurd degree of caution. "You'd better get that . . . that thing covered up," Buck said over his shoulder.

Left alone, the Doctor sat down on an empty box, holding his head with both hands. He was still sitting like this when the porch door slammed again. This time he did not start. He listened. The house door opened and closed. A voice cried, "Yoo-hoo! Yoo-hoo! I'm back."

The Doctor rose slowly to his feet. "I'm down here, Irene!" he called.

The cellar door opened. A young woman stood at the head of the steps. "Can you beat it?" she said. "I missed the damn train."

"Oh!" said the Doctor. "Did you come back across the field?"

"Yes, like a fool," she said. "I could have hitched a ride and caught the train up the line. Only I didn't think. If you'd run me over to the junction, I could still make it."

"Maybe," said the Doctor. "Did you meet anyone coming back?"

"Not a soul," she said. "Aren't you finished with that old job yet?"

"I'm afraid I'll have to take it all up again," said the Doctor. "Come down here, my dear, and I'll show you."

Evening Primrose

In a pad of Highlife Bond, bought by
Miss Sadie Brodribb at Bracey's for 25c

arch 21 Today I made my decision. I would turn my back for good and all upon the *bourgeois* world that hates a poet. I would leave, get out, break away——

And I have done it. I am free! Free as the mote that dances in the sunbeam! Free as a house-fly crossing first-class in the largest of luxury liners! Free as my verse! Free as the food I shall eat, the paper I write upon, the lamb's-wool-lined softly slithering slippers I shall wear.

This morning I had not so much as a car-fare. Now I am here, on velvet. You are itching to learn of this haven; you would like to organize trips here, spoil it, send your relations-in-law, perhaps even come yourself. After all, this journal will hardly fall into your hands till I am dead. I'll tell you.

I am at Bracey's Giant Emporium, as happy as a mouse in the middle of an immense cheese, and the world shall know me no more.

Merrily, merrily shall I live now, secure behind a towering pile of carpets, in a corner-nook which I propose to line with eiderdowns, angora vestments, and the Cleopatraean tops in pillows. I shall be cosy.

I nipped into this sanctuary late this afternoon, and soon heard the dying footfalls of closing time. From now on, my only effort will be to dodge the night-watchman. Poets can dodge.

I have already made my first mouse-like exploration. I tiptoed as far as the stationery department, and, timid, darted back with only these writing materials, the poet's first need. Now I shall lay them aside, and seek other necessities: food, wine, the soft furniture of my couch, and a natty smoking-jacket. This place stimulates me. I shall write here.

DAWN, NEXT DAY I suppose no one in the world was ever more astonished and overwhelmed than I have been tonight. It is unbelievable. Yet I believe it. How interesting life is when things get like that!

I crept out, as I said I would, and found the great shop in mingled light and gloom. The central well was half illuminated; the circling galleries towered in a pansy Piranesi of toppling light and shade. The spidery stairways and flying bridges had passed from purpose into fantasy. Silks and velvets glimmered like ghosts, a hundred pantie-clad models offered simpers and embraces to the desert air. Rings, clips, and bracelets glittered frostily in a desolate absence of Honey and Daddy.

Creeping along the transverse aisles, which were in deeper darkness, I felt like a wandering thought in the dreaming brain of a chorus girl down on her luck. Only, of course, their brains are not as big as Bracey's Giant Emporium. And there was no man there.

None, that is, except the night-watchman. I had forgotten him. As I crossed an open space on the mezzanine floor, hugging the lee of a display of sultry shawls, I became aware of a regular thudding, which might almost have been that of my own heart. Suddenly it burst upon me that it came from outside. It was footsteps, and they were only a few paces away. Quick as a flash I seized a flamboyant mantilla, whirled it about me and stood with one arm outflung, like a Carmen petrified in a gesture of disdain.

I was successful. He passed me, jingling his little machine on its chain, humming his little tune, his eyes scaled with refractions of the blaring day. "Go, worldling!" I whispered, and permitted myself a soundless laugh.

It froze on my lips. My heart faltered. A new fear seized me.

I was afraid to move. I was afraid to look around. I felt I was being watched by something that could see right through me. This was a very different feeling from the ordinary emergency caused by the very ordinary nightwatchman. My conscious impulse was the obvious one: to glance behind me. But my eyes knew better. I remained absolutely petrified, staring straight ahead.

My eyes were trying to tell me something that my brain refused to believe. They made their point. I was looking straight into another pair of eyes, human eyes, but large, flat, luminous. I have seen such eyes among the nocturnal creatures, which creep out under the artificial blue moonlight in the zoo.

The owner was only a dozen feet away from me. The watchman had passed between us, nearer him than me. Yet he had not seen him. I must have been looking straight at him for several minutes at a stretch. I had not seen him either.

He was half reclining against a low dais where, on a floor of russet leaves, and flanked by billows of glowing

home-spun, the fresh-faced waxen girls modeled spectator
sports suits in herringbones, checks, and plaids. He leaned
against the skirt of one of these Dianas; its folds concealed
perhaps his ear, his shoulder, and a little of his right side.
He, himself, was clad in dim but large patterned Shetland
tweeds of the latest cut, suède shoes, a shirt of a rather
broad *motif* in olive, pink, and grey. He was as pale as a
creature found under a stone. His long thin arms ended in
hands that hung floatingly, more like trailing, transparent
fins, or wisps of chiffon, than ordinary hands.

He spoke. His voice was not a voice; it was a mere whistling under the tongue. "Not bad, for a beginner!"

I grasped that he was complimenting me, rather satiri-
cally, on my own, more amateurish, feat of camouflage. I
stuttered. I said, "I'm sorry. I didn't know anyone else
lived here." I noticed, even as I spoke, that I was imitating
his own whistling sibilant utterance.

"Oh, yes," he said. "*We* live here. It's delightful."

"We?"

"Yes, all of us. Look!"

We were near the edge of the first gallery. He swept his
long hand round, indicating the whole well of the shop. I
looked. I saw nothing. I could hear nothing, except the
watchman's thudding step receding infinitely far along
some basement aisle.

"Don't you see?"

You know the sensation one has, peering into the half-
light of a vivarium? One sees bark, pebbles, a few leaves,
nothing more. And then, suddenly, a stone breathes—it is
a toad; there is a chameleon, another, a coiled adder, a
mantis among the leaves. The whole case seems crepitant
with life. Perhaps the whole world is. One glances at one's
sleeve, one's feet.

So it was with the shop. I looked, and it was empty. I
looked, and there was an old lady, clambering out from

behind the monstrous clock. There were three girls, elderly *ingénues*, incredibly emaciated, simpering at the entrance of the perfumery. Their hair was a fine floss, pale as gossamer. Equally brittle and colourless was a man with the appearance of a colonel of southern extraction, who stood regarding me while he caressed mustachios that would have done credit to a crystal shrimp. A chintzy woman, possibly of literary tastes, swam forward from the curtains and drapes.

They came thick about me, fluttering, whistling, like a waving of gauze in the wind. Their eyes were wide and flatly bright. I saw there was no colour to the iris.

"How raw he looks!"

"A detective! Send for the Dark Men!"

"I'm not a detective. I am a poet. I have renounced the world."

"He is a poet. He has come over to us. Mr. Roscoe found him."

"He admires us."

"He must meet Mrs. Vanderpant."

I was taken to meet Mrs. Vanderpant. She proved to be the Grand Old Lady of the store, almost entirely transparent.

"So you are a poet, Mr. Snell? You will find inspiration here. I am quite the oldest inhabitant. Three mergers and a complete rebuilding, but they didn't get rid of me!"

"Tell how you went out by daylight, dear Mrs. Vanderpant, and nearly got bought for Whistler's *Mother*."

"That was in pre-war days. I was more robust then. But at the cash desk they suddenly remembered there was no frame. And when they came back to look at me——"

"—She was gone."

Their laughter was like the stridulation of the ghosts of grasshoppers.

"Where is Ella? Where is my broth?"

"She is bringing it, Mrs. Vanderpant. It will come."

"Tiresome little creature! She is our foundling, Mr. Snell. She is not quite our sort."

"Is that so, Mrs. Vanderpant? Dear, dear!"

"I lived alone here, Mr. Snell, for many years. I took refuge here in the terrible times in the eighties. I was a young girl then, a beauty, people were kind enough to say, but poor Papa lost his money. Bracey's meant a lot to a young girl, in the New York of those days, Mr. Snell. It seemed to me terrible that I should not be able to come here in the ordinary way. So I came here for good. I was quite alarmed when others began to come in, after the crash of 1907. But it was the dear Judge, the Colonel, Mrs. Bilbee——"

I bowed. I was being introduced.

"Mrs. Bilbee writes plays. *And* of a very old Philadelphia family. You will find us quite *nice* here, Mr. Snell."

"I feel it a great privilege, Mrs. Vanderpant."

"And of course, all our dear *young* people came in '29. *Their* poor papas jumped from skyscrapers."

I did a great deal of bowing and whistling. The introductions took a long time. Who would have thought so many people lived in Bracey's?

"And here at last is Ella with my broth."

It was then I noticed that the young people were not so young after all, in spite of their smiles, their little ways, their *ingénue* dress. Ella was in her teens. Clad only in something from the shop-soiled counter, she nevertheless had the appearance of a living flower in a French cemetery, or a mermaid among polyps.

"Come, you stupid thing!"

"Mrs. Vanderpant is waiting."

Her pallor was not like theirs; not like the pallor of something that glistens or scuttles when you turn over a stone. Hers was that of a pearl.

Ella! Pearl of this remotest, most fantastic cave! Little mermaid, brushed over, pressed down by objects of a deadlier white—tentacles—! I can write no more.

MARCH 28   Well, I am rapidly becoming used to my new and half-lit world, to my strange company. I am learning the intricate laws of silence and camouflage which dominate the apparently casual strollings and gatherings of the midnight clan. How they detest the night-watchman, whose existence imposes these laws on their idle festivals!

"Odious, vulgar creature! He reeks of the coarse sun!"

Actually, he is quite a personable young man, very young for a night-watchman, so young that I think he must have been wounded in the war. But they would like to tear him to pieces.

They are very pleasant to me, though. They are pleased that a poet should have come among them. Yet I cannot like them entirely. My blood is a little chilled by the uncanny ease with which even the old ladies can clamber spider-like from balcony to balcony. Or is it because they are unkind to Ella?

Yesterday we had a bridge party. Tonight, Mrs. Bilbee's little play, *Love in Shadowland*, is going to be presented. Would you believe it?—another colony, from Wanamaker's, is coming over *en masse* to attend. Apparently people live in all the great stores. This visit is considered a great honour, for there is an intense snobbery in these creatures. They speak with horror of a social outcast who left a high-class Madison Avenue establishment, and now leads a wallowing, beachcomberish life in a delicatessen. And they relate with tragic emotion the story of a man in Altman's, who conceived such a passion for a model plaid dressing jacket that he emerged and wrested it from the hands of a purchaser. It seems that all the Altman colony, dreading an investigation, were forced to remove beyond the social pale, into a five-and-dime. Well, I must get ready to attend the play.

APRIL 14   I have found an opportunity to speak to Ella. I dared not before; here one has a sense always of pale eyes secretly watching. But last night, at the play, I developed a fit of hiccups. I was somewhat sternly told to go and secrete myself in the basement, among the garbage cans, where the watchman never comes.

There, in the rat-haunted darkness, I heard a stifled sob. "What's that? Is it you? Is it Ella? What ails you, child? Why do you cry?"

"They wouldn't even let me see the play."

"Is that all? Let me console you."

"I am so unhappy."

She told me her tragic little story. What do you think? When she was a child, a little tiny child of only six, she strayed away and fell asleep behind a counter, while her mother tried on a new hat. When she woke, the store was in darkness.

"And I cried, and they all came around, and took hold of me. 'She will tell, if we let her go,' they said. Some said, 'Call in the Dark Men.' 'Let her stay here,' said Mrs. Vanderpant. 'She will make me a nice little maid.' "

"Who are these Dark Men, Ella? They spoke of them when I came here."

"Don't you know? Oh, it's horrible! It's horrible!"

"Tell me, Ella. Let us share it."

She trembled. "You know the morticians, 'Journey's End,' who go to houses when people die?"

"Yes, Ella."

"Well, in that shop, just like here, and at Gimbel's, and at Bloomingdale's, there are people living, people like these."

"How disgusting! But what can they live upon, Ella, in a funeral home?"

"Don't ask me! Dead people are sent there, to be embalmed. Oh, they are terrible creatures! Even the people here are terrified of them. But if anyone dies, or if some poor burglar breaks in, and sees these people, and might tell——"

"Yes? Go on."

"Then they send for the others, the Dark Men."

"Good heavens!"

"Yes, and they put the body in Surgical Supplies—or the burglar, all tied up, if it's a burglar—and they send for these others, and then they all hide, and in they come, the others—— Oh! they're like pieces of blackness. I saw them once. It was terrible."

"And then?"

"They go in, to where the dead person is, or the poor burglar. And they have wax there—and all sorts of things. And when they're gone there's just one of these wax models left, on the table. And then our people put a dress on it, or a bathing suit, and they mix it up with all the others, and nobody ever knows."

"But aren't they heavier than the others, these wax models? You would think they'd be heavier."

"No. They're not heavier. I think there's a lot of them —gone."

"Oh, dear! So they were going to do that to you, when you were a little child?"

"Yes, only Mrs. Vanderpant said I was to be her maid."

"I don't like these people, Ella."

"Nor do I. I wish I could see a bird."

"Why don't you go into the pet-shop?"

"It wouldn't be the same. I want to see it on a twig, with leaves."

"Ella, let us meet often. Let us creep away down here

and meet. I will tell you about birds, and twigs and leaves."

MAY 1   For the last few nights the store has been feverish with the shivering whisper of a huge crush at Blooming-dale's. Tonight was the night.

"Not changed yet? We leave on the stroke of two." Roscoe has appointed himself, or been appointed, my guide or my guard.

"Roscoe, I am still a greenhorn. I dread the streets."

"Nonsense! There's nothing to it. We slip out by two's and three's, stand on the sidewalk, pick up a taxi. Were you never out late in the old days? If so, you must have seen us, many a time."

"Good heavens, I believe I have! And often wondered where you came from. And it was from here! But, Roscoe, my brow is burning. I find it hard to breathe. I fear a cold."

"In that case you must certainly remain behind. Our whole party would be disgraced in the unfortunate event of a sneeze."

I had relied on their rigid etiquette, so largely based on fear of discovery, and I was right. Soon they were gone, drifting out like leaves aslant on the wind. At once I dressed in flannel slacks, canvas shoes, and a tasteful sport shirt, all new in stock today. I found a quiet spot, safely off the track beaten by the night-watchman. There, in a model's lifted hand, I set a wide fern frond culled from the florist's shop, and at once had a young, spring tree. The carpet was sandy, sandy as a lake-side beach. A snowy napkin; two cakes, each with a cherry on it; I had only to imagine the lake and to find Ella.

"Why, Charles, what's this?"

"I'm a poet, Ella, and when a poet meets a girl like you he thinks of a day in the country. Do you see this tree? Let's call it *our* tree. There's the lake—the prettiest lake imaginable. Here is grass, and there are flowers. There are birds, too, Ella. You told me you like birds."

"Oh, Charles, you're so sweet. I feel I hear them singing."

"And here's our lunch. But before we eat, go behind the rock there, and see what you find."

I heard her cry out in delight when she saw the summer dress I had put there for her. When she came back the spring day smiled to see her, and the lake shone brighter than before. "Ella, let us have lunch. Let us have fun. Let us have a swim. I can just imagine you in one of those new bathing suits."

"Let's just sit there, Charles, and talk."

So we sat and talked, and the time was gone like a dream. We might have stayed there, forgetful of everything, had it not been for the spider.

"Charles, what are you doing?"

"Nothing, my dear. Just a naughty little spider, crawling over your knee. Purely imaginary, of course, but that sort are sometimes the worst. I had to try to catch him."

"Don't, Charles! It's late. It's terribly late. They'll be back any minute. I'd better go home."

I took her home to the kitchenware on the sub-ground floor, and kissed her good-day. She offered me her cheek. This troubles me.

MAY 10   "Ella, I love you."

I said it to her just like that. We have met many times. I have dreamt of her by day. I have not even kept up my journal. Verse has been out of the question.

"Ella, I love you. Let us move into the trousseau department. Don't look so dismayed, darling. If you like, we will go right away from here. We will live in that little restaurant in Central Park. There are thousands of birds there."

"Please—please don't talk like that!"

"But I love you with all my heart."

"You mustn't."

"But I find I must. I can't help it. Ella, you don't love another?"

She wept a little. "Oh, Charles, I do."

"Love another, Ella? One of these? I thought you dreaded them all. It must be Roscoe. He is the only one that's any way human. We talk of art, life, and such things. And he has stolen your heart!"

"No, Charles, no. He's just like the rest, really. I hate them all. They make me shudder."

"Who is it, then?"

"It's him."

"Who?"

"The night-watchman."

"Impossible!"

"No. He smells of the sun."

"Oh, Ella, you have broken my heart."

"Be my friend, though."

"I will. I'll be your brother. How did you fall in love with him?"

"Oh, Charles, it was so wonderful. I was thinking of birds, and I was careless. Don't tell on me, Charles. They'll punish me."

"No. No. Go on."

"I was careless, and there he was, coming round the corner. And there was no place for me; I had this blue dress on. There were only some wax models in their underthings."

"Please go on."

"I couldn't help it. I slipped off my dress, and stood still."

"I see."

"And he stopped just by me, Charles. And he looked at me. And he touched my cheek."

"Did he notice nothing?"

"No. It was cold. But Charles, he said—he said—'Say, honey, I wish they made 'em like you on Eighth Avenue.' Charles, wasn't that a lovely thing to say?"

"Personally, I should have said Park Avenue."

"Oh, Charles, don't get like these people here. Sometimes I think you're getting like them. It doesn't matter what street, Charles; it was a lovely thing to say."

"Yes, but my heart's broken. And what can you do about him? Ella, he belongs to another world."

"Yes, Charles, Eighth Avenue. I want to go there. Charles, are you truly my friend?"

"I'm your brother, only my heart's broken."

"I'll tell you. I will. I'm going to stand there again. So he'll see me."

"And then?"

"Perhaps he'll speak to me again."

"My dearest Ella, you are torturing yourself. You are making it worse."

"No, Charles. Because I shall answer him. He will take me away."

"Ella, I can't bear it."

"Ssh! There is someone coming. I shall see birds—real birds, Charles—and flowers growing. They're coming. You must go."

MAY 13   The last three days have been torture. This evening I broke. Roscoe had joined me. He sat eying me for a long time. He put his hand on my shoulder.

He said, "You're looking seedy, old fellow. Why don't you go over to Wanamaker's for some skiing?"

His kindness compelled a frank response. "It's deeper than that, Roscoe. I'm done for. I can't eat, I can't sleep. I can't write, man, I can't even write."

"What is it? Day starvation?"

"Roscoe—it's love."

"Not one of the staff, Charles, or the customers? That's absolutely forbidden."

"No, it's not that, Roscoe. But just as hopeless."

"My dear old fellow, I can't bear to see you like this. Let me help you. Let me share your trouble."

Then it came out. It burst out. I trusted him. I think I trusted him. I really think I had no intention of betraying Ella, of spoiling her escape, of keeping her here till her heart turned towards me. If I had, it was subconscious, I swear it.

But I told him all. All! He was sympathetic, but I detected a sly reserve in his sympathy. "You will respect my confidence, Roscoe? This is to be a secret between us."

"As secret as the grave, old chap."

And he must have gone straight to Mrs. Vanderpant. This evening the atmosphere has changed. People flicker to and fro, smiling nervously, horribly, with a sort of frightened sadistic exaltation. When I speak to them they answer evasively, fidget, and disappear. An informal dance has been called off. I cannot find Ella. I will creep out. I will look for her again.

LATER   Heaven! It has happened. I went in desperation to the manager's office, whose glass front overlooks the whole shop. I watched till midnight. Then I saw a little group of them, like ants bearing a victim. They were carrying Ella. They took her to the surgical department. They took other things.

And, coming back here, I was passed by a flittering, whispering horde of them, glancing over their shoulders in a thrilled ecstasy of panic, making for their hiding places. I, too, hid myself. How can I describe the dark inhuman creatures that passed me, silent as shadows? They went there—where Ella is.

What can I do? There is only one thing. I will find the watchman. I will tell him. He and I will save her. And if we are overpowered——Well, I will leave this on a counter. Tomorrow, if we live, I can recover it.

If not, look in the windows. Look for the three new figures: two men, one rather sensitive-looking, and a girl. She has blue eyes, like periwinkle flowers, and her upper lip is lifted a little.

Look for us.

Smoke them out! Obliterate them! Avenge us!

Witchs Money

Foiral had taken a load of cork up to the high road, where he met the motor truck from Perpignan. He was on his way back to the village, walking harmlessly beside his mule, and thinking of nothing at all, when he was passed by a striding madman, half naked, and of a type never seen before in this district of the Pyrénées-Orientales.

He was not of the idiot sort, with the big head, like two or three of them down in the village. Nor was he a lean, raving creature, like Barilles' old father after the house burned down. Nor had he a little, tiny, shrunken-up, chattering head, like the younger Lloubes. He was a new sort altogether.

Foiral decided he was a kind of *bursting* madman, all blare and racket, as bad as the sun. His red flesh burst out of his little bits of coloured clothes; red arms, red knees, red neck, and a great round red face bursting with smiles, words, laughter.

Foiral overtook him at the top of the ridge. He was staring down into the valley like a man thunderstruck.

"My God!" he said to Foiral. "Just look at it!" Foiral looked at it. There was nothing wrong.

"Here have I," said the mad Jack, "been walking up and down these goddam Pyrénées for weeks—meadows, birch trees, pine trees, waterfalls—green as a dish of *haricots verts!* And here's what I've been looking for all the time. Why did no one tell me?"

There's a damned question to answer! However, madmen answer themselves. Foiral thumped his mule and started off down the track, but the mad fellow fell in step beside him.

"What is it, for God's sake?" said he. "A bit of Spain strayed over the frontier, or what? Might be a crater in the moon. No water, I suppose? God, look at that ring of red hills! Look at that pink and yellow land! Are those villages down there? Or the bones of some creatures that have died?

"I like it," he said. "I like the way the fig trees burst out of the rock. I like the way the seeds are bursting out of the figs. Ever heard of surrealism? This is surrealism come to life. What are those? Cork forests? They look like petrified ogres. Excellent ogres, who bleed when these impudent mortals flay you, with my little brush, on my little piece of canvas, I shall restore to you an important part of your life!"

Foiral, by no means devout, took the sensible precaution of crossing himself. The fellow went on and on, all the way down, two or three kilometres, Foiral answering with a "yes," a "no," and a grunt. "This is *my* country!" cried the lunatic. "It's *made* for me. Glad I didn't go to Morocco! Is this your village? Wonderful! Look at those houses —three, four stories. Why do they look as if they'd been piled up by cave-dwellers, cave-dwellers who couldn't find a cliff? Or are they caves from which the cliff has crumbled away, leaving them uneasy in the sunlight, huddling together? Why don't you have any windows? I like that yellow belfry. Sort of Spanish. I like the way the bell hangs in that iron cage. Black as your hat. Dead. Maybe that's why it's so quiet here. Dead noise, gibbeted against the blue! Ha! Ha! You're not amused, eh? You don't care for surrealism? So much the worse, my friend, because you're the stuff that sort of dream is made of. I like the black clothes all you people wear. Spanish touch again, I suppose? It makes you look like holes in the light."

"Goodbye," said Foiral.

"Wait a minute," said the stranger. "Where can I put up in this village? Is there an inn?"

"No," said Foiral, turning into his yard.

"Hell!" said the stranger. "I suppose someone has a room I can sleep in?"

"No," said Foiral.

That set the fellow back a bit. "Well," said he at last, "I'll have to look around, anyway."

So he went up the street. Foiral saw him talking to Madame Arago, and she was shaking her head. Then he saw him trying it on at the baker's, and the baker shook his head as well. However, he bought a loaf there, and some cheese and wine from Barilles. He sat down on the bench outside and ate it; then he went pottering off up the slope.

Foiral thought he'd keep an eye on him, so he followed to the top of the village, where he could see all over the hillside. The fellow was just mooning about; he picked up nothing, he did nothing. Then he began to drift over to the little farm-house, where the well is, a few hundred yards above the rest of the houses.

This happened to be Foiral's property, through his wife: a good place, if they'd had a son to live in it. Seeing the stranger edging that way, Foiral followed, not too fast, you understand, and not too slow either. Sure enough, when he got there, there was the fellow peering through the chinks in the shutters, even trying the door. He might have been up to anything.

He looked round as Foiral came up. "Nobody lives here?" he said.

"No," said Foiral.

"Who does it belong to?" said the stranger.

Foiral hardly knew what to say. In the end he had to admit it was his.

"Will you rent it to me?" said the stranger.

"What's that?" said Foiral.

"I want the house for six months," said the stranger.

"What for?" said Foiral.

"Damn it!" said the stranger. "To live in."

"Why?" said Foiral.

The stranger holds up his hand. He picks hold of the thumb. He says, very slowly, "I am an artist, a painter."

"Yes," says Foiral.

Then the stranger lays hold of his forefinger. "I can work here. I like it. I like the view. I like those two ilex trees."

"Very good," says Foiral.

Then the stranger takes hold of his middle finger. "I want to stay here six months."

"Yes," says Foiral.

Then the stranger takes hold of his third finger. "In this house. Which, I may say, on this yellow ground, looks interestingly like a die on a desert. Or does it look like a skull?"

"Ah!" says Foiral.

Then the stranger takes hold of his little finger, and he says, "How much—do you want—to let me—live and work—in this house—for six months?"

"Why?" says Foiral.

At this the stranger began to stamp up and down. They had quite an argument. Foiral clinched the matter by saying that people didn't rent houses in that part of the world; everyone had his own.

"It is necessary," said the stranger, grinding his teeth, "for me to paint pictures here."

"So much the worse," said Foiral.

The stranger uttered a number of cries in some foreign gibberish, possibly that of hell itself. "I see your soul," said he, "as a small and exceedingly sterile black marble, on a waste of burning white alkali."

Foiral, holding his two middle fingers under his thumb, extended the first and fourth in the direction of the stranger, careless of whether he gave offence.

"What will you take for the shack?" said the stranger. "Maybe I'll buy it."

It was quite a relief to Foiral to find that after all he was just a plain, simple, ordinary lunatic. Without a proper pair of pants to his backside, he was offering to buy this excellent sound house, for which Foiral would have asked twenty thousand francs, had there been anyone of whom to ask it.

"Come on," said the stranger. "How much?"

Foiral, thinking he had wasted enough time, and not objecting to an agreeable sensation, said, "Forty thousand."

Said the stranger, "I'll give you thirty-five."

Foiral laughed heartily.

"That's a good laugh," said the stranger. "I should like to paint a laugh like that. I should express it by a *mélange* of the roots of recently extracted teeth. Well, what about it? Thirty-five? I can pay you a deposit right now." And, pulling out a wallet, this Croesus among madmen rustled one, two, three, four, five thousand-franc notes under Foiral's nose.

"It'll leave me dead broke," he said. "Still, I expect I can sell it again?"

"If God wills," said Foiral.

"Anyway, I could come here now and then," said the other. "My God! I can paint a showful of pictures here in six months. New York'll go crazy. Then I'll come back here and paint another show."

Foiral, ravished with joy, ceased attempting to understand. He began to praise his house furiously: he dragged the man inside, showed him the oven, banged the walls, made him look up the chimney, into the shed, down the well—— "All right. All right," said the stranger. "That's grand. Everything's grand. Whitewash the walls. Find me some woman to come and clean and cook. I'll go back to Perpignan and turn up in a week with my things. Listen, I want that table chucked in, two or three of the chairs, and the bedstead. I'll get the rest. Here's your deposit."

"No, no," said Foiral. "Everything must be done properly, before witnesses. Then, when the lawyer comes, he can make out the papers. Come back with me. I'll call Arago, he's a very honest man. Guis, very honest. Vigné, honest as the good earth. And a bottle of old wine. I have it. It shall cost nothing."

"Fine!" said the blessed madman, sent by God.

Back they went. In came Arago, Guis, Vigné, all as honest as the day. The deposit was paid, the wine was opened, the stranger called for more, others crowded in; those who were not allowed in stood outside to listen to the laughter. You'd have thought there was a wedding going on, or some wickedness in the house. In fact, Foiral's old woman went and stood in the doorway every now and then, just to let people see her.

There was no doubt about it, there was something very magnificent about this madman. Next day, after he had gone, they talked him over thoroughly. "To listen," said little Guis, "is to be drunk without spending a penny. You think you understand; you seem to fly through the air; you have to burst out laughing."

"I somehow had the delectable impression that I was rich," said Arago. "Not, I mean, with something in the chimney, but as if I—well, as if I were to spend it. And more."

"I like him," said little Guis. "He is my friend."

"Now you speak like a fool," said Foiral. "He is mad. And it is I who deal with him."

"I thought maybe he was not so mad when he said the house was like an old skull looking out of the ground," said Guis, looking sideways, as well he might.

"Nor a liar, perhaps?" said Foiral. "Let me tell you, he said also it was like a die on a desert. Can it be both?"

"He said in one breath," said Arago, "that he came from Paris. In the next, that he was an American."

"Oh, yes. Unquestionably a great liar," said Quès. "Perhaps one of the biggest rogues in the whole world, going up and down. But, fortunately, mad as well."

"So he buys a house," said Lafago. "If he had his wits about him, a liar of that size, he'd take it—like that. As it is, he buys it. Thirty-five thousand francs!"

"Madness turns a great man inside out, like a sack," said Arago. "And if he is rich as well——"

"—money flies in all directions," said Guis.

Nothing could be more satisfactory. They waited impatiently for the stranger's return. Foiral whitewashed the house, cleaned the chimneys, put everything to rights. You may be sure he had a good search for anything that his wife's old man might have left hidden there years ago, and which this fellow might have heard of. They say they're up to anything in Paris.

The stranger came back, and they were all day with the

mules getting his stuff from where the motor truck had left it. By the evening they were in the house, witnesses, helpers, and all—there was just the little matter of paying up the money.

Foiral indicated this with the greatest delicacy in the world. The stranger, all smiles and readiness, went into the room where his bags were piled up, and soon emerged with a sort of book in his hand, full of little *billets*, like those they try to sell for the lottery in Perpignan. He tore off the top one. "Here you are," he said to Foiral, holding it out. "Thirty thousand francs."

"No," said Foiral.

"What the hell now?" asked the stranger.

"I've seen that sort of thing," said Foiral. "And not for thirty thousand francs, my friend, but for three million. And afterwards—they tell you it hasn't won. I should prefer the money."

"This is the money," said the stranger. "It's as good as money anyway. Present this, and you'll get thirty thousand-franc notes, just like those I gave you."

Foiral was rather at a loss. It's quite usual in these parts to settle a sale at the end of a month. Certainly he wanted to run no risk of crabbing the deal. So he pocketed the piece of paper, gave the fellow good-day, and went off with the rest of them to the village.

The stranger settled in. Soon he got to know everybody. Foiral, a little uneasy, cross-examined him whenever they talked. It appeared, after all, that he *did* come from Paris, having lived there, and he *was* an American, having been born there. "Then you have no relations in this part of the world?" said Foiral.

"No relations at all."

Well! Well! Well! Foiral hoped the money was all right. Yet there was more in it than that. No relations! It was quite a thought. Foiral put it away at the back of his mind:

he meant to extract the juice from it some night when he couldn't sleep.

At the end of the month, he took out his piece of paper, and marched up to the house again. There was the fellow, three parts naked, sitting under one of the ilex trees, painting away on a bit of canvas. And what do you think he had chosen to paint? Roustand's mangy olives, that haven't borne a crop in living memory!

"What is it?" said the mad fellow. "I'm busy."

"This," said Foiral, holding out the bit of paper. "I need the money."

"Then why, in the name of the devil," said the other, "don't you go and get the money, instead of coming here bothering me?"

Foiral had never seen him in this sort of mood before. But a lot of these laughers stop laughing when it comes to hard cash. "Look here," said Foiral. "This is a very serious matter."

"Look here," said the stranger. "That's what's called a cheque. I give it to you. You take it to a bank. The bank gives you the money."

"Which bank?" said Foiral.

"Your bank. Any bank. The bank in Perpignan," said the stranger. "You go there. They'll do it for you."

Foiral, still hankering after the cash, pointed out that he was a very poor man, and it took a whole day to get to Perpignan, a considerable thing to such an extremely poor man as he was.

"Listen," said the stranger. "You know goddamn well you've made a good thing out of this sale. Let me get on with my work. Take the cheque to Perpignan. It's worth the trouble. I've paid you plenty."

Foiral knew then that Guis had been talking about the price of the house. "All right, my little Guis, I'll think that over some long evening when the rains begin." However, there was nothing for it, he had to put on his best black, take the mule to Estagel, and there get the bus, and the bus took him to Perpignan.

In Perpignan they are like so many monkeys. They push you, look you up and down, snigger in your face. If a man has business—with a bank, let us say—and he stands on the pavement opposite to have a good look at it, he gets elbowed into the roadway half a dozen times in five minutes, and he's lucky if he escapes with his life.

Nevertheless, Foiral got into the bank at last. As a spectacle it was tremendous. Brass rails, polished wood, a clock big enough for a church, little cotton-backs sitting among heaps of money like mice in a cheese.

He stood at the back for about half an hour, waiting, and no one took any notice of him at all. In the end one of the little cotton-backs beckoned him up to the brass railing. Foiral delved in his pocket, and produced the cheque. The cotton-back looked at it as if it were a mere nothing. "Holy Virgin!" thought Foiral.

"I want the money for it," said he.

"Are you a client of the bank?"

"No."

"Do you wish to be?"

"Shall I get the money?"

"But naturally. Sign this. Sign this. Sign on the back of the cheque. Take this. Sign this. Thank you. Good-day."

"But the thirty thousand francs?" cried Foiral.

"For that, my dear sir, we must wait till the cheque is cleared. Come back in about a week."

Foiral, half dazed, went home. It was a bad week. By day he felt reasonably sure of the cash, but at night, as soon as he closed his eyes, he could see himself going into that bank, and all the cotton-backs swearing they'd never seen him before. Still, he got through it, and as soon as the time was up, presented himself at the bank again.

"Do you want a cheque-book?"

"No. Just the money. The money."

"All of it? You want to close the account? Well! Well! Sign here. Sign here."

Foiral signed.

"There you are. Twenty-nine thousand eight hundred and ninety."

"But, sir, it was thirty thousand."

"But, my dear sir, the charges."

Foiral found it was no good arguing. He went off with his money. That was good. But the other hundred and ten! That sticks in a man's throat.

As soon as he got home, Foiral interviewed the stranger. "I am a poor man," said he.

"So am I," said the stranger. "A damned sight too poor to pay you extra because you can't get a cheque cashed in a civilized way."

This was a peculiarly villainous lie. Foiral had, with his own eyes, seen a whole block of these extraordinary thirty-thousand-franc *billets* in the little book from which the stranger had torn this one. But once more there was nothing to be done about it; a plain honest man is always being baffled and defeated. Foiral went home, and put his crippled twenty-nine thousand-odd into the little box behind the stone chimney. How different, if it had been a round thirty thousand! What barbarous injustice!

Here was something to think about in the evenings. Foiral thought about it a lot. In the end he decided it was impossible to act alone, and called in Arago, Quès, Lafago, Vigné, Barilles. Not Guis. It was Guis who had told the fellow he had paid too much for the house, and put his back up. Let Guis stay out of it.

To the rest he explained everything very forcefully. "Not a relation in the whole countryside. And in that book, my dear friends—you have seen it yourselves—ten, twelve, fifteen, maybe twenty of these extraordinary little *billets*."

"And if somebody comes after him? Somebody from America?"

"He has gone off, walking, mad, just as he came here. Anything can happen to a madman, walking about, scattering money."

"It's true. Anything can happen."

"But it should happen before the lawyer comes."

"That's true. So far even the curé hasn't seen him."

"There must be justice, my good friends, society cannot exist without it. A man, an honest man, is not to be robbed of a hundred and ten francs."

"No, that is intolerable."

The next night, these very honest men left their houses, those houses whose tall uprights of white plaster and black shadow appear, in moonlight even more than in sunlight, like a heap of bleached ribs lying in the desert. Without much conversation they made their way up the hill and knocked upon the stranger's door.

After a brief interval they returned, still without much conversation, and slipped one by one into their extremely dark doorways, and that was all.

For a whole week there was no perceptible change in the village. If anything, its darks and silences, those holes in the fierce light, were deeper. In every black interior sat a man who had two of these excellent *billets*, each of which commanded thirty thousand francs. Such a possession brightens the eyes, and enhances the savour of solitude, enabling a man, as the artist would have said, to partake of the nature of Fabre's tarantula, motionless at the angle of her tunnel. But they found it no longer easy to remember the artist. His jabbering, his laughter, even his final yelp, left no echo at all. It was all gone, like the rattle and flash of yesterday's thunderstorm.

So apart from the tasks of the morning and the evening,

performing which they were camouflaged by habit, they sat in their houses alone. Their wives scarcely dared to speak to them, and they were too rich to speak to each other. Guis found it out, for it was no secret except to the world outside, and Guis was furious. But his wife rated him from morning till night, and left him no energy for reproaching his neighbours.

At the end of the week, Barilles sprang into existence in the doorway of his house. His thumbs were stuck in his belt, his face was flushed from lead colour to plum colour, his bearing expressed an irritable resolution.

He crossed to Arago's, knocked, leaned against a doorpost. Arago, emerging, leaned against the other. They talked for some little time of nothing at all. Then Barilles, throwing away the stump of his cigarette, made an oblique and sympathetic reference to a certain small enclosure belonging to Arago, on which there was a shed, a few vines, a considerable grove of olives. "It is the very devil," said Barilles, "how the worm gets into the olive in these days. Such a grove as that, at one time, might have been worth something."

"It is worse than the devil," said Arago. "Believe me or not, my dear friend, in some years I get no more than three thousand francs from that grove."

Barilles burst into what passes for laughter in this part of the world. "Forgive me!" he said. "I thought you said three thousand. Three hundred—yes. I suppose in a good year you might make that very easily."

This conversation continued through phases of civility, sarcasm, rage, fury and desperation until it ended with a cordial handshake, and a sale of the enclosure to Barilles for twenty-five thousand francs. The witnesses were called in; Barilles handed over one of his *billets*, and received five thousand in cash from the box Arago kept in his chimney. Everyone was delighted by the sale: it was felt that things were beginning to move in the village.

They were. Before the company separated, *pourparlers* were already started for the sale of Vigné's mules to Quès for eight thousand, the transfer of Lloubes' cork concession to Foiral for fifteen thousand, the marriage of Roustand's daughter to Vigné's brother with a dowry of twenty thousand, and the sale of a miscellaneous collection of brass objects belonging to Madame Arago for sixty-five francs, after some very keen bargaining.

Only Guis was left out in the cold, but on the way home, Lloubes, with his skin full of wine, ventured to step inside the outcast's doorway, and looked his wife Filomena up and down, from top to toe, three times. A mild interest, imperfectly concealed, softened the bitter and sullen expression upon the face of Guis.

This was a mere beginning. Soon properties began to change hands at a bewildering rate and at increasing prices. It was a positive boom. Change was constantly being dug out from under flagstones, from the strawy interiors of mattresses, from hollows in beams, and holes in walls. With the release of these frozen credits the village blossomed like an orchid sprung from a dry stick. Wine flowed with every bargain. Old enemies shook hands. Elderly spinsters embraced young suitors. Wealthy widowers married young brides. Several of the weaker sort wore their best black every day. One of these was Lloubes, who spent his evenings in the house of Guis. Guis in the evenings would wander round the village, no longer sullen, and was seen cheapening a set of harness at Lafago's, a first-rate gun at Roustand's. There was talk of something very special by way of fiesta after the grape harvest, but this was only whispered, lest the curé should hear of it on one of his visits.

Foiral, keeping up his reputation as leader, made a staggering proposal. It was nothing less than to improve the mule track all the way from the metalled road on the rim of the hills, so that motor trucks could visit the village. It was objected that the wage bill would be enormous. "Yes," said Foiral, "but we shall draw the wages ourselves. We shall get half as much again for our produce."

The proposal was adopted. The mere boys of the village now shared the prosperity. Barilles now called his little shop "Grand Café Glacier de l'Univers et des Pyrénées." The widow Loyau offered room, board, and clothing to certain unattached young women, and gave select parties in the evenings.

Barilles went to Perpignan and returned with a sprayer that would double the yield of his new olive grove. Lloubes went and returned with a positive bale of ladies' underclothing, designed, you would say, by the very devil himself. Two or three keen card players went and returned with new packs of cards, so lustrous that your hand seemed to be all aces and kings. Vigné went, and returned with a long face.

The bargaining, increasing all the time, called for more and more ready money. Foiral made a new proposal. "We will all go to Perpignan, the whole damned lot of us, march to the bank, thump down our *billets*, and show the little cotton-backs whom the money belongs to. Boys, we'll leave them without a franc."

"They will have the hundred and ten," said Quès.

"To hell with the hundred and ten!" said Foiral. "And, boys, after that—well—ha! ha! all men sin once. They say the smell alone of one of those creatures is worth fifty francs. Intoxicating! Stair carpets, red hair, every sort of wickedness! Tomorrow!"

"Tomorrow!" they all cried, and on the morrow they went off, in their stiffest clothes, their faces shining. Every man was smoking like a chimney, and every man had washed his feet.

The journey was tremendous. They stopped the bus at

every café on the road, and saw nothing they didn't ask the price of. In Perpignan they kept together in a close phalanx; if the townspeople stared, our friends stared back twice as hard. As they crossed over to the bank, "Where is Guis?" said Foiral, affecting to look for him among their number. "Has he nothing due to him?" That set them all laughing. Try as they might, they couldn't hold their faces straight. They were all choking with laughter when the swing doors closed behind them.

The Touch of Nutmeg Makes It

dozen big firms subsidize our mineralogical institute, and most of them keep at least one man permanently on research there. The library has the intimate and smoky atmosphere of a club. Logan and I had been there longest and had the two tables in the big window bay. Against the wall, just at the edge of the bay, where the light was bad, was a small table which was left for newcomers or transients.

One morning a new man was sitting at this table. It was not necessary to look at the books he had taken from the shelves to know that he was on statistics rather than formulae. He had one of those skull-like faces on which the skin seems stretched painfully tight. These are almost a hallmark of the statistician. His mouth was intensely disciplined but became convulsive at the least relaxation. His hands were the focal point of a minor morbidity. When he had occasion to stretch them both out together—to shift an open book, for example—he would stare at them for a full minute at a time. At such times the convulsive action of his mouth muscles was particularly marked.

The newcomer crouched low over his table when anyone passed behind his chair, as if trying to decrease the likelihood of contact. Presently he took out a cigarette, but his eye fell on the "No smoking" sign, which was universally disregarded, and he returned the cigarette to its pack. At mid-morning he dissolved a tablet in a glass of water. I guessed at a long-standing anxiety neurosis.

I mentioned this to Logan at lunchtime. He said, "The poor guy certainly looks as miserable as a wet cat."

I am never repelled or chilled, as many people are, by the cheerless self-centredness of the nervous or the unhappy. Logan, who has less curiosity, has a superabundance of good nature. We watched this man sitting in his solitary cell of depression for several days while the pleasant camaraderie of the library flowed all around him. Then, without further discussion, we asked him to lunch with us.

He took the invitation in the typical neurotic fashion, seeming to weigh half-a-dozen shadowy objections before he accepted it. However, he came along, and before the meal was over he confirmed my suspicion that he had been starving for company but was too tied-up to make any move toward it. We had already found out his name, of course—J. Chapman Reid—and that he worked for the Walls Tyman Corporation. He named a string of towns he had lived in at one time or another, and told us that he came originally from Georgia. That was all the information he offered. He opened up very noticeably when the talk turned on general matters, and occasionally showed signs of having an intense and painful wit, which is the sort I like best. He was pathetically grateful for the casual invitation. He thanked us when we got up from the table, again as we emerged from the restaurant, and yet again on the

threshold of the library. This made it all the more natural
to suggest a quiet evening together sometime soon.

During the next few weeks we saw a good deal of J.
Chapman Reid and found him a very agreeable companion. I have a great weakness for these dry, reserved charac-
ters who once or twice an evening come out with a vivid,
penetrating remark that shows there is a volcanic core
smouldering away at high pressure underneath. We might
even have become friends if Reid himself hadn't prevented
this final step, less by his reserve, which I took to be part of
his nature, than by his unnecessary gratitude. He made no
effusive speeches—he was not that type—but a lost dog
has no need of words to show his dependence and his appreciation. It was clear our company was everything to J.
Chapman Reid.

One day Nathan Trimble, a friend of Logan's, looked in
at the library. He was a newspaperman and was killing an
hour while waiting for a train connection. He sat on Logan's table facing the window, with his back to the rest of
the room. I went round and talked to him and Logan. It
was just about time for Trimble to leave when Reid came
in and sat down at his table. Trimble happened to look
around, and he and Reid saw each other.

I was watching Reid. After the first startled stare, he did
not even glance at the visitor. He sat quite still for a minute
or so, his head dropping lower and lower in little jerks,
as if someone was pushing it down. Then he got up and
walked out of the library.

"By God!" said Trimble. "Do you know who that is?
Do you know who you've got there?"

"No," said we. "Who?"

"Jason C. Reid."

"Jason C.?" I said. "No, it's J. Chapman. Oh, yes, I
see. So what?"

"Why, for God's sake, don't you read the news? Don't you remember the Pittsburgh cleaver murder?"

"Nô," said I.

"Wait a minute," said Logan. "About a year or so ago, was it? I read something."

"Damn it!" said Trimble. "It was a front-page sensation. This guy was tried for it. They said he hacked a pal of his pretty nearly to pieces. I saw the body. Never seen such a mess in my life. Fantastic! Horrible!"

"However," said I, "it would appear this fellow didn't do it. Presumably he wasn't convicted."

"They tried to pin it on him," said Trimble, "but they couldn't. It looked hellish bad, I must say. Alone together. No trace of any outsider. But no motive. I don't know. I just don't know. I covered the trial. I was in court every day, but I couldn't make up my mind about the guy. Don't leave any meat cleavers round this library, that's all."

With that, he bade us goodbye. I looked at Logan. Logan looked at me. "I don't believe it," said Logan. "I don't believe he did it."

"I don't wonder his nerves are eating him," said I.

"No," said Logan. "It must be damnable. And now it's followed him here, and he knows it."

"We'll let him know, somehow," said I, "that we're not even interested enough to look up the newspaper files."

"Good idea," said Logan.

A little later Reid came in again, his movements showing signs of intense control. He came over to where we were sitting. "Would you prefer to cancel our arrangement for tonight?" said he. "I think it would be better if we cancelled it. I shall ask my firm to transfer me again. I——"

"Hold on," said Logan. "Who said so? Not us."

"Didn't he tell you?" said Reid. "Of course he did."

"He said you were tried," said I. "And he said you were acquitted. That's good enough for us."

"You're still acquitted," said Logan. "And the date's on, and we *won't* talk."

"Oh!" said Reid. "Oh!"

"Forget it," said Logan, returning to his papers.

I took Reid by the shoulder and gave him a friendly shove in the direction of his table. We avoided looking at him for the rest of the afternoon.

That night, when we met for dinner, we were naturally a little self-conscious. Reid probably felt it. "Look here," he said when we had finished eating, "would either of you mind if we skipped the movie tonight?"

"It's O.K. by me," said Logan. "Shall we go to Chancey's?"

"No," said Reid, "I want you to come somewhere where we can talk. Come up to my place."

"Just as you like," said I. "It's not necessary."

"Yes it is," said Reid. "We may as well get it over."

He was in a painfully nervous state, so we consented and went up to his apartment, where we had never been before. It was a single room with a pull-down bed and a bathroom and kitchenette opening off it. Though Reid had now been in town over two months, there was absolutely no sign that he was living there at all. It might have been a room hired for the uncomfortable conversation of this one night.

We sat down, but Reid immediately got up again and stood between us, in front of the imitation fireplace.

"I should like to say nothing about what happened today," he began. "I should like to ignore it and let it be forgotten. But it can't be forgotten.

"It's no use telling me you won't think about it," said he. "Of course you'll think about it. Everyone did back there. The firm sent me to Cleveland. It became known there, too. Everyone was thinking about it, whispering about it, wondering.

"You see, it would be rather more exciting if the fellow *was* guilty after all, wouldn't it?

"In a way, I'm glad this has come out. With you two, I mean. Most people—I don't want them to know anything. You two—you've been decent to me—I want you to know all about it. All.

"I came up from Georgia to Pittsburgh, was there for ten years with the Walls Tyman people. While there I met —I met Earle Wilson. He came from Georgia, too, and we became very great friends. I've never been one to go about much. Earle was not only my best friend: he was almost my only friend.

"Very well. Earle's job with our company was a better paid one than mine. He was able to afford a small house just beyond the fringe of the town. I used to drive out there two or three evenings a week. We spent the evenings very quietly. I want you to understand that I was quite at home in the house. There was no host-and-guest atmosphere about it. If I felt sleepy, I'd make no bones about going upstairs and stretching out on a bed and taking a nap for half an hour. There's nothing so extraordinary about that, is there?"

"No, nothing extraordinary about that," said Logan.

"Some people seemed to think there was," said Reid. "Well, one night I went out there after work. We ate, we sat about a bit, we played a game of checkers. He mixed a couple of drinks, then I mixed a couple. Normal enough, isn't it?"

"It certainly is," said Logan.

"I was tired," said Reid. "I felt heavy. I said I'd go upstairs and stretch out for half an hour. That always puts me right. So I went up.

"I sleep heavily, very heavily, for half an hour, then I'm all right. This time I seemed to be dreaming, a sort of nightmare. I thought I was in an air raid somewhere, and heard Earle's voice calling me, but I didn't wake, not until the usual half-hour was up anyway.

"I went downstairs. The room below was dark. I called out to Earle and started across from the stairs toward the light switch. Halfway across, I tripped over something—it turned out to be the floor lamp, which had fallen over. And I went down, and I fell flat on him.

"I knew he was dead. I got up and found the light. He was lying there. He looked as if he had been attacked by a madman. He was cut to pieces, almost. God!

"I got hold of the phone at once and called the police. Naturally, while they were coming, I looked round. But first of all I just walked about, dazed. It seems I must have gone up into the bedroom again. I've got no recollection of that, but they found a smear of blood on the pillow. Of course, I was covered with it. Absolutely covered; I'd fallen on him. You can understand a man being dazed, can't you? You can understand him going upstairs, even, and not remembering it? Can't you?"

"I certainly can," said Logan.

"It seems very natural," said I.

"They thought they had trapped me over that," said Reid. "They said so to my face. The idiots! Well, I remember looking around, and I saw what it had been done with. Earle had a great equipment of cutlery in his kitchen. One of our firm's subsidiaries was in that line. One of the things was a meat cleaver, the sort of thing you see usually in a butcher's shop. It was there on the carpet.

"Well, the police came. I told them all I could. Earle was a quiet fellow. He had no enemies. Does *anyone* have that sort of enemy? I thought it must be some maniac. Nothing was missing. It wasn't robbery, unless some half-crazy tramp had got in and been too scared in the end to take anything.

"Whoever it was had made a very clean getaway. Too

clean for the police. And too clean for me. They looked for fingerprints, and they couldn't find any.

"They have an endless routine in this sort of thing. I won't bore you with every single detail. It seemed their routine wasn't good enough—the fellow was too clever for them. But of course they wanted an arrest. So they indicted me.

"Their case was nothing but a negative one. God knows how they thought it could succeed. Perhaps they didn't think so. But, you see, if they could build up a strong presumptive case, and I only got off because of a hung jury—well, that's different from having to admit they couldn't find hair or hide of the real murderer.

"What was the evidence against me? That they couldn't find traces of anyone else! That's evidence of their own damned inefficiency, that's all. Does a man murder his best friend for nothing? Could they find any reason, any motive? They were trying to find some woman first of all. They have the mentality of a ten-cent magazine. They combed our money affairs. They even tried to smell out some subversive tieup. God, if you knew what it was to be confronted with faces out of a comic strip and with minds that match the faces! If ever you are charged with murder, hang yourself in your cell the first night.

"In the end they settled on our game of checkers. Our poor, harmless game of checkers! We talked all the while we were playing, you know, and sometimes even forgot whose turn it was to move next. I suppose there are people who can go berserk in a dispute over a childish game, but to me that's something utterly incomprehensible. Can *you* understand a man murdering his friend over a game? I can't. As a matter of fact, I remember we had to start this game over again, not once but twice—first when Earle mixed the drinks, and then when I mixed them. Each time we forgot who was to move. However, they fixed on that.

They had to find some shadow of a motive, and that was the best they could do.

"Of course, my lawyer tore it to shreds. By the mercy of God there'd been quite a craze at the works for playing checkers at lunchtime. So he soon found half-a-dozen men to swear that neither Earle nor I ever played the game seriously enough to get het up about it.

"They had no other motive to put forward. Absolutely none. Both our lives were simple, ordinary, humdrum, and open as a book. What was their case? They couldn't find what they were paid to find. For that, they proposed to send a man to the death cell. Can you beat that?"

"It sounds pretty damnable," said I.

"Yes," said he passionately. "Damnable is the word. They got what they were after—the jury voted nine to three for acquittal, which saved the faces of the police. There was plenty of room for a hint that they were on the right track all the time. You can imagine what my life has been since! If you ever get into that sort of mess, my friends, hang yourselves the first night, in your cell."

"Don't talk like that," said Logan. "Look here, you've had a bad time. Damned bad. But what the hell? It's over. You're here now."

"And we're here," said I. "If that helps any."

"Helps?" said he. "God, if you could ever guess how it helped! I'll never be able to tell you. I'm no good at that sort of thing. See, I drag you here, the only human beings who've treated me decently, and I pour all this stuff out and don't offer you a drink, even. Never mind, I'll give you one now—a drink you'll like."

"I could certainly swallow a highball," said Logan.

"You shall have something better than that," said Reid, moving toward the kitchenette. "We have a little specialty down in our corner of Georgia. Only it's got to be fixed properly. Wait just a minute."

He disappeared through the door, and we heard corks being drawn and a great clatter of pouring and mixing. While this went on, he was still talking through the doorway. "I'm glad I brought you up here," he said. "I'm glad I put the whole thing to you. You don't know what it means—to be believed, understood by God! I feel I'm alive again."

He emerged with three brimming glasses on a tray. "Try this," he said proudly.

"To the days ahead!" said Logan, as we raised our glasses.

We drank and raised our eyebrows in appreciation. The drink seemed to be a sort of variant of sherry flip, with a heavy sprinkling of nutmeg.

"You like it?" cried Reid eagerly. "There's not many people know the recipe for that drink, and fewer still can make it well. There are one or two bastard versions which some damned fools mix up—a disgrace to Georgia. I could —I could pour the mess over their heads. Wait a minute. You're men of discernment. Yes, by God, you are! You shall decide for yourselves."

With that, he darted back into the kitchenette and rattled his bottles more furiously than before, still talking to us disjointedly, praising the orthodox version of his drink, and damning all imitations.

"Now, here you are," said he, appearing with the tray loaded with drinks very much like the first but rather differently garnished. "These abortions have mace and ginger on the top instead of nutmeg. Take them. Drink them. Spit them out on the carpet if you want to. I'll mix some more of the real thing to take the taste out of your mouth. Just try them. Just tell me what you think of a barbarian who could insist that *that* was a Georgian flip. Go on. Tell me."

We sipped. There was no considerable difference. However, we replied as was expected of us.

"What do you think, Logan?" said I. "The first has it, beyond doubt."

"Beyond doubt," said Logan. "The first is the real thing."

"Yes," said Reid, his face livid and his eyes blazing like live coals. "And *that* is hogwash. The man who calls *that* a Georgian flip is not fit to mix bootblacking. It hasn't the nutmeg. The touch of nutmeg makes it. A man who'd leave out the nutmeg——! I could——!"

He put out both his hands to lift the tray, and his eyes fell on them. He sat very still, staring at them.

Three Bears Cottage

ur hen has laid two eggs," said Mrs. Scrivener, "and I have boiled them for breakfast." As she spoke she unfolded a snowy napkin, and displayed the barnyard treasures, and she placed the white one in her husband's egg-cup, and the brown one in her own.

The Scriveners lived in a house with a steep roof and a white gable, set in a woodland tract, among juvenile birch trees. It was extremely small, but so was the rent, and they called it *Three Bears Cottage*. Their ménage was frugal, for Henry had retired at forty, in order to study Nature. Nevertheless, everything was as neat as a pin, and everything was carefully regarded. Each week, in their tiny garden, a new lettuce approached perfection. Its progress was minutely inspected from day to day, and, at that hour when it reached the crest and pinnacle of its development, they cut it, and ate it.

Another day, they had the cauliflower.

People who live thus, from one cherished detail to the next, invariably have complexions clear to the point of transparency, and bright and bird-like eyes. They are also keenly sensitive to the difference between one new-laid egg and another, which, like many other fine points, is often overlooked by the hurrying multitudes in cities. The Scriveners were both well aware that, contrary to a commercially fostered superstition, it is the brown egg that is superior in nourishment, in appearance, and in flavour. Mr. Scrivener noted that his wife had retained the brown egg for herself, and his eyes grew rounder and more bird-like than before. "Ella," said he, "I notice that you have given me the white egg, and retained the brown one for yourself."

"Well," said she, "why not? Why should I not have the brown egg? It is I who keep everything neat and trim in the house, and polish the canary's cage, which you, if you were a man, would do for me. You do nothing but scratch about in the garden, and then go lounging about the woods, studying Nature."

"Do not call Dickie 'the canary' in that fashion," responded her husband. "I sometimes think you have no affection for any living creature about you, least of all for myself. After all, it is I who feed our dear hen every day, and, when she lays a brown egg, I think I should at least be *asked* if I would like it."

"I think I know what the answer would be," said his wife with a short laugh. "No, Henry. I have not forgotten your conduct when the tomato ripened. I think the less said about who has what in this house, the better."

Henry was unable to think of a fitting reply. He gazed moodily at the white egg, which seemed more than ever contemptible to him. His wife sawed off the top of her own egg with a grating and offensive sound. Henry took another look at his. "By God," thought he, "it is not only white! It is smaller!"

This was altogether too much. "Ella," said Henry, "you probably are uninterested in Ripley's *Believe It or Not*, for you despise the marvels of Nature. I am not sure he did not have a picture of a boiled egg, with an undigested worm coiled up inside it. I believe the egg was a brown one."

"There is no worm in this egg," replied Ella, munching away imperturbably. "Look in your own. Very likely you will find one there."

Henry, like an unskillful operator of a boomerang, was forcibly struck by the idea he had launched at Ella, in the hope of making her abandon her egg to him. He looked closely at his own egg, essayed a spoonful, and found he had no taste for it. "Hell and damn it!" he muttered, for like many a mild man he was subject to fits of fury, in which he was by no means guarded as to his language.

His wife looked at him quickly, so that he was ashamed without being mollified. "Selfishness and greed," said he, "have made the world what it is today." Ella, with unconcealed relish, devoured a heaping spoonful. With tight lips and burning eyes, Henry rose from the table, reached for his cap, and stamped out of the house. Ella, with a lift of her eyebrows, took over his neglected egg, which she found not noticeably inferior in flavour to the first. This put her in an excellent humour, and it was with a whimsical rather than a gloating smile that she set about her household tasks.

Henry, on the other hand, slashed savagely at the tall weeds and grasses as he strode along the path to the woods. "What a fool I was," muttered he to himself, "to retire so early, believing that happiness is to be found in a cottage! I conceived a simplicity as pleasurable as a tale for children. Two cups, one adorned with roses, and the other with cornflowers. Two plates, one with a blue ring, and the other with a red ring. Two apples on the tree, both rosy, but one slightly larger than the other. *And that should be for me!* I am a man, and it is right that I should have the larger one. Yes, it could be a divine life, if Ella had only a sense of the fitness of things. How happy I might be, if only she was less greedy, better tempered, not addicted to raking up old grudges, more affectionate, with slightly yellower hair, slimmer, and about twenty years younger! But what is the good of expecting such a woman to reform?"

He had just reached this point in his meditation when his eye fell upon a singularly handsome mushroom, of the genus *Clavaria*, and he uttered an exclamation of delight. It was part of their frugal economy at *Three Bears Cottage* to enliven their menus with all kinds of gleanings from the woods and fields, with wild berries and hedge salads, and above all with various sorts of edible fungi, which they found singularly palatable and nutritious.

Henry therefore gathered this one, and wrapped it in his handkerchief. His natural impulse was to make tracks for the cottage, and burst in radiant upon his mate (or perhaps enter lugubriously, holding his treasure trove behind his back for a surprise), but in any case sooner or later to come out with it exultingly, with, "Here it is, my love, an admirable specimen of the genus *Clavaria!* Rake together your fire, my dear, and serve it up piping hot for lunch. You shall nibble a little, and I will nibble a little, and thus we shall have half each." This generous urge was dashed by the thought that Ella was neither as good-tempered, nor as yellow-haired, nor as slim, nor as young as she ought to be. "Besides," thought he, "she will certainly contrive to keep the better half for herself, and in any case, it is a mistake to cut a mushroom, for it allows the nutritious juices to escape."

He looked about on all sides in the hope of finding another, but this was the only one. "How eagerly I would take it home," thought he, "if I might be greeted by such a creature as I have often imagined! I would willingly sacrifice the juices. As it is, I had better toast it on a stick. It is a pity, for they tend to dry up that way."

He began to hunt about for some twigs with which to make a little fire, and almost at once his eye fell upon another fungus, of singularly interesting shape, and of a pearly pallor that spoke volumes to the student of Nature. He recognized it at once as the Death Angel, that liberal scientists give a grosser name, calling it *Amanita phalloides*, if the ladies will pardon the Latin. It combines the liveliest of forms with the deadliest of material, and the smallest morsel will fell a man like a thunderbolt. Henry gazed respectfully at this formidable fungus, and was unable to repress a shudder. "Nevertheless," said he, "it is certainly very appropriately named. It is around such a toadstool that one might expect to see a fairy tripping, a delicious little creature with golden hair . . .

"And, by all that's wonderful," cried he, "figuratively speaking, I believe that is just what I *do* see!"

With trembling hands he garnered the lethal tidbit, and wrapped it in his handkerchief beside the other, carefully interposing a fold of the linen to avoid any contact between them. "Ella has always made nasty cracks at Nature," said he. "Now Nature shall have a crack at her."

He at once hurried back to the cottage, where Ella greeted him with a smile. "It is easy to smile when you have had two eggs for breakfast," thought our hero. "Let us see how you'll manage after having *Amanita phalloides* for lunch." This reflection struck him as being highly diverting, and he accorded his wife a very creditable smirk in return, from which she concluded their little tiff was all forgotten. This she found especially gratifying, for she was a simple, primitive creature, and her double breakfast ration had caused the blood to flow warm and sluggish in her veins.

"See what I have found," said Henry. "Two mush-rooms, and of different varieties. This one is a *Clavaria*, a wholesome fungus, with a decent, satisfying flavour."

"And what," said she, "is the other, which looks so white and pearly?"

"Oh, that," said he deceitfully, "that is *Eheu fugaces*."

"What a pretty name!" said she. "But what a very odd shape! I mean, of course, for a mushroom."

"Pay no attention to that," said he. "It is more nutri-tious than you can possibly imagine: it is rich in vitamins D, E, A, T, and H. What's more, it has a flavour fit for a king, so I shall eat it myself, for you can hardly be called kingly, not being built that way."

"Ah, that is true," said she, with a giggle. "That is per-fectly true, darling. Ha! Ha! I am not built that way."

This reply set Henry back a hundred leagues, for he had expected her to assert a strong claim to the deadly mush-room, as soon as she heard him credit it with a superior vitamin content and flavour. However, he was quick-wit-ted, and at once changed his tack. "Nevertheless," said he, "you shall have this excellent mushroom, for I think you thoroughly deserve it."

"Why, Henry," she said, "that is very sweet of you. How can I reward you for your kindness? What can a mere woman do, to show how she appreciates a good husband?"

"Mince them up," said he, "and cook them separately, so as not to confuse the flavours. Serve them each on a toast, and cover them liberally with grated cheese."

"I will do that," she said, "though it goes to my heart to chop it." She gave him a nudge and went into the kitchen, and began to dress and prepare the mushrooms. Henry waited in the sitting-room, thinking of a delicious creature, not a day more than twenty years old. Ella, peeking lov-ingly round the door, recognized the glimmer in his bird-like eye, and continued her cookery with a song in her heart. "He deserves nothing but the best," thought she, "and he shall have it. He shall have the better mushroom, for he is a king among men, and he said it is highly nutritious. After all, I had two eggs for breakfast, and those, *tra-la-la*, were sufficient for me.

"Come, my dear," said she, when all was done. "Here is our lunch ready, and here are our two plates, mine with a blue ring and yours with a red one. Eat heartily, my angel, and soon you shall be rewarded for your kindness and consideration."

Henry, who was peckish by reason of his diminished breakfast, wished moreover to fortify his tissues against the day when the true Goldilocks should arrive at *Three Bears Cottage*. He therefore sawed himself off a sizable morsel and crammed it into his maw. He at once shot out of his chair, and began to leap, writhe, stagger, spin, curvet, gyrate, loop, and flounder all over the room. Simultaneously he was seized with giddiness, nausea, spots before the eyes, palpitations, convulsions, flatulence, and other symptoms too hideous to mention.

"What on earth is the matter, darling?" said his wife. "Are you feeling unwell?"

"The Devil!" he gasped. "I have eaten the Death Angel! I have eaten *Amanita phalloides!*"

"Really, my dear!" said she in amazement. "What an expression! Whatever can you be thinking of?"

"You b——!" cried he. "Will you stand there bandying words? I am dying! I am poisoned! Run for a doctor. Do you hear?"

"Poisoned?" said she. "By that mushroom? Why, Henry, that is the one you tried to palm off on me!"

"I confess it," said he. "I was feeling aggrieved and resentful. Forgive me. And, for heaven's sake, fetch me a doctor, or in five minutes I shall be dead."

"I forgive you for trying to poison me," said Ella. "But

I cannot forget that awful name you called me just now. No, Henry, a lady dog cannot run for a doctor. I shall go no further than to that powerfully built young wood-cutter who is chopping away at an elm tree down in the hollow. He has often whistled when I passed him, like an oriole in full song. I shall ask him what *he* thinks of a man who calls his wife such a name, and what he thinks of a man who brings home a thing like that to his wife. And I have no doubt at all he will tell me."

Wet Saturday

t was July. In the large, dull house they were imprisoned by the swish and the gurgle and all the hundred sounds of rain. They were in the drawing-room, behind four tall and weeping windows, in a lake of damp and faded chintz.

This house, ill-kept and unprepossessing, was necessary to Mr. Princey, who detested his wife, his daughter, and his hulking son. His life was to walk through the village, touching his hat, not smiling. His cold pleasure was to recapture snapshot memories of the infinitely remote summers of his childhood—coming into the orangery and finding his lost wooden horse, the tunnel in the box hedge, and the little square of light at the end of it. But now all this was threatened—his austere pride of position in the village, his passionate attachment to the house—and all because Millicent, his cloddish daughter Millicent, had done this shocking and incredibly stupid thing. Mr. Princey turned from her in revulsion and spoke to his wife.

"They'd send her to a lunatic asylum," he said. "A criminal-lunatic asylum. We should have to move away. It would be impossible."

His daughter began to shake again. "I'll kill myself," she said.

"Be quiet," said Mr. Princey. "We have very little time. No time for nonsense. I intend to deal with this." He called to his son, who stood looking out of the window. "George, come here. Listen. How far did you get with your medicine before they threw you out as hopeless?"

"You know as well as I do," said George.

"Do you know enough—did they drive enough into your head for you to be able to guess what a competent doctor could tell about such a wound?"

"Well, it's a—it's a knock or blow."

"If a tile fell from the roof? Or a piece of the coping?"

"Well, guv'nor, you see, it's like this——"

"Is it possible?"

"No."

"Why not?"

"Oh, because she hit him several times."

"I can't stand it," said Mrs. Princey.

"You have got to stand it, my dear," said her husband. "And keep that hysterical note out of your voice. It might be overheard. We are talking about the weather. If he fell down the well, George, striking his head several times?"

"I really don't know, guv'nor."

"He'd have had to hit the sides several times in thirty or forty feet, and at the correct angles. No, I'm afraid not. We must go over it all again. Millicent."

"No! No!"

"Millicent, we must go over it all again. Perhaps you have forgotten something. One tiny irrelevant detail may save or ruin us. Particularly you, Millicent. You don't *want* to be put in an asylum, do you? Or be hanged?

They might hang you, Millicent. You must stop that shaking. You must keep your voice quiet. We are talking of the weather. Now."

"I can't. I . . . I . . ."

"Be quiet, child. Be quiet." He put his long, cold face very near to his daughter's. He found himself horribly revolted by her. Her features were thick, her jaw heavy, her whole figure repellently powerful. "Answer me," he said. "You were in the stable?"

"Yes."

"One moment, though. Who knew you were in love with this wretched curate?"

"No one. I've never said a——"

"Don't worry," said George. "The whole god-damned village knows. They've been sniggering about it in the Plough for three years past."

"Likely enough," said Mr. Princey. "Likely enough. What filth!" He made as if to wipe something off the backs of his hands. "Well, now, we continue. You were in the stable?"

"Yes."

"You were putting the croquet set into its box?"

"Yes."

"You heard someone crossing the yard?"

"Yes."

"It was Withers?"

"Yes."

"So you called him?"

"Yes."

"Loudly? Did you call him loudly? Could anyone have heard?"

"No, Father. I'm sure not. I didn't call him. He saw me as I went to the door. He just waved his hand and came over."

"How *can* I find out from you whether there was anyone about? Whether he *could* have been seen?"

"I'm sure not, Father. I'm quite sure."

"So you both went into the stable?"

"Yes. It was raining hard."

"What did he say?"

"He said 'Hullo, Milly.' And to excuse him coming in the back way, but he'd set out to walk over to Bass Hill."

"Yes."

"And he said, passing the park, he'd seen the house and suddenly thought of me, and he thought he'd just look in for a minute, just to tell me something. He said he was so happy, he wanted me to share it. He'd heard from the Bishop he was to have the vicarage. And it wasn't only that. It meant he could marry. And he began to stutter. And I thought he meant me."

"Don't tell me what you thought. Exactly what he said. Nothing else."

"Well . . . Oh dear!"

"Don't cry. It is a luxury you cannot afford. Tell me."

"He said no. He said it wasn't me. It's Ella Brangwyn-Davies. And he was sorry. And all that. Then he went to go."

"And then?"

"I went mad. He turned his back. I had the winning post of the croquet set in my hand——"

"Did you shout or scream? I mean, as you hit him?"

"No. I'm sure I didn't."

"Did he? Come on. Tell me."

"No, Father."

"And then?"

"I threw it down. I came straight into the house. That's all. I wish I were dead!"

"And you met none of the servants. No one will go into

the stable. You see, George, he probably told people he was going to Bass Hill. Certainly no one knows he came here. He might have been attacked in the woods. We must consider every detail . . . A curate, with his head battered in——"

"Don't, Father!" cried Millicent.

"Do you want to be hanged? A curate, with his head battered in, found in the woods. Who'd want to kill Withers?"

There was a tap on the door, which opened immediately. It was little Captain Smollett, who never stood on ceremony. "Who'd kill Withers?" said he. "I would, with pleasure. How d'you do, Mrs. Princey. I walked right in."

"He heard you, Father," moaned Millicent.

"My dear, we can all have our little joke," said her father. "Don't pretend to be shocked. A little theoretical curate-killing, Smollett. In these days we talk nothing but thrillers."

"Parsonicide," said Captain Smollett. "Justifiable parsonicide. Have you heard about Ella Brangwyn-Davies? I shall be laughed at."

"Why?" said Mr. Princey. "Why should you be laughed at?"

"Had a shot in that direction myself," said Smollett, with careful sang-froid. "She half said yes, too. Hadn't you heard? She told most people. Now it'll look as if I got turned down for a white rat in a dog collar."

"Too bad!" said Mr. Princey.

"Fortune of war," said the little captain.

"Sit down," said Mr. Princey. "Mother, Millicent, console Captain Smollett with your best light conversation. George and I have something to look to. We shall be back in a minute or two, Smollett. Come, George."

It was actually five minutes before Mr. Princey and his son returned.

"Excuse me, my dear," said Mr. Princey to his wife. "Smollett, would you care to see something rather interesting? Come out to the stables for a moment."

They went into the stable yard. The buildings were now unused except as odd sheds. No one ever went there. Captain Smollett entered, George followed him, Mr. Princey came last. As he closed the door he took up a gun which stood behind it. "Smollett," said he, "we have come out to shoot a rat which George heard squeaking under that tub. Now, you must listen to me very carefully or you will be shot by accident. I mean that."

Smollett looked at him. "Very well," said he. "Go on."

"A very tragic happening has taken place this afternoon," said Mr. Princey. "It will be even more tragic unless it is smoothed over."

"Oh?" said Smollett.

"You heard me ask," said Mr. Princey, "who would kill Withers. You heard Millicent make a comment, an unguarded comment."

"Well?" said Smollett. "What of it?"

"Very little," said Mr. Princey. "Unless you heard that Withers had met a violent end this very afternoon. And that, my dear Smollett, is what you are going to hear."

"Have you killed him?" cried Smollett.

"Millicent has," said Mr. Princey.

"Hell!" said Smollett.

"It *is* hell," said Mr. Princey. "You would have remembered—and guessed."

"Maybe," said Smollett. "Yes. I suppose I should."

"Therefore," said Mr. Princey, "you constitute a problem."

"Why did she kill him?" said Smollett.

"It is one of these disgusting things," said Mr. Princey. "Pitiable, too. She deluded herself that he was in love with her."

"Oh, of course," said Smollett.

"And he told her about the Brangwyn-Davies girl."

"I see," said Smollett.

"I have no wish," said Mr. Princey, "that she should be proved either a lunatic or a murderess. I could hardly live here after that."

"I suppose not," said Smollett.

"On the other hand," said Mr. Princey, "*you* know about it."

"Yes," said Smollett. "I am wondering if I could keep my mouth shut. If I promised you——"

"I am wondering if I could believe you," said Mr. Princey.

"If I promised," said Smollett.

"If things went smoothly," said Mr. Princey. "But not if there was any sort of suspicion, any questioning. You would be afraid of being an accessory."

"I don't know," said Smollett.

"I do," said Mr. Princey. "What are we going to do?"

"I can't see anything else," said Smollett. "You'd never be fool enough to do me in. You can't get rid of two corpses."

"I regard it," said Mr. Princey, "as a better risk than the other. It could be an accident. Or you and Withers could both disappear. There are possibilities in that."

"Listen," said Smollett. "You can't——"

"Listen," said Mr. Princey. "There may be a way out. There *is* a way out, Smollett. You gave me the idea yourself."

"Did I?" said Smollett. "What?"

"You said you would kill Withers," said Mr. Princey. "You have a motive."

"I was joking," said Smollett.

"You are always joking," said Mr. Princey. "People think there must be something behind it. Listen, Smollett, I can't trust you, therefore you must trust me. Or I will kill you now, in the next minute. I mean that. You can choose between dying and living."

"Go on," said Smollett.

"There is a sewer here," said Mr. Princey, speaking fast and forcefully. "That is where I am going to put Withers. No outsider knows he has come up here this afternoon. No one will ever look there for him unless you tell them. You must give me evidence that you have murdered Withers."

"Why?" said Smollett.

"So that I shall be dead sure that you will never open your lips on the matter," said Mr. Princey.

"What evidence?" said Smollett.

"George," said Mr. Princey, "hit him in the face, hard."

"Good God!" said Smollett.

"Again," said Mr. Princey. "Don't bruise your knuckles."

"Oh!" said Smollett.

"I'm sorry," said Mr. Princey. "There must be traces of a struggle between you and Withers. Then it will not be altogether safe for you to go to the police."

"Why won't you take my word?" said Smollett.

"I will when we've finished," said Mr. Princey. "George, get that croquet post. Take your handkerchief to it. As I told you. Smollett, you'll just grasp the end of this croquet post. I shall shoot you if you don't."

"Oh, hell," said Smollett. "All right."

"Pull two hairs out of his head, George," said Mr. Princey, "and remember what I told you to do with them. Now, Smollett, you take that bar and raise the big flagstone with the ring in it. Withers is in the next stall. You've got to drag him through and dump him in."

"I won't touch him," said Smollett.

"Stand back, George," said Mr. Princey, raising his gun.

"Wait a minute," cried Smollett. "Wait a minute." He did as he was told.

Mr. Princey wiped his brow. "Look here," said he. "Everything is perfectly safe. Remember, no one knows that Withers came here. Everyone thinks he walked over to Bass Hill. That's five miles of country to search. They'll never look in our sewer. Do you see how safe it is?"

"I suppose it is," said Smollett.

"Now come into the house," said Mr. Princey. "We shall never get that rat."

They went into the house. The maid was bringing tea into the drawing-room. "See, my dear," said Mr. Princey to his wife, "we went to the stable to shoot a rat and we found Captain Smollett. Don't be offended, my dear fellow."

"You must have walked up the back drive," said Mrs. Princey.

"Yes. Yes. That was it," said Smollett in some confusion.

"You've cut your lip," said George, handing him a cup of tea.

"I . . . I just knocked it."

"Shall I tell Bridget to bring some iodine?" said Mrs. Princey. The maid looked up, waiting.

"Don't trouble, please," said Smollett. "It's nothing."

"Very well, Bridget," said Mrs. Princey. "That's all."

"Smollett is very kind," said Mr. Princey. "He knows all our trouble. We can rely on him. We have his word."

"Oh, have we, Captain Smollett?" cried Mrs. Princey. "You *are* good."

"Don't worry, old fellow," Mr. Princey said. "They'll never find anything."

Pretty soon Smollett took his leave. Mrs. Princey pressed

his hand very hard. Tears came into her eyes. All three of them watched him go down the drive. Then Mr. Princey spoke very earnestly to his wife for a few minutes and the two of them went upstairs and spoke still more earnestly to Millicent. Soon after, the rain having ceased, Mr. Princey took a stroll round the stable yard.

He came back and went to the telephone. "Put me through to Bass Hill police station," said he. "Quickly . . . Hullo, is that the police station? This is Mr. Princey, of Abbott's Laxton. I'm afraid something rather terrible has happened up here. Can you send someone at once?"

Squirrels Have Bright Eyes

I had what appeared to be the misfortune to fall in love with a superb creature, an Amazon, a positive Diana. Her penthouse *pied-à-terre* was a single, enormous room, liberally decorated with the heads and skins of the victims of her Lee-Enfield, her Ballard, her light Winchester repeater. Bang—a hearth-rug! Crack—a fur coat! Pop, pop—a pair of cosy mittens!

But, as a matter of fact, clothes suffocated her. Supremely Nordic, she ranged her vast apartment clad only in a sort of kirtle. This displayed four magnificent limbs, sunburned several tones darker than her blonde and huntress hair. So I fell in love. What limbs! What hair! What love!

She only laughed. "Squirrel," she said—she called me Squirrel—"it's no good. You're a real pet, though; you remind me a little of Bopotiti. He lived in a tree on the Congo.

"Bogey," she said to her hateful little female adorer, who was always curled up on some skin or other, "Bogey," she said, "show him that snap of Bopotiti."

"Really," I said, "this is not like me at all. I am more graceful, more bird-like."

"Yes, but he used to bring me *mjna-mjnas*. Every morning."

"I will bring you love, at all hours. Marry me."

"No."

"Live with me."

"No, no. I live with my guns. The world cannot utter its gross libidinous sneers at a girl who lives chastely with her Lee-Enfield, her Ballard, her light Winchester."

"Love is better."

"Ha! Ha! Forgive me. I must laugh now." And she flung herself upon a polar-bear skin in a paroxysm of giant mirth.

Utterly crushed, I went out to do myself in. Racking my brain for the most expressive method, I suddenly remembered a man called Harringay, a taxidermist who was often at her cocktail parties, where he had eyed me with a friendly interest.

I went to his shop. He was there alone. "Harringay! Stuff me!"

"Sure. What shall it be? Steak? Chop suey? Something fancy?"

"No, Harringay, bitumen. Harringay, I want you to employ your art upon me. Send me to Miss Bjornstjorm with my compliments. For her collection. I love her." Here I broke down.

Harringay, that owl-like man, acted magnificently. He gave me his philosophy, put new heart into me. "Go just as you are," said he. "Perhaps love will come. Fortunately your eyes are somewhat glassy by nature. You have only to hold the pose."

"You think love will come?"

"She must at any rate recognize you as an admirably motionless companion for a—it's on the tip of my tongue —one of those things up in a tree to shoot from."

"It's on the tip of mine, too. I'll gamble on it. Harringay, you are a friend."

"No, no. It will be an advertisement for me."

"No, no. You are a friend. In one moment I shall be ready."

I was. He carried me to her apartment. "Brynhild, here is something more for your natural history museum."

"Why, it's Squirrel! Is he stuffed?"

"For love of you, Brynhild."

"How life-like! Harringay, you are the king of taxidermists."

"Yes, and I service him every day. It's a new method. It's all arranged for. Shall I put him in that alcove?"

"Yes, and we'll have a cocktail party. Right away. Everybody must come. Bogey, call everybody."

"Even Captain Fenshawe-Fanshawe?"

"Yes, by all means the Captain."

She collapsed, roaring with laughter, upon a flamboyant tiger-skin. She was still laughing when the guests poured in. The gigantic Captain Fenshawe-Fanshawe, my rival with the monocle and the Habsburg chin, taller than Brynhild herself, towered among them.

Everybody laughed, chattered, and admired. "Marvellous work, Mr. Harringay! When our dear Pongo dies, I shall send him to you."

"I hope you will do our Fifi, Mr. Harringay."

Harringay bowed and smiled.

"He did it for love, they say."

"Love!" boomed the Captain, filliping me under the nose. I trembled with rage and mortification.

"Be careful! He's very delicately wired," said Harringay.

"Love!" boomed the Captain. "A squirrel! Ha! Ha! It takes a full-sized man to hold a worth-while amount of love. What sort of heart did you find in him, Harringay?"

"Quite a good sort," said Harringay. "Broken of course."

Brynhild's laughter, which had been continuous, stopped.

"A squirrel!" sneered the Captain. "Didn't know you went in for small deer, Brynhild. Send you a stuffed mouse for Christmas."

He had not observed Brynhild's expression. I had. It looked like one of those bird's-eye views of the world you see before a news-reel, with everything going round and round: clouds, continents, seas, one thing after another. Suddenly, in a single convulsive movement, she was off her flamboyant tiger-skin, and stretched superbly prone on the funeral pelt of a black panther. "Leave me!" she cried chokingly. "Go away, everybody. Go away! Go away!"

The guests felt something was wrong. They edged out.

"Does that mean me?" said the Captain.

"Go away!" she cried.

"Me, too?" said Bogey.

"Everybody," sobbed Brynhild. Nevertheless a woman must have a friend: she clutched her by the hand.

"Brynhild! What is it? You are crying. I have never seen you cry. Tell me. We are alone."

"Bogey, he did it for love."

"Yes."

"I've just realized what that means, Bogey. I didn't know. I've been all my life hunting things—killing them—having them stuffed. Bogey, that's all done now. He's everything to me. I'll marry him."

"I don't think you can, if he's stuffed, Brynhild darling."

"Live with him, then."

"The world——?"

"The world's gross libidinous sneers can't touch a girl who lives with a man who's stuffed, Bogey. But I shall seat him at table, and talk to him, just as if he were alive."

"Brynhild, you're wonderful!"

I agreed. At the same time my position was a difficult one. It is no joke to have to seem stuffed when your beloved adores you, passionately, remorsefully, seats you up at table, talks to you in the firelight, tells you all, weeps even. And yet, if I unbent, if I owned up, I felt her newborn love might wither in the bud.

Sometimes she would stroke my brow, press a burning kiss upon it, dash off, fling herself down on a leopard-skin, and do her exercises, frantically, hopelessly. I needed all my control.

Harringay called every morning, "to service me" as he said. He insisted that Brynhild should go out for an hour, pretending that a professional secret was involved. He gave me my sandwich, my glass of milk, dusted me thoroughly, massaged my joints where they were stiff.

"You can't massage the stiffness out of this absurd situation," said I.

"Trust me," he said.

"All right," I said. "I will."

Brynhild returned, as usual, five minutes or so too early. She couldn't stay away the full hour. "I miss him so," she said, "when I'm out. And yet, when I come back, he's stuffed. It's too terrible."

"Perhaps I can help you," said Harringay.

"I dare not believe it," she said, clutching her heart.

"What?" cried he. "And you the little girl who shoots tigers? Pluck up your courage. Would you be too scared to believe in an artificial leg?"

"No," said she. "I could face that."

"One of those modern ones," said he, "that walk, kick, dance even, all by machinery?"

"Yes," she said. "I believe in it."

"Now," said he, "for his sake, believe in two of them."

"I will. I do."

"Be brave. Two arms as well."

"Yes. Yes."

"And so forth. I can make his jaw work. He'll eat. He'll open and shut his eyes. Everything."

"Will he speak to me?"

"Well, maybe he'll say 'Mamma.'"

"Science! It's wonderful! But—what will the world say?"

"I don't know. 'Bravo!' Something of that sort."

"No. Gross libidinous sneers. If I live with him, and he says 'Mamma.' And I can't marry him because he's stuffed. Oh, I knew it would be no good."

"Don't worry," said Harringay. "These are just technicalities. I'll straighten it all out. More tomorrow."

She saw him out, and came back shaking her head. She was in despair. So was I. I knew the Diana element in her. So did she. She spent the afternoon on the skin of an immense grizzly. I longed to be with her. I felt myself as if I were on the skin of a porcupine.

Suddenly, just as the shadows were falling thick in the vast apartment, there was a knock at the door. She opened. It was the abominable Fenshawe-Fanshawe.

"What do you want?" said she.

"Guess," said he.

"I wouldn't dream of it," said she.

"No need to," said he, removing his jacket.

"What are you doing?" said she.

"I have waited long enough," said he. "Listen, I don't like that kirtle. It doesn't suit you."

She made a bound, however, and reached the wall. Her guns were there. She pointed the Lee-Enfield. "Stand back!" she cried.

The Captain, sneering, continued to advance.

She pulled the trigger. A hollow click sounded. The Captain smiled and came nearer.

She caught up to the Ballard. Click. The Winchester light repeater. Click! Click! Click!

"I removed the cartridges," said the Captain, "when you where laughing so heartily at the cocktail party."

"Oh, Squirrel. If you could help me!"

"He can't. He's stuffed"

"Oh, Squirrel! Help me! Squirrel! Squirre——" At that moment, he seized her. She broke free. "Help me!"

"You're durn tootin' I will," said I, rising stiffly from my seat. The effect, in the shadowy alcove, was probably uncanny. The Captain gave a throbbing cry. He turned and fled for the door. My blood was up, however, and regardless of the pins and needles I pursued him, snatching a prize elephant's tusk as I ran. While yet he scrabbled at the latch I let him have it. He fell.

I felt Brynhild beside me, a true comrade. "Forgive me," I said. "I have deceived you."

"You have saved me. My hero!"

"But I'm not stuffed," I murmured.

"At least," said she, "you have more stuffing in you than that great beast."

"He will need it now, Brynhild. Or the mountainous carcass will become offensive."

"Yes, We'll call in Harringay."

"Good old Harringay!"

"A clean kill, Squirrel mine! Great hunting!"

"Thank you."

I put one foot on the mighty torso, then the other. Our lips were on a level.

"Brynhild! May I?"

"Yes."

"Really?"

"Yes."

It was a divine moment. We sank upon the skin of a giant panda. Bogey knocked in vain.

Next day, of course, we were married.

Halfway to Hell

ouis Thurlow, having decided to take his own life, felt that at least he might take his own time also. He consulted his bank-book; there was a little over a hundred pounds left. "Very well," said he. "I'll get out of this flat, which stinks, and spend a really delightful week at Mutton's. I'll taste all the little pleasures just once more, to say good-bye to them."

He engaged his suite at Mutton's, where he kept the pageboys on the run. At one moment they had to rush round into Piccadilly to buy him chrysanthemums, in which to smell the oncoming autumn, which he would never see. Next they were sent to Soho to get him some French cigarettes, to put him in mind of a certain charming hotel which overlooked the Seine. He had also a little Manet sent round by the Neuilly Galleries—"To try living with," he said, with the most whimsical smile. You may be sure he ate and drank the very best; just a bite of this and a glass of that, he had so many farewells to take.

On the last night of all he telephoned Celia, whose voice he felt inclined to hear once more. He did not speak, of course, though he thought of saying, "You should really not keep on repeating 'Hallo,' but say 'Goodbye.'" However, she had said that already, and he had been taught never to sacrifice good taste to a bad *mot*.

He hung up the receiver, and opened the drawer in which he had stored his various purchases of veronal tablets.

"It seems a great deal to get down," he thought. "Everything is relative. I prided myself on not being one of those panic-stricken, crack-brained suicides who rush to burn out their guts with gulps of disinfectant; now it seems scarcely less civilized to end this pleasant week with twenty hard swallows and twenty sips of water. Still, life is like that. I'll take it easy."

Accordingly he arranged his pillows very comfortably, congratulated himself on his pyjamas, and propped up a photograph against his bedside clock. "I have no appetite," he said. "I force myself to eat as a duty to my friends. There is no bore like a despairing lover." And with that he began to toy with this last, light, plain little meal.

The tablets were not long in taking effect. Our hero closed his eyes. He put on a smile such as a man of taste would wish to wear when found in the morning. He shut off that engine which drives us from one moment to the next, and prepared to glide into the valley of the shadow.

The glide was a long one. He anticipated no landing, and was the more surprised to learn that there is no such thing as nothing, while there is quite definitely such a thing as being dead in the most comfortable bedroom in all Mutton's Hotel.

"Here I am," he said. "Dead! In Mutton's Hotel!"

The idea was novel enough to make him get out of bed at once. He noticed that his corpse remained there, and was glad to observe that the smile was still in place, and looked extremely well.

He strolled across to the mirror to see if his present face was capable of an equally subtle expression, but when he came to look in he saw nothing at all. Nevertheless he obviously had arms and legs, and he felt that he could still do his old trick with his eyebrows. From this he assumed that he was much the same, only different.

"I am just invisible," he said, "and in that there are certain advantages."

He decided to go out at once, in order to have a bit of fun. He went down the stairs, followed a departing guest through the revolving door, and in two minutes he was walking down Cork Street. It appeared to be just after midnight; there was a bobby, a taxi or two, and a few ladies, none of whom took any notice of him at all.

He had not gone twenty yards, however, and was, as a matter of fact, just passing his tailor's, when a lean dark figure detached itself from the shadows which hung about the railings in front of the shop, and coming up close behind his elbow, said, "Damn and blast it, man, you *have* been a time!"

Louis was a little put out at finding himself not so invisible as he had thought. Still, he glanced at the stranger and saw that his eyes were as luminous as a cat's eyes, from which it was plain that he could see better than most.

"Do you mean," said Louis, "that I've been keeping you waiting?"

"I've been hanging about here, freezing, for a week," said the stranger peevishly.

Now it was only September, and the nights, though nippy, were not as cold as all that. Louis put two and two together. "Is it possible," said he, "that you have been waiting to—to take me in charge, so to speak, on account of my recent suicide?"

"I have," said the fiend. "You'll come quietly, I suppose."

"My dear fellow," said Louis, "I know you have your duty to do, and in any case I'm not the sort of person to make a scene in the street. I'm sorry if I've kept you hanging about in the cold, but the truth is I had no idea of your existence, so I hope there'll be no ill feeling."

"I've got an ill feeling all right," replied the other, grumpily. "I swear I've got the 'flu, curse it!" And with that he sneezed miserably. "The worst of it is," he added, "we've got such a *human* of a way to go. I shall be fit for nothing for weeks."

"Really, I can't bear to hear you sneeze like that," cried our hero. "Have you ever tried the Quetch at the Rat Trap Club?"

"What Quetch?" asked the other, between sneezes.

"It tastes like liquid fire," replied Louis. "I believe it's made from plum stones, though why I can't tell you. Possibly to cure your cold."

"Liquid fire, eh?" observed the stranger, his eyes glowing like cigarette ends.

"Come and try it," said Louis.

"I don't know," said the other. "We're a week late through your fault. I don't see why we shouldn't be half an hour later through mine. I suppose there'll be trouble if they hear of it."

Louis assured him that this last half-hour must be put down to his account also. "You caught the cold through my delay," said he. "Therefore I am responsible for the time you take to cure it." The fiend obviously believed this, which caused our hero to reflect that he must be a very simple fiend.

They set out for the Rat Trap Club. Passing through Piccadilly Circus, the fiend indicated the Underground, saying, "That's where I'm going to take you when we've had this drop of what-d'ye-call-it."

"That does not take you to Hell," said Louis, "but only to Barons Court. The mistake is pardonable."

"No mistake," replied the fiend. "Let's cross the road this way, and I'll show you what I mean."

They went in, and travelled down the escalator, chatting very affably. It was fairly crowded with more ordinary passengers, but our friends attracted no attention whatever. There are a great many fiendish-looking individuals travelling on this subway, and others of a corpsy appearance. Besides, now I come to think of it, they were invisible.

When they had reached the ordinary lowest level, where the trains run, "Come," said the fiend, and drew Louis into a passage he had never before noticed, up which there came a huger clanking and a sultrier blast. He saw a notice saying, KEEP TO THE WRONG. A few paces brought them to the top of an escalator such as our hero had never dreamed of: it swooped down from under their feet with a roar and a groan, down into the close innards of the earth. Its passage was lit by the usual lamps. Louis, whose sight seemed to have become extremely keen, saw that at some far point on its vast curve the black shades changed to blue, and the lamps gave place to stars. However, it seemed to go on the devil of a long way past that.

For the rest, it was made just like all other escalators, except in matters of details. Its sides were adorned with pictorial advertisements of temptations, some of which Louis thought might be very interesting. He could have stepped on, for there was no barrier or ticket collector, but, as we have seen, he liked to take his time.

Now and then, he and his companion were jostled by other fiends and their charges. I am afraid some of the latter were behaving in rather an undignified manner, and had to be marched along in a sort of policeman's grip. The effect was degrading. Louis was interested to see, however, how tremendously the escalator accelerated once it felt the weight of these infernal policemen and their victims. It was a tremendous spectacle to see this narrow moving chain, dimly lit, roaring, rushing down, looping the distance between Earth and Hell, which is greater than one would imagine.

"What did you do before this sort of thing was invented?" asked Louis.

"We had to leap down, like chamois, from star to star," replied the fiend.

"Splendid!" said Louis. "Now let's go and have that drink."

The fiend consenting, they went off to the Rat Trap, and, slipping into a cubby-hole behind the bar, they helped themselves to a full bottle of the famous Quetch. The fiend disdained a glass, and put the bottle to his lips, whereupon Louis saw, to his great amazement, this powerful form of brandy was actually brought to the boil. The fiend appeared to like it. When the liquid was gone he sucked away at the bottle, the melting sides of which collapsed like the skin of a gooseberry sucked at by a child. When he had drawn it all into his mouth, he smiled, pursed his lips, and blew out the glass again, this time more like a cigarette-smoker exhaling his first puff. What's more, he didn't blow the glass into bottle shape as formerly, but into the most delightful statuary piece, most realistic, most amusing. "Adam and Eve," said he laconically, placing it on the table to cool.

"Oh, very, very good!" cried Louis. "Can you do Mars and Venus?"

"Oh, yes," said the fiend. Louis immediately commandeered several more bottles of Quetch.

He called for one or two other subjects, of a nature that

would hardly interest the reader. The fiend, however, thought each more amusing than the last, and nearly split his sides over the effect of a hiccup on Lady Godiva. The fact is, he was getting rather tight. Louis encouraged him, not so much for the love of art as because he had no great desire to ride on that escalator.

At last the fiend could drink no more. He got up, jingled his money (fiends have money—that's where it's all gone to), puffed out his cheeks. "Whoops!" said he, with a hiccup. "My cold's better, I believe. If it isn't, well, then—to Hell with it! that's what I say. Ha! Ha!"

Louis, you may be sure, told him he was a fine fellow. "Well," said he, as they stood on the steps of the Club, "I suppose you're going that way; I'm going this." He made a bit of a face, pleasantly, raised his hat, and set off along the street, scarcely daring to breathe till he had rounded the corner.

When he thought himself in safety, "By Jove," said he, "I'm well rid of that fellow. Here I am, dead, invisible, and the night is yet young. Shall I go and see what Celia's doing?"

Before he could embark on this rash project, he felt a very hard hand on his arm, looked round, and saw his custodian.

"Oh, there you are," said he. "I wondered where you'd got to."

"Drunk as a lord," said the fiend, with a smile. "Got to see each other home, eh?"

There was nothing for it. They set out for Piccadilly Circus. The fiend kept his hand on Louis' wrist, quite inoffensively of course, only Louis would rather it had not been there.

So they went chatting into the subway again. Just as they got to the level of the Piccadilly line, which is where the infernal aperture gapes for those who are privileged to see it, whom should Louis see, in top hat, white silk scarf, and all the rest, but his damned nasty rival, catching a late train home.

"I bet," said Louis at once, addressing the fiend, "that you are not strong enough to carry me on your back from here to the escalator."

The fiend, with a sneer of contempt, immediately bent down. Louis, with a desperate effort, picked hold of his rival round the waist and dumped him on the back of the fiend, who gripped his legs, and started off like a race-horse.

"Carry you all the way to Hell for tuppence!" cried he, in drunken pride.

"Done!" cried Louis, who was skipping along beside them to enjoy the spectacle.

He had the delicious pleasure of seeing them jump on the escalator, whose terrific acceleration seemed even more marked and more admirable than before.

Louis returned to the street as happy as a king. He walked about for a bit, and suddenly decided to look in at Mutton's Hotel to see how his corpse was getting on.

He was rather annoyed to see, even as he stood looking at it, that the effective smile, over which he had taken so much trouble, was slipping. In fact, it was beginning to look altogether idiotic. Without giving the matter a thought, he instinctively nipped inside to hook it back into place. In doing so he twitched his nose, found it necessary to sneeze, opened his eyes, and, in a word, found himself quite alive and no longer kicking, in that excellent bed-room of Mutton's Hotel.

"Well, upon my word!" said he, glancing at the bedside table. "Is it possible I dropped off to sleep after taking only two of those tablets? There is really something to be said for taking one's time. It must have been just a vivid dream."

In short, he was glad to be alive, and still gladder a day or two afterwards, when some news came through that

made it seem that it was not a dream after all. Louis' rival
was announced as missing, having last been seen by two
friends at the entrance of Piccadilly Circus station shortly
after midnight on Tuesday.

"Who'd have thought it?" said Louis. "Anyway, I suppose I had better go and see Celia."

However, he had learned the advantage of taking his
time, and before he went he thought better of it, and, in
fact, did not go at all, but went to Paris for the autumn,
which shows that girls shouldn't play fast and loose with
the affections of small men with blue eyes, or they may
find themselves left in the lurch.

The Lady on the Grey

ingwood was the last of an Anglo-Irish family which had played the devil in County Clare for a matter of three centuries. At last all their big houses were sold up, or burned down by the long-suffering Irish, and of all their thousands of acres not a single foot remained. Ringwood, however, had a few hundred a year of his own, and if the family estates had vanished he at least inherited a family instinct, which prompted him to regard all Ireland as his domain, and to rejoice in its abundance of horses, foxes, salmon, game, and girls.

In pursuit of these delights Ringwood ranged and roved from Donegal to Wexford through all the seasons of the year. There were not many hunts he had not led at some time or other on a borrowed mount, nor many bridges he had not leaned over through half a May morning, nor many inn parlours where he had not snored away a wet winter afternoon in front of the fire.

He had an intimate by the name of Bates, who was another of the same breed and the same kidney. Bates was equally long and lean, and equally hard-up, and he had the same wind-flushed bony face, the same shabby arrogance, and the same seignorial approach to the little girls in the cottages and cowsheds.

Neither of these blades ever wrote a letter, but each generally knew where the other was to be found. The ticket collector, respecfully blind as he snipped Ringwood's third-class ticket in a first-class compartment, would mention that Mr. Bates had travelled that way only last Tuesday, stopping off at Killorglin for a week or two after the snipe. The chambermaid, coy in the clammy bedroom of a fishing inn, would find time to tell Bates that Ringwood had gone on up to Lough Corrib for a go at the pike. Policemen, priests, bagmen, game-keepers, even the tinkers on the roads, would pass on this verbal *pateran*. Then, if it seemed his friend was on to a good thing, the other would pack up his battered kit-bag, put rods and guns into their cases, and drift off to join in the sport.

So it happened that one winter afternoon, when Ringwood was strolling back from a singularly blank day on the bog of Ballyneary, he was hailed by a one-eyed horse dealer of his acquaintance, who came trotting by in a gig, as people still do in Ireland. This worthy told our friend that he had just come down from Galway, where he had seen Mr. Bates, who was on his way to a village called Knockderry, and who had told him very particularly to mention it to Mr. Ringwood if he came across him.

Ringwood turned this message over in his mind, and noted that it was a very particular one, and that no mention was made as to whether it was fishing or shooting his friend was engaged in, or whether he had met with some Croesus who had a string of hunters that he was prepared to lend. "He certainly would have put a name to it if it was anything of that sort! I'll bet my life it's a pair of sisters he's got on the track of. It must be!"

At this thought, he grinned from the tip of his long nose like a fox, and he lost no time in packing his bag and setting off for this place Knockderry, which he had never visited before in all his roving up and down the country in pursuit of fur, feathers, and girls.

He found it was a long way off the beaten track, and a very quiet place when he got to it. There were the usual low, bleak hills all around, and a river running along the valley, and the usual ruined tower up on a slight rise, girdled with a straggly wood and approached by the remains of an avenue.

The village itself was like many another: a few groups of shabby cottages, a decaying mill, half-a-dozen beer-shops and one inn at which a gentleman, hardened to rural cookery, might conceivably put up.

Ringwood's hired car deposited him there, and he strode in and found the landlady in the kitchen and asked for his friend Mr. Bates.

"Why, sure, your honour," said the landlady, "the gentleman's staying here. At least, he is, so to speak, and then, now, he isn't."

"How's that?" said Ringwood.

"His bag's here," said the landlady, "and his things are here, and my grandest room taken up with them (though I've another every bit as good), and himself staying in the house best part of a week. But the day before yesterday he went out for a bit of a constitutional, and—would you believe it, sir?—we've seen neither hide nor hair of him since."

"He'll be back," said Ringwood. "Show me a room, and I'll stay here and wait for him."

Accordingly he settled in, and waited all the evening, but Bates failed to appear. However, that sort of thing bothers no one in Ireland, and Ringwood's only impatience was in connection with the pair of sisters, whose acquaintance he was extremely anxious to make.

During the next day or two he employed his time in strolling up and down all the lanes and bypaths in the neighbourhood, in the hope of discovering these beauties, or else some other. He was not particular as to which it should be, but on the whole he would have preferred a cottage girl, because he had no wish to waste time on elaborate approaches.

It was on the second afternoon, just as the early dusk was falling, he was about a mile outside the village and he met a straggle of muddy cows coming along the road, and a girl driving them. Our friend took a look at this girl, and stopped dead in his tracks, grinning more like a fox than ever.

This girl was still a child in her teens, and her bare legs were spattered with mud and scratched by brambles, but she was so pretty that the seignorial blood of all the Ringwoods boiled in the veins of their last descendant, and he felt an over-mastering desire for a cup of milk. He therefore waited a minute or two, and then followed leisurely along the lane, meaning to turn in as soon as he saw the byre, and beg the favour of this innocent refreshment, and perhaps a little conversation into the bargain.

They say, though, that blessings never come singly, any more than misfortunes. As Ringwood followed his charmer, swearing to himself that there couldn't be such another in the whole country, he heard the fall of a horse's hoofs, and looked up, and there, approaching him at a walking pace, was a grey horse, which must have turned in from some bypath or other, because there certainly had been no horse in sight a moment before.

A grey horse is no great matter, especially when one is so urgently in need of a cup of milk, but this grey horse differed from all others of its species and colour in two respects.

First, it was no sort of a horse at all, neither hack nor hunter, and it picked up its feet in a queer way, and yet it had an arch to its neck and a small head and a wide nostril that were not entirely without distinction. And, second—and this distracted Ringwood from all curiosity as to breed and bloodline—this grey horse carried on its back a girl who was obviously and certainly the most beautiful girl he had ever seen in his life.

Ringwood looked at her, and as she came slowly through the dusk she raised her eyes and looked at Ringwood. He at once forgot the little girl with the cows. In fact, he forgot everything else in the world.

The horse came nearer, and still the girl looked, and Ringwood looked, and it was not a mere exchange of glances, it was wooing and a marriage, all complete and perfect in a mingling of the eyes.

Next moment the horse had carried her past him, and, quickening its pace a little, it left him standing on the road. He could hardly run after it, or shout; in any case he was too overcome to do anything but stand and stare.

He watched the horse and rider go on through the wintry twilight, and he saw her turn in at a broken gateway just a little way along the road. Just as she passed through, she turned her head and whistled, and Ringwood noticed that her dog had stopped by him, and was sniffing about his legs. For a moment he thought it was a smallish wolfhound, but then he saw it was just a tall, lean, hairy lurcher. He watched it run limping after her, with its tail down, and it struck him that the poor creature had had an appalling thrashing not so long ago; he had noticed the marks where the hair was thin on its ribs.

However, he had little thought to spare for the dog. As soon as he got over his first excitement, he moved on in the direction of the gateway. The girl was already out of sight when he got there, but he recognized the neglected avenue which led up to the battered tower on the shoulder of the hill.

Ringwood thought that was enough for the day, so made his way back to the inn. Bates was still absent, but that was just as well. Ringwood wanted the evening to himself in order to work out a plan of campaign.

"That horse never cost two ten-pound notes of any-body's money," said he to himself. "So she's not so rich. So much the better! Besides, she wasn't dressed up much; I don't know what she had on—a sort of cloak or some-thing. Nothing out of Bond Street, anyway. And lives in that old tower! I should have thought it was all tumbled down. Still, I suppose there's a room or two left at the bot-tom. Poverty Hall! One of the old school, blue blood and no money, pining away in this God-forsaken hole, miles away from everybody. Probably she doesn't see a man from one year's end to another. No wonder she gave me a look. God! if I was sure she was there by herself, I wouldn't need much of an introduction. Still, there might be a father or a brother or somebody. Never mind, I'll manage it."

When the landlady brought in the lamp: "Tell me," said he. "Who's the young lady who rides the cobby-look-ing, old-fashioned-looking grey?"

"A young lady, sir?" said the landlady doubtfully. "On a grey?"

"Yes," said he. "She passed me in the lane up there. She turned in on the old avenue, going up to the tower."

"Oh, Mary bless and keep you!" said the good woman. "That's the beautiful Murrough lady you must have seen."

"Murrough?" said he. "Is that the name? Well! Well! Well! That's a fine old name in the west here."

"It is so, indeed," said the landlady. "For they were kings and queens in Connaught before the Saxon came. And herself, sir, has the face of a queen, they tell me."

"They're right," said Ringwood. "Perhaps you'll bring

me in the whiskey and water, Mrs. Doyle, and I shall be comfortable."

He had an impulse to ask if the beautiful Miss Murrough had anything in the shape of a father or a brother at the tower, but his principle was, "least said soonest mended," especially in little affairs of this sort. So he sat by the fire, recapturing and savouring the look the girl had given him, and he decided he needed only the barest excuse to present himself at the tower.

Ringwood had never any shortage of excuses, so the next afternoon he spruced himself up and set out in the direction of the old avenue. He turned in at the gate, and went along under the forlorn and dripping trees, which were so ivied and overgrown that the darkness was already thickening under them. He looked ahead for a sight of the tower, but the avenue took a turn at the end, and it was still hidden among the clustering trees.

Just as he got to the end, he saw someone standing there, and he looked again, and it was the girl herself, standing as if she was waiting for him.

"Good afternoon, Miss Murrough," said he, as soon as he got into earshot. "Hope I'm not intruding. The fact is, I think I had the pleasure of meeting a relation of yours down in Cork, only last month. . . ." By this time he had got close enough to see the look in her eyes again, and all this nonsense died away in his mouth, for this was something beyond any nonsense of that sort.

"I thought you would come," said she.

"My God!" said he. "I had to. Tell me—are you all by yourself here?"

"All by myself," said she, and she put out her hand as if to lead him along with her.

Ringwood, blessing his lucky stars, was about to take it, when her lean dog bounded between them and nearly knocked him over.

"Down!" cried she, lifting her hand. "Get back!" The dog cowered and whimpered, and slunk behind her, creeping almost on its belly. "He's not a dog to be trusted," she said.

"He's all right," said Ringwood. "He looks a knowing old fellow. I like a lurcher. Clever dogs. What? Are you trying to talk to me, old boy?"

Ringwood always paid a compliment to a lady's dog, and in fact the creature really was whining and whimpering in the most extraordinary fashion.

"Be quiet!" said the girl, raising her hand again, and the dog was silent.

"A cur," said she to Ringwood. "Did you come here to sing the praises of a half-breed cur?" With that she gave him her eyes again, and he forgot the wretched dog, and she gave him her hand, and this time he took it and they walked toward the tower.

Ringwood was in the seventh heaven. "What luck!" thought he. "I might at this moment be fondling that little farm wench in some damp and smelly cowshed. And ten to one she'd be snivelling and crying and running home to tell her mammy. This is something different."

At that moment, the girl pushed open a heavy door, and, bidding the dog lie down, she led our friend through a wide, bare, stone-flagged hall and into a small vaulted room which certainly had no resemblance to a cowshed except perhaps it smelt a little damp and mouldy, as these old stone places so often do. All the same, there were logs burning on the open hearth, and a broad, low couch before the fire-place. For the rest, the room was furnished with the greatest simplicity, and very much in the antique style. "A touch of the Kathleen ni Houlihan," thought Ringwood. "Well, well! Sitting in the Celtic twilight, dreaming of love. She certainly doesn't make much bones about it."

The girl sat down on the couch and motioned him down

beside her. Neither of them said anything; there was no
sound but the wind outside, and the dog scratching and
whimpering timidly at the door of the chamber.

At last the girl spoke. "You are of the Saxon," said she
gravely.

"Don't hold it against me," said Ringwood. "My people
came here in 1656. Of course, that's yesterday to the Gaelic
League, but still I think we can say we have a stake in the
country."

"Yes, through its heart," said she.

"Is it politics we're going to talk?" said he, putting an
Irish turn to his tongue. "You and I, sitting here in the
firelight?"

"It's love you'd rather be talking of," said she with a
smile. "But you're the man to make a blunder and a
mockery of the poor girls of Eire."

"You misjudge me entirely," said Ringwood. "I'm the
man to live alone and sorrowful, waiting for the one love,.
though it seemed something beyond hoping for."

"Yes," said she. "But yesterday you were looking at
one of the Connell girls as she drove her kine along the
lane."

"Looking at her? I'll go so far as to say I did," said he.
"But when I saw you I forgot her entirely."

"That was my wish," said she, giving him both her
hands. "Will you stay with me here?"

"Ah, that I will!" cried he in a rapture.

"Always?" said she.

"Always," cried Ringwood. "Always and forever!" for
he felt it better to be guilty of a slight exaggeration than
to be lacking in courtesy to a lady. But as he spoke she
fixed her eyes on him, looking so much as if she believed
him that he positively believed himself.

"Ah," he cried. "You bewitch me!" And he took her in
his arms.

He pressed his lips to hers, and at once he was over the brink. Usually he prided himself on being a pretty cool hand, but this was an intoxication too strong for him; his mind seemed to dissolve in sweetness and fire, and at last the fire was gone, and his senses went with it. As they failed he heard her saying "For ever! For ever!" and then everything was gone and he fell asleep.

He must have slept some time. It seemed he was wakened by the heavy opening and closing of a door. For a moment he was all confused and hardly knew where he was.

The room was now quite dark, and the fire had sunk to a dim glow. He blinked, and shook his ears, trying to shake some sense into his head. Suddenly he heard Bates talking to him, muttering as if he, too, was half asleep, or half drunk more likely. "You *would* come here," said Bates. "I tried hard enough to stop you."

"Hullo!" said Ringwood, thinking he must have dozed off by the fire in the inn parlor. "Bates? God, I must have slept heavy! I feel queer. Damn it—so it was all a dream! Strike a light, old boy. It must be late. I'll yell for supper."

"Don't, for Heaven's sake," said Bates, in his altered voice. "Don't yell. She'll thrash us if you do."

"What's that?" said Ringwood. "Thrash us? What the hell are you talking about?"

At that moment a log rolled on the hearth, and a little flame flickered up, and he saw his long and hairy forelegs, and he knew.

Incident on a Lake

r. Beaseley, while shaving on the day after his fiftieth birthday, eyed his reflection, and admitted his remarkable resemblance to a mouse. "Cheep, cheep!" he said to himself, with a shrug. "What do I care? At least, I wouldn't except for Maria. I remember I thought her kittenish at the time of our marriage. How she has matured!"

He knotted his thread-like necktie and hurried downstairs, scared out of his life at the thought of being late for breakfast. Immediately afterwards he had to open his drugstore, which then, in its small-town way, would keep him unprofitably busy till ten o'clock at night. At intervals during the day, Maria would drop in to supervise, pointing out his mistakes and weaknesses regardless of the customers.

He found a brief solace every morning when, unfolding the newspaper, he turned first of all to the engaging feature originated by Mr. Ripley. On Fridays he had a greater treat: he then received his copy of his favourite magazine, *Nature Science Marvels*. This reading provided, so to speak, a hole in his otherwise hopeless existence, through which he escaped from the intolerable into the incredible.

On this particular morning the incredible was kind enough to come to Mr. Beaseley. It came in a long envelope and on the handsome note paper of a prominent law firm. "Believe it or not, my dear," Mr. Beaseley said to his wife, "but I have been left four hundred thousand dollars."

"Where? Let me see!" cried Mrs. Beaseley. "Don't hog the letter to yourself in that fashion."

"Go on," said he. "Read it. Stick your nose in it. Much good may it do you!"

"Oh! Oh!" said she. "So you are already uppish!"

"Yes," said he, picking his teeth. "I have been left four hundred thousand dollars."

"We shall be able," said his wife, "to have an apartment in New York or a little house in Miami."

"You may have half the money and do what you like with it," said Mr. Beaseley. "For my part, I intend to travel."

Mrs. Beaseley heard this remark with the consternation she always felt at the prospect of losing anything that belonged to her, however old and valueless. "So you would desert me," she said, "to go chasing about after some native woman? I thought you were past all that."

"The only native women I am interested in," said he, "are those that Ripley had a picture of—those with lips big enough to have dinner plates set in them. In the *Nature Science Marvels Magazine* they had some with necks like giraffes. I should like to see those, and pygmies, and birds of paradise, and the temples of Yucatan. I offered to give you half the money because I know you like city

life and high society. I prefer to travel. If you want to,
I suppose you can come along."

"I will," said she. "And don't forget I'm doing it for
your sake, to keep you on the right path. And when you
get tired of gawking and rubbering around, we'll have an
apartment in New York and a little house in Miami."

So Mrs. Beaseley went resentfully along, prepared to
endure Hell herself if she could deprive her husband of a
little of his Heaven. Their journeys took them into profound forests, where, from their bare bedroom, whose
walls, floor, and ceiling were austerely fashioned of raw
pine, they could see framed in every window a perfect little Cézanne, with the slanting light cubing bluely among
the perpendiculars of pine trees or exploding on the new
green of a floating spray. In the high Andes, on the other
hand, their window was a square of burning azure, with
sometimes a small, snow-white cloud like a tight roll of
cotton in a lower corner. In the beach huts on tropical
islands, they found that the tide, like an original and tasteful *hôtelier*, deposited a little gift at their door every
morning: a skeleton fan of violet seaweed, a starfish, or a
shell. Mrs. Beaseley, being one of the vulgar, would have
preferred a bottle of Grade A and a copy of *The Examiner*.
She sighed incessantly for an apartment in New York and
a house in Miami, and she sought endlessly to punish the
poor man for depriving her of them.

If a bird of paradise settled on a limb above her husband's head, she was careful to let out a raucous cry and
drive the interesting creature away before Mr. Beaseley
had time to examine it. She told him the wrong hour for
the start of the trip to the temples of Yucatan, and she
diverted his attention from an armadillo by pretending she
had something in her eye. At the sight of a bevy of the
celebrated bosoms of Bali, clustered almost like grapes
upon the quay, she just turned around and went straight

up the gangplank again, driving her protesting husband before her.

She insisted they should stay a long time in Buenos Aires so that she could get a permanent wave, a facial, some smart clothes, and go to the races. Mr. Beaseley humoured her, for he wanted to be fair, and they took a suite in a comfortable hotel. One afternoon when his wife was at the races, our friend struck up an acquaintance with a little Portuguese doctor in the lounge, and before long they were talking vivaciously of hoatzins, anacondas, and axolotls. "As to that," said the little Portuguese, "I have recently returned from the headwaters of the Amazon, where the swamps and lakes are terrific. In one of those lakes, according to the Indians, there is a creature entirely unknown to science: a creature of tremendous size, something like an alligator, something like a turtle, armour-plated, with a long neck, and teeth like sabres."

"What an interesting creature that must be!" cried Mr. Beaseley in a rapture.

"Yes, yes," said the Portuguese. "It is certainly interesting."

"If only I could get there!" cried Mr. Beaseley. "If only I could talk to those Indians! If only I could see the creature itself! Are you by any chance at liberty? Could you be persuaded to join a little expedition?"

The Portuguese was willing, and soon everything was arranged. Mrs. Beaseley returned from the races, and had the mortification of hearing that they were to start almost immediately for a trip up the Amazon and a sojourn on the unknown lake in the dysgenic society of Indians. She insulted the Portuguese, who did nothing but bow, for he had an agreeable financial understanding with Mr. Beaseley.

Mrs. Beaseley berated her husband all the way up the river, harping on the idea that there was no such creature as he sought, and that he was the credulous victim of a confidence man. Inured as he was to her usual flow of complaints, this one made him wince and humiliated him before the Portuguese. Her voice, also, was so loud and shrill that in all the thousands of miles they travelled up the celebrated river he saw nothing but the rapidly vanishing hinder parts of tapirs, spider monkeys, and giant ant-eaters, which hurried to secrete themselves in the impenetrable deeps of the jungle.

Finally they arrived at the lake. "How do we know this is the lake he was speaking of?" Mrs. Beaseley said to her husband. "It is probably just *any* lake. What are those Indians saying to him? You can't understand a word. You take everything on trust. You'll never see a monster. Only a fool would believe in it."

Mr. Beaseley said nothing. The Portuguese learned, from his conversation with the Indians, of an abandoned grass hut, which in due time and after considerable effort they located. They moved into it. The days passed by. Mr. Beaseley crouched in the reeds with binoculars and was abominably bitten by mosquitoes. There was nothing to be seen.

Mrs. Beaseley succeeded in taking on a note of satisfaction without in the least abating her tone of injury. "I will stand this no longer," she said to her husband. "I've allowed you to drag me about. I've tried to keep my eye on you. I've travelled hundreds of miles in a canoe with natives. Now I see you wasting our money on a confidence man. We leave for Para in the morning."

"You may, if you wish," said he. "I'll write you a check for two hundred thousand dollars. Perhaps you can persuade some native in a passing canoe to take you down the river. But I will not come with you."

"We will see about that," said she. She hadn't the faintest intention of leaving her husband alone, for she feared he might enjoy himself. Nevertheless, after he had written out the check and given it to her, she continued to threaten to leave him, for if he surrendered, it would be a triumph, and if he didn't, it would be another little black cross against him.

She happened to rise early one morning and went out to make her ungrateful breakfast on some of the delicious fruits that hung in profusion all around the hut. She had not gone far before she happened to glance at the sandy ground, and there she saw a footprint that was nearly a yard wide, splayed, spurred, and clawed, and the mate to it was ten feet away.

Mrs. Beaseley looked at these admirable footprints with neither awe nor interest—only annoyance at the thought of her husband's triumph and the vindication of the Portuguese. She did not cry out in wonder, or call to the sleeping menfolk, but only gave a sort of honking snort. Then, picking up a sizeable palm frond, this unscrupulous woman obliterated the highly interesting footprints, never before seen by a white person's eyes. Having done so, she smiled grimly and looked for the next, and she wiped out that one, too. A little farther on she saw another, and then still one more, and so on, till she had removed every trace down to the tepid lip of the lake, where the last was printed at the very edge of the water.

Having obliterated this final trace, Mrs. Beaseley straightened up and looked back toward the hut. "You shall hear of this," she said, addressing her sleeping husband, "when we are settled down at Miami and you are too old to do anything about it."

At that moment there was a swirl in the water behind her and she was seized by a set of teeth which quite exactly resembled sabres. She had no leisure to check up on the other points mentioned by the Portuguese doctor, but no doubt they came up to specification. She uttered one brief scream as she disappeared, but her voice was hoarse by reason of the strain she had put on it during the previous weeks, and her cry, even if it had been heard, could easily have been confused with the mating call of the Megatherium, thought to be extinct. In fact, the last surviving Megatherium emerged from the jungle only shortly afterward, looked around in all directions, shrugged his shoulders resignedly, and went back the way he had come.

Shortly afterward, Mr. Beaseley awoke, noted the absence of his wife, and finally went and woke the Portuguese. "Have you seen my wife?" said he.

"Really!" said the little Portuguese, and went to sleep again.

Mr. Beaseley went out and looked around, and at last returned to his friend. "I'm afraid my wife has run away," said he. "I have found her footprints leading down to the lake, where she has evidently encountered some native in a canoe and persuaded him to transport her down the river. She was always threatening to do so in order to take a small house at Miami."

"That is not a bad town," said the Portuguese, "but in the circumstances perhaps Buenos Aires is better. This monster is a great disappointment, my dear friend. Let us go back to Buenos Aires, where I will show you some extraordinary things—in quite a different line of course—such as your Ripley has never dreamed of."

"What an agreeable companion you are!" said Mr. Beaseley. "You make even city life sound attractive."

"Well, if you get tired of it, we can always move on," said the little Portuguese. "I know some tropical islands where the girls—though their lips are not designed to hold dinner plates—are nevertheless marvels of nature, and their dances are wonders of art."

Over Insurance

lice and Irwin were as simple and as happy as any young couple in a family-style motion picture. In fact, they were even happier, for people were not looking at them all the time and their joys were not restricted by the censorship code. It is therefore impossible to describe the transports with which Alice flew to embrace Irwin on his return from work, or the rapture with which Irwin returned her caresses.

It was at least two hours before they even thought about dinner. Even then, it took a long time to get the food on the table, there was so much patting and petting, nibbling at the nape of the neck, mumbling of ears, kissing, fondling, and foolishness to the carrying of every single dish.

When at last the meal was ready, you may be sure they ate with excellent appetite. Nevertheless, whatever was best on his plate, he found time to put it on hers, and she was no slower in picking out some dainty titbit to pop between his eager and rather rubbery lips.

After dinner they would sit in one chair, for all the world like two innocent love-birds in a cage, and he would entertain her with a detailed catalogue of her charms, which gave her the highest possible opinion of his taste and judgment. However, these delights did not endure very long, for they found it necessary to go to bed at an early hour, in order to rise bright and fresh in the morning.

It was a dull and heavy night when he did not wake up once or twice, and switch on the light to assure himself she was not merely a delightful dream. She, blinking through the rosy radiance, was not in the least annoyed at being thus awakened, and they would have a very delightful little conversation and soon would fall happily asleep again.

It is not likely that a husband whose evenings are so contentedly spent at home will often linger in saloons and barrooms when the day's work is done. It was only on rare occasions that Irwin suffered himself to be persuaded, and even then he would suddenly think of his darling; how plump, how soft, how deliciously rounded she was, and he would give a sort of frisk or leap into the air.

"Why the hell do you do that?" his friends would demand. "Did you think someone was giving you a hotfoot or something?"

"No, no," he would reply evasively. "I was just feeling peppy. I was just feeling full of beans."

With that, he would grin all over his face like a fool, and take hasty leave of them, and rush home at top speed, eager to reassure himself as to the genuine existence, and his own miraculous possession, of those tender, those rounded, those infinitely sweet details that made up his delectable little wife.

On one of these occasions he was darting home as fast as his legs would carry him, when he forgot to look about him in crossing the street, and a taxi came swiftly around the corner. Fortunately the driver jammed on his brakes;

otherwise Irwin would have been bowled over like a nine-pin, and might never have seen his honey bun any more. This idea appalled him, and he was unable to dismiss it from his mind.

That night they were seated as usual in their single chair, she tenderly stroking his somewhat sallow chops, and he protruding his lips, like some eager ape at the approach of a milk bottle, in the attempt to imprint kisses on her passing hand. In this interval it was his custom to recite all the events of the long day, and especially how he had missed her. "And that reminds me," said he, "I was very narrowly missed myself, by a taxi, as I was crossing the street, and if the driver had not put his brakes on I should have been bowled over like a ninepin. And then maybe I should never have seen my honey bun any more."

At these words her lips trembled, and her eyes brimmed over with tears. "If *you* didn't see me any more," she said, "then I wouldn't see *you* any more."

"I was just thinking of that," said Irwin.

"We always have the same thoughts," said she.

This, however, was no consolation; their thoughts that evening were so unutterably sad. "All day tomorrow," said Alice, weeping, "I shall be seeing you lying all squashed in the gutter. I'm sure it will be too much for me. I shall just lie down and die."

"Oh, I wish you had not said that," said Irwin. "Now I shall be thinking of you lying all crumpled on the hearth-rug. I shall go mad, or die."

"Oh no!" cried Alice. "Now I shall think of you dying because you think I might be dead. The thought will kill me."

"Now it's even worse," lamented Irwin. "Supposing you should die because you think that I've died because . . . It's too much! I can't bear it!"

"Nor can I," said she.

They hugged each other very tightly, and exchanged
kisses rendered surpassingly salty by their tears. This is
thought by some to add relish, as with peanuts, by bringing out the sweetness. Irwin and Alice were too overcome
to appreciate fine points of this nature; they could think
of nothing but of how each would feel if the other should
suddenly die. Consequently they got never a wink of sleep
all night long, and Irwin was deprived of the pleasure of
dreaming of his Alice, and of switching on the light to find
that she was true. She, on her side, was denied the joy
of blinking up in a sudden rosy radiance to see him hovering and goggling over her. They made up for this by
the passion and fervour of their embraces. Consequently,
when the dawn came cool and grey and rational in at
their window, the unhappy pair were themselves feeling
cooler, greyer, and more rational than at any time since
they had first met.

"Alice," said Irwin, "we must look at this bravely. We
must face up to what may happen, and do our best to provide what consolation we can."

"My only consolation will be to cry," said she.

"Yes, and mine, too," said he. "But would you rather
cry in a fireless garret, and have to stop and get up and do
your own housework, or would you rather cry in a fine
apartment, with a mink coat on, and plenty of servants to
bring in your meals?"

"I would rather have my meals brought in," said she.
"Because then I could go right on crying. And if I had a
mink coat on I should not catch cold, and sneeze in the
middle of it."

"And I would rather cry on a yacht," said he, "where my
tears could be ascribed to the salt spray, and I should not
be thought unmanly. Let us insure one another, darling, so
that if the worst happens we can cry without interruption.
Let us put nine-tenths of our money into insurance."

"It will leave us very little to live on now," said she. "But that is all the better, beloved, because then it will be all the more of a consolation."

"That was exactly my idea," said he. "We always have the same thoughts. This very day I will take out the policies."

"And let us," cried she, "insure our dear bird also," pointing to the feathered cageling, whom they always left uncovered at night, in order that his impassioned trills might grace their diviner raptures.

"You are right," said he. "I will put ten bucks on the bird. His chirpings would be as a string of pearls to me, if ever I were left alone."

That day Irwin made arrangements for the investment of nine-tenths of his earnings. "We are poor," said he, on his return, "but we have each other. If ever we are robbed of that joy we shall at least have many thousands of dollars."

"Do not speak of them," said she. "Hateful dollars!"

"By all means," said he. "Let us have dinner. I was very economical at lunchtime, and I am unusually hungry this evening."

"It will not take long," said she. "I was economical at the market, and have bought a new sort of food. It is amazingly cheap, and it contains a whole alphabet of vitamins, enough to keep a whole family in pep and energy for a week. It says so in the description on the packet."

"Splendid!" said he. "Depend upon it; your dear, sweet, tender little metabolism, and my great, gruff, bearish metabolism, will spell all the honey-dovey-love-words in creation out of that same alphabet of vitamins."

No prospect could be more agreeable, but as the days passed it appeared that their metabolism would have put on a poor show at any word-making game. Or perhaps the manufacturer of the product had been misled by some alien-minded scientist, and had thus erred slightly in the description on the packet. Irwin grew so weak that he could no longer leap into the air at the thought of his darling, his tender, his deliciously rounded little wife. On the other hand, Alice grew so thin that he no longer had any reason to do so.

Her stockings now wrinkled revoltingly upon her stick-like legs.

"I think," thought Irwin, "she no longer rushes to greet me with eager rapture as of yore. Perhaps it's as well. How much more delightful, to be greeted by a porterhouse steak!"

What with this new, disturbing thought, and his saw-dust diet, and the innumerable financial worries that increasingly beset the young lovers, now that nine-tenths of their income went into insurance, Irwin frequently passed wakeful nights, but he no longer felt impelled to switch on the light, and feast his eyes on his beloved. The last time he had done so, she had mistaken his face for an omelette. "Oh, it's only you," she had murmured, turning crossly away.

They fed their new diet to the bird, who soon afterwards flopped on his back, threw up his feet, and died. "At least we get fifty bucks on him," said Irwin. "And he is only a bird!"

"I hope we are not thinking the same thought," said Alice.

"Of course not," said he. "How can you imagine it?"

"I certainly am not," said she. "How shall we spend the money? Shall we buy another canary?"

"No," said he. "Let us have something bigger. Let us buy a big, fat roasting chicken."

"So we will," said she, "and potatoes and mushrooms and string beans, and chocolate cake, and cream and coffee."

"Yes," said he. "And coffee. Get some good, strong,

bitter coffee; something with a real kick to it, if you know what I mean."

"I will get," said she, "the best, the strongest, and the bitterest I can."

That night they were not long in carrying in the dishes, nor in emptying them when they were on the table.

"This is certainly good strong coffee," said Irwin. "And bitter."

"Is it not?" said she. "You didn't by any chance, change the cups round while I was in the kitchen?"

"No, dear," said Irwin. "I was just wondering if you had. It certainly seems to have a kick in it."

"Oh, Irwin!" cried Alice. "Is it possible we had the same thought after all?"

"It feels like it," cried Irwin, legging it for the door faster even than he had done in the old days, when he used to leave saloons and barrooms with such impetuous speed. "I must get to a doctor."

"So must I," said she, fumbling also for the latch.

The poison, however, acted extremely quickly on their weakened constitutions. Even as they scuffled for precedence they fell prone upon the door mat, and the postman came and covered them with bills.

Old Acquaintance

he apartment, on a fifth floor in the *huitième arrondissement*, was pervaded by the respectable smell of furniture polish. The Parisian *ménage* of 40,000 francs a year smells either thus, or of a certain perfume, which indicates quite a different way of living.

Monsieur et Madame Dupres, admirably fitted by temperament for the rotund connubialities of a more spicily scented dwelling, nevertheless had dwindled away twenty years of life in the austere aroma of furniture polish. This was because of an intense though unacknowledged jealousy, which had early inclined both parties to the mortification of their own flesh.

Monsieur had been jealous because he had suspected that Madame had not been altogether free from certain regrets when they married. Madame had been jealous rather in the manner of a miser who underpays his servant and therefore suspects his honesty. It is true that on the rare occasions when they visited the café, Monsieur would look round for a copy of *La Vie Parisienne*, and if there was a picture in it that interested him, his eyes would remain riveted on it for five minutes at a stretch.

Hence the unvoluptuous furniture of Parisian puritanism, and hence its weekly anointings with the pungent resins of respectability.

Now, in the bedroom, the smell of medicine was added. Madame Dupres lay dying of a frugal pneumonia. Her husband sat beside the bed, unfolding his handkerchief in hopeful expectation of a tear, and craving damnably for a smoke.

"My dear," said Madame faintly, "what are you thinking about? I said, 'Get the gloves at Pascal's. There the prices are not beyond all reason.'"

"My dear," replied her husband, "excuse me. I was thinking of long ago; how we used to go about together, you and I and Robert, in the days before he went to Martinique, before you and I were married. What friends we were! We would have shared our last cigarette."

"Robert! Robert!" murmured Madame Dupres. "I wish you could be at my funeral."

At these words a ray of light fell into a long-neglected corner of Monsieur's mind. "Holy saints!" cried he, slapping his knee. "It was Robert, then, all the time?"

Madame Dupres made no reply; only smiled, and expired. Her husband, a little at a loss as to what to do, kissed her lifeless brow once or twice, tried kneeling by the bedside, got up, and brushed his knees. "Twenty years!" he murmured, stealing a glance at the mirror. "Now I must let the doctor know, the notary, the undertaker, Aunt Gabrielle, the cousins, the Blanchards. I must call at the Mairie. I can hardly get a smoke at the Mairie.

"I could have a puff here, but people coming in would smell it. It would savour of a lack of respect for the dead.

Perhaps if I went down to the street door, just for five minutes... After all, what are five minutes, after twenty years?"

So Monsieur Dupres descended to the street door, where he stood on the step, conscious of the soft air of early evening, and inhaling the smoke from his long-awaited cigarette. As he drew in his first puff, a smile of the utmost satisfaction overspread his plump features.

"Ah, my poor Monsieur Dupres!" said the concierge, emerging suddenly from her den. "How goes it with Madame? She suffers?"

Conscious of his cigarette and his smile, Monsieur Dupres felt he could hardly explain that his wife had passed away but a minute before. "Thank you," said he, "she suffers no longer. She sleeps."

The concierge expressed optimism. "After all," she said, "Madame is from Angers. You know the proverb about the women of Angers."

She prattled on in this vein; Monsieur Dupres paid no attention. "I will go upstairs," thought he, "and make the sad discovery. Then I can return and confront this old cow with a more appropriate countenance.

"And then, my God! there is the doctor, the notary, the funeral arrangements, aunts, cousins ... My cigarette is done already, and I scarcely noticed I was smoking it. In a civilized country a bereaved should be left alone with his regrets."

The concierge retired, but would undoubtedly soon return to the attack. Monsieur Dupres felt that he could do with another cigarette, but this time a cigarette smoked under better conditions, so that its healing task might be accomplished unhindered. His nervous condition demanded a seat in a modest café, a glass of Pernod before him, and all about him the salutary air of cafés, which is infinitely more fragrant than furniture polish.

"A cigarette, a Pernod," thought Monsieur Dupres,

"and then a good meal! A good meal calls for a glass of cognac afterwards; the digestion requires it, the doctors recommend it. And yet—what is one glass of cognac?

"I will tell you," said he to a passing dog. "The first glass of cognac is utilitarian merely. It is like a beautiful woman, who has, however, devoted herself entirely to doing good, to nursing, for example. Nothing is more admirable, but one would like to meet her sister. The second glass, on the other hand, is that self-same sister, equally beautiful, and with leisure for a little harmless diversion. . . . Twenty years!"

Monsieur Dupres went upstairs for his hat.

He decided to go to the Victoire on the Boulevard Montparnasse. It was there they used to celebrate, he and she and Robert, in the old student days, whenever they were in funds. "It will be, in effect, an act of homage," thought he, "far better than disturbing her rest with doctors and cousins. And the cuisine used to be superb."

Soon he was comfortably seated at the Victoire, with a monster Pernod before him. Every sip was like a caress, and, like a caress, led to another. Monsieur Dupres ordered a second glass, and permitted himself to glance at the pages of *La Vie Parisienne*.

"There is no doubt about it," said he to himself, "life is what you choose to make it." He looked about him in search of a little raw material. "Those two girls over there," thought he, "are probably good-natured to a fault. I wonder if they wear little articles like those in this picture."

His imagination conjured up a scene which he found incredibly diverting. He was compelled to snigger through his nose. He experienced an ardent desire to slap somebody. "What in the world have I been doing," thought he, "all these twenty years? Nothing!"

He looked up again, with the intention of darting a certain sort of glance at the two young ladies who had ap-

pealed to his fancy. He was mortified to see that they were
gone.

He looked around the café, in the hope that they had
only changed their table, and saw, to his overwhelming
surprise, sitting only a few feet away from him, with a
monster Pernod before her, none other than Madame Dupres herself, apparently in the best of health, and wearing
her grey hat.

She was at once aware of his regard, compressed her
lips, and stifled a giggle, which exploded like a soda-water
within. She then fixed him with an eye as quizzical as a
parrot's eye. Monsieur Dupres, taking up his glass, made
haste to join his spouse. "My dear," said he, "I came out
to recover my calm."

Madame made no answer, only downed the second half
of her Pernod at a single swig, and, replacing the glass on
the table, fixed her eye unwaveringly upon it till her husband signalled the waiter. "Another Pernod," said he. "In
fact, bring two."

The power of conscience is so great, in a small way, that
Monsieur Dupres, on being discovered in the café, could
not help feeling that his wife knew his most secret intentions, even those concerning the two young ladies. He anticipated a volley of reproaches. You may imagine his relief when he saw that Madame was cocking her eye at him
in the most tolerant and understanding fashion over the
rim of her glass, the contents of which were drawn up as
if by magic into the refined pouting of her lips. "Marie,"
said he with a smile, "perhaps we have lived too narrowly,
as it were. After all, this is the twentieth century. What a
magnificent figure of a woman you really are!"

Madame Dupres smiled indulgently. At that moment
the door swung violently open, and a man entered, who
looked about him on all sides. Monsieur Dupres looked at
this man. "Impossible!" said he. "As I was saying, Marie,

I have a delicious idea. Prepare yourself to be shocked."

Madame Dupres, however, had noticed the newcomer. She smiled delightedly, and waved her hand. Smiling also, but not evincing any surprise, the newcomer hastened over.

"Robert!" cried Madame Dupres.

"God in heaven!" cried Monsieur. "It *is* Robert."

No words can express the felicity of these three old friends, bound together by memories which were only mellowed by the passage of twenty years. Besides, they were already half tight, for it was apparent that Robert also had been indulging in an *apéritif* or two. "Fancy seeing you!" said he to Monsieur Dupres. "What a small world it is! There is really no room to do anything."

Monsieur Dupres was equally incoherent. He could do nothing but slap Robert on the back. They had a last round, and moved into the restaurant on the other side of the partition.

"What have you been doing all these years?" asked Robert as they seated themselves.

"Nothing very much," said Madame Dupres.

"Oho!" cried Robert, smiling all over his face. "Is that so? What a magnificent evening we shall have! Tonight we drink the wine we could never afford in the old days. You know the wine I mean, Marie?"

"You mean the Hermitage," said Monsieur Dupres, who already had his nose in the list. "Eighty francs! Why not? To the devil with eighty francs! A wine like that puts all sorts of ideas into one's head. Champagne first. Why not? Like a wedding. Only better."

"Bravo!" cried Robert. "You have neatly expressed it."

"What shall we eat?" said Monsieur Dupres. "Study the menu, my children, instead of looking at one another as if you were raised from the dead. We must have something spicy. Marie, if you eat garlic, I must eat garlic. He! He! He!"

"No garlic," said Robert.

"No garlic," said Madame Dupres.

"What?" said her husband. "You know you adore it."

"One's tastes change," said Madame.

"You are right," said her husband. "That was what I was saying when Robert came in. I wish the fal-lal shops were open. Marie, I would like to buy you a little present. Something I saw in a magazine. Heavens, what wickedness there is in the world! The air seems full of it. Marie, we have wasted our time. Here is the champagne. Here is a toast. After Lent, the Carnival!"

"After Lent, the Carnival!" cried the others, in the highest good humour, touching their glasses together.

"Why be ashamed?" said Monsieur Dupres, laughing heartily. "We have been married twenty years, Marie. Robert has been in Martinique. There, they are black. What of it?"

"What of it?" echoed Madame, filliping Robert on the nose and giggling uncontrollably.

"Embrace one another!" cried Monsieur Dupres, suddenly, and in a voice of thunder. He rose in his chair to put an arm round each of them. "Go on! Give her a kiss! She had a weakness for you in the old days. You didn't know that, my boy. But I know. I know everything. I remember on the night of our nuptials, I thought: 'She has a weakness for somebody.' Twenty years! Marie, you have never looked more beautiful than you look tonight. What is twenty times three hundred and sixty-five?" Overcome by the enormous figure that resulted, Monsieur Dupres burst into tears.

While he wept, the others, who were as drunk as he was, leaned across the table, their foreheads now and then colliding, while they chuckled inanely.

With the arrival of the brandy, Monsieur Dupres emerged

into a calmer mood. "The thing to do," said he, "is to
make up for lost time. Do you not agree with me?"

"Perfectly," said Robert, kissing him on both cheeks.

"Regard her," said Monsieur Dupres. "A woman of
forty. Oh, if only those little shops were open! Robert, old
friend, a word in your ear."

Robert inclined that organ, but Monsieur Dupres was
unable to utter the promised confidence. He was capable
of nothing but a sputter of laughter, which obliged Robert
to use his napkin as a towel.

"To the devil with your little shops!" said Robert. "We
need nothing. There are cafés, bars, *bistros*, *boîtes*, night
clubs, cabarets, everything. To the boulevard, all three!"

With that, he sprang up. The others unsteadily followed
him. On the street everyone looked at them with a smile.
Madame's respectable grey hat fell over her nose. She gave
it a flick, and sent it equally far over the back of her head.
They linked arms, and began to sing a song about a broken
casserole.

They visited several bars, and emerged from each more
hilarious than before. The men, crouching down so that
their overcoats trailed along the ground, shuffled along in
imitation of dwarfs, as they had done in their student days.
Madame was so excessively amused that she was compelled to retire into the midnight shadows of the little alley
that runs between the Rue Guillaume and the Avenue des
Gascons.

"I suppose," hiccuped Monsieur Dupres, when she rejoined them, "I suppose we should soon be going home."

Robert expressed his contempt for this notion wordless-
ly though not soundlessly. "*Mes amis,*" said he, facing
round, and putting a hand on a shoulder of each, while he
surveyed them with a comical and a supplicating face,
"*mes amis, mes amis, pourquoi pas le bordel?*" At this he

was overcome by a fit of silly laughter, which was soon echoed by the others.

"It is, after all, the twentieth century," chuckled Monsieur Dupres. "Besides, we must consider our friend Robert."

"It is in the nature of an occasion," said Madame. "It is a little reunion."

Accordingly they staggered in the direction of an establishment known as the *Trois Jolies Japonaises*, the staff of which would no doubt have worn kimonos were it not for the excessive warmth of the premises. This warmth was the undoing of Monsieur Dupres. They had no sooner seated themselves at a table in the lower salon than he found it necessary to cool his face on the glass table top, and immediately fell sound asleep.

After a humane interval, gentle hands must have guided him to the door, and perhaps given him a gentle push, which set his legs in motion after the manner of clockwork. At all events, he somehow or other got home.

Next morning he woke on the narrow sofa in the dining-room of his apartment, and smelled again the refreshing odour of furniture polish. He found his head and stomach disordered, and his mind half crazy. He had only a vague memory of great dissipation the night before.

"Thank heaven she has been spared this!" thought he, looking guiltily at the closed door of the bedroom. "It would have upset her appallingly. But what? Am I mad? Do I remember her somewhere last night? What poison they serve in these days! Yet... No, it is impossible!

"I must call the doctor," he said. "The undertaker, too. Notary, aunts, cousins, friends, all the damned fry. Oh, my poor head!" As he spoke he was proceeding towards the bedroom, and now he opened the door. His brain reeled when he found his family business would not after all be necessary. The bed was empty. Madame Dupres was gone.

Clasping his brow, Monsieur Dupres staggered from the room, and more fell than walked down the five flights of stairs to the conciergerie. "Madame!" cried he to that experienced vigilant. "My wife is gone!"

"I saw her go out last night," replied the concierge. "I saw her grey hat go by soon after you had left."

"But she is dead!" cried Monsieur Dupres.

"Impossible," replied the concierge. "I would not discompose you, Monsieur, but Madame was from Angers. You know the proverb."

With that she retired into her lodge, shrugging her shoulders.

"It was, then," cried Monsieur Dupres, "a plot, between her and that abominable Robert! I had better notify the police."

He took the street car to the Châtelet, and, just as it was jolting along at its fastest, he thought he saw them, still drunk, in broad daylight, staggering round a corner in the Rue de Clichy. By the time he had stopped the car and hurried back, they had utterly disappeared.

Feeling completely overcome, Monsieur Dupres gave up his errand, and decided to go home and rest a little, and took a taxi-cab to get there the sooner. This taxi was halted in a traffic block, and from it Monsieur Dupres saw quite distinctly, in a cab passing across the very nose of his own taxi, his wife and his friend, locked in each other's arms, scandalously drunk, and quite oblivious of his existence. "Follow that cab!" cried he.

The driver did his best. They followed a cab all the way to the Porte de Neuilly, only to see an elderly gentleman, probably an ambassador, descend from it.

Monsieur Dupres paid the fare, which was no trifle, and made his way back on the Métro. He had just descended from the train, when he saw two people getting in at the very far end, who were experiencing some difficulty in negotiating the narrow door, for each had an arm around the other's waist. He started towards them but the doors slammed all along the train, and in a moment it had pulled out of the station.

Monsieur Dupres leaned against the wall. "Is it not my old friend, Dupres?" asked a man who had just come onto the platform. "I see it is. My dear fellow, are you ill?"

"Ill enough," replied Monsieur Dupres, utterly shattered. "My wife has left me, my dear Labiche. She has left me for Robert Crespigny, and they are behaving abominably all over the town."

"No. No, my dear friend," replied the other. "Set your mind at rest, I implore you. We husbands are sometimes even more suspicious than we should be. Crespigny cannot have taken your wife, my dear fellow. I saw him only three months ago, back from Martinique and in hospital. He died a week later. Out there, their excesses are something formidable."

The Frog Prince

wo young men were discussing life. Said the richer of them to the poorer, "Paul, you had better marry my sister."

"That is a very strange thing to say," said Paul, "considering I have told you all about my debts."

"I am not worldly," replied Henry Vanhomry. "I should prefer my sister to marry a clean, decent, and kindly fellow like yourself, than some rich but blasé roué, cynic, near-man, sub-man, or half-man."

"I am certainly not blasé," said Paul. "On the other hand, I had not the pleasure of meeting your family when I was in Boston."

"I am very fond of my sister," said Henry, "in a way."

"How delightful! No doubt she was a mother to you when you were small. A little mother!"

"No. No. She is ten years younger than I am; only twenty-eight, in fact."

"Aha! She would have come into her fortune just in the rockiest year of our financial history."

"Fortunately it is well invested, and yields her an income of forty thousand dollars."

"An objection occurs to me. We are men of the world, Henry. If we were of the other sex, we might also make mistakes. Fond as I am of children——"

"That would be a matter entirely for you to decide."

"Henry, your sister sounds charming. Tell me more about her. She is not by any chance a *teeny* little woman?" And Paul held his hand some thirty inches from the floor.

"Quite the reverse."

"*Quite* the reverse, eh?"

"My dear Paul, I do not mean that she is six feet four."

"Six feet three, perhaps?"

"And a half. But perhaps I should tell you she is rather plump. Disproportionately so, in fact."

"Upon my word! I hope she is good-tempered."

"Angelically. You should hear her petting her dolls."

"Pardon me, Henry, but is she at all—backward?"

"A matter of opinion. She reads and writes admirably."

"How delightful. We could correspond, if I happened to be away."

"I will be frank with you, Paul; her letters to famous boxers are quite amazingly expressive, though by no means perfect in orthography."

"Henry, she is capable of hero worship; she has an affectionate nature."

"Almost embarrassingly so. It appears from these letters of hers, which we censor, that she would make a devoted wife. However, my family are old-fashioned, and the boxers are cowardly brutes. I should like to see her safely married."

"But, as yet, if I understand you, she is pure as the driven snow? Charming!"

"Hers has been a cloistered girlhood. Yet there is something romantic in her nature which causes me alarm. Supposing one of the boxers responded. He might not treat her politely."

"I, on the other hand, would write her the most devoted letters, and bow, with old-world courtesy, whenever we met. Hm! All I fear, to be perfectly candid, is that a certain confounded coldness, a defect of my nature, might be a cause of pain, dissatisfaction, or longing."

"Well, my dear Paul, that is hardly a matter for me to speculate upon. I can only remind you that faint heart never won fair lady."

"Very well, Henry. I will at least come with you and see your sister."

"I am afraid I cannot accompany you. You forget that I am off to Europe next week. However, I'll give you a letter of introduction to the family."

All this being arranged, our good Paul took leave of his friend, and after walking about for a little with an air of distraction, he paid a visit to the apartment of another friend of his.

"My dear Olga," he said, after a time, "I'm afraid I have some very ridiculous news for you. I am going to be poor no longer."

"Tell me only one thing, Paul. Is she beautiful?"

"Not very, it seems. I have not seen her, but she is over six feet three, and disproportionately fat."

"My poor Paul! She is simply bound to have hair on her face. What will become of you?"

"Besides all this, she is not very bright, I hear."

"And, now I come to think of it, what will become of me?"

"She has forty thousand a year, my dear Olga."

"Paul, we women are given to incredible follies when we are jealous. I might refuse everything. I find myself capable of jealousy."

"But, on the other hand, are you, or am I, capable of living any longer without a little of that forty thousand a year?"

"Or some other."

"But what other, my dear Olga? Where is another forty thousand?"

"It is true, Paul. Am I right in believing that your gigantic bride-to-be is mentally nine years, or is it twelve years old?"

"Seven, I should think, by all that Henry told me of her. She has an exuberant innocence. She writes to boxers, but caresses dolls."

"Really? That is very interesting. Dolls are so featureless. Now, is there any great hurry, Paul? I have still that bracelet you found at Palm Beach. It would provide us with a few last weeks together."

"I was going to suggest, as a matter of fact, that it should be my present to the bride, for I like to do things in good style. However, something may turn up. I admit that I love you."

"You shall promise me not to go near Boston for at least a month. I shall be busy; I have decided to wear my hair short, but at least we shall meet at week ends. In between, you may say farewell to all your bachelor life."

"Yes, that is true, Olga. I shall have to do that, I suppose."

Everything being agreed, this young couple spent the next month or so as Olga had suggested, and at the end of it, she saw him off to Boston, with a restraint that he found almost too admirable.

He arrived at Boston, presented his letter of introduction, and was very well received by old Mrs. Vanhomry.

They got on admirably. "You are still a bachelor?" she asked.

"I cannot," he replied, "bring myself to regard the mod-

ern girl as a true mate. Those clipped locks, that flat masculine figure, that hardness, that ultra-sophistication!
Where are the curves, the innocence, the warm-hearted-
ness of yesteryear? But why am I telling you all this——?"

"You would have liked our dear Ethel. Such a big,
healthy, affectionate, old-fashioned girl! You must meet
her, and her fiancé. Perhaps you will come to the wedding?"

"Nothing could be more delightful. Unfortunately, I
have to return to New York almost immediately."

On his return, Paul called at once on Olga, but found
that her flat was locked up. She had left no address; you
may depend he sought her everywhere.

He saw in the papers an account of the wedding of Miss
Vanhomry to a Mr. Colefax. It appeared that the happy
pair were on their way to the Ritz-Carlton.

"I really must go and sit in the lobby," said he, "and
console myself with a peep at the disadvantages attached
to that forty thousand a year."

Very well, he sat in the lobby. Before very long, he saw
the enormous form of what was evidently the happy bride
crossing from the elevator.

"Upon my word!" he thought. "There is a great deal to
be said for the simple life after all. One at least preserves
one's individuality."

He peered about for the husband. At last he saw a sensitive face in the neighbourhood of the bride's hips. "That
must be the husband," he said. "Very charming! Very
charming indeed. But surely I have seen him before."

In order to make sure, he edged closer, and was amazed
to find that this husband was none other than his own
Olga, in male attire.

He at once applied for a private interview. "My dear
Olga, this is a very pretty trick you have played on me.
And what can your bride—*soi-disant*—think of it all?"

"You must regard the matter rationally, my dear Paul."

"I am so afraid there may be a scandal. You have no idea what spiteful tongues might make of it."

"You underestimate the innocence of my wife, whose dolls, as I suspected, were very ordinary dolls. And you must admit, Paul, that if either of us is to be in this position, I at least offer less grounds for jealousy. You had better be my secretary."

Paul submitted with a good grace, and for a long time enjoyed his occupation very tolerably. Fortunately, Henry Vanhomry remained in Europe.

On one occasion there was a dinner party at the Colefax home, and a few of the male guests, with Paul the friendly secretary, and dapper little Mr. Colefax, remained smoking together long after the gigantic bride had retired to bed. The conversation turned on women, a subject which the so-called Mr. Colefax enjoyed more than his secretary. They talked of attractions.

"My wife," said this charming imposter, "is disarmingly simple; why try to disguise it? Nevertheless, she has an amazing personality buried, as it were, beneath her *naïveté*. I am convinced it is there, I sense it, and yet I could hardly find an example to describe. How do you account for that?"

"It is very simple, my dear Colefax," said a very eminent doctor. "Your wife, if I may say so, owes her adorable simplicity, as she does her admirably robust physique, to a little glandular maladjustment, which (always supposing you should desire what professionally we should regard as an improvement) could easily be put right. Who knows what she is like underneath?"

"It would certainly be interesting to find out," said her false husband, intrigued.

"She might be slim, vivacious, a positive butterfly," continued the doctor.

"It would be like carving out ambergris from a whale," observed a well-known adventurer who was present.

"Or opening a neolithic barrow," added a famous archaeologist.

"Or undressing an Eskimo girl at Christmas," put in a notorious Don Juan.

"You might find more than you bargain for," observed Paul, overcome by an inexplicable foreboding.

He spoke too late. Everyone was desperately keen on the experiment.

"You must bring your dear wife to a little home that I have in Paris," said the doctor, "where I have every facility for the treatment."

"We shall come at once. You, Paul, had better remain behind, to deal with everything we shall have to leave unsettled."

Paul, therefore, was left. Ethel and her spouse went on the next boat to Paris, accompanied by the doctor, and, as a matter of fact, by the adventurer, the archaeologist, and the Don Juan as well.

My Dear Paul,

You will be amazed at the result of our experiment, and possibly a little disconcerted, though you were always a connoisseur of poetic justice. Under the treatment Ethel has lost no less than a hundred pounds. The removal of this prodigious quantity of blubber has left her exposed as a lean, agile, witty, and very handsome man. "How absurd that I should have been called Ethel so long!" he observed to me when first he was apprised of this transformation. In order to put him at his ease, I replied at once, "No more absurd than that I should have been called your husband." After all, the cat was, so to speak, out of the bag, and there was nothing else to do.

He took it extremely well, saying with a smile, "We must make the punishment fit the crime." On my part, I was not long in promising never to deceive him again.

We are remaining on this side to avoid gossip, for the situation has a ludicrous side which we might find painful. But not nearly so ludicrous or painful, my dear Paul, as it might have proved, in all the circumstances, had you had your original wish.

Once more,
Olga

Season of Mists

I was ready for anything when I came to the town of T——. It was already late in the year. Dead leaves crawled like crabs over the asphalt of the deserted esplanade. Winds raced along the corridors of the larger hotels, barging into the wrong rooms.

It is at such a place, and at such a season, that one finds the desperate grass widow, or young things whose natural credulity snaps starvingly at the grossest counterfeit. The illusion of teeming possibilities had gone with the licentious carnival of summer, the masks of coarse sunburn, and he who may be sitting alone among the sand dunes. Ravenous dreams pace the unvisited sitting-rooms of villas, or stalk between rising waves and falling leaves.

The concealed smile in my smile, and the concealed meaning in my words, would have made me seem a sort of scheme-riddled Machiavelli in the ephemeral mating dance of July. I should have been condemned as heavy going, would-be clever, even unpleasant or dangerous. Now, on the other hand, my slightly involved personality would be as welcome as a jig-saw puzzle in hands already fidgety with boredom. Nevertheless, I had gone so far as to purchase a ready-made sports jacket, and had my black mustache had any objective existence I should have taken the precaution of shaving it off.

I still had a little money. I was not after profit, but pleasure. I desired to intoxicate myself on a real emotion, and I wondered in which of the still occupied villas, in what sort of absurd drawing-room, treading softly in fear of what husband or what aunt, I should perform what drunken antics my chosen potion would inspire in me.

Meticulous in my observance of protective mimicry, I could not of course omit the *snorter* or *quick one* before dinner on my first evening in the hotel. I entered the bar in jaunty style, my mouth already writhing with a classy catch-phrase, like the eye socket of a provincial actor (but all actors are provincial) in travail with his waggish monocle.

This witticism was never uttered. I thought I saw a golden fish. It was the honey head of the barmaid, bent over a love story, but, as the place had the appearance of the tourist cocktail lounge of a liner sunk two years previously in a hundred fathoms of grey-green ocean, I thought it was a golden fish. I was sharply corrected when she raised a face so dappled with flush and sun-gleam that I looked instinctively for the orchard boughs above her head.

All this was disconcerting, and effective in shattering my pose. It happens that these fresh and almost eatable faces have a peculiar effect on me. "Farewell before hail," I thought, "to the sailor's languishing wife, and to the ardent anaemia at the Vicarage! I am off."

I ordered one of the far inferior intoxicants that stood ranked behind her, and retired a pace, changing my name to Bert, a young man already doing well, at once cheeky and shy, but probably capable of being serious. One never knew what I could come out with next.

I was wondering about that myself when I saw that she, affecting to take no particular notice of me, had retired into the flowery thicket of her reverie. I realized that this must have grown very wild and tangly in the last month or two, because, before she could turn and peep out from it, it swallowed her up entirely, like a prospective sleeping beauty, and indeed she yawned.

I analyzed this yawn with the aloof precision of one of those scientists who are always helping Scotland Yard. I discovered it to be heavy with a super-saturation of sigh, its origin a plaintive protest against the difference between dreams and reality. Though this was only the middle of November, I diagnosed it as a premature December yawn, *and in December they settled for reality*. This emboldened me to act at once.

Affecting to consult my heart, exactly as if it had been a pocket watch, I gasped, bit my lip, and stared at her in wild surmise. You could never tell when I was joking. "Do you believe," I said fervently, "in love at first sight?"

"No, sir," she said severely. "That sort of thing doesn't appeal, thank you."

It was clear she had not been a barmaid more than seven or eight weeks. From behind her professional hauteur she peeped out to watch for its effect, as bewitchingly as if she were a child wearing her mother's terrible hat.

"I'm not fooling," I said (taken down a peg or two, you understand). "The fact is, believe it or not, I'm a bit psychic." On this word, the most useful though not the most beautiful in our language, she raised her eyes to mine, which I had baited with pieces of an old sincerity which I carry about for just such purposes. I put a little in my voice too, as I added, "Do you know what I thought, the minute I saw you?"

"What?" said she.

"I'll tell you," said I. " 'That girl's tragic,' I thought. 'She's being wasted. There's a sort of bar between her and all sorts of delightful surprises. I wish it could be melted away.' "

"Not really!"

"I did," said I. "Give me your hand. I can read it like a book, probably by your favourite author. Oh, I'm psychic all right. I had a sort of premonition when I came here. I knew I was going to fall desperately in love."

"I know you're kidding," said she, but she offered me her open hand, which proved to be quite illegible.

Nevertheless I spoke with confidence. "You've been thinking of love today. You've been dreaming of a stranger. Now don't deny it, because it's written in your hand. And that's not all."

"What else does it say?" said she.

"Call it Fate," said I solemnly. "Call it Kismet if you like; I can deny you nothing. Or, look here, let's call it Destiny. You can't go back on Destiny, you know. It would absolutely ruin it. It says . . . Guess what!"

"I can't," she said. "Do tell me."

I couldn't guess either. Dumbly I scrutinized her palm. She leaned a little farther over the bar, joining me in the study. Our foreheads touched. I remained conscious, but the shock had dislocated all connection between awareness and volition. With a divine shudder I heard myself reply, "It says we are going to be married."

"Oh," said she. "I don't know about that."

"What?" I cried, hurt to the quick, all caution forgotten. "Is this mutual understanding? Is this two hearts beating as one? Don't let's start off with a rift like this between us."

"I didn't mean it that way," she replied remorsefully.

"Splendid," I said. "Our first little quarrel healed already. And don't we sort of know one another better for it? Aren't we somehow closer? If not, we ought to be. Lean over a little farther."

Fate had evidently triumphed. Her kiss was like cowslips and cream. I was unquestionably in love, and felt no longer responsible for my actions.

At that moment, however, a gong sounded in the echoing depths of the hotel. "Better go," she said, already wifely. "Go and get your dinner. I'll be here later on."

I bowed before the importance of Bert's dinner, and went. When I returned the bar was still empty of intruders, and she was still there. I rushed forward, I flung my arms about her, and resumed the kiss that had been so coarsely interrupted.

I had just been struck by the nice thought that perhaps after all it tasted of cream and honeysuckle, rather than cowslips, when I was also struck by a tremendous blow in the face.

"What?" I said, staggering back. "Are you tired of me already? You might at least have broken it more gently."

"I'll call the manager," said she.

"Do so," said I. "Call the boots, too. Call the waiters. Call all the principal residents of T—— on Sea. Let them hear how you promised to marry me before dinner, and socked me in the puss for a kiss immediately afterwards."

"Promised to marry you?" she cried. "Before dinner. Oooh! It must have been Bella. Fancy! Bella!"

"What is your name?" said I.

"Nellie," said she.

"That's who it was," said I. "Nellie. You. To the devil with this interfering, designing Bella, who . . ." But, as I spoke, she turned and darted through the door behind her.

I heard some delicious squeals and giggles. "I hope," I thought, "she is giving that abominable Bella a good pinch. Pretending to be her! She had the poor girl all confused." At that moment the door opened again, and out they came, hand in hand.

"I'm Nellie."

"I'm Bella."

"Keep quite still," said I, clowning astonishment. "I must think for a little while about this."

"Look! He's all bowled over."

"Isn't he sweet?"

"Yes, he's a duck. Bella, you *are* lucky."

"Your turn next."

That was the rub. My mind darkened at the thought of a brother-in-law. You know what beasts men are. A thousand intricate jealousies tangled themselves before me. The girls were so exactly alike; they *went together*, as we say. Besides, who can choose between cowslips and honeysuckle?

It was time I said something. "Well!" said I. "By all that's wonderful! I wish old Fred were here tonight!"

"Who's Fred?"

"Fred? You'll like Fred. He's a splendid fellow. We're twins."

"No!"

"Yes, identical twins. More alike than you are. Same looks. Same tastes. Same thoughts. I always know what he's thinking. Listen! He's sort of trying to get through to me now. I bet he knows I'm happy. He does. He's sending congratulations. In waves. He's asking something. What is it, Fred, old boy? Is there what? Oh, *Is there one for me, Bert?* That's what he's trying to say. What shall I tell him, Nellie?"

"Don't know, I'm sure."

"Why don't you bring him along one day?" said Bella.

"I can't," said I. "We're on a very special job. It's just half the time off for each of us. But I'll tell you what; I'll *send* him along."

This was agreed upon. I spent the rest of the evening delightfully, and in the morning bought a new sports coat, brushed my hair differently, and returned as Fred.

I entered the bar peering through my fingers. "Which are you?" I cried. "I don't want to look at you properly till I know. I might fall in love with the wrong one."

"I'm Nellie."

"Good! To make it absolutely perfect, I'm Fred." With that I dropped my hand. "Good old Bert!" I cried. "Wonderful taste he's got! Wonderful fellow!"

"He's nice. But you're nice, too."

"Do you really think so?"

In short, we were happy. Soon afterwards Bella came in. There was nothing but giggles, comparisons, talk of future joys.

"It really ought to be a double wedding," they said.

"Can't be done," I replied. "Truly. Ask Bert if you don't believe me. He'll tell you it's out of the question."

The next few days passed like lightning. All went twice as merrily as the ordinary marriage bell. I rented two bungalows, semi-detached, furnished them from the same store, took a week off for my honeymoon as Bert, and the next week for my honeymoon as Fred.

I then settled down to lives of singular contentment and regularity. One evening Nellie and I would have Bella to dinner, and spend the time saying what a grand fellow Bert was, and the next evening Bella and I would entertain Nellie and do the same for Fred.

It was a full month before I asked myself, which is the happier of the two, Fred or Bert? I was unable to answer. The doubt persisted until it tortured me.

I became a little moody, and sometimes would retire to the next room, under the pretense of a headache, in order to ponder the question over again. On one of these occasions, I went into the hallway to get cigarettes from my overcoat and I heard the girls' voices through the flimsy door of the drawing-room. "The darlings!" I thought. "They are discussing their husbands again. This may shed some light on my problem. Bella thinks Bert has the nicer voice. Nellie claims that Fred knows more songs. What is this? Really, Bella! Come, come, Nellie, you flatter me! Bella, what an exaggeration! Nellie, that is a downright lie!"

Soon afterwards I heard Nellie go home. I rejoined Bella, who was obviously much exercised in her mind. "Bert," she said, "who is the best swimmer, you or Fred?"

"We never compete, darling, we are so sure we are equal."

"I wonder if you would be if you tried," said Bella, still looking extremely thoughtful.

When I returned to the other bungalow next evening, I found Nellie equally ill at ease. "Tell me something," said she. "Of course I know Bella's my sister, my twin. Nobody could love her more than I do. But tell me, Fred, would you say she was absolutely truthful?"

"Absolutely," said I. "I'd stake my life on it. Bert's life, too. She is incapable of a lie."

"Oh!" said Nellie, lapsing into a deeper reverie than before.

It was with a sardonic pleasure that I watched the increasing wistfulness of both my wives. "I have an idea," said I to myself, "that I shall soon learn whether Bert or Fred is the happier."

Sure enough, it was not long before Nellie sent round one evening to ask if Bert would help her move some heavy furniture. I went to her aid, and afterwards we sat talking for a while on twins, likeness, differences, marriage, conventions, love, and what would have happened if Fred had met Bella before I had, and whether what hurts nobody can really be said to be wrong.

It took a long time to resolve all these problems to our complete satisfaction, and I was deprived of a good deal of Bella's company that evening. But this was made up to me on the following day, for she came round to ask if Fred would help her with a leaky tap, and we had an almost identical discussion which took just as long for its complete resolution.

I was now in a state of extreme and complicated bliss. It was clear that Bert had no reason to envy Fred, and that Fred's happiness was in all respects equal to Bert's. Not only had I two charming wives, but my double domestic happiness was multiplied by a dual and delicious infidelity.

But I was one day in the character of Bert, sitting before the fire enjoying the more legal of my happiness with Bella, charmed by her prattle and pleased by the complete restoration of her good spirits, when suddenly I was struck, as if by a thunderbolt, by the thought: "This woman is deceiving me!"

I leapt up with a muttered excuse, and rushed out of the now hateful house. I walked on the shore till late that night, a prey to the most bitter reflections. I had to admit that I was largely responsible, but I at least knew that it made no difference. She had no such excuse; it was she who had blighted our Eden.

I went home long after midnight, slept uneasily, and hurried off in the morning, eager to exchange the pitiful personality of the deceived husband for the roguish character of his betrayer.

As Fred, I returned with a jaunty sneer. Nellie greeted me. "How was Bert," said she, "when you left him?"

"Bert?" said I. "Bert?"

Without another word I went heavily upstairs, and looked at myself in the mirror. The sight maddened me. I itched to get my fingers round my throat. I longed to rush next door and pour out my troubles to my adorable mistress, but I knew in my heart that she was as false as her sister below.

I thought of divorce, working out the actions and counteractions on my fingers, and badly spraining two of them in the process. Besides, there was the unsavory publicity.

At last I made up my mind. I hurried off to catch the last train to the town. Arrived there, I wrote two notes, as follows:

"Dear Nellie, I have found you out. I am asking Bert to come for a swim. He will never return. Fred."

"Dear Bella. I know all. Am persuading Fred to take a midnight bathe. He will not come back, Bert."

Having posted my letters, I took my two sports coats to the beach, where I left them side by side.

There was just time to get the train for B——, and it was there that I met Mrs. Wilkinson.

Great Possibilities

here are certain people who do not come to full flower until they are well over fifty. Among these are all males named Murchison. A Mr. Murchison is nothing without pink cheeks, white whiskers, and vintage port. There are no females of this name, except by accident. In fact, one wonders how the breed is continued, since bachelorhood is a fourth essential attribute of a true Murchison. Fortunately, they tend to be lawyers of the old-fashioned school, and old-fashioned family lawyers know all sorts of peculiar secrets.

By keeping at it twenty-four hours a day, and for considerably more than fifty years, Mr. Benjamin Murchison had succeeded in becoming a nearly perfect specimen of his race. He was fit to be stuffed and put in a museum, although there, of course, he could not have beamed and twinkled so benevolently.

He was very comfortably off, and could have been really

wealthy, but certain of the more remunerative fields of law were not entirely to his taste. Indeed, he had become so fastidious that he would have retired completely, but many of his old friends had died and had left estates to be divided among their children, and to all these numerous broods Mr. Murchison was guardian, trustee, adviser, friend, and uncle.

Nothing delighted him more than to pay visits to his young friends, and nothing delighted them more than to have him.

Although nearly perfect, Mr. Murchison had one little eccentricity, which he kept extremely private. It was a mere nothing, a thought, a whim; it seems almost unfair to mention it. The fact is, he felt that nothing in the world would be nicer than to set fire to a house and watch it blaze.

What is the harm in that? Who has not had a similar bright vision at some time or other? There is no doubt about it; it *would* be nice, very nice indeed, absolutely delightful. But most of us are well broken in and we dismiss the idea as impracticable. Mr. Murchison found that it took root in his mind and blossomed there like a sultry flower.

When thoughts of this delightful description occurred to him, which was increasingly often, he would smile all over his face and rub his hands together with a zest that was very pleasant to behold. Having rubbed them, he would spread them out, as if to enjoy the cheerful blaze of a Christmas fire. Nothing could be more benevolent than his aspect when indulging in this little mannerism. Young wives who had married into the circle of his wards and protégés would at once think of him as a godfather.

Mr. Murchison was always the first to inspect and praise a new home. "Ah!" said he, on looking over Millicent and Rodney's, "I am glad you have chosen the Colonial style.

I am glad you have built in wood; it is a fine tradition. It is cool in summer, and can be warm, very warm, in winter. Of course you have a good cellar? Excellent! Excellent! And there is your front door; the back door, I suppose, is through there? Yes, that is beautifully planned. A fine current of air—there is nothing like it. I like these long draperies, Millicent. Some people like little, skimpy, short draperies; I vastly prefer long ones. Well, you have a delightful home, my dears, I hope you have it completely insured."

"Oh, yes. We have the house covered," Rodney said. "But as for Millie's precious antiques—you know how she absolutely wore herself to death going round picking them up at auctions. Well, you can't insure blood and sweat, of course. She'd be absolutely broken-hearted if anything happened. Still, touching wood, let's hope it won't. How did we get talking about this sort of thing anyway?"

At this, Mr. Murchison lost a little of his sparkle, for the thought of distressing his young friends cast cold water upon all his pleasant fancies. The following week he motored up to Buck and Ida's, a fine old place on a hill in the Berkshires, and four miles from a one-horse fire station. The situation was superb. Probably on a clear, windy night the house, ablaze, would have been visible fifty miles away. But Buck was an architect, and his competition plans were all done in his spare time at home. His study was full of them.

At Dick and Lucy's there were three high gables, rich with promise of the most dramatic effects imaginable, so Mr. Murchison rubbed his hands like an Indian rubbing two sticks of wood together. "You rub your hands so briskly, Uncle Ben," said Lucy, smiling happily at the sight of him. "One would almost expect to see sparks flying from your fingers. Electricity, you know." She went on to tell how Dick's book on insect civilizations was nearly finished, notes and draft chapters littered all over the house —five years of work—and soon he would be famous.

So Mr. Murchison travelled on. Cecily had all her father's books. John had the family portraits, Tom and Lisbeth had little Tom and little Lisbeth.

Sometimes, when Mr. Murchison went walking in the mornings during his week-end visits, he was almost reduced to hailing some passing farmhand and asking to whom that old barn belonged, and if the owner might be likely to take a price for it just as it stood. But he speedily dismissed impulses of that sort as altogether unworthy.

Pity this sweet-natured old gentleman, compelled to visit a tantalizing succession of highly combustible houses and always finding some little obstacle which would have deterred no one less good-hearted than himself.

At length a letter reached Mr. Murchison from Mark and Vicky, whom he had not seen for rather a long time, begging him, with exclamation marks, to come and inspect their new, magnificent abode. "Come and warm the place for us!" they said. He went the very next week end, and Mark and Vicky met him at the station.

"Now, what is all this?" said he. "A new house, and this is the first I hear of it! You may imagine I am all agog. Tell me, is it one you have built, or——"

"Ask Mark," said Vicky in a disgruntled tone. "It's nothing to do with me. Except I have to live in it."

"It was my mother's uncle's," said Mark, dealing ferociously with the gears of the car. "And now it's mine."

"The sins of the mother's uncles are visited on the children," said Vicky, with an obvious effort at good humor.

"But what about your little place at Willowdale?" asked Mr. Murchison. "I thought you were so very fond of it."

"We were," said Mark.

"Don't make me weep," said Vicky. "When I think of the garden——"

"Yes, don't make her weep," said Mark. "We had to rent Willowdale. You see, we have to pay the taxes on this place. Twenty-eight rooms! You can't rent it, you can't sell it. So we had to move in. Here's the gate. Now you'll see it. Look."

"Dear me!" said Mr. Murchison. "Dear me!"

"That's what everyone says," said Vicky. "A castle on the Rhine, built in clapboard!"

"The other side has a touch of the Taj Mahal," said Mark.

"Well, well, well!" said Mr. Murchison. "And yet—and yet, you know, perhaps you think I am old-fashioned, but I feel it has possibilities. Those pinnacles! Those things which conceivably may have been meant to suggest flying buttresses! And that minaret-like structure at the very top of all! Seen under the right conditions . . ." And he beamed more jovially than he had beamed for months.

"Oh, come, Uncle Ben!" said Vicky.

"Never mind me," said he, rubbing his hands. "Never mind an old fogy. Perhaps I am a little eccentric. I must confess it needs a spark of imagination. But then—yes, it has possibilities. The insurance must be very high."

"The rascals have had a fortune in premiums," said Mark. "I'm going to stop it. However, let me take your bags."

"Mind the big box," said Murchison. "It's just a dozen of a little wine I thought you'd like. Put it down in the cellar and I'll unpack it myself before dinner."

Mr. Murchison frequently took presents of wine to his young friends. He felt it was one of the gracious duties of a quasi-uncle. He also felt the straw bottle-wrappers might somehow come in handy.

They went into the house, and Vicky, with bitter mirth,

showed him a vast succession of rooms through which the wind whistled, as if to keep up its spirits.

"We just live in a corner of the damned place," said Vicky, "and we'll end up all thin and dry and pale, with great, long nails, among cobwebs."

"Oh, come!" said Mr. Murchison. "I'm sure something will turn up. We must get the neighbours to come around. A little light, a little warmth, a little bustle and the old place will seem quite different. Believe me, my dear, things may change over-night."

And, indeed, when Mr. Murchison went down to unpack the wine, it really seemed as if they would. He made admirable disposition of the straw wrappers in which the bottles were packed, and he emerged from the cellar in the highest of spirits, rubbing his hands with a gusto that would have warmed the cockles of your heart. It was as well that he was so jovial, for otherwise dinner would have been a very gloomy meal. Mark and Vicky were already far into the bickering stage.

"I can't help it," said Mark, in reply to complaints he had obviously heard before. "I've told you a hundred times we'll clear out as soon as we can afford to."

"Can you beat that, Uncle Ben?" cried Vicky. "As soon as we can *afford* to live in tiny six-roomed Willowdale!"

"Oh, *please* forget it!" said Mark, rather loudly. "Just for a little while."

"Don't shout," said Vicky. "I don't wonder Uncle Ben sniffs at you."

"What?" said Mr. Murchison. "Sniff? At Mark? Never in my life."

"Good heavens! Can it be the fish?" cried Vicky. "Please say so, Uncle Ben, if it is."

"No, no," said he. "It is excellent."

"But you don't eat it," said she. "You do nothing but sniff."

"On my word, Vicky," said Mr. Murchison, defending his plate, "I am enjoying myself enormously."

"Don't tell me," said Vicky. "If the fish is all right, you must have a cold. Oh, dear!"

"No, I have not," said he. "But that reminds me. The nights are getting brisk. I hope you have a warm wrap handy, my dear?"

"Oh, I am warm enough," said Vicky. "But are *you* cold? The heating here is like everything else."

"Thank you," said he. "I am very comfortable. I just thought—if we should go outside. On the lawn, you know."

"The lawn?" said Mark. "Go out on the lawn? Why should we go out on the lawn?"

"Ah, yes! You are right. Why should we?" said Mr. Murchison in some confusion. "A very sensible question. Now, what put the idea into my head? How ridiculous! Let us forget it. Tell me, Mark, who built this amazing place?"

"It was my great-uncle Coxon," said Mark.

"Coxon? Do you mean the banker?" asked Mr. Murchison.

"Yes," said Mark. "And they used to wonder why banks failed!"

"He was the father of the famous Annabel Coxon," said Vicky. "The great beauty. You must have known her, Uncle Ben. Were you one of her admirers?"

"Well . . ." said Mr. Murchison, his smile fading.

"This," said Mark, "is the scene of her adorable girlhood. Her little white bedroom was presumably in some goddam turret."

"She was born here. Yes, of course. She was a child here," murmured Mr. Murchison, now not smiling at all.

"It was her bower," said Mark, "the scene of her maiden dreams. Her lovely ghost is probably scampering around upstairs at this moment. In pantalettes, or whatever they wore. I wish I could meet it."

"Uncle Ben is not amused," said Vicky. "I bet you *were* in love with her, Uncle Ben. Do tell."

"I? What a notion! Dear me!" said Mr. Murchison, looking quite shaken. "At all events, she was a lovely creature. Yes. 'Her lovely ghost,' you said. Quite a felicitous expression! Well, well, well!"

"But seriously," said Mark, "isn't it extraordinary? She probably loved this place, which is driving us melancholy mad."

"She did," said Mr. Murchison. "I remember her describing it. Yes, she did indeed."

"Was she pretty?" asked Vicky. "Was she full of life?"

"Oh, yes," said Mr. Murchison. "Very lovely. Very alive. Alive in a way—well, perhaps I'm growing old. In these days people don't seem to be alive that way. Alive like a bird singing. Except, of course, you, my dear," he added politely.

"And was she nice?" said Vicky.

"Yes," said Mr. Murchison. "Very nice. Later on, some people thought, she grew a little—different. But she was so young when first I knew her. She must have just come from this house. Yes, very nice. 'Her lovely ghost!' Dear me! Well, I'm glad you are looking after the old place, my boy. It would be a pity if—if it went to ruin. Oh, my God!"

"What? What is it, Uncle Ben?"

"What is that I smell?" cried he. "Do I smell burning? I do!"

"Burning?" said Mark.

"I know!" cried Mr. Murchison. "Keep your heads, pray! Remain precisely where you are! I shall be back in a moment." And he hastened from the room.

"Well, I'll be damned!" said Mark to Vicky after they had stared at one another for a time. "Has the old boy gone crazy, or what?"

"I think I did smell smoke," said she. "Can he have left a cigarette in the cellar, do you think?"

"Maybe," said Mark. "I suppose he'll shout if it's anything serious."

Soon afterwards, Mr. Murchison returned. "Nothing at all," said he, smiling. "Just my fancy. I knew it."

"But you have a great smear of black on your face," said Vicky. "And look at your hands! Uncle Ben, you left a cigarette in the cellar."

"Well," said he, "perhaps I did. I confess I did. Don't be angry with me, Vicky."

"Angry!" said Mark, laughing. "We are, though—for putting it out. Why didn't you let the confounded place burn down?"

"My dear boy," said Mr. Murchison, "I know you are joking. That would be a very serious crime. Arson, in fact. Besides, a house, you know, is not like a—a haystack. There is something alive about an old house, Mark. It has its memories."

"When *we* go," said Mark, "this house will have a hangover."

"I can't help feeling you somehow don't care very much for the place," said Mr. Murchison. "You said you find it hard to rent or sell?"

"Not hard," said Mark. "Impossible."

"Not impossible," said Mr. Murchison. "You could sell it to me."

"*You*, Uncle Ben?" cried Vicky. "You live in this dismal place? Alone?"

"I don't think it dismal," said Mr. Murchison. "I don't think I should feel lonely."

Everything was speedily arranged. In a very few weeks, Mark and Vicky were back at Willowdale. Various other friends of Mr. Murchison's dropped in to see them. "How is he getting on?" they asked. "Does he like it?"

"He thinks it's fine," said Mark. "You know, the old boy really is marvellous. Always the perfect type. He's the eccentric squire nowadays. Have you heard about him and the fire brigade?"

"No. Let's hear it," they cried.

"Well," said Mark, "first of all he raised hell. He said the service wasn't efficient. He wrote letters, called a meeting, went round to all the farmers—God knows what all."

"And then?"

"Then he must have waved a check at them or something. They elected him chairman, captain, the whole works. We were over that way last week; they all said he drills hell out of 'em. And we saw them charge through the village with the new engine, and there was Uncle Ben sitting up by the driver, smiling all over his face, with a damned great axe in his hand."

"He always was a bit fussy about the chance of fire," said the others.

Without Benefit of Galsworthy

he minute I left the golf links, I gave a sort of sniff. "Damn it! Poetry about!" I said. I can always tell it; I've got that sort of streak in me. "Where does it come from?" I said. "Sunset tints? Going round in eighty? Or what?" Passed a couple of schoolgirls, giggling in a gateway. I could just imagine their conversation: one saying to the other, "Who's the wicked mustache?" and the other replying, "Why, that's our handsome Major."

Life suddenly seemed like a bottle of champagne. Cheltenham looked like a first-class oil painting, only with a lot of decent people living in it. There was *Poona Lodge*. "Good old *Poona Lodge!*" There was *Amritsar*. "Cheerio, *Amritsar!*" There was my little box, *The Laurels*. Poetic streak again, you see, calling it that. Better, maybe, if I'd just been an ordinary, damfool, wooden-headed soldier man. Still, if it wasn't for these sneaking Socialists——

Well, in I went. Adela looked out of the drawing-room.

Good old Adela! Sound through and through. Troop-ships, kids, marvellous head of hair, everything. She gave me a sort of hiss. "She's come," she said.

I knew who she meant. We had that sort of understanding. It was the new parlourmaid. "Grand!" I said. "Tell her to bring my tea into the Den."

I went into the Den. Snug little cubbyhole. Mixed myself a peg. "Hullo! What's this? Poetry's getting stronger!" Had a good look round; caught sight of my mustache in the looking glass. "Wicked mustache, eh?" That was the word. Gave it a pat. "Well," I said, "damn it!" Very nearly burst out laughing.

In she came with the tea. Ten minutes past five; the moment my life changed completely. Here had I been going about with a streak of poetry all my life; this was the woman it was meant for. Woman, did I say? Little more than a girl. Slip of a girl. Yet, mind you, a touch of the goddess.

I was down. I was out. "Jack," I said, "You're done for." Talk about poetry—I tell you I saw that girl, nude, on a beach, in a sort of dawn. The impression was overwhelming. Do you know what I very nearly said? I very nearly said, "Look here, my dear! Bathing costume, please! Might be trippers about."

Of course I said nothing of the sort. But I looked it. She seemed to understand. You know what I mean. Goddess—all very well. Mustache—all very well. But if a woman doesn't understand a man, and if a man doesn't understand a woman, there isn't much in it, is there? Still, she seemed to. If it wasn't for these bloody Bolsheviks——

Anyway, there I was, sparring for time, fighting like a madman to get on my feet, face up to it, grip the controls, anything. I said, "What's your name?" She said, "Gladys."

After that neither of us said anything for a while. There we were.

Then she said, "Please, sir, shall I pour out your tea?"

I said, "Yes. Always." Just that, you see? Nothing about the beach. Nothing about anything. Just "Always."

And all she said was, "Very well, sir."

You see the delicacy? I thought, "That girl's got breeding." I'm the true democrat, you see. Or was, rather. I thought, "There was some young dog of a subaltern hovering round the cottage where you were born, my dear." But I didn't say so, naturally. Might have been someone in the Diplomatic, anyway. "*Very well, sir.*"

That was all. She went out. Went up to her little room, I expect. I was left alone, staring at the fire, like a fellow in a play.

I heard Adela going upstairs. "Good God," I thought, "there's Adela!" I'd forgotten her. "And the kids!" Clean, decent youngsters. "God," I thought, "there's the Carrington-Joneses, too!" Bitch of a woman. Tongue like a Gurkha's kukri. I thought of the old General, over at Lucknow Grange; dear old boy! Thought of the regiment; young chaps in the mess, keen as mustard, lead 'em to Hell and back. What would they say? Thought of my round in eighty. Thought of a fellow called Uglow. Met him one day in the bar of the Chutna Club. Never saw him again. Don't know why I thought of *him*.

But Adela was in my thoughts all the time, dodging in and out among the others. Then there was a sort of mirage, only not upside down, of this little goddess, on a beach, as it were. Pretty hard to concentrate.

Shall I tell you the words that came into my mind then? "Play the game!" Woman's heart broken, life ruined, old campaigner like Adela. No! Thought of the day we found a snake in the bed up at Chundrapore. That's another story. Still, it's a link, you know, that sort of thing. Only what's a snake against a goddess? If it wasn't for these blasted agitators——

I did my best. I ignored her all Sunday. Monday morning I came out into the hall. There she was, sweeping the stairs. With a dustpan and broom. You know what I mean. I found Adela in the drawing-room. I said, "Adela, I've got to go up to town. I've got to see Doggie Weaver."

She saw something was up. When I'm in a tight place I like to see Doggie Weaver. Been in tight places together. "You go," she said. "Come back on the eight-forty-five." I said, "All right, I will."

So I went up to town. I saw Doggie. I told him everything. I said, "I've got to choose. And I can't face it." He said, "I advise a compromise." I said, "What?" He gave a sort of wink. He said, "Least said, soonest mended." I said, "What?" He said, "What the eye doesn't see, the heart doesn't grieve for." I said, "Doggie, you and I have been in some tight places. Now I think you're a dirty rotten cynic. You don't know what a good woman is, and I wish I'd never been in a single tight place with you."

So I went out. Then I thought of Piggy Hawkins. Can't say he was ever the most popular man in our mess; still I had an idea Piggy was all right—a sort of intuition. I looked him up. I told him everything. "Jack," he said, "there's nothing for it. There it is—as clear as daylight. You've got to play the game."

You see? The very words I'd said to myself. So I knew he was right. I shook hands with him. I said, "Piggy, we've never been in very many tight places together, but if ever I'm in a tight place again, I hope you'll be there beside me."

I went back. I had another look at her, just to make sure. I called Adela into the Den. I said, "Adela, keep a stiff upper lip. You're a soldier's daughter."

She said, "Yes, Jack. A soldier's wife, too."

I said, "Well, yes. Up to the present."

She said, "Don't tell me it's another woman."

I said, "I won't. It's a goddess."

She said, "I see. Now I'm just the mother of a couple of soldier's children."

I said, "Clean, decent kids, Adela. Keen as a couple of well-bred, sporting terriers."

She said, "Yes, clean. I must have them, Jack. I'll keep them——clean."

I said, "Take them, Adela."

She said, "Keep a stiff upper lip, Jack. They've got to have the right sort of school."

I said, "Yes, Adela."

She said, "And the right sort of home to come home to. The right sort of mother, too. Do you know what they call me?" she said. And she almost broke down as she said it. "They call me their 'lovely mother.' I can't be a 'lovely mother,' Jack, in a ragged old last-season's frock, can I?"

I said, "All right. I want nothing. I shall be living at Waikiki or somewhere. On a beach."

She said, "You must have your baccy, Jack." The way she said it—I almost broke down myself.

Then, of course, there was her family, and her lawyers, and resigning from everything, and being cut, and the Carrington-Joneses—bitch of a woman—everything. I kept a stiff upper lip, signed everything, never said a word, kept my eyes to myself in the house—didn't want to drag the little goddess into it. Time enough for that when we got to Waikiki or wherever it was.

In the end they took all the furniture out. There I was with my polo cup and a bag of golf clubs in the old Den. Never mind—off to Waikiki or somewhere before you could say knife. Damn these reptiles from Moscow— they're un-English.

I called for Gladys. She came in. I gave her a look. Suddenly the words burst out of me. Did you ever see a

light drumfire barrage moving briskly forward in advance
of a battalion of the best men God ever made? That's
how it sounded to me.

"Here I am," I said. "Take me. Play with my mustache.
Cut it off if you like. It's yours. So's all the rest of me."
She said, "What?"

I said, "I've given it up. Everything. Adela. Children.
The old General—dear old boy, but never mind. Carrington-Joneses. Cheltenham. Club. Regiment. Money.
Even a fellow called Uglow—met him in the Chutna Club
—never mind him, either. I'm yours. I saw you, nude, on
a beach—dawn, everything. Get your hat on, Gladys.
We're going into that dawn. We're going to find that
beach. Not a tripper for miles!"

She looked at me. Of course I knew she'd be surprised.
Hadn't liked to say anything, not while Adela was in the
house. Kept it clean, you know. Still, there was that word
"Always." And "Very well, sir."

I thought she was going to say it again. Going to say
it, not as she'd said it before, like a mouse talking out of
a hole with all the cats of wealth, rank, station, convention, and God knows what prowling about the room, if
you know what I mean, but loudly, triumphantly, and
with a sort of spring at the end of it.

She was loud enough. Did you ever see a buzz bomb go
off? With some poor fellow under it? That's how it seemed
to me. I thought, "Jack, you're knocked out. You're done
for." I looked round. She was gone.

I saw what it was. They'd been at her. The scum! From
Moscow. The blasted agitators. The cursed Reds. Nobody's too young for 'em, or too pure. Damn it, they're
in the Sunday schools—everywhere. Goddess—what's that
to them? Eyes, little ears, everything—they don't give a
damn. Class against class, that's their motto. Class hatred.
Class war.

Back for Christmas

D octor," said Major Sinclair, "we certainly must have you with us for Christmas." Tea was being poured, and the Carpenters' living-room was filled with friends who had come to say last-minute farewells to the Doctor and his wife.

"He shall be back," said Mrs. Carpenter. "I promise you."

"It's hardly certain," said Dr. Carpenter. "I'd like nothing better, of course."

"After all," said Mr. Hewitt, "you've contracted to lecture only for three months."

"Anything may happen," said Doctor Carpenter.

"Whatever happens," said Mrs. Carpenter, beaming at them, "he shall be back in England for Christmas. You may all believe me."

They all believed her. The Doctor himself almost believed her. For ten years she had been promising him for dinner parties, garden parties, committees, heaven knows what, and the promises had always been kept.

The farewells began. There was a fluting of compliments on dear Hermione's marvellous arrangements. She and her husband would drive to Southampton that evening. They would embark the following day. No trains, no bustle, no last-minute worries. Certain the Doctor was marvellously looked after. He would be a great success in America. Especially with Hermione to see to everything. She would have a wonderful time, too. She would see the skyscrapers. Nothing like that in Little Godwearing. But she must be very sure to bring him back. "Yes, I will bring him back. You may rely upon it." He mustn't be persuaded. No extensions. No wonderful post at some super-American hospital. Our infirmary needs him. And he must be back by Christmas. "Yes," Mrs. Carpenter called to the last departing guest, "I shall see to it. He shall be back by Christmas."

The final arrangements for closing the house were very well managed. The maids soon had the tea things washed up; they came in, said goodbye, and were in time to catch the afternoon bus to Devizes.

Nothing remained but odds and ends, locking doors, seeing that everything was tidy. "Go upstairs," said Hermione, "and change into your brown tweeds. Empty the pockets of that suit before you put it in your bag. I'll see to everything else. All you have to do is not to get in the way."

The Doctor went upstairs and took off the suit he was wearing, but instead of the brown tweeds, he put on an old dirty bath gown, which he took from the back of his wardrobe. Then, after making one or two little arrangements, he leaned over the head of the stairs and called to his wife, "Hermione! Have you a moment to spare?"

"Of course, dear. I'm just finished."

"Just come up here for a moment. There's something rather extraordinary up here."

Hermione immediately came up. "Good heavens, my dear man!" she said when she saw her husband. "What are you lounging about in that filthy old thing for? I told you to have it burned long ago."

"Who in the world," said the Doctor, "has dropped a gold chain down the bathtub drain?"

"Nobody has, of course," said Hermione. "Nobody wears such a thing."

"Then what is it doing there?" said the Doctor. "Take this flashlight. If you lean right over, you can see it shining, deep down."

"Some Woolworth's bangle off one of the maids," said Hermione. "It can be nothing else." However, she took the flashlight and leaned over, squinting into the drain. The Doctor, raising a short length of lead pipe, struck two or three times with great force and precision, and tilting the body by the knees, tumbled it into the tub.

He then slipped off the bathrobe and, standing completely naked, unwrapped a towel full of implements and put them into the washbasin. He spread several sheets of newspaper on the floor and turned once more to his victim.

She was dead, of course—horribly doubled up, like a somersaulter, at one end of the tub. He stood looking at her for a very long time, thinking of absolutely nothing at all. Then he saw how much blood there was and his mind began to move again.

First he pushed and pulled until she lay straight in the bath, then he removed her clothing. In a narrow bathtub this was an extremely clumsy business, but he managed it at last and then turned on the taps. The water rushed into the tub, then dwindled, then died away, and the last of it gurgled down the drain.

"Good God!" he said. "She turned it off at the main."

There was only one thing to do: the Doctor hastily wiped his hands on a towel, opened the bathroom door with a clean corner of the towel, threw it back onto the bath stool, and ran downstairs, barefoot, light as a cat. The cellar door was in a corner of the entrance hall, under the stairs. He knew just where the cut-off was. He had reason to: he had been pottering about down there for some time past—trying to scrape out a bin for wine, he had told Hermione. He pushed open the cellar door, went down the steep steps, and just before the closing door plunged the cellar into pitch darkness, he put his hands on the tap and turned it on. Then he felt his way back along the grimy wall till he came to the steps. He was about to ascend them when the bell rang.

The Doctor was scarcely aware of the ringing as a sound. It was like a spike of iron pushed slowly up through his stomach. It went on until it reached his brain. Then something broke. He threw himself down in the coal dust on the floor and said, "I'm through. I'm through!

"They've got no *right* to come," he said. Then he heard himself panting. "None of this," he said to himself. "None of this."

He began to revive. He got to his feet, and when the bell rang again the sound passed through him almost painlessly. "Let them go away," he said. Then he heard the front door open. He said, "I don't care." His shoulder came up, like that of a boxer, to shield his face. "I give up," he said.

He heard people calling. "Herbert!" "Hermione!" It was the Wallingfords. "Damn them! They come butting in. People anxious to get off. All naked! And blood and coal dust! I'm done! I'm through! I can't do it."

"Herbert!"

"Hermione!"

"Where the dickens can they be?"

"The car's there."

"Maybe they've popped round to Mrs. Liddell's."

"We must see them."

"Or to the shops, maybe. Something at the last minute."

"Not Hermione. I say, listen! Isn't that someone having a bath? Shall I shout? What about whanging on the door?"

"Sh-h-h! Don't. It might not be tactful."

"No harm in a shout."

"Look, dear. Let's come in on our way back. Hermione said they wouldn't be leaving before seven. They're dining on the way, in Salisbury."

"Think so? All right. Only I want a last drink with old Herbert. He'd be hurt."

"Let's hurry. We can be back by half-past six."

The Doctor heard them walk out and the front door close quietly behind them. He thought, "Half-past six. I can do it."

He crossed the hall, sprang the latch of the front door, went upstairs, and taking his instruments from the wash-basin, finished what he had to do. He came down again, clad in his bath gown, carrying parcel after parcel of towelling or newspaper neatly secured with safety pins. These he packed carefully into the narrow, deep hole he had made in the corner of the cellar, shovelled in the soil, spread coal dust over all, satisfied himself that everything was in order, and went upstairs again. He then thoroughly cleansed the bath, and himself, and the bath again, dressed, and took his wife's clothing and his bath gown to the incinerator.

One or two more like touches and everything was in order. It was only quarter past six. The Wallingfords were always late; he had only to get into the car and drive off. It was a pity he couldn't wait till after dusk, but he could make a detour to avoid passing through the main street, and even if he was seen driving alone, people would only think Hermione had gone on ahead for some reason and they would forget about it.

Still, he was glad when he had finally got away, entirely unobserved, on the open road, driving into the gathering dusk. He had to drive very carefully; he found himself unable to judge distances, his reactions were abnormally delayed, but that was a detail. When it was quite dark he allowed himself to stop the car on the top of the downs, in order to think.

The stars were superb. He could see the lights of one or two little towns far away on the plain below him. He was exultant. Everything that was to follow was perfectly simple. Marion was waiting in Chicago. She already believed him to be a widower. The lecture people could be put off with a word. He had nothing to do but establish himself in some thriving out-of-the-way town in America and he was safe for ever. There were Hermione's clothes, of course, in the suitcases; they could be disposed of through the porthole. Thank heaven she wrote her letters on the typewriter —a little thing like handwriting might have prevented everything. "But there you are," he said. "She was up-to-date, efficient all along the line. Managed everything. Managed herself to death, damn her!"

"There's no reason to get excited," he thought. "I'll write a few letters for her, then fewer and fewer. Write myself—always expecting to get back, never quite able to. Keep the house one year, then another, then another; they'll get used to it. Might even come back alone in a year or two and clear it up properly. Nothing easier. But not for Christmas!" He started up the engine and was off.

In New York he felt free at last, really free. He was safe. He could look back with pleasure—at least after a meal, lighting his cigarette, he could look back with a sort of pleasure—to the minute he had passed in the cellar listening to the bell, the door, and the voices. He could look forward to Marion.

As he strolled through the lobby of his hotel, the clerk, smiling, held up letters for him. It was the first batch from England. Well, what did that matter? It would be fun dashing off the typewritten sheets in Hermione's downright style, signing them with her squiggle, telling everyone what a success his first lecture had been, how thrilled he was with America but how certainly she'd bring him back for Christmas. Doubts could creep in later.

He glanced over the letters. Most were for Hermione. From the Sinclairs, the Wallingfords, the vicar, and a business letter from Holt & Sons, Builders and Decorators.

He stood in the lounge, people brushing by him. He opened the letters with his thumb, reading here and there, smiling. They all seemed very confident he would be back for Christmas. They relied on Hermione. "That's where they make their big mistake," said the Doctor, who had taken to American phrases. The builders' letter he kept to the last. Some bill, probably. It was:

Dear Madam,
 We are in receipt of your kind acceptance of estimate as below and also of key.
 We beg to repeat you may have every confidence in same being ready in ample time for Christmas present as stated. We are setting men to work this week.
 We are, Madam,

       Yours faithfully,
       PAUL HOLT & SONS

To excavating, building up, suitably lining one sunken wine bin in cellar as indicated, using best materials, making good, etc.

   . . . . £18/ 0/ 0/

Another American Tragedy

young man entered the office of a prominent dentist, and seated himself in the chair. He scornfully waved aside the little probe and mirror with which the dentist smilingly approached him. "Rip 'em all out," he said.

"But," said the dentist, "your teeth seem perfectly good."

"So," said the young man, "is my money."

The dentist hestitated a little. "It would hardly be ethical," said he, "to take out teeth which are sound—unless there is a very good reason for it."

The young man, who had begun to smile at the word "ethical," here extended his smile into a cavernous gape, which laid bare the hindermost of his ivories. At the same time he twitched out a small roll of bills from his vest pocket, and held them noticeably in his hand.

The dentist utterly ignored these bills. "If you want those excellent teeth out," said he, "you must certainly be mad. Now I have a little theory: *mental* derangement is caused by *dental* derangement. It is a sign of something wrong way up behind the roots of the teeth, especially those of the upper row. Viewed from that angle——"

"Cut it, and pull them, out," said the young man, impatient of these professional niceties.

The dentist shrugged and obeyed. As if in fear that the young man might become altogether too sane at the end of the operation, he humorously tweaked away the roll of bills with a thirty-third frisk of his forceps.

The young man made no comment, but only called for a mirror, in which he surveyed his numb and fallen chaps with every appearance of satisfaction. He asked when his denture would be ready, made the appointment, and went his way.

"Dear me!" thought the dentist. "Perhaps the trouble was not in his teeth after all. Certainly he is still as crazy as a coot."

Here the dentist made a big mistake. The young man was perfectly sane, and knew very well what he was about. It happened that he had spent all his money, in some years of the vilest dissipation, but he had a very far-reaching and water-tight plan for getting some more. His views on the subject of teeth were directly opposite to the common attitude towards insurance. He held it is better not to have them, and to need them, than to have them but to find no sort of use for them.

He accordingly returned to the dentist on the appointed day, and was equipped with his artificial grinders, which he sucked at and gnashed in the most ordinary fashion. He paid for them with almost his last dollar, went out, and got into his racy-looking roadster, and drove out of town as if pursued by the finance company, as he certainly would have been had they caught sight of him.

He drove till nightfall, and resumed his journey next

day. Late in the afternoon he arrived in that part of the country where old and miserly uncles live in remote, dilapidated farmhouses. Our young man was more or less fortunate in possessing one of the oldest and richest of these uncles, whose house was the remotest and most dilapidated of all.

Arriving at this secluded dwelling, our hero drew up before a porch upon which no money had been squandered for years. "So much the more in the old sock," reflected the nephew, as he knocked upon the door.

He was a little disconcerted to hear the tap of high heels within, instead of the shuffle of a deaf and surly retainer, and his jaw dropped when the door was opened by a plump and squarish blonde, a baby of some thirty-odd years and about a hundred and fifty pounds. Her mouth was as wide and as red as a slice of watermelon; she had well-darkened lashes and brows, and an abundance of phony gold hair flowing girlishly down over her shoulder. Our friend was to some extent reassured when he realized that she was dressed in what might be called a nurse's uniform, but the extreme shortness of the skirt and the fact that her garters were bright scarlet, and adorned with enormous bows, caused him to wonder if his dear uncle was getting the very best of professional care.

Nevertheless it is important to get on the right side of the nurse, especially when she stands solidly in the doorway. Our hero removed his hat, and put on so soapy a smile that his false teeth nearly dropped out of his head. "I have driven all the way from the big city," said he, "to see my poor, dear, bed-ridden old uncle—God bless him! I did not expect to see so charming a nurse."

The nurse, not budging an inch, responded with a surly and suspicious stare.

"I fear he must be sinking," continued the nephew. "In fact, I had an intuition, a sort of telephonic S.O.S., telling me to hasten out here before it was too late. Let me rush to his bedside."

The nurse still hesitated, but at that moment a peculiar sound, resembling the croaking of giant bull-frogs, arose in the dim depths of the house. This was the good old uncle himself, vociferating toothlessly for an immediate sight of his nephew, whose expressions of affection and concern had been audible in every corner of the dwelling. The old boy knew very well that his young relative was after his money, and he was eager for the pleasure of turning him down.

The nurse somewhat grudgingly stepped aside. Our hero, with a well-rehearsed whinny of delight, scuttled into the bedroom.

Nothing is more affecting than the greetings of near relatives after a long separation, especially when they are as fond of each other as these two. "My dear Uncle!" cried the nephew. "What a pleasure it is to see you again! But why does your hand tremble so? Why are your eyes so sunken? Why are you so thin and pale?"

"If it comes to that," said his uncle, "you are not too stout and rosy yourself. Yes, you are very worn and emaciated, my boy. Your hair is thin and grey; you have lines, bags, and creases all over your face. If it were not for your handsome white teeth, I believe you would look every bit as old as I do."

"That," said the nephew, "is the effect of ceaseless toil and moil. It is a hard struggle, Uncle, to make good in these days, especially without any capital."

"So you are making good?" said the old man. "Do you not drink any more?"

"No, Uncle, I never drink now," replied the nephew.

"Well, that's tough," said his uncle, producing a giant flask from under his pillow. "In that case I can't ask you to join me." With that, he took a mighty swig, and, wiping his lips, he continued, "I have, thank heaven, a good doctor. A typical tough, bluff, hard-hitting, straight-shooting country sawbones of the old school. We call him the horse 'n' buggy doc. He recommends me this as medicine."

"Perhaps that is why your hand trembles so," said his nephew.

"Your own is none too steady," rejoined his uncle. "Evidently you work too hard. Tell me, Nephew, do you ever take a little flutter with the cards?"

"Good heavens, no!" cried the nephew. "I cured myself of that folly long ago."

"I am sorry to hear it," replied his uncle. "We might have played a little cut-throat. The old horse 'n' buggy doc says the excitement keeps me lively. We often play together till after midnight."

"That is why your eyes are sunken so deep," said the nephew.

"I think yours are equally hollow," replied the old man. "You should take a little rest now and then. I suppose, my dear Nephew, you still have an occasional frolic with the girls."

"Girls!" cried the nephew, lifting up his hands. "What an odious suggestion! It is years since I have even looked at a girl."

"Well, that's too bad," said his uncle. "The old horse 'n' buggy doc has up-to-date views. It was he who sent me Birdie." And, turning to the nurse, who happened to be arranging his pillows, he gave her a certain sort of caress, such as is mentioned nowhere in the pharmacopoeia.

"No wonder!" cried his nephew, when the nurse had gone bridling and smirking from the room. "No wonder, my poor Uncle, that you are so extremely thin and pale!"

"You are equally so," replied his uncle, "and you are only half my age."

"Well," said the nephew, trying a new tack, "perhaps your doctor is right. Perhaps I had better take your treatment."

"I heartily advise it," said the old man.

"The only thing is," said the nephew, "that I can hardly work at the same time. I suppose you would not care to give me a little money, so that I can enjoy the benefits of the system."

"Well, no," said his uncle. "I would not. Definitely not."

"I thought as much," said his nephew. "I fear I shall have to keep on toiling. How upset your good horse 'n' buggy doc would be! Tell me one thing, however; indulge my curiosity in one trifling respect. Is there any hope I shall come into your money? Have you arranged it in your will?"

"Oh, come!" said his uncle. "Why bother your head with matters of that sort?"

"Do tell me," pressed the nephew. "You have no idea how interested I am."

"Well, if you really want to know," said his uncle, "I have left it all to the old horse 'n' buggy doc, a true, downright, straight-living, hard-faced, crusty, soft-hearted country croaker of the old school, and you cannot imagine how agreeable his treatment is to me."

"Is that really so?" said the nephew. "I must say I expected something of the sort. Fortunately I have made my plans against just such a contingency. Allow me, my dear Uncle."

With that he twitched a pillow from under the old man's head, and pressed it over his face. The old uncle gave a petulant kick or two, but what with one thing and another there was very little life left in him, and soon that little was gone.

The nephew, with a wary glance at the door, quickly divested himself of his clothing, which he stowed under the bed. Next, possibly feeling a little chilly, he took the liberty of borrowing his uncle's nightshirt. Then, stowing his uncle's shrunken body under the bed also, he climbed into his place between the sheets. Finally he expectorated his false teeth into a clean pocket handkerchief, which he had brought especially for the purpose, and leaned back upon the pillows, the very spit and image of the old man.

Soon he set up a pipe: "Birdie! Birdie!"

At his call the nurse came hurrying in. "Why, honey-boy," said she, "where's your worthless nephew gone?"

"He has just slipped out for a stroll around the old place," croaked our hero. "Moreover, I don't think you should call him worthless. No, I have misjudged that young man, and I want you to send for the lawyer, so that I can do him justice in my will."

"Why, Daddy?" cried the nurse. "What's made this change in you?"

"Change?" said the nephew hastily. "There's no change in me, my dear, except perhaps I feel my latter end approaching. Otherwise I am just the same." And to reassure her on this point, he gave her a friendly little caress, exactly as his uncle had done. She emitted an hilarious squeal and went giggling on her errand.

The nephew lay at his ease, waiting only for the arrival of the lawyer. "I shall dictate a new will," thought he, "and sign it before the very eyes of the lawyer, in a shaky imitation of the old man's crabbed hand. I shall then express a desire to be left alone for a short nap, replace my poor uncle in the bed, put on my clothes, put back my teeth, and step out of the window, to march in at the front door as if newly returned from my walk. What bucketfuls of tears I shall shed, when we discover that the poor old boy has passed peacefully away!"

Pretty soon there was a heavy footstep on the porch,

and a large and rough-hewn individual strode into the room, bearing a sizable black bag.

"I am glad you have come," said our hero. "I am eager to make out a new will. I wish to leave everything to my nephew."

"My dear old friend," replied the newcomer, "I fear your malady has reached the brain. Who would have thought my old pal could have mistaken me for the lawyer? You must let me make a brief examination." With that, he pulled down the sheet, and began to probe the nephew with a hard and horny finger. The nephew realized too late that this was no lawyer, but the horse 'n' buggy doc himself, and he uttered a hollow groan.

"I feared as much," said the Doctor. "There is something very wrong somewhere in here. I must act at once if you are to recover your reason." As he spoke, he turned the nephew over in the bed, and whisked out a monster hypodermic from his black bag. "Fortunately," said he, "I am always ready for emergencies."

Our hero tried to protest, but he hardly knew what to say, fearing that his uncle would be discovered under the bed, and the circumstance would tend to his prejudice. The Doctor, all in a moment, injected a pint of icy fluid into the small of his back, which numbed his whole middle, and paralyzed all his faculties, except that of rolling the eyes, which he indulged to the point of excess.

"I am only an old, rough, goldarn horse 'n' buggy doc," observed the Doctor, "but I keep abreast of the times. Mental derangement is often caused by abdominal derangement. If you will get out my instruments, nurse, I think we shall soon find the source of the trouble."

In a moment the unfortunate nephew was laid open under his own eyes, which he never ceased to roll. The Doctor, unpacking him like a Gladstone bag, kept up a running commentary. "Take this," said he to the nurse, "and put it on the washstand. Put these on the chair. Don't get them mixed up, or I shall have the devil of a job getting them back again. It is a pity that nephew is not back; it is more ethical to have the consent of a relative before operating. I see nothing wrong with this pancreas, considering the age of the patient. Put it on the chest of drawers. Hang these over the bed-rail.

"Hold the light a little closer," he continued. "I still have not found the cause of his madness. Don't let the candle drip; that is hardly hygienic. Anyway, he is certainly mad, or he would not think of leaving his money to that scallawag of a nephew. It is as well you let me know, my dear, instead of bothering the lawyer. When this is all over, we must take a little trip together."

Saying this, he gave the nurse a caress, similar to that which both uncle and nephew had bestowed on her. The sight of this caress not only shocked our hero, but depressed him beyond description, and lowered his powers of resistance. "It is most unprofessional," thought he, "and, what's even worse, it smacks abominably of conspiracy." This thought caused him to roll his eyes for the last time, and the next moment he was a goner.

"Dear me," said the Doctor, "I fear I have lost my patient. Sometimes I quite envy the city doctor, with his well-appointed operating theatre. However, their biographies usually sell very poorly, and, after all, I did my best for the old boy, and he has remembered me in his will. Had he lived, he might have altered it. What an extraordinary trick of fate! Pass me over the various organs, my dear, and I will put them roughly into position, for I expect the nephew will be back very shortly, and he would hate to see them lying around."

Midnight Blue

r. Spiers came in extremely late. He shut the door very quietly, switched on the electric light, and stood for quite a long time on the door-mat.

Mr. Spiers was a prosperous accountant with a long, lean face, naturally pale; a cold eye, and a close mouth. Just behind his jaw bones a tiny movement was perceptible, like the movement of gills in a fish.

He now took off his bowler hat, looked at it inside and out, and hung it upon the usual peg. He pulled off his muffler, which was a dark one, dotted with polka dots of a seemly size, and he scrutinized this muffler very carefully and hung it on another peg. His overcoat, examined even more scrupulously, was next hung up, and Mr. Spiers went quickly upstairs.

In the bathroom he spent a very long time at the mirror. He turned his face this way and that, tilted it sideways to expose his jaw and neck. He noted the set of his collar, saw that his tiepin was straight, looked at his cuff links, his buttons, and finally proceeded to undress. Again he examined each garment very closely; it was as well Mrs. Spiers did not see him at this moment, or she might have thought he was looking for a long hair, or traces of powder. However, Mrs. Spiers had been asleep for a couple of hours. After her husband had examined every stitch of his clothing, he crept to his dressing room for a clothes-brush, which he used even upon his shoes. Finally he looked at his hands and his nails, and scrubbed them both very thoroughly.

He then sat down on the edge of the bath, put his elbows on his knees and his chin on his hands, and gave himself up to a very profound train of thought. Now and then he marked the checking-off of some point or other by lifting a finger and bringing it back again onto his cheek, or even onto the spot behind his jawbone where there was that little movement, so like the movement of the gills of a fish.

At last Mr. Spiers seemed satisfied, and he turned out the light and repaired to the conjugal bedroom, which was decorated in cream, rose, and old gold.

In the morning, Mr. Spiers arose at his usual hour and descended, with his usual expression, to the breakfast room.

His wife, who was his opposite in all respects, as some say a wife should be, was already busy behind the coffee service. She was as plump, as blonde, as good-humored, and as scatterbrained as any woman should be at a breakfast table, perhaps even more so. The two younger children were there; the two older ones were late.

"So here you are!" said Mrs. Spiers to her husband, in a sprightly tone. "You were late home last night."

"About one," said he, taking up the newspaper.

"It must have been later than that," said she. "I heard one o'clock strike."

"It might have been half past," said he.

"Did Mr. Benskin give you a lift?"

"No."

"All right, my dear, I only asked."

"Give me my coffee," said he.

"A dinner's all right," said she. "A man ought to have an evening with his friends. But you ought to get your rest, Harry. Not that I had much rest last night. Oh, I had such a terrible dream! I dreamed that——"

"If there's one thing," said her husband, "that I hate more than a slop in my saucer——Do you see this mess?"

"Really, dear," said she, "you asked so brusquely for your coffee——"

"Father spilled the coffee," piped up little Patrick. "His hand jerked—liked that."

Mr. Spiers turned his eye upon his younger son, and his younger son was silent.

"I was saying," said Mr. Spiers, "that if I detest anything more than a filthy mess in my saucer, it is the sort of fool who blathers out a dream at the breakfast table."

"Oh, my dream!" said Mrs. Spiers with the utmost good humor. "All right, my dear, if you don't want to hear it. It was about you, that's all." With that, she resumed her breakfast.

"Either tell your dream, or don't tell it," said Mr. Spiers.

"You said you didn't want to hear it," replied Mrs. Spiers, not unreasonably.

"There is no more disgusting or offensive sort of idiot," said Mr. Spiers, "than the woman who hatches up a mystery, and then——"

"There is no mystery," said Mrs. Spiers. "You said you didn't want——"

"Will you," said Mr. Spiers, "kindly put an end to this, and tell me, very briefly, whatever nonsense it was that you dreamed, and let us have done with it? Imagine you are dictating a telegram."

"Mr. T. Spiers, Normandene, Radclyffe Avenue, Wrexton Garden Suburb," said his wife. "I dreamed you were hung."

"*Hanged*, Mother," said little Daphne.

"Hullo, Mums," said her big sister, entering at that moment. "Hullo, Dads. Sorry I'm late. Good morning, children. What's the matter, Daddy? You look as if you'd heard from the Income Tax."

"Because of a murder," continued Mrs. Spiers, "in the middle of the night. It was so vivid, my dear! I was quite glad when you said you were back by half-past one."

"Half-past one, nothing," said the elder daughter.

"Mildred," said her mother, "that's film talk."

"Daddy's an old rip," said Mildred, tapping her egg. "Freddy and I got back from the dance at half-past two, and his hat and coat wasn't there then."

"*Weren't* there," said little Daphne.

"If that child corrects her elder sister, or you, in front of my face once again——" said Mr. Spiers.

"Be quiet, Daphne," said her mother. "Well, that was it, my dear. I dreamed you committed a murder, and you were hanged."

"Daddy hanged?" cried Mildred in the highest glee. "Oh, Mummy, who did he murder? Tell us all the grisly details."

"Well, it really was grisly," said her mother. "I woke up feeling quite depressed. It was poor Mr. Benskin."

"What?" said her husband.

"Yes, you murdered poor Mr. Benskin," said Mrs. Spiers. "Though why you should murder your own partner, I don't know."

"Because he insisted on looking at the books," said Mildred. "They always do, and get murdered. I knew it would be one or the other for Daddy—murdered or hung."

"*Hanged*," said little Daphne. "And *whom* did he murder."

"Be *quiet!*" said her father. "These children will drive me mad."

"Well, my dear," said his wife, "there you were, with Mr. Benskin, late at night, and he was running you home in his car, and you were chatting about business—you know how people can dream the most difficult talk, about things they don't know anything about, and it sounds all right, and of course it's all nonsense. It's the same with jokes. You dream you made the best joke you ever heard, and when you wake up——"

"Go on," Mr. Spiers said firmly.

"Well, my dear, you were chatting, and you drove right into his garage, and it was so narrow that the doors of the car would only open on one side, and so you got out first, and you said to him, 'Wait a minute,' and you tilted up the front seat of that little Chevrolet of his, and you got in at the back where your coats and hats were. Did I say you were driving along without your overcoats on, because it was one of these mild nights we're having?"

"Go on," said Mr. Spiers.

"Well, there were your coats and hats on the back seat, and Mr. Benskin still sat at the wheel, and there was that dark overcoat he always wears, and your light cheviot you wore yesterday, and your silk mufflers, and your hats and everything, and you picked up one of the mufflers—they both had white polka dots on them—I think he was wearing one like yours last time he came to lunch on Sunday. Only his was dark blue. Well, you picked up the mufflers, and you were talking to him, and you tied a knot in it, and all of sudden you put it round his neck and strangled him."

"Because he'd asked to look at the books," said Mildred.

"Really it's—it's too much," said Mr. Spiers.

"It was nearly too much for me," said his spouse. "I was so upset, in my dream. You got a piece of rope, and tied it to the end of the scarf, and then to the bar across the top of the garage, so it looked as if he'd hanged himself."

"Good heavens!" said Mr. Spiers.

"It was so vivid, I can't tell you," said his wife. "And then it all got mixed up, as dreams do, and I kept on seeing you with that muffler on, and it kept on twisting about your neck. And then you were being tried, and they brought in—the muffler. Only, seeing it by daylight, it was Mr. Benskin's, because it was dark blue. Only by the artificial light it looked black."

Mr. Spiers crumbled his bread. "Very extraordinary," he said.

"It's silly, of course," said his wife. "Only you *would* have me tell you."

"I wonder if it *is* so silly," said her husband. "As a matter of fact, I *did* ride home with Benskin last night. We had a very serious talk. Not to go into details, it happened I'd hit on something very odd at the office. Well, I had it out with him. We sat talking a long time. Maybe it *was* later than I thought when I got home. When I left him, do you know, I had the most horrible premonition. I thought, 'That fellow's going to make away with himself.' That's what I thought. I very nearly turned back. I felt like a—well, I felt responsible. It's a serious business. I spoke to him very forcefully."

"You don't say Mr. Benskin's a fraud?" cried Mrs. Spiers. "We're not ruined, Harry?"

"Not ruined," said her husband. "But there's been some pretty deep dipping."

"Are you sure it's him?" said Mrs. Spiers. "He—he seems so honest."

"Him or me," said her husband. "And it wasn't me."

"But you don't think he's—he's hanged himself," said Mrs. Spiers.

"Heaven forbid!" said her husband. "But considering that feeling I had—well, perhaps the dream came just from the feeling."

"It's true Rose Waterhouse dreamed of water when her brother was away sailing," said Mrs. Spiers, "but he wasn't drowned."

"There are thousands of such cases," said her husband. "They're generally wrong on all the details."

"I hope so, indeed!" cried Mrs. Spiers.

"For example," said her husband, "it happens we both kept our coats on, and our mufflers too, all the time last night. The atmosphere was hardly intimate."

"I should say not," said Mrs. Spiers. "Who would have thought it of Mr. Benskin?"

"His wife, poor woman, would not have thought it," said Mr. Spiers gravely. "I have resolved to spare her. So, Mildred, children, whatever has happened or has not happened, not a word, not one word, is to be said about this to anyone. Do you hear? To anyone! You know nothing. A single word might lead to disgrace for the whole wretched family."

"You are quite right, my dear," said his wife. "I will see to the children."

"Morning, Mum," cried Fred, bursting into the room.

"Morning, Guv'nor. No time for breakfast. I'll just get the train by the skin of my teeth, if I'm lucky. Whose muffler's this, by the way? It's not yours, is it, Dad? This is dark blue. Can I bag it? Why—what's the matter? What on earth's the matter?"

"Come in, Fred," said Mrs. Spiers. "Come in here and shut the door. Don't worry about your train."

Gavin O'Leary

here was a young, bold, active, and singularly handsome flea, who lived as blissful as a shepherd in Arcady upon the divine body of Rosie O'Leary. Rosie was an eighteen-year-old nursemaid in the comfortable home of a doctor in Vermont, and no flea has been better pastured than this one since the beginning of the world. He considered himself a landowner in a country overflowing with milk and honey, and he delighted in every undulation of the landscape.

Rosie was the merriest, most ardent, laughing, bounding, innocent, high-spirited creature that ever trod on earth, from which it follows that our flea was equally blessed in temperament and general physical tone. It is widely known that the flea imbibes more than half his weight at a single repast, from which it follows that not only the bodily health but the nervous conditions, the emotions, the inclinations, and even the moral standards of whoever provides the meal are very directly transmitted to his diminutive guest.

Thus it came about that this particular flea bounded higher than most, and ceaselessly extolled his good fortune. All his nourishment came fresh and ruby from her untroubled heart and there was never such a gay, silly, glossy, high-jumping, well-developed flea as Gavin O'Leary. Gavin was his given name; the other he took from Rosie, as a nobleman takes his title from his domain.

There came a time when Gavin found something a little heady in his drink, and his whole being was filled with delicious dreams. On Thursday evening this sensation rose to a positive delirium. Rosie was being taken to the movies.

Our flea at that time had no great interest in the art of the motion picture. He sat through the first half of the performance in a nook that offered no view of what was going on. At ten o'clock he began to feel ready for his supper, and, as Rosie showed no signs of going home to bed, he resolved to picnic, as it were, on the spot. He inserted his privileged proboscis in the near neighborhood of her heart. His earlier exhilaration should have warned him that great changes were taking place in the nature and quality of the nectar on which he lived, but as Rosie was guileless and heedless, so therefore was Gavin O'Leary. Thus he was taken by surprise when his light and sparkling sustenance changed to a warm and drowsy syrup, with a fire smouldering under its sweetness, which robbed him of all his bounding enterprise. A tremor ran through his body, his eyes half closed, and when his shy retreat was suddenly and inexplicably invaded by an alien hand, he was neither amazed nor hopping mad, but crawled half-reluctantly away, looking over his shoulder with a languid simper, for all the world as if he were a mere bug.

Gavin took refuge in a cranny of the plush seat, and surrendered himself to the throbbing intoxication that filled his veins. He awoke from his drunken sleep several hours later, with a slight sense of shame. It was early morning; Rosie and her companion were gone; the picture house was empty and no food was in sight. Gavin waited eagerly for the place to re-open, for his appetite was of the best. At the proper hour people began to file in. Gavin's seat was taken by a pale youth, who fidgeted impatiently until the performance began, and when the performance began he sighed. Gavin, brushing his forefoot over his proboscis, for all the world like a toper who wipes his lips before taking a swig, entered between a pair of waist-coat buttons, and, without any affectation of saying grace, tapped his new host between the fourth and fifth rib, in order that he might drink as fresh and pure as it came.

I think it is Dante who describes a lover's blood as running pale and fiery like old wine. By this comparison, the draught now sucked up by Gavin was vodka or absinthe at the very least. No sooner had he swallowed his potent philter than he began to pant, moan, and roll his eyes like a madman, and he could not clamber up fast enough out of the young man's shirt to where he could catch a glimpse of the object of what was now their joint adoration. It was none other than Miss Blynda Blythe, whose infinitely famous, infinitely glamorous face at this moment filled the greater part of the screen.

Gazing upon her, our flea was in the condition of one who has made a whole meal of a love potion. He felt his host's blood positively boiling within him. He was devoured, wrought-up, hysterical; his proboscis burned, throbbed, and tingled at the sight of that satiny skin; he wept, laughed, and finally began to rhyme like a demon, for his host was a poet, or he could never have been such a lover. In short, no flea has ever loved, longed, and hungered as Gavin did, at his very first sight of Miss Blynda Blythe. (Except that one, dear Madame, which was availing itself of my hospitality, when you passed in your limousine last Thursday.)

All too soon the film came to its end, and Gavin rode home to a hall bedroom, where he spent the night on the young man's coat collar, looking over his shoulder at the fan magazines which this youth incessantly studied. Every now and then he would take a quick shot of that burning brew that was the cause of his furious passion. A number of lesser fleas, and other creatures of a baser sort, refreshed themselves at the same source and shared a night-long bacchanal. Their besotted host, confused between his itches, was too far gone even to scratch. The crazy drinkers were free to take their perilous fill, and the scene was worse than any opium den. Some wept and moaned their lives away in corners; some, dirty, unkempt, lost to the world, lay abandoned in feverish reverie; others sprang from the window, drowned themselves in the slop-pail, or took Keatings. Many, mad with desire, blunted their proboscises on one or other of the glossy photographs of Blynda Blythe which adorned the mantelpiece and the screen.

Gavin, though he sipped and sipped till the potent liquor entered into the very tissues of his being, was made of sterner stuff. It was not for nothing that he had spent his youth on the finest flower of the indomitable immigrant stock. With the dawn his bold plan was made. His host rose from his uneasy slumbers, dashed off a few lines, and went out to seek his breakfast at a drugstore. Gavin rode boldly on the rim of his hat, taking his bearings from the position of the sun.

The poet walked westward for two or three blocks, and Gavin was grateful for the lift. But no sooner did the fellow veer off in a northerly direction in quest of his coffee and doughnut than Gavin was down on the sidewalk, and hopping furiously on the first stage of his three-thousand-mile trek to the Coast. He hitch-hiked when he could, but as he left the town behind him these opportunities grew fewer. The dust choked him, the hard surface proved lacerating to those sensitive feet, accustomed to nothing coarser than the silken skin of Rosie O'Leary. Nevertheless, when the red sunset beaconed where the long trail crossed the distant hills, a keen eye might have discerned the speck-like figure of Gavin, jigging lamely but gamely on.

It was afterwards, and after Heaven knows what adventures by prairie, desert, and mountain, that a travel-worn, older, and gaunter Gavin entered Hollywood. He was gaunt, not merely by reason of his incredible exertions, but because of the knight-errant asceticism he had practiced through all the hungry miles of the way. Fearing lest any full meal should fill him with some baser, alien mood, he had disciplined himself to take the merest semi-sip, except where he was well assured that his entertainer was also an adoring fan of Blynda Blythe.

He now hastened along Hollywood Boulevard in search of the world-famous Chinese Theatre. There, sinking on one knee, he reverently pressed his long proboscis to a certain beloved footprint set here in the cement of eternity. A keen-eyed producer noticed the knightly gesture as he drove by, and instantly conceived the idea of doing a new version of Cyrano de Bergerac. Gavin, having accomplished this act of homage, took the innocent equivalent of a glass of milk from the dimpled shoulder of a baby star, and began to ponder on how he might make contact with his idol.

He thought at first of striking up an acquaintance with some of the lounging, idle, disappointed fleas of the town, to find out from them which laundry she patronized, so that he might arrive like a male Cleopatra rolled up in some intimate article of her apparel. His wholesome pride rejected this backstairs approach. He dallied for a shuddering moment with the fierce temptation to perch on the cuff of an autograph hunter, and make a Fairbanks leap upon her as she signed the book. "To spring upon her!" he muttered. "To wreak my will upon her regardless of her cries and struggles! To plunge my cruel proboscis into her delicate epidermis!" But Gavin O'Leary was no brutal, cowardly rapist. There was something upright and manly in his nature that demanded he meet his mate as a friend and as an equal. He was fully conscious of the immense social gulf that lay between a poor, unknown flea and a rich and famous film star. Painful as the thought was to him, he did not avert his eyes from the racial barrier. But to Gavin barriers were made to be over-leaped. He felt that he must be recognized as a fellow being, and respected as . . . as what? "Why, that's it!" he cried as the inspiration struck him. "Respected as a fellow artist! Who has not heard of performing fleas? Whenever did a troupe of players travel without a numerous companionship of my dark, brittle, and vivacious kin?"

The decision made, nothing remained but to crash the studios, as the ambitious phrase it. Gavin had certain misgivings at the thought of permitting an agent to handle him. The only alternative was to mingle with the ranks of shabby extras who hung about the gates of Blynda's studio in the hope of being called in on some emergency. Fortune favors the brave; he had not been waiting there many weeks when an assistant director dashed out, crying in an urgent voice: "Say! Any of you guys got a performing flea? Anybody know where I can hire one?"

The word was spread. The extras on the sidewalk began to search themselves hastily. Genuine professional flea masters patrolled the boulevards rounding up and corralling their troupes, which they had, with the inhumanity of their kind, turned out to forage for themselves during the bad times. While all this *brouhaha* was spreading through the town, with "Yipee i ay! Yipee i ay!" re-echoing from Gower Street to Culver City, Gavin boldly entered the studio, and took up a point of vantage on the producer's desk. "At least," thought he, "I am first in the queue."

Some flea masters soon entered, carrying their recaptured artistes in pill boxes and phials. Gavin surveyed his rivals, and saw that every one of them bore the indefinable stamp of the bit player. He could hardly suppress a sneer.

When all were assembled: "We've got a part here for the right flea," said the producer. "It's not big, but it's snappy. Listen, this flea's going to have the chance to play opposite Blynda Blythe. It's a bedroom scene, and there's a close two-shot. He's going to bite her on the shoulder in a lodging-house scene. Say, where are your fleas from, feller?"

"Dey're Mex, boss," replied the impresario he had addressed. "Mexican flea, him lively, him jumpa, jumpa . . ."

"That's enough," replied the producer coldly. "This scene's laid in the East, and when I shoot a scene it's authentic. You can't fool the public these days. Come on, boys, I want a New England flea."

As he spoke he spread the contract out before him. A babble rose from the flea masters, all of whom swore their fleas had been bred on Plymouth Rock and raised on none but Lowells, Cabots, and Lodges. While they still argued, Gavin dipped his proboscis in the ink bottle and scrawled his minute signature on the dotted line.

The effect was electrifying. "The darned little guy!" said the producer. "He's got what it takes. While all you fellers are shooting off your mouths, he muscles right in and gets his moniker on the contract. Reminds me of the time when *I* broke into this industry," he added to a sycophant who nodded smiling agreement. Gavin was hurried on to the set, where his coming was eagerly awaited. "You wouldn't like your stand-in to do this scene, Miss Blythe?" said an over-obsequious assistant. Gavin's heart sank.

"No," said Miss Blythe. "When it's a champagne scene,

I want real champagne, and when I get bitten by a flea I stand for a real flea bite."

"Get that written down and over to the publicity department," said the producer to another hanger-on. "O.K., Jack," to the director. "I'll watch you shoot."

"Better run it over once or twice in rehearsal," said the director. "Somebody stand by with a glass of brandy for Miss Blythe."

"It's all right, Benny," said Blynda. "It's for my art."

"Look how it is, Blynda," said the director, taking up the script. "This is where you've walked out on Carew, just because you're nuts about him. You want to see if he'll follow you down to the depths. You're yearning for him. And you're lying on the lodging-house bed, crying. And you feel a bite, just where he kissed you in the scene we're going to shoot when that goddam Art Department gets the country-club revel set done. Get the point, Blynda? You feel the bite. For a moment you think it's Carew."

"Yes, Jack. I think I see that. I think I understand."

"And, Jesus! you turn your head, hoping against hope it's him . . ."

". . . and it's only the flea!" she nodded gravely. "Yes, I can feel that. I can play it."

"Bet your life you can play it! Okay, get on the bed. Where's Make-up? Got Miss Blythe's tears ready?"

Blynda waved the crystal vial aside. She shook her head and smiled bravely at the director. "I shan't need phony tears, Jack. Not if it's Carew."

At these words a look and a murmur passed through all the numerous company. Actors and technicians alike felt sympathy and admiration for the plucky girl, for her unrequited real-life passion for the handsome, sneering leading man was no secret. In fact it was the subject of almost hourly bulletins from the Publicity Department.

It was whispered that "Repressed Carew," as he was

nicknamed by the psychology-conscious younger set of Hollywood, was a man contemptuous of love in any form whatever. Only those who had seen him at his mirror knew that he made an exception in favour of his own supercilious profile. This was the man Blynda hopelessly adored, and Blynda was the girl Gavin was about to bite.

Next moment the director had said a quiet word to his assistant, and the assistant, like a human megaphone, blared the command to the farthest corner of the vast sound stage. "QUIET for Miss Blythe and Mr. Gavin O'Leary rehearsing."

Gavin's heart swelled. To become at one stroke a successful film actor and a happy lover is enough to intoxicate a more down-to-earth personality than a flea's. Blynda pressed her face to the pillow and wept. Her delicious shoulder blades heaved with emotion, and Gavin stood ready for the leap. He wished only that he had a delicate scrap of cambric, that he might wipe his proboscis and fling it into the hands of a nearby grip. He felt the gesture would have shown a nice feeling.

His regrets were cut short by a crisp word: "Mr. O'Leary!" He sprang high into the air, landed and struck deep.

"Boy! did you see that jump?" cried the director to the producer. "Watch him bite! The little guy gives it all he's got."

"Make a note for me to get him under long-term contract," said the producer to his secretary.

"What the hell am I doing on this floozy's shoulder?" murmured Gavin in a petulant voice. "I wonder when this fellow Carew is going to make his entrance." Forgive him, reader! It was the drink speaking.

At that very moment a deep, rich jocular voice was heard. "Hey, what goes on here? New talent, eh? Stealing my scene!"

All turned to eye the newcomer with respect; Blynda and Gavin with something more. Blynda wallowed as invitingly as she could upon the bed; Gavin, with a leap that approached if not surpassed the world's record, flung himself upon his new idol's breast, sobbing in mingled ecstasy and shame.

"The little fellow seems to take to me," said the actor good-humouredly. "Going to be buddies, eh? Good material that, Jack, for the Publicity Department." These words marked the beginning, and, as far as the speaker was concerned, the motivation, of a friendship between the oddly assorted pair. Soon they became inseparable.

The biographer prefers to draw a veil over the next stage of Gavin's career. To know all is to excuse all, but to know less in a case of this sort is to have less to excuse. Suffice it to say that Carew's love for himself continued what Blynda's love for Carew had begun, and as it was marked by a fervour and a constancy very rare in Hollywood, fervid and constant was Gavin's unhallowed passion for Carew.

It was not long before ugly rumors were in circulation concerning the flea star. People whispered of his fantastic costumes, his violet evening suits, his epicene underwear, his scent-spray shower-bath, and of strange parties at his bijou house in Bel Air. A trade paper, naming no names, pointed out that if individuals of a certain stripe were considered bad security risks by the State Department, they must be even more of a danger in the most influential of all American industries. It seemed only a matter of time before Gavin would be the centre of an open scandal, and his pictures be picketed by the guardians of our morals.

But time works in many ways, and the actor's face withered even faster than Gavin's reputation. Soon he was rejected everywhere for the rôle of the lover, and must either play character parts or go in for production. Character never having been his strong point, he felt himself better fitted to be a producer. Now, producers are known to be God-like creatures, and the chief point of resemblance is that they must either create new stars or have no public.

Carew, of course, had Gavin as an ace up his sleeve. Splendid parts, full of nimble wit and biting satire, were written for the flea actor, but nowhere could a new beauty be found who was worthy to play opposite him. The talent scouts ranged far and wide, but their eulogies carried little conviction. At last, however, a short list was made. Carew read it over, shook his head, and threw it down on his dressing table. "There's not a winner among them," he muttered. "That means I'm not a genius as a producer."

He retired to bed feeling thoroughly dissatisfied with himself for the first time in many years. To Gavin, his supper that night seemed to have a smack of clean and salutary bitterness about it. His nerves steadied themselves, his mind cleared; he saw Carew for what he was, and the hour of his salvation was upon him. At such moments the mind naturally reverts to thoughts of old times, early days, youth, innocence, and the bright faces of the past.

Gavin O'Leary rose and ripped off the flimsy, decadent night attire he had recently affected. He sought, with a leap that was already less mincing and effeminate, the list upon the writing table. The ink-well stood open; to him its sable depths were a positive Jordan, in which, if he dipped seven times, he might yet cease to be a social leper. He immersed himself with a shudder, and, clambering painfully out, he stood for a moment upon the dark rim of the ink-well, nude, shivering, gasping, yet tensing his muscles for a leap to a certain spot at the head of the list. He made it, and made it without splash or blot. With the accuracy of a figure skater, but with all the slow difficulty of a treacle-clogged fly, he described the word "Rosie" in a perfect imitation of the sprawling hand of the chief talent scout.

Another painful leap, and he was back, sobbing and choking, in the bitter, glutinous ink. The hot weather had thickened it. This time he completed the word "O'Leary." Five times more, and her address was written. Gavin, utterly worn out, black as your hat, half-poisoned by ink, sank exhausted on the blotting pad. But a great gladness had dawned in his heart.

The ruse was successful. Rosie was brought to the Coast for a screen test. Needless to say, she passed it triumphantly. Gavin, with a thankful sigh, nestled once more upon her heart, and drank deep of its cleansing, life-giving vintage. With that draught the last of his aberration fell away from him like a shoddy outworn garment. The past was dead. He was a new flea and had earned his right to be the lover of the most beautiful Irish colleen, and the greatest little actress, and the most important human being, in the world. And as Miss O'Leary soon began to think of herself in the same terms, you may be sure they lived happily ever after.

If Youth Knew If Age Could

The first thing one noticed about Henri Maurras was inevitably his gaunt and quixotic Spanish nose, flanked by a pair of enormous eyes, extremely dark and melancholy, but capable of fire. This romantic equipment was unfortunately betrayed by the childish, petulant mouth of a Parisian, and a ridiculous little mustache.

For the rest, he was a mere thread of a young man, a veritable nailparing, and wore a paper-thin grey suit, under which his little buttocks presented all the appearance of a hair-pin. He worked as assistant book-keeper in a big general store in Marseilles, and he desired ardently to be married.

Frequently he would lose count of a column of figures, and turn up his dark eyes, as he visualized the bride of his dreams, youthful, devoted, passionate, deliciously rounded, and yet of immaculate reputation. Our passionate *petit bourgeois* was especially set upon the immaculate reputation.

His little mustache would twitch as he imagined the promenades they would take on Sundays, envied by all who beheld them. She would hang fondly on his arm, driving all the men to despair; he would wear a smart suit from Marquet's, and carry a fashionable cane.

"Pleasure is all very well," said he to his fellow clerks, when they proposed some little frolic on pay-day. "But what pleasure can compare to being married? I mean, to a beautiful wife, gay, amiable, sympathetic, and——" His hands sketched certain outlines in the air. "For that," said he, "one must save. One must wait."

"Nonsense," said the others. "Come with us to Madame Garcier's. It may make saving a little harder, but the waiting becomes infinitely more tolerable. After all, a young man is entitled to a little happiness on account."

"No. No," said he. "I have certain ideals. You would hardly understand."

Henri's ideals, as lofty as the bridge of his nose, preserved him from the venal affections so popular among the youth of Marseilles. Yet that phrase, *"A little happiness on account,"* took fatal root. Under its influence he succumbed to the attractions of a superb malacca cane, displayed in the window of the most expensive shop in all the Rue St. Ferréol. "After all," said he to himself, "I shall have to buy one sooner or later. Why not now?"

As soon as he had paid over the money, he was almost ready to kill himself, he was so mortified at his extravagance. Yet he trembled with joy as he twirled his new treasure, leaned upon it, and hung it over his arm. On leaving the shop, he fancied that several well-dressed men eyed it with envious interest. "Wait," thought he, "till they see me in a suit from Marquet's, and with my lovely wife walking by my side."

When he got home he put his new acquisition into his wardrobe. It would never do to get it scratched, or even to have the least gloss taken off it, before the day of his nuptials. On that day, everything was to be immaculate; everything must have its gloss absolutely unimpaired.

Nevertheless, every night, before he undressed, he put on his hat again, and took out his cane for a few minutes, holding it this way and that way in front of the mirror. He swung it as gracefully as the narrowness of his bedchamber allowed, and seating himself on the side of his bed, he drew a heart on the carpet.

This cane had a horn ferrule of the highest quality. It was as smooth and round as anything you can possibly imagine, and it was girdled with a slim circlet of gold, for all the world like a wedding ring.

Now that he possessed such a cane as this, Henri could no longer resist casting glances at the girls, although his saving was at far too early a stage to justify such boldness. He was a little bothered by a certain look on the more attractive faces he saw, a look which can only be described as suggesting worldly experience. "Where shall I find a bride," thought Henri, "as fresh, immaculate, and shining as my new cane?" He did not reflect that this cane had come to him, not leafy from the swamp in which it had grown, but smooth and sophisticated from the hands of the polisher.

However, Henri still hoped, and every evening he rode home on the bus to his dwelling at the far end of the Prado. At this hour, at the beginning of May, the streets of Marseilles are full of a golden light. The new leaves of the innumerable plane trees exude their soft yellow into the radiance of the declining sun.

One evening a girl got on to the bus. Henri looked up; his magnificent nose made a true point, his dark eyes flamed, his little mustache quivered, and his childish mouth pouted as if it had been stung by a bee. She was an Italianate Marseillaise; and as lovely as a black grape; her skin had that sort of bloom upon it. This dusky bloom concentrated into a delicate, adorable down along the line of her upper lip, which was bewitchingly lifted. Her eye was like the eye of a gazelle, her cheek was soft, and her figure was at once young and ample, such as any man must admire, but especially he whose buttocks are as lean as a hair-pin under his skimpy pants.

To crown it all, she was dressed very simply, in one of those nondescript black dresses affected by the well-to-do peasantry, who are so much better off than the little book-keepers. She wore black cotton gloves. It must have been a careful family, of the proper old-fashioned type, that had brought her up so completely out of the dubious mode. Such old-fashioned people are usually extremely conscientious about the *dot*. Henri admired, approved, and loved.

"It is true," he thought, "I have yet to win her affections, gain the approval of her family, and save up a whole mountain of francs. All that is possible, but how am I to make her acquaintance? At any moment she may get off the bus. If I speak to her, she will either answer me, in which case she cannot be as virtuous as she looks, or she will not answer me, and I shall never see her again." Here Henri experienced one of the greatest dilemmas known to mankind, and one which has been sadly neglected by the philosophers.

Fate, however, was altogether on his side. The bus stopped for a whole minute at a corner where a family of gipsies were giving the traditional exhibition. A goat mounted precariously upon a step-ladder, a mangy bear stood by, shifting his feet in melancholy reminiscence of his training, a nervous monkey presented a miniature tambourine for the sous of the passers-by.

The girl, as simple as a child, was ravished by this familiar spectacle. She pressed her face against the glass, smiled in rapture, and turned a bright gaze on the other

passengers, to see if they were enjoying it, too. Henri, leaning over, was emboldened to offer the comments of a man
of the world.

"Very amusing, the little monkey," said he.

"Yes, Monsieur, very amusing."

"The bear, he is droll."

"But yes, Monsieur, very droll."

"The goat, also. For a domestic animal, he is droll, too."

"Yes, Monsieur, he is truly droll."

"The *gitanos* are very picturesque, but they are a bad
type."

At this point the bus jolted on. A brilliant conversation
had been interrupted, but acquaintance was established,
and in such a simple and innocent fashion that the most
fastidious of future husbands could find nothing to object
to. Henri ventured to seat himself beside her. The jolting of
the bus provided the briefest but most delicious of con-
tacts. A *rapport* was established; their tongues uttered
banalities, but their shoulders were supremely eloquent.
"Mademoiselle," said Henri at last, "dare I hope that you
will take a little promenade with me on Sunday."

"Oh, but I am afraid that would hardly be possible,"
replied the young girl, with an adorable appearance of
confusion.

Henri urged his plea with all the feeling at his command, and at length his charmer, whose name was Marie,
decided that she might overcome the obstacles, which
doubtless had their origin in the excessive respectability of
her upbringing.

The rendezvous was made. Henri, left alone upon the
bus, rode far past his destination, lost in an ecstasy far
transcending any description. The excess fare amounted to
two francs.

That night he spent a whole hour before his mirror,
conducting his cane in the manner in which he hoped to

parade it on Sunday. "There is no doubt about it," said he to himself, "such a cane and such a girl, absolutely demand that new suit from Marquet's. Tomorrow I will pay them a visit." He drew several hearts, all of them transfixed by arrows, and surrounded by initials. "I will take her to the *calanque*," said he to himself, "and there, seated beside her on a rock, I will draw something of this sort on the sand. She will guess what I mean."

On Sunday everything went as well as any lover could wish. Henri was first at the trysting place, and soon saw her tripping along. This time she was wearing a summer frock and white cotton gloves. She had the happy air of a little girl let out from school. "Her parents must be very severe," thought Henri. "So much the better. I wonder by what artless excuses she managed to get away."

Their greeting was all the heart could desire. Every true lover, and some whose aims are less creditable, knows the delicious promise of those first meetings in which both parties act as frankly and simply as children, and take hands even as they make their way to the bus. Days beginning thus should always be spent in the open air, and no place under all the sky is more propitious to them than those deep and cliffy creeks near Marseilles, which are called the *calanques*. Snow-white rocks descend into water as clear as glass, edged by tiny beaches of sand, perfectly suited for the inscription of hearts and arrows. Little pine trees cover all the slopes, and, when the afternoon sun is hot, there is all the more reason to take advantage of their shade.

Henri and his Marie did this. "Take off your gloves," said he, "and I will tell your fortune."

She willingly removed the glove from her right hand, which she extended to him with the utmost grace.

"No," said he, "I beg you to take off both."

Marie blushed, and hesitated, and began with tantalizing slowness to draw off the other glove.

"It does not seem to come off very easily," said Henri.

"You demand too much," said she. "This is only the first time I have been out with you. I did not think you would ask me to remove my gloves."

"At last," thought Henri, "I have found a girl of a simplicity, of a virtue, such as must be absolutely unique in the world of 193—. Marie," cried he, pressing his lips to her hands, "I adore you with every fibre of my being. I implore you to be mine. I long, I burn, I die for the happiness of being married to you."

"Oh, no," said she. "That is impossible."

"Then you do not love me," said he. "I have spoken too soon."

"No," said she. "Perhaps I do. But how can I answer you? It could not be for a year, perhaps two, possibly even three."

"What of that?" cried he. "I will wait. In fact, I still have a great deal of money to save." He told her of the prospects of the furniture business, and of the situation of his old mother, who had been treated abominably by certain relatives.

Marie was less explicit in her description of her background. She said, though, that she was treated very strictly, and could hardly introduce into her home a young man she had met so unconventionally on a bus.

"It is inconvenient," said Henri, "but it is as it should be. Sooner or later we will manage something. Till then, we are affianced, are we not? We will come here every Sunday."

"It will be very hard for me to get away," said she.

"Never mind," said he. "It will arrange itself. Meanwhile, we are affianced. Therefore I may embrace you."

An interlude followed in which Henri experienced that happiness which is only revealed to young men of the meagrest proportions in the company of girls as delight-

fully rounded as Marie. At the close of the day Henri had
drawn almost as deeply on his future marriage as he had
upon his costume and his cane. "They are right," thought
he, "one is entitled to a little happiness on account."

He went home the happiest young man in Marseilles,
or in all France for that matter, and next day he actually
carried his cane to the office with him, for he could not
bear to part with it.

That evening, on the bus, he fixed his eyes on the people
waiting at every stopping place. He felt that fortune might
grant him an unappointed glimpse of his beloved. Sure
enough, after a false alarm or two, he caught sight of her
shoulder and the line of her neck as she stood in a knot of
people two or three hundred yards up the street. He recognized this single curve immediately.

His heart pounded, his hands shook, his cane almost fell
from his grasp. The bus came to a stop, and he turned to
greet her as she entered. To his horror and dismay, she appeared not to recognize him, and, as he blundered toward
her, she gave him a warning frown.

Henri saw that behind her was an old man, a man of
nearly eighty, a colossal ruin of a man, with dim and hollow eyes, a straggly white mustache horribly stained, and
two or three yellow tusks in a cavernous mouth. He took
his seat beside the adorable Marie, and folded his huge
and grimy hands, on which the veins stood out like whip-
cord, over the handle of a cheap and horrible cane, an
atrocity, fashioned out of bamboo. He wore the expensive
and ugly broadcloth of the well-to-do peasant.

Henri fixed his eyes on the pair. "Possibly he is her
father," thought he.

A lover, however, has an eye which is not easily deceived. Henri knew perfectly well that this old man was
not her father. He tried to repress a feeling of acute
uneasiness. "He is very old," thought Henri. "It is more

likely he is her grandfather. Possibly she has something to endure from him. He seems to be sitting beside her in a very familiar way. How I wish we could be married at once!"

At this point the conductor approached the old man, and jingled his little ticket machine under his nose. "Demand it of Madame," said the old man in a low and thunderous rumble.

Henri sat as if struck by lightning. "It is impossible," said he to himself over and over again. "After all, what is more natural than for a man to speak of his female companion as Madame, whether she is married or not, when he is addressing a waiter, a bus conductor, or someone of that sort? Besides, the old fool dotes; he doesn't know what the hell he is saying. He thinks it's his wife, her grandmother; his mind is in the past."

As he said this, he saw before his eyes a picture of her left hand, with the white gloves on it, which she had removed so slowly and with so much trouble.

"She is a pure, sincere, serious, straightforward girl," thought he. "Yes, but that is why she had so much trouble with that glove. An artful girl would have removed her wedding ring before meeting me. So much the more terrible!

"No, no. I am going mad. He *is* her grandfather. Possibly her great-grandfather. See how old he is! People should be killed before reaching that age. Look at his mouth, his teeth! If he *should* be her husband, and fondle her! Nonsense! I am mad. The idea is absurd."

Nevertheless he lived in torment till the end of the week, when a note reached him saying that Marie could slip out for an hour or two on Sunday. She would be at the same rendezvous at two o'clock.

Nothing could be more simple and reassuring than this note, which breathed innocence and affection. One or two words were artlessly misspelled, which always gives an effect of sincerity. Henri's suspicions departed as suddenly as they had come. "What a brute I was!" he thought, as he hastened to meet her. "I will beg her forgiveness. I will go down on my knees. But no, not in this suit. On the whole, I had better say nothing about it. What sort of a husband will she think I will make if I am already suspicious of a disgusting old man? Ah, here she comes! How lovely she is! How radiant! I certainly deserve to be thrashed with my own cane."

She came smiling up to him, and put out her hand with the white cotton glove upon it. Henri's eyes fell upon this glove, and his debonair welcome died upon his lips. "Who," said he hoarsely, "who was that old man who was with you?"

Marie dropped her hand and stared at Henri.

"He is not your father," said Henri, in a tone of rage and despair.

"No," said she, obviously terror-stricken.

"He is not your grandfather!" cried Henri. "He is your husband."

"How did you know?" cried she.

"You have deceived me!" cried Henri. "I thought you pure, true, artless, without fault. I—I—I—— Never mind. *Adieu*, Madame! Be so good as to look at the newspaper in the morning, and see if any unfortunate has fallen from the ramparts of the Château d'If."

With that he turned on his heel and strode away, in the ominous direction of the port, where the little boats take sightseers out to the Château d'If. Marie, with a cry, ran after him, and clasped his arm in both her hands.

"Do nothing rash," she begged. "Believe me, I adore you."

"And yet," said he, "you marry a disgusting old man."

"But that was before I knew you."

"So be it, Madame. I wish you every felicity."

"But, beloved," said she, "you do me an injustice. He is rich. I was young. My parents urged me. You cannot think I love him."

"Leave me, prostitute!" cried Henri.

"Ah, you are unkind!" said she. "Why should you be jealous? You are young. You are dressed in the mode, even to your cane. You are handsome. You are my dream. How could you threaten to commit a desperate act? The old man will not live forever. You and I would be rich. We could be happy. Henri, were we not happy last Sunday, out at the *calanque?* I am just the same."

"What?" cried Henri. "Do you think I care for his dirty money? Could I be happy with you again, thinking of that old man?"

"Nevertheless," said she, "it is nearly a million francs."

"To the devil with it!" said Henri. "Supposing we stayed at the best hotels, travelled, had an apartment in Paris even, how could I enjoy anything, thinking of you and him together?"

"But he is so old," said she. "He is nearly blind. He can scarcely speak. He is deaf. He has lost the use of all his senses. Yes, Henri, *all* his senses."

"What do you mean, *all* his senses?" said Henri, halting in his stride.

"All his senses," said she, facing round and nodding gravely at Henri. "All. All. All.

"He is eighty years of age," said she. "Who is jealous of a man of eighty? What is there to be jealous of? Nothing. Nothing at all."

"All the same," said Henri. "They are sometimes worse than the rest. Yes, a thousand times worse. Leave me. Let me go."

"He is a log of wood," said she earnestly. "Henri, is it

possible to be jealous of a log of wood? It is not what you
would choose, perhaps, or me either, but, after all, it is
nothing. The same cannot be said of a million francs."

Henri demanded ten thousand assurances, and was
given them all. The Parisian in him urged a common-sense
view of the situation. "After all, we must be broad-mind-
ed," thought he. "Provided, of course, that it is really
nothing. Absolutely and certainly nothing!"

"I shall be able to see you every Sunday afternoon," said
Marie. "I have suggested to him that he take a little stroll
and a drink at the café between two and six. I made very
poor excuses for not accompanying him, but to my surprise
he assented eagerly. I expected a lot of trouble."

"He is jealous, then?" cried Henri. "A log of wood is
not jealous."

"But all the more," said Marie. "After all, is it so un-
reasonable, darling?"

"Nevertheless," said Henri, "I cannot understand why
he should be jealous. I am jealous; that is natural. But a
log of wood——"

Marie soothed him again with another ten thousand
assurances, and when at last he bade her farewell his happiness was completely restored.

Only one fly remained in his ointment. "When I consider," thought he, "how extremely scrupulous I have
been, unlike any other young man in Marseilles, it certainly seems very unfair. I have never spent my money on
girls. I have never visited an establishment such as Madame Garcier's. And now I am to marry a girl who——It
is true he is eighty. At eighty a man is no better than a log
of wood. Nevertheless, it is a difference between us. It will
give rise to a thousand bitter reflections when we are married. She is so beautiful. And there is the million francs.
What a pity there should be any cause for bitterness!

How lovely she looked today! I wish we could have been reconciled under that little pine tree out in the *calanque*. I should be able to view matters more calmly."

At this moment a certain idea came into his head. It is impossible to say where it came from. Probably it was from the Parisian in him. "It would certainly balance accounts between us," said he to himself. "It would go far to prevent bitterness. She would be all the happier for it. After all, it is not my fault we could not go to the *calanque*."

Reflecting thus, he bent his steps toward the famous establishment of Madame Garcier, so highly recommended by his fellow clerks. This discreet haven had all the appearance of a private house; the door was answered by a maidservant, who ushered callers into an anteroom.

"Madame will be with you immediately," said this maidservant to Henri, taking his hat and stick and depositing them in an old-fashioned hall-stand. With that she showed him into the anteroom and departed, leaving the door open behind her.

"This is an excellent idea," thought Henri. "Now there will be two of us, and I shall be the worse of the two, as a man should be! So I shall not feel bitter. How happy we shall be! And after all, what is a little extravagance, when we are going to inherit a million francs?"

At that moment he heard footsteps on the stairs, and the voice evidently of the Madame, who was ushering out some favourite patron.

"This has been a delightful surprise," she was saying. "When I heard of your marriage, I declared we had seen the last of you. Delphine and Fifi were inconsolable."

"What would you?" came the reply in a thunderous rumble, which caused Henri's hair to stand erect upon his head. "A man must settle down, Madame, especially when he is no longer as young as he was. It is, so to speak, a duty to the Republic. But, Madame, I am, thank God, still in my prime, and, when he is in his prime, a man demands variety. Besides, Madame, the young women in these days——"

Henri nearly fainted. He heard the front door close, and the footsteps of the proprietress approaching the room in which he sat. He felt he must get out at all costs.

"Pardon me, Madame," he muttered. "I fear I have changed my mind. A sudden indisposition."

"Just as you please, Monsieur," said the old trot. "There is no compulsion in this establishment. But if Monsieur would like at least to *inspect* a young lady—to exchange a few pleasant remarks——"

"No, no, thank you," said Henri desperately, edging into the hallway. "I must go. Ah, here is my hat. But my cane! Where is my cane?"

He stared, but his cane was gone. In its place the last visitor had left a cheap, nasty, battered old bamboo.

Thus I Refute Beelzy

There goes the tea bell," said Mrs. Carter. "I hope Simon hears it."

They looked out from the window of the drawing-room. The long garden, agreeably neglected, ended in a waste plot. Here a little summer-house was passing close by beauty on its way to complete decay. This was Simon's retreat. It was almost completely screened by the tangled branches of the apple tree and the pear tree, planted too close together, as they always are in the suburbs. They caught a glimpse of him now and then, as he strutted up and down, mouthing and gesticulating, performing all the solemn mumbo-jumbo of small boys who spend long afternoons at the forgotten ends of long gardens.

"There he is, bless him!" said Betty.

"Playing his game," said Mrs. Carter. "He won't play with the other children any more. And if I go down there —the temper! And comes in tired out!"

"He doesn't have his sleep in the afternoons?" asked Betty.

"You know what Big Simon's ideas are," said Mrs. Carter. "'Let him choose for himself,' he says. That's what he chooses, and he comes in as white as a sheet."

"Look! He's heard the bell," said Betty. The expression was justified, though the bell had ceased ringing a full minute ago. Small Simon stopped in his parade exactly as if its tinny dingle had at that moment reached his ear. They watched him perform certain ritual sweeps and scratchings with his little stick, and come lagging over the hot and flaggy grass toward the house.

Mrs. Carter led the way down to the play-room, or garden-room, which was also the tea-room for hot days. It had been the huge scullery of this tall Georgian house. Now the walls were cream-washed, there was coarse blue net in the windows, canvas-covered armchairs on the stone floor, and a reproduction of Van Gogh's *Sunflowers* over the mantelpiece.

Small Simon came drifting in, and accorded Betty a perfunctory greeting. His face was an almost perfect triangle, pointed at the chin, and he was paler than he should have been. "The little elf-child!" cried Betty.

Simon looked at her. "No," said he.

At that moment the door opened, and Mr. Carter came in, rubbing his hands. He was a dentist, and washed them before and after everything he did. "You!" said his wife. "Home already!"

"Not unwelcome, I hope," said Mr. Carter, nodding to Betty. "Two people cancelled their appointments: I decided to come home. I said, I hope I am not unwelcome."

"Silly!" said his wife. "Of course not."

"Small Simon seems doubtful," continued Mr. Carter. "Small Simon, are you sorry to see me at tea with you?"

"No, Daddy."

"No, what?"

"No, Big Simon."

"That's right. Big Simon and Small Simon. That sounds more like friends, doesn't it? At one time little boys had to call their father 'sir.' If they forgot—a good spanking. On the bottom, Small Simon! On the bottom!" said Mr. Carter, washing his hands once more with his invisible soap and water.

The little boy turned crimson with shame or rage.

"But now, you see," said Betty, to help, "you can call your father whatever you like."

"And what," asked Mr. Carter, "has Small Simon been doing this afternoon? While Big Simon has been at work."

"Nothing," muttered his son.

"Then you have been bored," said Mr. Carter. "Learn from experience, Small Simon. Tomorrow, do something amusing, and you will not be bored. I want him to learn from experience, Betty. That is my way, the new way."

"I have learned," said the boy, speaking like an old, tired man, as little boys so often do.

"It would hardly seem so," said Mr. Carter, "if you sit on your behind all the afternoon, doing nothing. Had *my* father caught me doing nothing, I should not have sat very comfortably."

"He played," said Mrs. Carter.

"A bit," said the boy, shifting on his chair.

"Too much," said Mrs. Carter. "He comes in all nervy and dazed. He ought to have his rest."

"He is six," said her husband. "He is a reasonable being. He must choose for himself. But what game is this, Small Simon, that is worth getting nervy and dazed over? There are very few games as good as all that."

"It's nothing," said the boy.

"Oh, come," said his father. "We are friends, are we not? You can tell me. I was a Small Simon once, just like you, and played the same games you play. Of course there were no aeroplanes in those days. With whom do you play this fine game? Come on, we must all answer civil questions, or the world would never go round. With whom do you play?"

"Mr. Beelzy," said the boy, unable to resist.

"Mr. Beelzy?" said his father, raising his eyebrows inquiringly at his wife.

"It's a game he makes up," said she.

"Not makes up!" cried the boy. "Fool!"

"That is telling stories," said his mother. "And rude as well. We had better talk of something different."

"No wonder he is rude," said Mr. Carter, "if you say he tells lies, and then insist on changing the subject. He tells you his fantasy: you implant a guilt feeling. What can you expect? A defence mechanism. Then you get a real lie."

"Like in *These Three*," said Betty. "Only different, of course. *She* was an unblushing little liar."

"I would have made her blush," said Mr. Carter, "in the proper part of her anatomy. But Small Simon is in the fantasy stage. Are you not, Small Simon? You just make things up."

"No, I don't," said the boy.

"You do," said his father. "And because you do, it is not too late to reason with you. There is no harm in a fantasy, old chap. There is no harm in a bit of make-believe. Only you have to know the difference between day dreams and real things, or your brain will never grow. It will never be the brain of a Big Simon. So come on. Let us hear about this Mr. Beelzy of yours. Come on. What is he like?"

"He isn't like anything," said the boy.

"Like nothing on earth?" said his father. "That's a terrible fellow."

"I'm not frightened of him," said the child, smiling. "Not a bit."

"I should hope not," said his father. "If you were, you would be frightening yourself. I am always telling people, older people than you are, that they are just frightening themselves. Is he a funny man? Is he a giant?"

"Sometimes he is," said the little boy.

"Sometimes one thing, sometimes another," said his father. "Sounds pretty vague. Why can't you tell us just what he's like?"

"I love him," said the small boy. "He loves me."

"That's a big word," said Mr. Carter. "That might be better kept for real things, like Big Simon and Small Simon."

"He is real," said the boy, passionately. "He's not a fool. He's real."

"Listen," said his father. "When you go down the garden there's nobody there. Is there?"

"No," said the boy.

"Then you think of him, inside your head, and he comes."

"No," said Small Simon. "I have to make marks. On the ground. With my stick."

"That doesn't matter."

"Yes, it does."

"Small Simon, you are being obstinate," said Mr. Carter. "I am trying to explain something to you. I have been longer in the world than you have, so naturally I am older and wiser. I am explaining that Mr. Beelzy is a fantasy of yours. Do you hear? Do you understand?"

"Yes, Daddy."

"He is a game. He is a let's-pretend."

The little boy looked down at his plate, smiling resignedly.

"I hope you are listening to me," said his father. "All you have to do is to say, 'I have been playing a game of

let's-pretend. With someone I make up, called Mr. Beelzy.'
Then no one will say you tell lies, and you will know the
difference between dreams and reality. Mr. Beelzy is a
day dream."

The little boy still stared at his plate.

"He is sometimes there and sometimes not there," pursued Mr. Carter. "Sometimes he's like one thing, sometimes another. You can't really see him. Not as you see me.
I am real. You can't touch him. You can touch me. I can
touch you." Mr. Carter stretched out his big, white, dentist's hand, and took his little son by the nape of the neck.
He stopped speaking for a moment and tightened his
hand. The little boy sank his head still lower.

"Now you know the difference," said Mr. Carter, "between a pretend and a real thing. You and I are one thing;
he is another. Which is the pretend? Come on. Answer
me. What is the pretend?"

"Big Simon and Small Simon," said the little boy.

"Don't!" cried Betty, and at once put her hand over her
mouth, for why should a visitor cry "Don't!" when a father is explaining things in a scientific and modern way?
Besides, it annoys the father.

"Well, my boy," said Mr. Carter, "I have said you must
be allowed to learn from experience. Go upstairs. Right
up to your room. You shall learn whether it is better to
reason, or to be perverse and obstinate. Go up. I shall
follow you."

"You are not going to beat the child?" cried Mrs. Carter.

"No," said the little boy. "Mr. Beelzy won't let him."

"Go on up with you!" shouted his father.

Small Simon stopped at the door. "He said he wouldn't
let anyone hurt me," he whimpered. "He said he'd come
like a lion, with wings on, and eat them up."

"You'll learn how real he is!" shouted his father after

him. "If you can't learn it at one end, you shall learn it at the other. I'll have your breeches down. I shall finish my cup of tea first, however," said he to the two women.

Neither of them spoke. Mr. Carter finished his tea, and unhurriedly left the room, washing his hands with his invisible soap and water.

Mrs. Carter said nothing. Betty could think of nothing to say. She wanted to be talking for she was afraid of what they might hear.

Suddenly it came. It seemed to tear the air apart. "Good God!" she cried. "What was that? He's hurt him." She sprang out of her chair, her silly eyes flashing behind her glasses. "I'm going up there!" she cried, trembling.

"Yes, let us go up," said Mrs. Carter. "Let us go up. That was not Small Simon."

It was on the second-floor landing that they found the shoe, with the man's foot still in it, like that last morsel of a mouse which sometimes falls unnoticed from the side of the jaws of the cat.

Special Delivery

t was with his eyes wide open, and with a reluctance amounting to dread, that Albert Baker slowly surrendered to the passion that was to change his whole life. "Am I mad?" he asked.

He addressed this inquiry, at the end of a long letter, to a certain Big Brother Frank, who gave candid advice in the Heart Correspondence Column of the popular *Tails Up Weekly*. They printed his letter in full.

Dear Sir,

Excuse my writing to you, but you say write your difficulties. I am in a difficulty, and cannot ask anyone else, they will say I am mad. I am in love. Only the young lady is not like others. She is different.

Have you been along Oxford Street at eight in the morning? I have to go every morning, that is where I work. In the shop windows you can see the young men carrying in the artificial young ladies they have to dress for the day. All the way along you can see them, like the old master picture of the Romans and the stolen women, only not so fat. Some struggle, some have their arms round the young men's necks but are looking out of the window. She does not struggle or look out of the window. She is one of those young ladies and I am one of the young men.

Surely it is not much difference from falling in love with a film star. I have been in London on this job four years, no one to really talk to. She seems to know everything I try to say. She has those very long blue eyes, thinking about the Riveera, but very kind.

After all, what do you really want with a girl if not higher things? It isn't only the Riveera, either, but I look after her every way, and you would really think she knew. Ordinary girls don't know, take it from me.

I take her in and keep well in front of her till she is full-dressed, no one shall write to the papers about her. Anyway, what is it they make all the fuss about— *nothing*. I am not mad, she is what I want, not everybody wants a lot of chatter or a family. You want someone to understand you, so you can be happy. I would look after her. But they cost £30, you might as well cry for the moon. Besides, if I got £30, they would say to me, you are mad. Or immoral purposes. It is not like that.

In the shop they heard me speak to her and are ribbing me all the time. I shall know what to do if I know what I am. My plans are made. Please tell me Big Brother if you think they are right. Am I mad?

Yours truly,
Albert Baker

Big Brother Frank's reply was printed below. "Take cold baths and plenty of open air exercise," said this amiable adviser. "Change your occupation. If you find yourself unable to put aside this degraded and perverse attachment, by all means consult a reliable psychiatrist, and if necessary enter an institution for treatment."

"So I'm crazy," said Albert, when the paper was delivered on Friday morning. "All right, then. My plans are made." There was a touch of braggadocio in this speech.

Albert's only plan was to keep quiet and see what he could do.

At half-past seven in the morning there is only one thing a shop assistant can do; that is, hurry off to work as fast as he may, especially if he has to walk from Paddington. To be crazy is one thing; to be late at Rudd & Agnew Ltd. is quite another; Albert was not as mad as all that.

So he started out from his lodgings with his mouth open and his eyes wide. "If I'm late," said he, "they're bound to get hold of her. They'll bend her over. They'll do anything. I must hurry.

"I'll be in time," said Albert to Eva, speaking across the desolate glory of the new day's sunlight, the sunlight, that is, of the day on which he was definitely crazy, and anything was possible; the sunlight in which he and she were utterly and terribly alone. "I wouldn't let you down."

Unfortunately, Albert now abandoned himself to a dream, the dream of his every morning rush toward Rudd & Agnew's. This was of entering first upon the empty salon, lifting the dust-sheet. "Wake up," he would say. "Is it all right? Put your arms round my neck. Helpless, aren't you? Here's your brassière. Here's your things." (The models at Rudd & Agnew's were life-like to a degree, perfect in almost every particular.) "Come on," Albert would say. "Nobody can see you. Hurry up, and we'll have a minute before they come in. What did you dream about? Did you dream about the house?"

In abandoning himself to this rehearsal, Albert unconsciously fell into his normal pace. Awakening, he found himself in the glazed brick employee's entrance, devoured by the dry smell of big shops, facing a time clock that stood at three minutes past eight. "They'll be here," he said.

He fled through the catacombs below, into the main shop, downstairs, upstairs, over an interior bridge. From the gallery on the other side he could look down into the long aisles behind the principal windows. Like laden ants in a disturbed ant-hill, the shop-men ran to and fro with their still, pale burdens. Albert could see the daily joke pass, from the lips of one to the eyes of another, wherever their paths crossed, as they carried their waxen Circassians, these proud, long-suffering, far-eyed, enchanted princesses, out of their mad mysterious night to their odious toilettes, to make them ready for the long slave-market of the day. There was a slap, and a guffaw.

"Here, none of that," said the shopwalker, himself unable to restrain a scurvy grin at what Clarkie was doing.

But, rounding the gallery, Albert could see three or four gathered in the corner where Eva lay, where he put her to sleep properly, after they had all gone at night. They were out of sight of the shopwalker. They were bending over. Miller's hateful voice sounded out of the middle of the group. "Oh, my God!" cried Albert. "They've got her."

He went down the stairs as one flies downstairs in a nightmare, heedless of the steps, round the satins, into the French models. "Living statue, number three," he heard Miller say. "Albert's 'oneymoon, or——" His hands dived out before him, without waiting to be told; his fingers were on the back of Miller's neck. They slipped on the brilliantine. He drove his nails in.

Next moment, Miller was up, facing him. "You think you can do that to me?" said Miller. "You poor loony!" There was a crack, shatteringly loud; Miller had struck him open-handed on the cheek.

"You leave her alone," said Albert, "or by heaven I'll be the death of you."

"What in the world is this?" cried the shopwalker, hurrying up.

"Stuck his nails in the back of my neck, that's what,"

said Miller, truculent, standing up for his rights, justified. "I reckon I'm bleeding."

Albert's lower lip was jerking, as if something quite independent of himself had got inside it. "He had hold of her," he said at last.

They all looked down at Eva, naked, her eyes staring out far beyond her shame, like a lion's eyes staring past the bars and the crowd. Albert bent down, and pressed her into a more seemly position. She ignored him. Properly let down, angry, she ignored him.

"What if he had got hold of her?" said the shopwalker. "You think Rudd & Agnew's waits for *you* to come in any time and fix the windows?"

"I'm sorry sir," said Albert.

"I shall have to make a report on you," said the shopwalker. "Get on with your work."

Albert was left alone with Eva. "If they give me the sack," he murmured, "who'll look after you? Don't be hard, Eva. I couldn't help it. And I had something to tell you. Don't you want to know what it is? You do? Really? Well, listen——"

Eva had given him an unmistakable look of understanding and forgiveness. It raised Albert to a precarious exaltation. Twice he actually risked slipping out into the entrance, where he could catch the side-long glance from her eyes. It seemed to him impossible he could get the sack.

After the midday break, however, things took a different turn. Albert spent his lunchtime walking up and down in front of the shop, an exercise which was not forbidden because no one had ever thought it possible. Soon after he got in, Miller entered, full-blown, triumphant, carrying a copy of *Tails Up Weekly*. As he passed Albert he showed it to him, and grinned.

"What a fool!" said Albert. "What a fool I've been!"

"Look here, boys," cried Miller as loudly as he dared. "Come in behind here. Clarkie! Sid! Come on. Just half a tick. It's worth it."

"Get back to your counters," said the shopwalker, perceiving the excitement. "What is it now, Miller, for heaven's sake?"

"Only something that proves something," said Miller with an air of righteousness, handing the shopwalker the fatal page.

"This is serious!" cried the shopwalker, staring at Albert. "This is a matter for the Secretary. I'm taking this paper, Miller. I'm taking it to Mr. Schilberg himself."

He went, and Albert was left alone; standing, stared at, like a man brought out to be hanged. "It's the sack all right," he said to himself. "Who knows? They might have me shut up."

The thought set his legs in motion. "Here, you'd better stand by," cried a good-natured man. "They'll be sending for you in a minute."

"Let 'em," said Albert. "I'm off."

"Well, I ain't seen you go," said the other defensively.

"I'm off!" cried Albert aloud, as he passed others of the department. They all stared at him, then pretended not to notice. He went up the stairs and round the gallery, through the corridors, out past the time-keeper. "I'm off," said he, punching the clock for the last time.

"You look it," said the time-keeper indifferently.

He went into the street, and round into Oxford Street, crossing to the other side in the hope of making some undetected signal to Eva. As soon as he saw her, he knew what his real purpose was. He walked on without a change of pace, and entered the farther doorway, into the hardware department, where as yet the news could hardly be known, and where he himself would be unrecognized.

He went through a staff door, into a maze of corridors,

and found his way to a nook in a store-room, where he could lie hidden till closing time. There he lay, with his eyes closed and his hands folded, like a dead man, but there was a clock ticking in his brain.

At exactly seven o'clock he got up and stepped out quietly. He was cool, collected, utterly different. The whole place was different. A little daylight leaked in through the blinds at the back of the windows; the high glass dome was blueing, the galleries were drowned in darkness; flying staircases leapt out where the light struck them, and stopped short in mid-air where darkness bit them off. Vast stacks of shadow, the leaning façades of towering dreams, mounted like the skyscrapers of a new-risen city from floor to unsubstantial floor, up to the dome itself. The watchman, a being of the shadows, drifted unhurriedly across the diminishing territories of the light. Albert, a deeper shade, followed him, blacker and quieter than the watchman, more utterly of the dark.

The watchman entered the main hall, crossed the region of the French models, and disappeared into a deep vista of darkness on the farther side. Albert, absolutely master of the situation, knowing exactly how many minutes were his before the watchman could stumble round again, ran noiselessly forward.

He pulled aside the dust-sheets. The models were huddled there, grouped like victims in the sack of some forgotten city. Some stood upright, unable to relax, tense to meet new outrage; some, on hands and knees, bowed their faces to the floor, straining for the relief of tears. Others, their wits wiped out by horror, sat with their legs straight out, their hands flat and dead beside them, staring idiotically into a darkness deeper than that of the night.

"Eva!" whispered Albert. "Where are you?" She was a little apart from the others, sitting as if waiting to be taken away.

"You knew I'd come," said Albert, lifting her. Her face fell forward on his, her lips touched his cheek. "You're cold," said Albert. "You're used to your bed."

He caught up the dust-sheet and tucked it about her neck. Its pale folds fell over her and him.

This cloaked double figure, this walking embrace of life and death, this beautiful nightmare under its carapace of cotton cloud, now ran noiselessly, staggering a little, up the light spirals of fretted iron, over the flying bridges, now to be seen rounding some high gallery, now swallowed by darkness, now seen higher, still mounting like a spider, till at last it reached the uppermost corridors, and the sanctuary of the little store-room.

Albert closed the door, spread a bed of wrapping papers, laid Eva upon it, took her head upon his lap, and spread the dust-sheet over them. Eva gazed up at him. There was still light here, through a little round window like a porthole. He could see her eyes, steady and cool, gazing at him, weighing him up: his weak face with its tremulous, rickety outline, his flossy, inconsiderable hair. All the same, he was her saviour. More than that, for that was a job merely, he was for her the only man in the world. If ever she loved, she must love him. Whatever her memories were, there was no one else now. All the rest were monsters, raging in blindness. In all his unworthiness he was the only living creature she could love. "What can I do?" thought Albert, overwhelmed by the responsibilities laid on him by this tremendous act of chance, which blackmailed her into the necessity of loving him, and left it to him to make himself worthy.

The dawn, with its threat, recalled him from a thousand fine spiritual issues to a very practical one. "I can't leave you here," said he. "What can I do?"

Albert was not a man of action. His mind was weak, broken, bound by the hundred habits of timid servitude.

He crouched, with his head in his hand, conscious, less of the problem than of Eva's blue gaze, which expected a decision.

Suddenly Albert stood up. "I've got it," said he. "They've driven me to it. Never mind. You do what I tell you. You trust *me*." He actually emphasized the word "me." He lifted Eva, and set her in the corner, as if she were a mere dummy. "Keep quiet," he said. "I'm going to deliver you, like a chap in a book."

He went out into the twilight of the vast shop; a dawn twilight, altogether different from that of the evening. Albert was equally changed. He was no longer a shadow scurrying ratlike from dark to dark, but a young man of nerve and decision. He was perfectly prepared, if he met him in the silks, to stun the night-watchman with a roll of art-shade ninon, or to hood him with a girdle if their paths crossed in the lingerie, or gag him with gloves in the gloves, or strangle him with a stocking in the hosiery, or fell him with a cucumber in the fruit. He devoutly hoped the encounter would not take place in the hardware or cutlery, for Albert was the mildest, gentlest creature that ever breathed, and abhorred the sight of blood. As it happened the night-watchman was no believer in burglaries at six o'clock on a June morning, and was now in his cubby-hole far away in the basement, engaged in the nice preparation of a cup of cocoa to keep at bay the ill effects of the night air.

Albert, not knowing this, and resolved to deal with a dozen night-watchmen if necessary, was intoxicated by his only experience of courageous action, and rose from height to height. When he had gathered up a complete wardrobe for Eva, of a rather gayer fashion than she had enjoyed before, he went boldly up to the main office, to a desk where forms were made out for special deliveries, and, finding a block of such forms, he chose a name from a list of customers on the desk: "Raymond Pinckney Esq., 14 Mulberry Grove, Hampstead." This he scribbled on the form; filled in the words, "One model, special arrangement: deliver 9 A.M.——" "Now what the hell day is this?" murmured Albert. His heart sank; he was done for; he had come upon that blind spot which brings the greatest criminals to their downfall. But no! There was a calendar: yesterday was a Friday because his washing had to be made up; this, therefore, was Saturday. "Who says I'm crazy?" said Albert. "Deliver 9 A.M. Saturday, 14 June, without fail." Now for the rubber stamp. He looked in the middle drawer, and there it was. Everything was going swimmingly. It was with a light heart that he drew out the cash for expenses and hurried back to Eva.

She looked at him questioningly. "Don't worry," said he. "I been man enough. Here, I'm going to wrap you up. When I've got you dressed, of course."

Albert dressed Eva. That was no difficult task. He wrapped the grey-white paper about her, leaving a chink for light and air to come through. Then he set himself to wait for the striking of eight o'clock. In the long interval he was as still as Eva was. He dared not move, nor think, nor scarcely breathe even; he sat holding a tourniquet on his courage, which had already begun to ebb away. He did not hear seven o'clock strike at all, or the clashing of the scrub-women's pails, or the drone of the vacuum cleaners; he heard only one bronzy reverberation, and knew it for the last stroke of eight.

He picked Eva up and ran down the back stairs, out to where a raw service-lift clanked him down into the goods yard, whence, without stopping, he walked straight out, holding up his form to the indifferent custodian. "Special delivery," he said. "Got to get a cab."

Albert looked around: he was in the street. "Oh, good heavens!" he said. "What have I done?" People were looking at him, only waiting a split second before they knew and would begin to hound him down. He forgot all about the cab; all his thought and will were concentrated on the single effort of keeping himself from breaking into a run.

Automatically, he took the way to his lodgings. Four times he saw a policeman in the distance, and walked step by leaden step under the awful eyes till he drew abreast of him, crossed the razor edge between brazen approach and guilt-proclaiming flight, felt the eyes on his back, and waited for the shout.

He passed a knot of children on their way to school. "Look what he's got!" they cried. "Hi, Crippen!"

He had had no lunch, no supper, no breakfast, no sleep. The morning sun was already sultry. Eva, whom he could carry like a baron or a brigand when he was in the shop, now became an insupportable weight. He ached in every joint, his knees gave, his head swam; every one of the thousands in the streets was a pursuer: never was creature so universally hunted, nor moved so pitiably slow.

He turned at last into the mean street where he lived. He stumbled into the smelly passage. His landlady, who had spied him from the basement window, now called to him up the kitchen stairs. "Is that you, Mr. Baker?" cried she.

Albert stopped dead. His room was two floors above, but he could already see it as if he were in the doorway: its dimness, its frowsiness, its promise of a few hours' safety with Eva. He had thought of nothing beyond that. All he wanted was just a few hours in that room. He had gone through the hellish streets for that, and now, from the tone of his landlady's voice, he knew he would never see his room again. He began to cry.

"Yes, it's me, Mrs. Budgen," he said haltingly, using the breaths between his sobs.

"Mr. Baker, there's been inquiries," shouted the land-lady. "Looked like the plain-clothes to me. I'd like a word, *now*. I——"

"All right, Mrs. Budgen," said Albert. "I'll be down in half a tick. Just got to go to the W.C."

He allowed himself a few seconds to breathe, then took up Eva again, and crept out of the front door and into the hideous street. He reached the corner, and saw Praed Street with its taxi-cabs. "Got to take a cab," he said aloud, as if he were still addressing the man in the goods yard. "*I* dunno where I'm going.

"Hi!" called Albert to a passing taxi. It went on unheeding. "Hi!" he called. "Stop, won't you? Are you mad?" He actually galvanized his bending knees into a pitiable stagger, and overtook the taxi a few yards on, where it had stopped at a crossing. The driver looked at him as he panted alongside.

"Here you are," said Albert, staring at the delivery slip he had held all this time in his hand. "Pinckney, 14 Mulberry Grove, Hampstead."

"O.K." said the driver. Albert fell into the cab, and they were off.

Albert held Eva propped against him, and closed his eyes. A jerk, such as the dead will feel on the last day, recalled him to his sense. There was sunlight, altogether unlike the menacing glare in the loud streets: it was filtered through the leaves of lime trees. There was a heavenly quiet, a green iron gate, a gravel drive, a smiling housefront, peaceful, prosperous, and not unfriendly.

Albert stood in a wide porch, with his arm round Eva. A soft-faced man, in blue serge trousers and waistcoat stood in the doorway. "Never 'eard of a tradesman's entrance?" said he mildly.

"This 'ere's special," said Albert, holding out his slip.

"Well, you've come wrong," said the man. "Mr. Pinck-

ney's down at the Hall. Two Rivers Hall, Baddingly,
Suffolk. They ought to have known at the shop. You take
it back quick."

"Wanted very special," murmured Albert in despair,
proffering his slip.

The man weighed up the situation for a moment. "Hand
it over," said he. "The chauffeur's going down. He'll take
it."

"He'll take me, too," said Albert. "This is special."

"All right," said the man. "You'll have to get back by
yourself though."

"Don't you worry about me," said Albert.

There followed another dream, with Albert sitting in
the back of a large touring car, Eva beside him, and the
wrapping dislodged a little so that she could get the fresh
air and see the fields go by. Not a word was said. Albert
ceased trying to fit things together in his brain. He wished
the drive would go on for ever, but, since it had to end, he
was glad that it ended at a quiet house, standing on a
gentle Suffolk knoll, surrounded by red walls and green
gardens, full of the shade of senior trees.

"The master's in the studio," said an old woman to the
chauffeur.

"You come along with me," said the chauffeur to Albert.

Albert followed with his precious burden into a cobbled
stable yard. The chauffeur knocked at a door. "Young
man from Rudd & Agnew's. Special delivery," said he.

"What's that?" said a voice. "Send him in."

Albert found himself in a giant room. It was a loft and
stable knocked into one, with a vast cool window all down
one side. A large canvas stood on an easel; there were
hundreds of brushes, several palettes, boxes of colours. On
a cane sofa was a young man reclining in great comfort,
reading a thriller.

This young man looked up at Albert. He was a true

monkeyface, hideously ugly, with a quick brown eye, hair fallen over his forehead; cotton jersey, beach trousers, straw shoes, and a pipe. "Well, what is it?" said he.

"I've brought——" said Albert. "I've brought—I've brought this." He pulled aside a little more of the wrapping.

"I didn't order anything of this sort," said the young man. "You've brought her to the wrong place."

"Here it is," said Albert, offering his slip. "Written down."

"I don't use that sort of model," said the young man. "Might be an idea, though. However, you ask them to give you some beer in the kitchen, and then take her back."

"No," said Albert. He began to shake and tremble. He stared at Mr. Pinckney with a rabbit desperation. Mr. Pinckney stared back at him. "What *is* all this?" said he.

"Mister," said Albert, "have you ever been in love?"

"We won't discuss that," said the ugly young man.

"If you don't know, it's no good me talking," said Albert. "All right, I'll get out. Come on, Eva. I can't help it. We got to get out."

"Wait a little," said Mr. Pinckney. "Take it easy. Tell me all about it. I shall understand."

"It's like this," said Albert, and told, very strangely, his strange story.

"You are quite mad," said Pinckney at the end of it.

"So they say," said Albert. "I'm a human being, ain't I? I could be happy."

"I like your philosophy," said Pinckney. "Mad but happy."

"Have I ever been happy?" said Albert.

"Go on," said Pinckney.

"And what about her?" said Albert. "But you are laughing. You're ribbing me." His voice rose dangerously.

"What would you do with her?" said Pinckney.

"I'd look after her," said Albert. "But not to be ribbed. No. I'll get out."

"Listen you," said Pinckney. "If you want to look after her, don't leave her propped against the table there. Set her in the armchair comfortably."

"Yes, sir, I will," said Albert. "I didn't like to ask."

"Take off those stuffy wrappings," said Mr. Pinckney harshly. Albert smiled at Mr. Pinckney.

"So, you're in love with her," said Mr. Pinckney, "and you want to be happy. What's your name, by the way?"

"Albert Baker. Hers is Eva."

"Well, Baker," said Pinckney, in a tone of command. "I'm not making you any promises; you're just here in peace and quiet for the present. How long, depends on a lot of things. Most of all, on how you behave. You're mad. Don't forget it. It doesn't matter a bit, but you've got to be sensible about it. Listen to this. If ever you feel an overpowering impulse—if ever you feel you simply must do something—whatever it is, you're to tell me first. Do you hear?"

"Yes, sir," cried Albert. "If you please, I must—I must go to the lavatory. I'm so happy."

"Excellent!" said Pinckney. "Then go and sit under the tree over there. Eva will be perfectly all right. She's resting."

"She's all right," said Albert. "She trusts you."

When he had gone, Pinckney went to the telephone, and he called his lawyer.

"I'm going to keep him here," said he, in conclusion. "Well, I'm going to, that's all—Yes, but you tell them their damned model's going to be paid for. That's all they care about—Yes. I'm responsible for him—That's it, our respected client—As long as you fix it—Oh, hideous, absolutely hideous—Might do to paint for a lark—Well, you'll let me know? Good man! That's fine."

Pinckney hung up. "He'll fix it," said he to himself. "But I'll keep that bit of news, in case he needs calling to order. If he seems depressed, I'll tell him."

Albert, however, did not seem depressed. The journey through the London streets had left him with some comfortable blanks in his mind. He wore a slightly dazed look; his mouth hung open, and his eyes filled with tears now and then, when a thought came to a happy end, transforming itself into a feeling, like a flower opening inside his mind. To the outward view there was nothing very odd about him. "He's a bit queer, isn't he?" said Mabel the housemaid.

"Nervous breakdown," said the housekeeper. "That's what Mr. Pinckney says. My sister's boy had one. They put him in a home."

"He's no trouble," said Mabel. "Does his own room, anyway. Funny, he locks that door as if he had the Crown Jewels to look after."

"He's very willing and obliging," said the housekeeper. "And he's got to be let alone."

Albert had an old chauffeur's room, away over the end of the stables. He shone the shoes, he fetched and carried for the housekeeper, who was told never to send him down to the village. Most of the time he helped the gardeners in the green gardens that were almost all lawn and trees. From the dusty window Eva watched him working for her in the yellow shade of the limes, in the black shade of the mulberries, and in the green shade of the mighty beech.

In the evening Albert had his supper in the housekeeper's room. At the end of it, "Thank you, ma'am," said he, and, "Thank you, miss," to Mabel. He was very polite; to him they were lesser angels, instruments of the great power that kept the world at bay. Then he hurried away to his room, to tell Eva all about it.

"He came up to me today," he would say, "Oh he's so

nice, Eva. I can't tell you how nice he is. Always speaks rough, only it's in a joking way. But when he mentions you—it's most respectful. He knows what you are. I ought to have told you: it was his idea about bringing up the roses. Only I thought you'd like it to be me."

This was only the beginning of their evening, which stretched far into the light summer night, for Albert slept very little, and when he did Eva came to life in his dreams. "Are you miserable?" he asked her. "Are you still longing for the Riveera?"

"Not me," she replied softly.

"It's better than the shop, isn't it?" said he, anxiously.

"It's nice being with you," said Eva.

"Do you mean it?" cried Albert eagerly. "With me?"

These tender passages passed between them in dreams so mingled with his summer wakefulness that he passed from one to another as easily and unnoticingly as he passed from one shade of beech to shade of lime on the lawn. Sometimes Albert and Eva never lay down at all, but passed the night at the window, watching the glow fade from the red roofs of the village at the foot of the slope, and not moving till the dawn brought them into sight again.

One evening, under one of these friendly red roofs, a meeting was in progress. The proceedings were concerned with the organization of the village flower-show and fête. Officials were appointed to the charge of the show-tent, the gate, the sideshows, and the collection of subscriptions. "I propose Mr. Bly be asked to go round for subscriptions," said the vicar's gardener. "I beg to second that," said the blacksmith. "If Mr. Bly will be so kind," said the secretary, cocking an inquiring eye at the village constable, whose official position marked him out for this responsible office. Mr. Bly nodded formidable assent, the proposal was unanimously accepted, entered in the minutes, and the meeting was adjourned.

Next morning Mr. Bly mounted his bicycle, and pedaled slowly in the direction of the Hall.

"Oh, God!" cried Albert, peering from behind a hedge. "They've tracked us down."

Bending double, he ran to his little stable-room. "Come on, Eva," he said. "It's no good. It couldn't last. He can't save us this time. It's the police."

He took Eva in his arms and ran down under the field hedges to a wood in the bottom, and there across country, along the edges of dusty summer fallows, crawling through standing corn, taking to the woods whenever possible, scuttling across the roads when he came to them, shouted at by one or two men in the fields, flown at by a dog when he blundered on a keeper's hut in a clearing, stared at by an awful eye from above. All around he could sense a network of cars and men, policemen, shopwalkers, the Secretary himself, searching for him and Eva.

Night came. He could now creep only a hundred yards at a time, and then must lie still a long time, feeling the earth turn over and over, and the network of pursuit close in. "Eva," said he, "we've got to go on all night. Can you stand it?"

Eva made no response. "You're weak," said he. "Your head's going round. You can feel your heart giving way. But we've got to go on. I've let you down again, Eva. We've got to go on."

The last part of that night journey was a blank to Albert. They must have come to a common. He found himself sprawled in a deep bay in a clump of furze. Eva lay tumbled beside him, in a horrible attitude, as she had lain that fatal morning in the shop. "Stretch yourself out," he said. "I'll come to in a minute. I'll look after you."

But the sun was already high when he sat up, and Eva was still sprawled as she had been before. A yellow fly crawled on her cheek: before he could move, it had crawled right over her unwinking blue eye. "Eva!" he cried. "What's up? Wake up. Has it been too much for you? Say something, do.

"She's dead!" he cried to the world at large. "Carrying her about like that—I've killed her."

He flung himself upon the sprawling figure. He opened her dress, he listened for her heart. He lay like that for a long time. The sun poured down, glimmering on the worn blue suit, parching the flossy hair, devouring the waxen cheeks, fading the staring blue eyes.

Albert's face was as dead as Eva's, till suddenly it was galvanized by an expression too distracted and too fleeting to be called hope. Thump, thump, thump, he heard: he thought it was her heart beating again. Then he realized it was footsteps coming near.

He raised his head. Someone was on the other side of the bushes. "They shan't disturb you, my darling," he said to Eva, and got up and stumbled round to face the intruders.

It was not policemen: it was two ordinary men, filthy, unshaven, looking at Albert out of wicked eyes.

"Nice goings on," said one of them.

"We seen you," said the other.

"There's a law against that sort of thing," said the first. He gazed up at the sky. "Might be worth a couple of quid, not to be run in for that sort of thing."

"For a decent girl it would," said the other.

"Not to be dragged along to the copper-station with her thin-gummys hanging round her ankles," said the first.

"You keep off," said Albert. "I haven't got no money. Straight. You can search me if you like."

"Perhaps the young lady 'as," said the first man, having verified this point.

"If she *is* a young lady, she 'as," said the second.

"And if not," said the first. "If not, Alf——What do you say? Looked O.K. to me. Nice bit of goods!"

"I'm game," said Alf, glancing round.

The men made a move. Albert got in front of them, his arms spread wide. "Keep back," he said again, feeling how light and flat and useless the words were.

"Sit on him, Alf," said the first man. "Then I will."

There was a scuffle. Albert, heaven knows how, tore himself away from Alf, and rushed after the first man, seizing him by the collar and raining blows on his hard head. "Strewth!" cried the man. " 'Ere, take him off, Alf, 'e's stinging me."

Albert felt a hand seize him. He turned; there was Alf's grinning face. "Come on, dearie," said Alf. Albert, yielding for a moment, suddenly kicked as hard and viciously as he could. There was a terrifying howl. Alf was rolling on the ground.

"What'll they do to me?" thought Albert. "Eva! I did it for you."

"He's done it to me!" cried Alf. "He's done it to me. Kill the——Kill 'im!"

Something hit Albert on the side of the jaw, and a bombshell burst in his brain. "The knock-out," said the first man, turning again to go round to where Eva lay.

"Let me get my boots on him," said Alf, scrambling to his feet.

"Gawd's trewth! Look here, Alf," cried the first man from the other side of the bushes. "It's a bloody dummy."

"You come back here," said Alf. "You 'it 'im. *I* didn't!"

"What's up?" cried the other, hurrying round.

"He's a goner," said Alf. "I'm off."

"Wait a minute, pal," cried the first man. "Have some sense. You're in it as much as me. Look here, you kicked him. Do you think I can't see? Never mind. Let's get him hid; that's the main thing."

"Chuck 'em down in the chalk pit, both of 'em," said the other. "Come on! It'll look as if he fell in of his own accord. We've never seen him, have we?"

A few minutes later the men were gone. The sun poured down on the glinting common, scorching everywhere except in the cool bottom of the chalk pit, where Eva and Albert lay unsought and undisturbed. His head lay limp on her neck; her stiff arm was arched over him. In the autumn, when the over-hang crumbled down on them, it pressed him close to her for ever.

Little Memento

A young man who was walking fast came out of a deep lane onto a wide hilltop space, where there was a hamlet clustered about a green. The setting encompassed a pond, ducks, the Waggoner Inn, with white paint and swinging sign; in fact, all the fresh, clean, quiet, ordinary appurtenances of an upland Somerset hamlet.

The road went on, and so did the young man, over to the very brink of the upland, where a white gate gave upon a long garden well furnished with fruit trees, and at the end of it a snug little house sheltered by a coppice and enjoying a view over the vast vale below. An old man of astonishingly benevolent appearance was pottering about in the garden. He looked up as the walker, Eric Gaskell, approached his gate.

"Good morning," said he. "A fine September morning!"

"Good morning," said Eric Gaskell.

"I have had my telescope out this morning," said the old

man. "I don't often get down the hill these days. The way back is a little too steep for me. Still, I have my view and my telescope. I think I know all that goes on."

"Well, that's very nice," said Eric.

"It is," said the old man. "You are Mr. Gaskell?"

"Yes," said Eric. "I know. We met at the vicarage."

"We did," said the old man. "You often take your walk this way. I see you go by. Today I thought, 'Now this is the day for a little chat with young Mr. Gaskell!' Come in."

"Thanks," said Eric. "I will, for a spell."

"And how," said the old man, opening his gate, "do you and Mrs. Gaskell like Somerset?"

"Enormously," said Eric.

"My housekeeper tells me," said the old man, "that you come from the East Coast. Very bracing. Her niece is your little maid. You don't find it too dull here? Too backward? Too old-fashioned?"

"We like that part of it best," said Eric, sitting with his host on a white seat under one of the apple trees.

"In these days," said the old man, "young people like old-fashioned things. That's a change from my day. Now most of us who live about here are old codgers, you know. There's Captain Felton, of course, but the Vicar, the Admiral, Mr. Coperus, and the rest—all old codgers. You don't mind that?"

"I like it," said Eric.

"We have our hobbies," said the old man. "Coperus is by way of being an antiquarian; the Admiral has his roses."

"And you have your telescope," said Eric.

"Ah, my telescope," said the old man. "Yes, yes, I have my telescope. But my principal pastime—what I really plume myself on—is my museum."

"You have a museum?" said Eric.

"Yes, a museum," said the old man. "I should like you to have a look at it and tell me what you think."

"I shall be delighted," said Eric.

"Then come right in," said the old man, leading him toward the house. "I seldom have the chance of showing my collection to a newcomer. You must bring Mrs. Gaskell one of these days. Does she find enough entertainment in this quiet part, would you say?"

"She loves it," said Eric. "She can't see too much of the country here. She drives out almost every day."

"All by herself in that little red roadster of hers," said the old man. "Does she like the house?"

"Well, I don't know," said Eric. "She did when we chose it last spring. She liked it very much."

"It is a very nice house," said the old man.

"She finds it a little oppressive lately, I'm afraid," said Eric. "She says she has to get out to breathe."

"It is the difference in the air," said the old man. "After living on the East Coast."

"Probably it's that," said Eric.

By this time they had reached the front door. The old man ushered Eric in. They entered a very snug, trim little room, the furniture all well polished and everything meticulously arranged. "This is my little sitting-room," the old man said. "My dining-room, too, these days. The drawing-room and the little study beyond I have given over entirely to my museum. Here we are."

He threw open a door. Eric stepped in, looked around, and stared in amazement. He had been expecting the usual sort of thing: a neat cabinet or two with Roman coins, flint implements, a snake in alcohol, perhaps a stuffed bird or some eggs. But this room and the study, seen through the connecting doorway, were piled high with the most broken, battered, frowzy, gimcrack collection of junk he had ever seen in his life. What was oddest of all was that no item in this muddle of rubbish had even the excuse of a decent antiquity. It was as if several cartloads of miscellaneous material had been collected from the village dump and spilled over the tables, sideboards, chairs, and floors of these two rooms.

The old man observed Eric's astonishment with the greatest good humour. "You are thinking," said he, "that this collection is not the sort of thing one usually finds in a museum. You are right. But let me tell you, Mr. Gaskell, that every object here has a history. These pieces are pebbles rolled and broken by the stream of time as it flows over the villages in our quiet little district. Taken together, they are a—a record. Here is a souvenir from the War: a telegram to the Bristows in Upper Medlum, saying their boy was killed. It was years before I could get that from poor Mrs. Bristow. I gave her a pound for it."

"Very interesting," said Eric.

"That wheelbarrow," said the old man, pointing out a splintered wreck, "was the cause of two deaths. It rolled down a bank into the lane here just as a car was coming along. It was in all the papers. 'Local Tragedy.'"

"Extraordinary!" said Eric.

"It all makes up life," said the old man. "Here is a belt dropped by one of the Irish haymakers when they fought the gipsies. This hat belonged to the man who had Church Farm, near you. He won a prize in the Irish Sweep and drank himself to death, poor fellow! These are bricks from my gardener's cottage. It burned down, you know, and nobody knows how the fire started. This is a snake which somehow got into the church during service last year. Captain Felton killed it. He's a very handsome man, don't you think?"

"Yes. I suppose so. I hardly know him."

"That's funny. I thought you and Mrs. Gaskell were very great friends of Captain Felton."

"What gave you that idea?"

"Perhaps it was just my fancy. Here is a rather sad exhibit. These horns came from a bull that Farmer Lawson put into my meadow. Somebody left the gate open; it got out and gored a man on the road."

"We scarcely know Captain Felton," said Eric. "We met him when first we came here, but——"

"Quite, quite," said the old man. "Here is an anonymous letter. We have them now and then in this district, as in most places. Mr. Coperus gave me this."

"Are they usually well founded, the hints in your local brand of anonymous letters?" asked Eric.

"I believe they are," said the old man. "Someone seems to know what goes on. Here's something that I fear won't last very long: a giant puffball from the graveyard. They grow larger there than anywhere else. Feel how light it is."

He thrust it toward Eric. Eric had been fumbling with his pipe and tobacco pouch and now put them down to take the puffball. "Very light," said he. "Wonderful."

"Come through here," cried the old man eagerly. "I was forgetting my boots." Eric followed him, still carrying the giant fungus. "These boots," said the old man, "came off a tramp found drowned in a pond. That little pond near Captain Felton's house."

"What does Felton do?" asked Eric.

"He has an income," said the old man. "He amuses himself."

"What is his amusement?" said Eric very casually.

"I'm afraid," said the old man, with a twinkle, "that Captain Felton is rather one for the ladies."

"Indeed?" said Eric.

"There are stories," said the old man. "The Captain is very discreet, but—you know how it is. That big crystal up there—that was found in the quarry half a mile down our little road here. Well now, that quarry has been out of use for many years. You can drive into it from the road, and I'm told the Captain finds it a very secluded rendezvous. Dear me, I ought not to gossip. But the fact is the shepherd boys have been known to look over the top, and of course stories get around. People love to chuckle over such matters. I'm afraid that some day one of the worthy gentlemen whose domestic relations the Captain has, so to speak, trespassed upon will look over the top and—well, there are some very large stones lying about. Here is a cat I had stuffed. Now there is a very extraordinary story connected with this cat."

"Tell me," said Eric, "is Felton here now or is he away?"

"He's here," said the old man. "I saw his car go by only an hour ago. It's a red car. One doesn't often see a red car, though as a matter of fact another red one came by just after his."

"I—I think I must be off," said Eric.

"Must you go?" said the old man. "I was just going to tell you about this unhappy cat."

"Another time," said Eric.

"Another time then," said the old man. "I shall always be delighted. Let me see you to the gate."

Eric hurried through the gate.

"You are not going back the way you came?" said the old man. "It's quicker."

"No. No. I have to go round this way," said Eric.

"That will lead you past the Captain's quarry," said the old man. "Well, goodbye. Come again soon."

He watched Eric stride rapidly down the road and even climbed a bank to watch him farther. When he saw him leave the road and strike over the face of the down, toward the up lip of the quarry, he went placidly back to his museum.

There he took up Eric's pipe and tobacco pouch and fondled them with infinite affection. It was quite a long time before he could bring himself to place them carefully on a shelf and return to his pottering in the garden.

Green Thoughts

Annihilating all that's made
To a green thought in a green shade. MARVELL

he orchid had been sent among the effects of his friend, who had come by a lonely and mysterious death on the expedition. Or he had brought it among a miscellaneous lot, "unclassified," at the close of the auction. I forget which it was, but it was certainly one or the other of these. Moreover, even in its dry, brown, dormant root state, this orchid had a certain sinister quality. It looked, with its bunched and ragged projections, like a rigid yet a gripping hand, hideously gnarled, or a grotesquely whiskered, threatening face. Would you not have known what sort of an orchid it was?

Mr. Mannering did not know. He read nothing but catalogues and books on fertilizers. He unpacked the new acquisition with a solicitude absurd enough in any case toward any orchid, or primrose either, in the twentieth century, but idiotic, foolhardy, doom-eager, when extended to an orchid thus come by, in appearance thus. And in his traditional obtuseness he at once planted it in what he called the "Observation Ward," a hothouse built against the south wall of his dumpy red dwelling. Here he set always the most interesting additions to his collection, and especially weak and sickly plants, for there was a glass door in his study wall through which he could see into this hothouse, so that the weak and sickly plants could encounter no crisis without his immediate knowledge and his tender care.

This plant, however, proved hardy enough. At the ends of thick and stringy stalks it opened out bunches of darkly shining leaves, and soon it spread in every direction, usurping so much space that first one, then another, then all its neighbours had to be removed to a hothouse at the end of the garden. It was, Cousin Jane said, a regular hop-vine. At the ends of the stalks, just before the leaves began, were set groups of tendrils, which hung idly, serving no apparent purpose. Mr. Mannering thought that very probably these were vestigial organs, a heritage from some period when the plant had been a climber. But when were the vestigial tendrils of an ex-climber half or quarter so thick and strong?

After a long time sets of tiny buds appeared here and there among the extravagant foliage. Soon they opened into small flowers, miserable little things; they looked like flies' heads. One naturally expects a large, garish, sinister bloom, like a sea anemone, or a Chinese lantern, or a hippopotamus yawning, on any important orchid; and should it be an unclassified one as well, I think one has every right to insist on a sickly and overpowering scent into the bargain.

Mr. Mannering did not mind at all. Indeed, apart from his joy and happiness in being the discoverer and godfather of a new sort of orchid, he felt only a mild and scientific interest in the fact that the paltry blossoms were so

very much like flies' heads. Could it be to attract other
flies for food or as fertilizers? But then, why like their heads?

It was a few days later that Cousin Jane's cat disappeared. This was a great blow to Cousin Jane, but Mr.
Mannering was not, in his heart of hearts, greatly sorry.
He was not fond of the cat, for he could not open the
smallest chink in a glass roof for ventilation but the creature would squeeze through somehow to enjoy the warmth,
and in this way it had broken many a tender shoot. But
before poor Cousin Jane had lamented two days something happened which so engrossed Mr. Mannering that
he had no mind left at all with which to sympathize with
her affliction, or to make at breakfast kind and hypocriti-
cal inquiries after the lost cat. A strange new bud appeared
on the orchid. It was clearly evident that there would be
two quite different sorts of bloom on this one plant, as
sometimes happens in such fantastic corners of the vegetable world, and that the new flower would be very different
in size and structure from the earlier ones. It grew bigger
and bigger, till it was as big as one's fist.

And just then—it could never have been more inoppor-
tune—an affair of the most unpleasant, the most distressing nature summoned Mr. Mannering to town. It was his
wretched nephew, in trouble again, and this time so deeply and so very disgracefully that it took all Mr. Mannering's generosity, and all his influence, too, to extricate the
worthless young man. Indeed, as soon as he saw the state
of affairs, he told the prodigal that this was the very last
time he might expect assistance, that his vices and his ingratitude had long ago cancelled all affection between
them, and that for this last helping hand he was indebted
only to his mother's memory, and to no faith on the part
of his uncle either in his repentance or his reformation. He
wrote, moreover, to Cousin Jane, to relieve his feelings,

telling her of the whole business, and adding that the only thing left to do was to cut the young man off entirely.

When he got back to Torquay, Cousin Jane was nowhere to be found. The situation was extremely annoying. Their only servant was a cook who was very old and very stupid and very deaf. She suffered besides from an obsession, owing to the fact that for many years Mr. Mannering had had no conversation with her in which he had not included an impressive reminder that she must always, no matter what might happen, keep the big kitchen stove up to a certain pitch of activity. For this stove, besides supplying the house with hot water, heated the pipes in the "Observation Ward," to which the daily gardener who had charge of the other hothouses had no access. By this time she had come to regard her duties as stoker as her chief *raison d'être*, and it was difficult to penetrate her deafness with any question which her stupidity and her obsession did not somehow transmute into an inquiry after the stove, and this, of course, was especially the case when Mr. Mannering spoke to her. All he could disentangle was what she had volunteered on first seeing him, that his cousin had not been seen for three days, that she had left without saying a word. Mr. Mannering was perplexed and annoyed, but, being a man of method, he thought it best to postpone further inquiries until he had refreshed himself a little after his long and tiring journey. A full supply of energy was necessary to extract any information from the old cook; besides, there was probably a note somewhere. It was only natural that before he went to his room Mr. Mannering should peep into the hothouse, just to make sure that the wonderful orchid had come to no harm during the inconsiderate absence of Cousin Jane. As soon as he opened the door his eyes fell upon the bud; it had now changed in shape very considerably, and had increased in size to the bigness of a human head. It is no exaggeration to state that Mr. Mannering remained rooted to the spot, with his eyes fixed upon this wonderful bud, for fully five minutes.

But, you will ask, why did he not see her clothes on the floor? Well, as a matter of fact (it is a delicate point), there were no clothes on the floor. Cousin Jane, though of course she was entirely estimable in every respect, though she was well over forty, too, was given to the practice of the very latest ideas on the dual culture of the soul and body— Swedish, German, neo-Greek and all that. And the orchid house was the warmest place available. I must proceed with the order of events.

Mr. Mannering at length withdrew his eyes from this stupendous bud, and decided that he must devote his attention to the grey exigencies of everyday life. But although his body dutifully ascended the stairs, heart, mind, and soul all remained in adoration of the plant. Although he was philosophical to the point of insensibility over the miserable smallness of the earlier flowers, yet he was now as much gratified by the magnitude of the great new bud as you or I might be. Hence it was not unnatural that Mr. Mannering while in his bath should be full of the most exalted visions of the blossoming of his heart's darling, his vegetable godchild. It would be by far the largest known, complex as a dream, or dazzlingly simple. It would open like a dancer, or like the sun rising. Why, it might be opening at this very moment! Mr. Mannering could restrain himself no longer; he rose from the steamy water, and, wrapping his bathrobe about him, hurried down to the hothouse, scarcely staying to dry himself, though he was subject to colds.

The bud had not yet opened; it still reared its unbroken head among the glossy, fleshy foliage, and he now saw, what he had had no eyes for previously, how very exuberant that foliage had grown. Suddenly he realized with astonishment that this huge bud was not the one which had appeared before he went away. That one had been lower down on the plant. Where was it now, then? Why, this new thrust and spread of foliage concealed it from him. He walked across, and discovered it. It had opened into a bloom. And as he looked at this bloom his astonishment grew to stupefaction, one might say to petrification, for it is a fact that Mr. Mannering remained rooted to the spot, with his eyes fixed on the flower, for fully fifteen minutes. The flower was an exact replica of the head of Cousin Jane's lost cat. The similitude was so exact, so life-like, that Mr. Mannering's first movement, after the fifteen minutes, was to seize his bathrobe and draw it about him, for he was a modest man, and the cat, though bought for a Tom, had proved to be quite the reverse. I relate this to show how much character, spirit, *presence* —call it what you will—there was upon this floral cat's face. But although he made to seize his bathrobe, it was too late. He could not move. The new lusty foliage had closed in unperceived; the too lightly dismissed tendrils were everywhere upon him; he gave a few weak cries and sank to the ground, and there, as the Mr. Mannering of ordinary life, he passes out of this story.

Mr. Mannering sank into a coma, into an insensibility so deep that a black eternity passed before the first faint elements of his consciousness reassembled themselves in his brain. For of his brain was the centre of a new bud being made. Indeed, it was two or three days before this at first almost hopeless and quite primitive lump of organic matter had become sufficiently mature to be called Mr. Mannering at all. These days, which passed quickly enough, in a certain mild, not unpleasant excitement, in the outer world, seemed to the dimly working mind within the bud to resume the whole history of the development of our species, in a great many epochal parts.

A process analogous to the mutations of the embryo was being enacted here. At last the entity which was thus being rushed down an absurdly foreshortened vista of the ages slowed up and came almost to a stop in the present. It became recognizable. The Seven Ages of Mr. Mannering were presented, as it were, in a series of close-ups, as in an educational film; his consciousness settled and cleared. The bud was mature, ready to open. At this point, I believe, Mr. Mannering's state of mind was exactly that of a patient who, wakening from under an anaesthetic, struggling up from vague dreams, asks plaintively, "Where am I?" Then the bud opened, and he knew.

There was the hothouse, but seen from an unfamiliar angle. There, through the glass door, was his study. There below him was the cat's head, and there—there beside him was Cousin Jane. He could not say a word, but then, neither could she. Perhaps it was as well. At the very least, he would have been forced to own that she had been in the right in an argument of long standing; she had always maintained that in the end no good would come of his preoccupation with "those unnatural flowers."

It must be admitted that Mr. Mannering was not at first greatly upset by this extraordinary upheaval in his daily life. This, I think, was because he was interested, not only in private and personal matters, but in the wider and more general, one might say the biological, aspects of his metamorphosis. For the rest, simply because he *was* now a vegetable, he responded with a vegetable reaction. The impossibility of locomotion, for example, did not trouble him in the least, or even the absence of body and limbs, any more than the cessation of that stream of rashers and tea, biscuits and glasses of milk, luncheon cutlets, and so forth, that had flowed in at his mouth for over fifty years, but which had now been reversed to a gentle, continuous, scarcely noticeable feeding from below. All the powerful influence of the physical upon the mental, therefore, inclined him to tranquillity. But the physical is not all. Although no longer a man, he was still Mr. Mannering. And from this anomaly, as soon as his scientific interest had subsided, issued a host of woes, mainly subjective in origin.

He was fretted, for instance, by the thought that he would now have no opportunity to name his orchid, or to write a paper upon it, and, still worse, there grew up in his mind the abominable conviction that, as soon as his plight was discovered, it was he who would be named and classified, and that he himself would be the subject of a paper, possibly even of comment and criticism in the lay press. Like all orchid collectors, he was excessively shy and sensitive, and in his present situation these qualities were very naturally exaggerated, so that the bare idea of such attentions brought him to the verge of wilting. Worse yet was the fear of being transplanted, thrust into some unfamiliar, draughty, probably public place. Being dug up! Ugh! A violent shudder pulsated through all the heavy foliage that sprang from Mr. Mannering's division of the plant. He became conscious of ghostly and remote sensations in the stem below, and in certain tufts of leaves that sprouted from it; they were somehow reminiscent of spine and heart and limbs. He felt quite a dryad.

In spite of all, however, the sunshine was very pleasant. The rich odour of hot, spicy earth filled the hothouse. From a special fixture on the hot-water pipes a little warm steam oozed into the air. Mr. Mannering began to abandon himself of a feeling of *laissez-aller*. Just then, up in a corner of the glass roof, at the ventilator, he heard a persistent buzzing. Soon the note changed from one of irritation to a more complacent sound; a bee had managed, after some difficulty, to find his way through one of the tiny chinks in the metal work. The visitor came drifting down and down through the still, green air, as if into some subaqueous world, and he came to rest on one of those petals which were Mr. Mannering's eyebrows. Thence he commenced to explore one feature after another, and at last he settled heavily on the lower lip, which drooped under his weight and allowed him to crawl right into Mr. Mannering's mouth. This was quite a considerable shock, of course, but on the whole the sensation was neither as alarming nor as unpleasant as might have been expected. "Indeed," thought the vegetable gentleman, "it seems quite agreeable."

But Mr. Mannering soon ceased the drowsy analysis of his sensations when he saw the departed bee, after one or two lazy circlings, settle directly upon the maiden lip of Cousin Jane. Ominous as lightning, a simple botanical principle flashed across the mind of her wretched relative. Cousin Jane was aware of it also, although, being the product of an earlier age, she might have remained still blessedly ignorant had not her cousin—vain, garrulous, proselytizing fool!—attempted for years past to interest her in the rudiments of botany. How the miserable man upbraided himself now! He saw two bunches of leaves just below the flower tremble and flutter, and rear themselves painfully upwards into the very likeness of two shocked and protesting hands. He saw the soft and orderly petals of his cousin's face ruffle and incarnadine with rage and embarrassment, then turn sickly as a gardenia with horror and dismay. But what was he to do? All the rectitude implanted by his careful training, all the chivalry proper to an orchid-collector, boiled and surged beneath a paralytically calm exterior. He positively travailed in the effort to activate the muscles of his face, to assume an expression of grief, manly contrition, helplessness in the face of fate, willingness to make honourable amends, all suffused with the light of a vague but solacing optimism; but it was in vain. When he had strained till his nerves seemed likely to tear under the tension, the only movement he could achieve was a trivial flutter of the left eyelid—worse than nothing.

This incident completely aroused Mr. Mannering from his vegetable lethargy. He rebelled against the limitations of the form into which he had thus been cast while subjectively he remained all too human. Was he not still at heart a man, with a man's hopes, ideals, aspirations—and capacity for suffering?

When dusk came, and the opulent and sinister shapes of the great plant dimmed to a suggestiveness more powerfully impressive than had been its bright noonday luxuriance, and the atmosphere of a tropical forest filled the orchid-house like an exile's dream or the nostalgia of the saxophone; when the cat's whiskers drooped, and even Cousin Jane's eyes slowly closed, the unhappy man remained wide awake, staring into the gathering darkness. Suddenly the light in the study was switched on. Two men entered the room. One of them was his lawyer, the other was his nephew.

"This is his study, as you know, of course," said the wicked nephew. "There's nothing here. I looked when I came over on Wednesday."

"I've sat in this room many an evening," said the lawyer with an expression of distaste. "I'd sit on this side of the fireplace and he on that. 'Mannering,' I'd think to myself, 'I wonder how you'll end up. Drugs? Sexual perversion? Or murder?' Well, maybe we'll soon know the answer. Until we do, I suppose you, as next of kin, had better take charge here."

Saying this, the lawyer turned, about to go, and Mr.

Mannering saw a malicious smile overspread the young man's face. The uneasiness which had overcome him at first sight of his nephew was intensified to fear and trembling at the sight of this smile.

When he had shown the lawyer out, the nephew returned to the study and looked round him with lively and sinister satisfaction. Then he cut a caper on the hearthrug. Mr. Mannering thought he had never seen anything so diabolical as this solitary expression of the glee of a venomous nature at the prospect of unchecked sway, here whence he had been outcast. How vulgar petty triumph appeared, beheld thus; how disgusting petty spite, how appalling revengefulness and hardness of heart! He remembered suddenly that his nephew had been notable, in his repulsive childhood, for his cruelty to flies, tearing their wings off, and for his barbarity toward cats. A sort of dew might have been noticed upon the good man's forehead. It seemed to him that his nephew had only to glance that way, and all would be discovered, although he might have remembered that it was impossible to see from the lighted room into the darkness of the hothouse.

On the mantelpiece stood a large unframed photograph of Mr. Mannering. His nephew soon caught sight of this, and strode across to confront it with a triumphant and insolent sneer. "What? You old Pharisee," said he, "taken her off for a trip to Brighton, have you? My God! How I hope you'll never come back! How I hope you've fallen over the cliffs, or got swept off by the tide or something! Anyway—I'll make hay while the sun shines. Ugh! you old skinflint, you!" And he reached forward his hand, and bestowed a contemptuous fillip upon the nose in the photograph. Then the usurping rascal left the room, leaving all the lights on, presumably preferring the dining-room with its cellarette to the scholarly austerities of the study.

All night long the glare of electric light from the study

fell upon Mr. Mannering and his Cousin Jane, like the glare of a cheap and artificial sun. You who have seen at midnight in the park a few insomniac asters standing stiff and startled under an arc light, all their weak colour bleached out of them by the drenching chemical radiance, neither asleep nor awake, but held fast in a tense, a neurasthenic trance, you can form an idea of how the night passed with this unhappy pair.

And toward morning an incident occurred, trivial in itself no doubt, but sufficient then and there to add the last drop to poor Cousin Jane's discomfiture and to her relative's embarrassment and remorse. Along the edge of the great earthbox in which the orchid was planted, ran a small black mouse. It had wicked red eyes, a naked, evil snout, and huge, repellent ears, queer as a bat's. This creature ran straight over the lower leaves of Cousin Jane's part of the plant. It was simply appalling. The stringy main stem writhed like a hair on a coal-fire, the leaves contracted in an agonized spasm, like seared mimosa; the terrified lady nearly uprooted herself in her convulsive horror. I think she would actually have done so, had not the mouse hurried on past her.

But it had not gone more than a foot or so when it looked up and saw, bending over it, and seeming positively to bristle with life, that flower which had once been called Tib. There was a breathless pause. The mouse was obviously paralyzed with terror, the cat could only look and long. Suddenly the more human watchers saw a sly frond of foliage curve softly outward and close in behind the hypnotized creature. Cousin Jane, who had been thinking exultantly, "Well, now it'll go away and never, never, never come back," suddenly became aware of hideous possibilities. Summoning all her energy, she achieved a spasmodic flutter, enough to break the trance that held the mouse, so that, like a clock-work toy, it swung round and fled. But already the fell arm of the orchid had cut off its retreat. The mouse leaped straight at it. Like a flash five tendrils at the end caught the fugitive and held it fast, and soon its body dwindled and was gone. Now the heart of Cousin Jane was troubled with horrid fears, and slowly and painfully she turned her weary face first to one side, then to the other, in a fever of anxiety as to where the new bud would appear. A sort of sucker, green and sappy, which twisted lightly about her main stem, and reared a blunt head, much like a tip of asparagus, close to her own, suddenly began to swell in the most suspicious manner. She squinted at it, fascinated and appalled. Could it be her imagination? It was not.

Next evening the door opened again, and again the nephew entered the study. This time he was alone, and it was evident that he had come straight from table. He carried in his hand a decanter of whiskey capped by an inverted glass. Under his arm was a siphon. His face was distinctly flushed, and such a smile as is often seen in saloon bars played about his lips. He put down his burdens and, turning to Mr. Mannering's cigar cabinet, produced a bunch of keys, which he proceeded to try upon the lock, muttering vindictively at each abortive attempt, until it opened, when he helped himself from the best of its contents. Annoying as it was to witness this insolent appropriation of his property, and mortifying to see the contempt with which the cigar was smoked, the good gentleman found deeper cause for uneasiness in the thought that, with the possession of the keys, his abominable nephew had access to every private corner that was his.

At present, however, the usurper seemed indisposed to carry on investigations; he splashed a great deal of whiskey into the tumbler and relaxed into an attitude of extravagant comfort. But after a while the young man began to tire of his own company. He had not yet had time to gather any of his pothouse companions into his uncle's home, and repeated recourse to the whiskey bottle only increased his longing for something to relieve the monotony. His eye fell upon the door of the orchid-house. Sooner or later it was bound to have happened. Does this thought greatly console the condemned man when the fatal knock sounds upon the door of his cell? No. Nor were the hearts of the trembling pair in the hothouse at all comforted by the reflection.

As the nephew fumbled with the handle of the glass door, Cousin Jane slowly raised two fronds of leaves that grew on each side, high upon her stem, and sank her troubled head behind them. Mr. Mannering observed, in a sudden rapture of hope, that by this device she was fairly well concealed from any casual glance. Hastily he strove to follow her example. Unfortunately, he had not yet gained sufficient control of his—his *limbs?*—and all his tortured efforts could not raise them beyond an agonized horizontal. The door had opened, the nephew was feeling for the electric light switch just inside. It was a moment for one of the superlative achievements of panic. Mr. Mannering was well equipped for the occasion. Suddenly, at the cost of indescribable effort, he succeeded in raising the right frond, not straight upwards, it is true, but in a series of painful jerks along a curve outward and backward, and ascending by slow degrees till it attained the position of an arm held over the possessor's head from behind. Then, as the light flashed on, a spray of leaves at the very end of this frond spread out into a fan, rather like a very fleshy horse-chestnut leaf in structure, and covered the anxious face below. What a relief! And now the nephew advanced into the orchid-house, and now the hidden pair simultaneously remembered the fatal presence of the cat. Simultaneously also, their very sap stood still in their veins. The nephew was walking along by the plant. The cat, a sagacious beast, "knew" with the infallible intuition of its kind that this was an idler, a parasite, a sensualist, gross and brutal, disrespectful of age, insolent to weakness, barbarous to cats. Therefore it remained very still, trusting to its low and somewhat retired position on the plant, and to protective mimicry and such things, and to the half-drunken condition of the nephew, to avoid his notice. But all in vain.

"What?" said the nephew. "What, a cat?" And he raised his hand to offer a blow at the harmless creature. Something in the dignified and unflinching demeanour of his victim must have penetrated into his besotted mind, for the blow never fell, and the bully, a coward at heart, as bullies invariably are, shifted his gaze from side to side to escape the steady, contemptuous stare of the courageous cat. Alas! His eye fell on something glimmering whitely behind the dark foliage. He brushed aside the intervening leaves that he might see what it was. It was Cousin Jane.

"Oh! Ah!" said the young man, in great confusion. "*You're* back. But what are you hiding there for?"

His sheepish stare became fixed, his mouth opened in bewilderment; then the true condition of things dawned upon his mind. Most of us would have at once instituted some attempt at communication, or at assistance of some kind, or at least have knelt down to thank our Creator that we had, by His grace, been spared such a fate, or perhaps have made haste from the orchid-house to ensure against accidents. But alcohol had so inflamed the young man's hardened nature that he felt neither fear, nor awe, nor gratitude. As he grasped the situation a devilish smile overspread his face.

"Ha! Ha! Ha!" said he. "But where's the old man?"

He peered about the plant, looking eagerly for his uncle. In a moment he had located him and, raising the inadequate visor of leaves, discovered beneath it the face of our hero, troubled with a hundred bitter emotions.

"Hullo, Narcissus!" said the nephew.

A long silence ensued. The spiteful wretch was so pleased that he could not say a word. He rubbed his hands together, and licked his lips, and stared and stared as a child might at a new toy.

"Well, you're properly up a tree," he said. "Yes, the tables are turned now all right, aren't they? Do you remember the last time we met?"

A flicker of emotion passed over the face of the suffering blossom, betraying consciousness.

"Yes, you can hear what I say," added the tormentor. "Feel, too, I expect. What about that?"

As he spoke, he stretched out his hand and, seizing a delicate frill of fine, silvery filaments that grew as whiskers grow around the lower half of the flower, he administered a sharp tug. Without pausing to note, even in the interests of science, the subtler shades of his uncle's reaction, content with the general effort of that devastating wince, the wretch chuckled with satisfaction and, taking a long pull from the reeking butt of the stolen cigar, puffed the vile fumes straight into his victim's centre. The brute!

"How do you like that, John the Baptist?" he asked with a leer. "Good for the blight, you know. Just what you want!"

Something rustled upon his coat sleeve. Looking down, he saw a long stalk, well adorned with the fatal tendrils, groping its way over the arid and unsatisfactory surface. In a moment it had reached his wrist, he felt it fasten, but knocked it off as one would a leech, before it had time to establish its hold.

"Ugh!" said he. "So that's how it happens, is it? I think I'll keep outside till I get the hang of things a bit. I don't want to be made an Aunt Sally of. Though I shouldn't think they could get you with your clothes on." Struck by a sudden thought, he looked from his uncle to Cousin Jane, and from Cousin Jane back to his uncle again. He scanned the floor, and saw a single crumpled bathrobe lying in the shadow.

"Why!" he said. "*Well!*—Haw! Haw! Haw!" And with an odious backward leer, he made his way out of the orchid-house.

Mr. Mannering felt that his suffering was capable of no increase. Yet he dreaded the morrow. His fevered imagination patterned the long night with waking nightmares, utterly fantastic visions of humiliation and torture. Torture! It was absurd, of course, for him to fear cold-blooded atrocities on the part of his nephew, but how he dreaded some outrageous whim that might tickle the youth's sense of humour, and lead him to *any* wanton freak, especially if he were drunk at the time. He thought of slugs and snails, espaliers and topiary. If only the monster would rest content with insulting jests, with wasting his substance, ravaging his cherished possessions before his eyes, with occasional pulling at the whiskers, even! Then it might be possible to turn gradually from all that still remained in him of man, to subdue the passions, no longer to admire or desire, to go native as it were, relapsing into the Nirvana of a vegetable dream. But in the morning he found this was not so easy.

In came the nephew and, pausing only to utter the most perfunctory of jeers at his relatives in the glass house, he sat at the desk and unlocked the top drawer. He was evidently in search of money, his eagerness betrayed that; no doubt he had run through all he had filched from his uncle's pockets, and had not yet worked out a scheme for getting direct control of his bank account. However, the drawer held enough to cause the scoundrel to rub his hands with satisfaction and, summoning the housekeeper, to bellow into her ear a reckless order upon the wine and spirits merchant.

"Get along with you!" he shouted, when he had at last made her understand. "I shall have to get someone a bit more on the spot to wait on me; I can tell you that. Yes," he added to himself as the poor old woman hobbled away, deeply hurt by his bullying manner, "yes, a nice little parlour-maid."

He hunted in the telephone book for the number of the local registry office. That afternoon he interviewed a succession of maidservants in his uncle's study. Those that happened to be plain, or too obviously respectable, he treated curtly and coldly; they soon made way for others. It was only when a girl was attractive (according to the young man's depraved tastes, that is) and also bore herself in a fast or brazen manner, that the interview was at all prolonged. In these cases the nephew would conclude in a fashion that left no doubt in the minds of any of his auditors as to his real intentions. Once, for example, leaning forward, he took the girl by the chin, saying with an odious smirk, "There's no one else but me, and so you'd be treated just like one of the family, d'you see, my dear?" To another he would say, slipping his arm round her waist, "Do you think we shall get on well together?"

After this conduct had sent two or three in confusion from the room, there entered a young person of the most regrettable description; one whose character, betrayed as it was in her meretricious finery, her crude cosmetics, and her tinted hair, showed yet more clearly in florid gesture and too facile smile. The nephew lost no time in coming to an arrangement with this creature. Indeed, her true nature was so obvious that the depraved young man only went through the farce of an ordinary interview as a sauce to his anticipations, enjoying the contrast between conventional dialogue and unbridled glances. She was to come next day. Mr. Mannering feared more for his unhappy cousin than for himself. "What scenes may she not have

to witness," he thought, "that yellow cheek of hers to incarnadine?" If only he could have said a few words!

But that evening, when the nephew came to take his
ease in the study, it was obvious that he was far more under the influence of liquor than he had been before. His
face, flushed patchily by the action of the spirits, wore a
sullen sneer; an ominous light burned in that bleared eye;
he muttered savagely under his breath. Clearly this fiend
in human shape was what is known as "fighting drunk";
clearly some trifle had set his vile temper in a blaze.

It is interesting to note, even at this stage, a sudden
change in Mr. Mannering's reactions. They now seemed
entirely egotistical, and were to be elicited only by stimuli
directly associated with physical matters. The nephew
kicked a hole in a screen in his drunken fury, he flung a
burning cigar-end down on the carpet, he scratched matches on the polished table. His uncle witnessed this with the
calm of one whose sense of property and of dignity has become numbed and paralyzed; he felt neither fury nor mortification. Had he, by one of those sudden strides by which
all such development takes place, approached much nearer to his goal, complete vegetation? His concern for the
threatened modesty of Cousin Jane, which had moved him
so strongly only a few hours earlier, must have been the
last dying flicker of exhausted altruism; that most human
characteristic had faded from him. The change, however,
in its present stage, was not an unmixed blessing. Nar-
rowing in from the wider and more expressly human re-
gions of his being, his consciousness now left outside its
focus not only pride and altruism, which had been responsible for much of his woe, but fortitude and detachment
also, which, with quotations from the Greek, had been
his support before the whole battery of his distresses. Moreover, within its constricted circle, his ego was not reduced
but concentrated; his serene, flower-like indifference to-

ward the ill-usage of his furniture was balanced by the absorbed, flower-like single-mindedness of his terror at the thought of similar ill-usage directed toward himself.

Inside the study the nephew still fumed and swore. On the mantelpiece stood an envelope, addressed in Mr. Mannering's handwriting to Cousin Jane. In it was the letter he had written from town, describing his nephew's disgraceful conduct. The young man's eye fell upon this and, unscrupulous, impelled by idle curiosity, he took it up and drew out the letter. As he read, his face grew a hundred times blacker than before.

"What," he muttered, " 'a mere race-course cad . . . a worthless vulgarian . . . a scoundrel of the sneaking sort' . . . and what's this? '. . . cut him off absolutely . . .' What?" said he, with a horrifying oath. "*Would* you cut me off absolutely? Two can play at that game, you old devil!"

And he snatched up a large pair of scissors that lay on the desk, and burst into the hothouse——

Among fish, the dory, they say, screams when it is seized upon by man; among insects, the caterpillar of the death's-head moth is capable of a still, small shriek of terror; in the vegetable world, only the mandrake could voice its agony—till now.

Romance Lingers Adventure Lives

There is a great deal of devilry in a bright and windy midnight in the month of March. A little naked moon rides high over Fairlawn Avenue in the heart of the Sweetholme building development. The new houses are chalk-masked by its light, except for their darkened windows, which glare broodingly, like deep-set eyes, or the sockets of eyes. There are some young almond trees, which ordinarily look as if drawn by a childish hand. Now, as the wind sets their weak branches gibbering, they seem like shamanistic scratches on the white bone of the brittle bright night.

The wind causes a man to tuck his chin into his coat collar, to become a mere rag, curved against the wind. His bowler-hatted moon-shadow, apparently cut from a sheet of tin, scythes its way implacably through the asphalt, and seems the better man of the two, probably the real man, the genuine Mr. Watkins. Around the bend, just out of sight, comes another figure, bowler-hatted also, scythe-curved also, also chopping its way through the icy air. It might be the shadow of the shadow. It might be Death. It is, however, only Mr. Gosport.

The carriage from which he alighted out of the midnight train was the farthest from the station barrier. Also, his shoelace came undone. There is an explanation for everything: sometimes two explanations. These two explain why Mr. Gosport was a hundred yards or so behind Mr. Watkins.

Mr. Watkins, with his little grin slipped in like a scarfpin behind his upturned lapels, observed with a stare of desolate and hopeless superiority the monotony of the houses of Fairlawn Avenue. This was the vilest ingratitude, for the uniformity was due to the fact that each was the best possible house at the figure. Watkins, however, having drunk and sung away the Saturday evening in exclusively male company, was full of blood and villainy, intolerant of caution and incapable of gratitude. He decided that on Monday he would rob the bank at which he was employed, and fly to South America, where he would set up a seraglio.

How different were the thoughts of Mr. Gosport, as out of sight, around the bend, he sheared his way into the wind and also regarded the monotony of Fairlawn Avenue! The good Gosport fully realized that each house was the best possible at the price; he knew that each chalky bump was a vertebra in the backbone of the country; he had read that the life of the little man was as full of romance and high adventure as that of any buccaneer of old; columnists had told him that the Fairlawn Avenues of the world are its very jewels, its necklaces of simple joys and sorrows, its rosaries in which each well matched home is a pearl. The only trouble was, he had no great fondness for jewelry, and wished that he was dead. "I am unfit to appreciate the best of all possible lives in the best of all possible building developments," said he. "Tomorrow I will put my affairs in order, and be specially nice to Milly. On Monday I will go far away, to where there are trees larger than these little almond trees, and I will hang myself upon the branch of one of them."

Watkins, away ahead, roller-coastered in imagination over the curves of his future seraglio. He was brought to a halt by the appearance of a dim light behind a hall door. "Here we are," said he. He went up the little path and opened the door, and was at once received into the warmth of domesticity and greeted by the beauty of a three-piece hallway set of a pattern very popular on Fairlawn Avenue.

In a moment, the vigorous Watkins had hung hat and coat upon the peg, switched out the hall light, and was creeping up the stairs to bed.

Still out in the cold, still shearing with sensitive nose the arctic currents of the wind, Mr. Gosport passed the now darkened house. Four doors farther up, his watering eyes perceived a dim light behind a hall-door pane. "Here I am!" said he with a sigh.

Upstairs in the first house, treading soft so as not to wake his sleeping wife, Watkins flung off his clothing, expanded his chest, scratched his rump, donned his pyjamas, and slipped into the bed. His wife acknowledged his entry with a muted whinny.

Here were two human caterpillars, immobile in a cotton cocoon, awaiting the pupescence of sleep, the wings of dream.

There is, however, a great deal of devilry at midnight on a Saturday. What was the influence that drew the lady up from sleep like Sheba's queen from glowing Africa, and reclaimed the gentleman like Solomon from the contemplation of his seraglio? Was it that which had been moribund three years, or was it something totally different? It felt like something totally different.

Something very much the same—that is to say, something totally different—was happening at the very same time to Mr. Gosport.

Both couples slept late on Sunday morning, and when they woke the ladies did what they had not done since honeymoon days. That is to say, they rose smiling in the darkness of the curtained rooms, and hastened downstairs to prepare a morning cup of coffee.

Watkins, waking to full consciousness, heard the clink of the crockery below. He smiled, stretched, sniffed, expanded his chest, and with a coy smile abandoned himself to a warm flood of happiness. This, like a Gulf Stream, bore his thoughts away from South America and set the almonds all ablossoming on Fairlawn Avenue.

Watkins descended the stairs, and entered the little kitchen. There was the steaming coffee; there was a beloved figure in a fresh and flowery wrapper, bending over the gas stove. He bestowed a jovial but appreciative pinch, and took up the newspaper.

"How manly!" thought she.

At the same moment Mr. Gosport was descending the stairs, and in a similar mood. To him also was accorded the scent of new-made coffee, and the sight of a sweet figure in flowered wrapper bending over the stove. He bestowed a lingering and grateful kiss just where the hair twirls in little tendrils at the back of the neck, and took up the newspaper.

"How refined!" thought she.

"Hey, what's this?" said Mr. Watkins, when he had sipped his coffee, and skimmed smilingly over an account of a fugitive bank clerk being arrested at Southampton. "Hey, what's this? Where is the true detective story feature in this Sunday's *Telegram?*"

"That is not the *Telegram*," said the lady, turning in surprise from the stove. "And you," said she on a rising note, "And you are not my husband."

With that she fell to the floor, in a faint of the third intensity. "I got into the wrong house last night," murmured Watkins. "I had better get off home."

He quickly assembled his clothes and left the house. On his way along the Avenue he passed Mr. Gosport, with whom he was unacquainted. Each was too busy concocting an excuse for staying in town overnight, to take any notice of the other.

Mr. Watkins found Mrs. Watkins, and Mr. Gosport found Mrs. Gosport, highly agitated at the unaccountable absence of their husbands, and too relieved at their return to scrutinize very closely the likelihood of the excuses they made.

They each had a nice cut of beef for their Sunday lunch, and after lunch they took a nap, while their wives looked out of the window. Their dreams were not unpleasant, and when they woke, Fairlawn Avenue no longer seemed so monotonous as to justify resort to crime or suicide. How long this cheerful mood would have lasted without reinforcement it is impossible to say. Fortunately Mrs. Gosport shortly afterwards made the acquaintance of Mrs. Watkins while seeking a strayed kitten, and the two families became the greatest of friends, and spent most of their evenings, their week ends, and their summer holidays together.

This happy relationship altogether banished monotony from Fairlawn Avenue, and it would have persisted to this day, had not a slight coolness arisen last spring owing to Mr. Gosport refusing Mr. Watkins the loan of his lawn mower.

Bird of Prey

he house they call the Engineer's house is now deserted. The new man from Baton Rouge gave it up after living less than a month in it, and built himself a two-room shack with his own money, on the very farthest corner of the company's land.

The roof of the Engineer's house has caved in, and most of the windows are broken. Oddly enough, no birds nest in the shelter of the eaves, or take advantage of the forsaken rooms. An empty house is normally fine harborage for rats and mice and bats, but there is no squeak or rustle or scamper to disturb the quiet of this one. Only creatures utterly foreign, utterly remote from the most distant cousinhood to man, only the termite, the tarantula, and the scorpion indifferently make it their home.

All in a few years Edna Spalding's garden has been wiped out as if it had never existed. The porch where she and Jack sat so happily in the evenings is rotten under its load of wind-blown twigs and sand. A young tree has already burst up the boards outside the living-room window, so that they fan out like the stiff fingers of someone who is afraid. In this corner there still stands a strongly made parrot's perch, the wood of which has been left untouched even by the termite and the boring beetle.

The Spaldings brought a parrot with them when first they came. It was a sort of extra wedding present, given them at the last moment by Edna's mother. It was something from home for Edna to take into the wilds.

The parrot was already old, and he was called Tom, and, like other parrots, he sat on his perch, and whistled and laughed and uttered his few remarks, which were often very appropriate. Edna and Jack were both very fond of him, and they were overwhelmingly fond of each other. They liked their house, and the country, and Jack's colleagues, and everything in life seemed to be delightful.

One night they had just fallen asleep when they were awakened by a tremendous squawking and fluttering outside on the porch. "Oh, Jack!" cried Edna. "Get up! Hurry! Run! It's one of those cats from the men's camp has got hold of poor Tom!"

Jack sprang out of bed, but caught his foot in the sheet, and landed on his elbow on the floor. Between rubbing his elbow and disentangling his foot, he wasted a good many seconds before he was up again. Then he dashed through the living-room and out upon the porch.

All this time, which seemed an age, the squawking and fluttering increased, but as he flung open the door it ceased as suddenly as it had begun. The whole porch was bathed in the brightest moonlight, and at the farther end the perch was clearly visible, and on the floor beneath it was poor old Tom parrot, gasping amid a litter of his own feathers, and crying, "Oh! Oh! Oh!"

At any rate he was alive. Jack looked right and left for

traces of his assailant, and at once noticed the long, heavy trailers of the trumpet vine were swinging violently, although there was not a breath of wind. He went to the rail and looked out and around, but there was no sign of a cat. Of course, it was not likely there would be. Jack was more interested in the fact that the swaying vines were spread over a length of several feet, which seemed a very great deal of disturbance for a fleeing cat to make. Finally he looked up, and he thought he saw a bird—a big bird, an enormous bird—flying away. He just caught a glimpse of it as it crossed the brightness of the moon.

He turned back and picked up old Tom. The poor parrot's chain was broken, and his heart was pounding away like mad, and still, like a creature hurt and shocked beyond all endurance, he cried, "Oh! Oh! Oh!"

This was all the more odd, for it was seldom the old fellow came out with a new phrase, and Jack would have laughed heartily, except it sounded too pathetic. So he carefully examined the poor bird, and finding no injury beyond the loss of a handful of feathers from his neck, he replaced him on the perch, and turned to reassure Edna, who now appeared in the doorway.

"Is he dead?" cried she.

"No," said Jack. "He's had a bit of shock, though. Something got hold of him."

"I'll bring him a piece of sugar," said Edna. "That's what he loves. That'll make him feel better."

She soon brought the sugar, which Tom took in his claw, but though usually he would nibble it up with the greatest avidity, this time he turned his lack-lustre eye only once upon it, and gave a short, bitter, despairing sort of laugh, and let it fall to the ground.

"Let him rest," said Jack. "He has had a bad tousling."

"It was a cat," said Edna. "It was one of those beastly cats the men have at the camp."

"Maybe," said Jack. "On the other hand—I don't know. I thought I saw an enormous bird flying away."

"It couldn't be an eagle," said Edna. "There are none ever seen here."

"I know," said Jack. "Besides, they don't fly at night. Nor do the buzzards. It might have been an owl, I suppose. But——"

"But what?" said Edna.

"But it looked very much larger than an owl," said Jack.

"It was your fancy," said Edna. "It was one of those beastly cats that did it."

This point was discussed very frequently during the next few days. Everybody was consulted, and everybody had an opinion. Jack might have been a little doubtful at first, for he had caught only the briefest glimpse as the creature crossed the moon, but opposition made him more certain, and the discussions sometimes got rather heated.

"Charlie says it was all your imagination," said Edna. "He says no owl would ever attack a parrot."

"How the devil does *he* know?" said Jack. "Besides, I said it was bigger than an owl."

"He says that shows you imagine things," said Edna.

"Perhaps he would like me to think I do," said Jack. "Perhaps you both would."

"Oh, Jack!" cried Edna. She was deeply hurt, and not without reason, for it showed that Jack was still thinking of a ridiculous mistake he had made, a real mistake, of the sort that young husbands sometimes do make, when they come suddenly into a room and people are startled without any real reason for it. Charlie was young and free and easy and good-looking, and he would put his hand on your shoulder without even thinking about it, and nobody minded.

"I should not have said that," said Jack.

"No, indeed you shouldn't," said Edna, and she was right.

The parrot said nothing at all. All these days he had been moping and ailing, and seemed to have forgotten even how to ask for sugar. He only groaned and moaned to himself, ruffled up his feathers, and every now and then shook his head in the most rueful, miserable way you can possibly imagine.

One day, however, when Jack came home from work, Edna put her finger to her lips and beckoned him to the window. "Watch Tom," she whispered.

Jack peered out. There was the old bird, lugubriously climbing down from his perch and picking some dead stalks from the vine, which he carried up till he gained a corner where the balustrade ran into the wall, and added his gatherings to others that were already there. He trod round and round, twisted his stalks in and out, and, always with the same doleful expression, paid great attention to the nice disposition of a feather or two, a piece of wood, a fragment of cellophane. There was no doubt about it.

"There's no doubt about it," said Jack.

"He's making a nest!" cried Edna.

"He!" cried Jack. "*He!* I like that. The old impostor! The old male impersonator! She's going to lay an egg. Thomasina—that's her name from now on."

Thomasina it was. Two or three days later the matter was settled beyond the shadow of a doubt. There, one morning, in the ramshackle nest, was an egg.

"I thought she was sick because of that shaking she got," said Jack. "She was broody, that's all."

"It's a monstrous egg," said Edna. "Poor birdie."

"What do you expect, after God knows how many years?" said Jack, laughing. "Some birds lay eggs nearly as big as themselves—the kiwi or something. Still, I must admit it's a whopper."

"She doesn't look well," said Edna.

Indeed, the old parrot looked almost as sick as a parrot can be, which is several times sicker than any other living creature. Her eyes closed up, her head sank, and if a finger was put out to scratch her she turned her beak miserably away. However, she sat conscientiously on the prodigious egg she had laid, though every day she seemed a little feebler than before.

"Perhaps we ought to take the egg away," said Jack. "We could get it blown, and keep it as a memento."

"No," said Edna. "Let her have it. It's all she's had in all these years."

Here Edna made a mistake, and she realized it a few mornings later. "Jack," she called. "Do come. It's Tom—Thomasina, I mean. I'm afraid she's going to die."

"We ought to have taken the egg away," said Jack, coming out with his mouth full of breakfast. "She's exhausted herself. It's no good, anyway. It's bound to be sterile."

"Look at her!" cried Edna.

"She's done for," said Jack, and at that moment the poor old bird keeled over and gasped her last.

"The egg killed her," said Jack, picking it up. "I said it would. Do you want to keep it? Oh, good Lord!" He put the egg down very quickly. "It's alive," he said.

"What?" said Edna. "What do you mean?"

"It gave me a turn," said Jack. "It's most extraordinary. It's against nature. There's a chick inside that egg, tapping."

"Let it out," said Edna. "Break the shell."

"I was right," said Jack. "It *was* a bird I saw. It must have been a stray parrot. Only it looked so big."

"I'm going to break the shell with a spoon," said Edna, running to fetch one.

"It'll be a lucky bird," said Jack when she returned. "Born with a silver spoon in its beak, so to speak. Be careful."

"I will," said Edna. "Oh, I do hope it lives!"

With that she gingerly cracked the shell, the tapping increased, and soon they saw a well-developed beak tearing its way through. In another moment the chick was born.

"Golly!" cried Jack. "What a monster!"

"It's because it's young," said Edna. "It'll grow lovely. Like its mother."

"Maybe," said Jack. "I must be off. Put it in the nest. Feed it pap. Keep it warm. Don't monkey with it too much. Goodbye, my love."

That morning Jack telephoned home two or three times to find out how the chick was, and if it ate. He rushed home at lunchtime. In the evening everyone came round to peep at the nestling and offer advice.

Charlie was there. "It ought to be fed every hour at least," said he. "That's how it is in nature."

"He's right," said Jack. "For the first month at least, that's how it should be."

"It looks as if I'm going to be tied down a bit," said Edna ruefully.

"I'll look in when I pass and relieve your solitude," said Charlie.

"I'll manage to rush home now and then in the afternoons," said Jack, a little too thoughtfully.

Certainly the hourly feeding seemed to agree with the chick, which grew at an almost alarming speed. It became covered with down, feathers sprouted; in a few months it was fully grown, and not in the least like its mother. For one thing, it was coal-black.

"It must be a hybrid," said Jack. "There *is* a black parrot; I've seen them in zoos. They didn't look much like this, though. I've half a mind to send a photograph of him somewhere."

"He looks so wicked," said Edna.

"He looks cunning," said Jack. "That bird knows everything, believe me. I bet he'll talk soon."

"It gave a sort of laugh," said Edna. "I forgot to tell you."

"When?" cried Jack. "A laugh?"

"Sort of," said Edna. "But it was horrible. It made Charlie nearly jump out of his skin."

"Charlie?" cried Jack. "You didn't say he'd been here."

"Well, you know how often he drops in," said Edna.

"Do I?" said Jack. "I hope I do. God! What was that?"

"That's what I meant," said Edna. "A sort of laugh."

"What a horrible sound!" said Jack.

"Listen, Jack," said Edna. "I wish you wouldn't be silly about Charlie. You are, you know."

Jack looked at her. "I know I am," said he. "I know it when I look at you. And then I think I never will be again. But somehow it's got stuck in my mind, and the least little thing brings it out. Maybe I'm just a bit crazy, on that one subject."

"Well, he'll be transferred soon," said Edna. "And that'll be the end of it."

"Where did you hear that?" said Jack.

"He told me this afternoon," said Edna. "He was on his way back from getting the mail when he dropped in. That's why he told me first. Otherwise he'd have told you first. Only he hasn't seen you yet. Do you see?"

"Yes, I see," said Jack. "I wish I could be psychoanalyzed or something."

Soon Charlie made his farewells, and departed for his job on the company's other project. Edna was secretly glad to see him go. She wanted no problems, however groundless, to exist between herself and Jack. A few days later she felt sure that all the problems were solved forever.

"Jack," said she when he came home in the evening.

"Yes," said he.

"Something new," said she. "Don't play with that bird. Listen to me."

"Call him Polly," said Jack. They had named it Polly

to be on the safe side. "You don't want to call him 'that bird.' The missus doesn't love you, Poll."

"Do you know, I don't!" said Edna, with quite startling vehemence. "I don't like him at all, Jack. Let's give him away."

"What? For heaven's sake!" cried Jack. "This rare, black, specially hatched Poll? This parrot of romantic origin? The cleverest Poll that ever——"

"That's it," said Edna. "He's too darned clever. Jack, I hate him. He's horrible."

"What? Has he said something you don't like?" said Jack, laughing. "I bet he will, when he talks. But what's the news, anyway?"

"Come inside," said Edna. "I'm not going to tell you with that creature listening." She led the way into the bedroom. "The news is," said she, "that I've got to be humoured. And if I don't like anything, it's got to be given away. It's not going to be born with a beak because its mother was frightened by a hateful monstrosity of a parrot."

"What?" said Jack.

"That's what," said Edna, smiling and nodding.

"A brat?" cried Jack in delight. "A boy! Or a girl! It's bound to be one or the other. Listen, I was afraid to tell you how much I wanted one, Edna. Oh, boy! This is going to make everything very, very fine. Lie down. You're delicate. Put your feet up. I'm going to fix dinner. This is practice. Stay still. Oh, boy! Oh, boy! Or girl as the case may be!"

He went out through the living-room on his way to the kitchen. As he passed the window he caught sight of the parrot on the dark porch outside, and he put his head through to speak to it.

"Have you heard the news?" said he. "Behold a father! You're going to be cut right out, my bird. You're going to be given away. Yes, sir, it's a baby."

The parrot gave a long low whistle. "You don't say so?" said he in a husky voice, a voice of apprehension, a quite astonishing imitation of Charlie's voice. "What about Jack?"

"What's that?" said Jack, startled.

"He'll think it's his," whispered the parrot in Edna's voice. "He's fool enough for anything. Kiss me, darling. Phew-w-w! You don't say so? What about Jack? He'll think it's his, he's fool enough for anything. Kiss me, darling. Phew-w-w!"

Jack went out into the kitchen, and sat down with his head in his hands for several minutes.

"Hurry up!" cried Edna from the bedroom. "Hurry up —*Father!*"

"I'm coming," said Jack.

He went to his desk, and took out the revolver. Then he went into the bedroom.

At the sound of the cry and the shot, the parrot laughed. Then, lifting its claw, it took the chain in its beak, and bit through it as if it were paper.

Jack came out, holding the gun, his hand over his eyes. "Fool enough for anything!" said the parrot, and laughed.

Jack turned the gun on himself. As he did so, in the infinitesimal interval between the beginning and the end of the movement of his finger on the trigger, he saw the bird grow, spread its dark wings, and its eyes flamed, and it changed, and it launched itself toward him.

The gun went off. Jack dropped to the floor. The parrot, or whatever it was, sailing down, seized what came out of his ruined mouth, and wheeled back through the window, and was soon far away, visible for a moment only as it swept on broader wings past the new-arisen moon.

The Steel Cat

The Hotel Bixbee is as commercial an hotel as any in Chicago. The brass-rail surmounts the banisters; the cuspidor gleams dimly in the shade of the potted palm. The air in the corridors is very still, and appears to have been de-odorized a few days ago. The rates are moderate.

Walter Davies' cab drew up outside the Bixbee. He was a man with a good deal of grey in his hair, and with a certain care-worn brightness on his face, such as is often to be seen on the faces of rural preachers, if they are poor enough and hopeful enough. Davies, however, was not a preacher.

The porter seized his suitcase, and would have taken the black box he held on his knees, but Davies nervously put out his hand. "No," he said. "Leave this one to me."

He entered the hotel carrying the box as if it were a baby. It was an oblong box, nearly two feet long, and perhaps a foot wide and a foot in depth. It was covered with a high-grade near-leather. It had a handle on the top side, but Davies preferred to cradle it in his arms rather than to swing it by this handle.

As soon as he had checked in and was shown to his room, he set the box on the bureau and made straight for the telephone. He called Room Service. "This is Room 517," said he. "What sort of cheese have you?"

"Well, we got Camembert, Swiss, Tillamook . . ."

"Now, the Tillamook," said Davies. "Is that good and red-looking?"

"Guess so," said the man at the other end. "It's like it usually is."

"All right, send me up a portion."

"What bread with it? Roll? White? Rye?"

"No bread. Just the cheese by itself."

"Okay. It'll be right up."

In a minute or two a bell-hop entered, carrying a platter with the wedge of cheese on it. He was a coloured man of about the same age as Davies, and had a remarkably round face and bullet head. "Is that right, sir? You wanted just a piece of cheese?"

"That's right," said Davies, who was undoing the clasps of his black box. "Put it right there on the table."

The bell-hop, waiting for him to sign the check, watched Davies fold down the front side of the box, which carried part of the top with it. Thus opened, it displayed an interior lined with black velvet, against which gleamed an odd-looking skeletal arrangement in chromium-plated metal. "Now look at that!" said the bell-hop, much intrigued. "Wouldn't be surprised if that ain't an *invention* you got there."

"Interesting, eh?" said Davies. "Catches the eye?"

"Sure does," said the bell-hop. "There ain't nothing much more interesting than an invention." He peered reverently at the odd-looking apparatus in the box. "Now what sort of invention would you say that might be?"

"That," said Davies proudly, "is the Steel Cat."

"Steel Cat?" cried the bell-hop. "No kidding?"

He shook his head, a plain man baffled by the wonders of science. "So that's the Steel Cat! Well now, what do you know?"

"Good name, you think?" asked Davies.

"Boy, that's a *title!*" replied the bell-hop. "Mister, how come I ain't never heard of this here Steel Cat?"

"That's the only one in the world," said Davies. "So far."

"I come from Ohio," said the bell-hop. "And I got folks in Ohio. And they're going to hear from me how I got to see this one and only Steel Cat."

"Glad you like it," said Davies. "Wait a minute. Fond of animals? I'll show you something."

As he spoke, he opened a small compartment that was built into one end of the box. Inside was a round nest of toilet tissues. Davies put his fingers against his nest. "Come on, Georgie," he said. "Peep! Peep! Come on, Georgie!"

A small, ordinary mouse, fat as a butter-ball, thrust his quick head out of the nest, turned his berry-black eyes in all directions, and ran along Davies' finger, and up his sleeve to his collar, where he craned up to touch his nose to the lobe of Davies' ear.

"Well, sir!" cried the bell-hop in delight. "If that ain't a proper tame, friendly mouse you got there!"

"He knows me," said Davies. "In fact, this mouse knows pretty near everything."

"I betcha!" said the bell-hop with conviction.

"He's what you might call a demonstration mouse," said Davies. "He shows off the Steel Cat. See the idea? You hang the bait on this hook. Mr. Mouse marches up this strip in the middle. He reaches for the bait. His weight tips the beam, and he drops into this jar. Of course, I fill it with water."

"And that's his name—Georgie?" asked the bell-hop, his eyes still on the mouse.

"That's what I call him," said Davies.

"You know what?" said the bell-hop thoughtfully. "If I had that mouse, mister, I reckon I'd call him Simpson."

"D'you know how I came to meet up with this mouse?" said Davies. "I was in Poughkeepsie—that's where I come from—and one night last winter I ran my bath, and somehow I sat on, reading the paper, and forgot all about it. And I felt something sort of urging me to go into the bathroom. So I went in, and there was the bath I'd forgotten all about. And there was Master Georgie in it, just about going down for the third time."

"Hey! Hey!" cried the bell-hop in urgent distress. "No third time for President Simpson!"

"Oh, no!" said Davies. "Life-guard to the rescue! I picked him out, dried him, and I put him in a box."

"Can you beat that?" cried the bell-hop. "Say, would it be all right for me to give him just a little bit of the cheese?"

"No. That's just demonstration cheese," said Davies. "Mice aren't so fond of cheese as most people think. He has his proper meal after the show. A balanced diet. Well, as I was saying, in a couple of days he was just as friendly as could be."

"Sure thing," said the bell-hop. "*He* knows who saved him."

"You know, a thing like that," said Davies, "it starts a fellow thinking. And what I thought of—I thought of the Steel Cat."

"You thought of that cat from seeing that mouse in that bath?" cried the bell-hop, overwhelmed by the processes of the scientific mind.

"I did," said Davies. "I owe it all to Georgie. Drew it

up on paper. Borrowed some money. Got a blue-print made; then this model here. And now we're going around together, demonstrating. Cleveland, Akron, Toledo—everywhere. Now here."

"Just about sweeping the country," said the bell-hop. "That's a real good-luck mouse, that is. He certainly ought to be called Simpson."

"Well, I'll tell you," said Davies. "It needs one really big concern to give the others a lead. Otherwise, they hang back. That's why we're in Chicago. Do you know who's coming here this afternoon? Mr. Hartpick of Lee and Waldron. They don't only manufacture; they own the outlets. Six hundred and fifty stores, all over the country! No middle-man, if you see what I mean. If they push it, oh, boy!"

"Oh, boy!" echoed the bell-hop with enthusiasm.

"He'll be here pretty soon," said Davies. "Three o'clock. By appointment. And Georgie'll show him the works."

"He don't never balk?" inquired the bell-hop. "He ain't afraid of being drowned?"

"Not Georgie," said Davies. "He trusts me."

"Ah, that's it!" said the bell-hop. "He trusts you."

"Of course I make the water luke-warm for him," said Davies. "All the same, it takes some character in a mouse to take the dip every time like that. Never mind—if he puts this deal over, we get him a little collar made."

"Mister," cried the bell-hop, "I want to see that mouse in that collar. You ought to get his photo taken. You could give it to anybody. They could send it back home to their families. Yes, sir, their folks 'ud sure be tickled to death to get a photo of that mouse in that collar."

"Maybe I will," said Davies, smiling.

"You do that thing, mister," said the bell-hop. "Well, I got to be getting. Goodbye, Georgie!" He went out, but at once re-opened the door. "All the same," he said, "if I had that mouse I sure would call him Simpson."

Davies, left alone, set out his apparatus to advantage, washed, even shaved, and powdered his face with talcum. When he had nothing more to do, he took out his billfold, and laid six dollar bills one by one on the top of the bureau, counting them out as if he had hoped to find there were seven. He added thirty-five cents from one pocket, and a nickel from another. "We've got to put it over this time," said he to the mouse, who was watching him brightly from the top of the box. "Never get down-hearted, Georgie! That gang of short-sighted, narrow-minded, small-town buyers, they just don't mean a thing. This fellow's the guy that counts. And he's our last chance. So do your stuff well, pal, and we'll be on top of the world yet."

Suddenly the telephone rang. Davies snatched it up. "Mr. Hartpick to see you," said the desk-clerk.

"Send Mr. Hartpick up right away," said Davies.

He stowed away the money, put Georgie back in his nest, and dried his moist palms on his handkerchief. He remembered, just as the tap came on the door, to banish the anxious expression from his face and put on a genial smile.

Mr. Hartpick was a square and heavy man, with fingers twice as thick as ordinary fingers, and the lower joints of them were covered with wiry, reddish hair.

"Mr. Hartpick," said Davies. "I certainly appreciate your coming up here like this."

"Long as I'm not wasting my time," returned Mr. Hartpick. "Let's see the goods. I got a rough idea from your letter."

Davies had set the box on the table. Now getting behind it, he attempted a persuasive, hearty, salesmanlike tone. "Mr. Hartpick, you know the old adage about the better mouse-trap. You've been good enough to beat a path to my door, and . . ."

"Show me an idea, and I'll beat a path to it," said Mr. Hartpick. "However nutty it sounds."

". . . and here," said Davies, "is the Steel Cat." With that he flung open the box.

"Selling name!" said Hartpick. "Might be able to use the name, anyway."

"Mr. Hartpick, the idea is this," said Davies, beginning to count off his points on his fingers. "More mice caught. More humanely. No mutilation of mice as with inferior traps. No mess. No springs to catch the fingers. Some women are just scared to death of those springs. No family disagreements, Mr. Hartpick. That's an important angle. I've gone into that angle psychologically."

His visitor paused in the rooting out of a back tooth, and stared at Davies. "Eh?" said he.

"Psychologically," said Davies. "The feminine angle, the masculine angle. Now, the wife doesn't generally like to see a cat playing with a mouse."

"She can poison 'em," said Hartpick.

"That's what *she* says," said Davies. "That's the woman angle. Poisoners throughout the ages. Lucrezia Borgia —lots of 'em. But a good many husbands are allergic to having their wives playing around with poison. I think a nation-wide poll would show most husbands prefer a cat. Remember, it was Nero—a man—fed the Christians to the lions. So that starts an argument. Besides, you've got to put a cat out, get it fed when on vacation."

"Any mice *we* catch, the missus flushes 'em down the toilet," said Mr. Hartpick, with a shrug.

"Feminine angle again," said Davies. "Cleopatra fed her slaves to the crocodiles. Only many women haven't the levelheadedness of Mrs. Hartpick to take a mouse out of a trap and get rid of it that way."

"Oh, I dunno," said Mr. Hartpick in tones of complete boredom.

"In one way this is the same sort of thing," said Davies, beginning to talk very fast. "Only more scientific and la-

bour-saving. See—I fill the glass jar here with water, luke-
warm water. It's glass in this demonstration model. In the
selling product it'd be tin to keep the cost down to what I
said in my letter. The frame needn't be chromium either.
Well, having filled it, I place it right here in position. Kindly observe the simplicity. I take a morsel of ordinary cheese,
and I bait the hook. If economy's the subject, a piece of
bread rubbed in bacon fat is equally effective. Now look!
Please look, Mr. Hartpick! I'll show you what the mouse
does. Come on, Georgie!"

"Live mouse, eh?" observed Hartpick, with a flicker of
interest.

"*Mus domesticus*, the domestic mouse," said Davies.
"Found in every home. Now watch him! He's found the
way in. See him go along that strip in the middle! Right to
the bait—see? His weight tilts the . . ."

"He's in!" cried Hartpick, his interest entirely regained.

"And the trap," said Davies triumphantly, "has automatically set itself for another mouse. In the morning you
just remove the dead ones."

"Not bad!" said Hartpick. "Gosh—he's trying to swim!
My friend, I think you may have something there."

"You know the old adage, Mr. Hartpick," said Davies,
smiling. "It's the better mouse-trap!"

"Like hell it is!" said Hartpick. "Pure nut, that's what
it is. But what I always say—there's a nut market for nut
inventions. Play up the humane angle . . . get the old
dames het up . . ."

"Gee, that's great!" said Davies. "I was beginning to
. . . Well, never mind! Excuse me! I'll just get him out."

"Wait a minute," said Hartpick, putting his heavy hand
on Davies' wrist.

"I think he's getting a bit tired," said Davies.

"Now look," said Hartpick, still watching the mouse.
"We've got our standard contract for notions of this sort.

Standard rate of royalties. Ask your attorney if you like; he'll tell you the same thing."

"Oh, that'll be all right, I'm sure," said Davies. "Just let me . . ."

"Hold on! Hold on!" said Hartpick. "We're talking business, ain't we?"

"Why sure," said Davies uneasily. "But he's getting tired. You see, he's a demonstration mouse."

Mr. Hartpick's hand seemed to grow heavier. "And what's this?" he demanded. "A demonstration—or what?"

"A demonstration? Yes," said Davies.

"Or are you trying to put something over on me?" said Hartpick. "How do I know he won't climb out? I was *going* to suggest you step around to the office in the morning, and we sign. If you're interested, that is."

"Of course, I'm interested," said Davies, actually trembling. "But. . ."

"Well, if you're interested," said Hartpick, "let him alone."

"But, my God, he's drowning!" cried Davies, tugging to free his wrist. Mr. Hartpick turned his massive face toward Davies for a moment, and Davies stopped tugging.

"The show," said Hartpick, "goes on. There you are! Look! Look! He's going!" His hand fell from Davies' arm. "Going! Going! Gone! Poor little bastard! Okay, Mr. Davies, let's say ten-thirty o'clock then, in the morning."

With that he strode out. Davies stood stock-still for a little, and then moved toward the Steel Cat. He put out his hand to take up the jar, but turned abruptly away and walked up and down the room. He had been doing this for some time when there came another tap on the door. Davies must have said "come in," though he wasn't aware of doing so. At all events the bell-hop entered, carrying a covered platter on a tray. "Excuse me," said he, smiling all over his face. "It's on the house, sir. Buttered corn-cob for Brother George Simpson!"

In the Cards

The Vascal System is the most reliable, the most up-to-date, and the most scientific method of foretelling the future by cards. It is true the operator cannot tell his own fortune, but that drawback seems to be common to all methods, and in every other way the successes of the Vascal System have been prodigious.

A wife, who studied a Vascal in her spare time, laid out the cards for her husband on the breakfast table. She revealed to him that he would be involved in an unfortunate collision, and suffer a severe jolt at the very least, if by any chance he drove his car home between three and five that afternoon. He now regularly desires his wife to lay out the cards for him, and never drives home before the hour she announces as propitious, with the result that he is almost the only person in the whole block who has not been severely jolted during the period in question.

A young girl, holder of a Grade A. Vascal Diploma,

was able to warn her still younger sister that she might that evening expect to lose something she had possessed all her life, through the agency of a tall, dark man, but though this would cause her some little distress at the out-set, it would in the end lead to lasting happiness and sat-isfaction. Sure enough, the young sister left for a blind date that evening in such haste that she forgot to lock the door behind her. A sneak thief, entering, took away her baby seed-pearl necklace, which was a tatty little number any-way, and she was successful in gypping the insurance peo-ple for at least three times its value, and bought that very same rhinestone clip which first attracted the attention of Mr. Jerry Horrabin, now her fiancé.

Mr. Brewster, when only half-way through the Vascal Course, laid out the cards for his wife, and told her she would be wrong to insist on going to the theatre that eve-ning, because the show would stink. She did insist, and it did stink.

Convinced by these, and by scores of other unsolicited testimonials, Myra Wilkins decided she could hardly do better than enroll as a student. Her idea was a big one; she meant to play her cards properly. She considered that sooner or later, among the numerous young men who would flock to consult her, she would strike one for whom she could forsee an enormous fortune arriving in the near future from some unsuspected source. She had no inten-tion of unsettling this happy young man by telling him what the future held, but thought rather she might warn him against any Queens of Hearts or Diamonds with whom he might be involved, and guide him gently toward a mar-riage with a high-grade Spade, for Myra was a brunette.

She graduated with the highest honours, and set up in a shadowy little nook in the West Forties, above the es-tablishment of a dancing instructress with whom she was acquainted. She figured that young men who suddenly took dancing lessons often had a great yearning to know what the future held for them, and she hoped these would form the nucleus of a clientele.

Myra had very little capital, and this was exhausted in furnishing her nook with bead-curtain, witch balls, images of Buddha, and similar junk, to create a convincing atmosphere for her visitors. She set her fee very low, in order to get the widest possible range of clients, and thus increase her chances of finding a future millionaire among them.

She shuffled and spread her greasy pack of cards, foretelling for innumerable insignificant young men the details of futures that were little better than pasts, which of course they would become one of these days. As far as the imminent fortune was concerned, the whole business was like a game of solitaire that never came out. The average future wealth of her clients was somewhere about the Two of Diamonds, and work and worry loomed up like a grand slam.

The months stretched on into years, and the dust lay thick upon the witch ball and the Buddha. Myra had nothing but her dreams of wealth, and these, like an old knife, were sharpened to a razor keenness. At last, late one afternoon, when the shadows were at their deepest, the stairway groaned beneath a heavy tread, and a hulking figure tried to get four ways at once through the bead-curtain that screened her alcove.

The new customer was an ugly one, and a more prosperous fortune teller would probably have sent him straight back to the Zoo. Myra, however, could not afford to pass up a dollar, so she wearily laid out her pack. The Two of Clubs frisked around fairly actively in the near foreground, in a context that gave it the significance of a copper's night stick. She saw he was in some danger of visiting a large building, full of men in strange clothes, but vaguer influences seemed to indicate a postponement of this necessity.

Suddenly she had to repress a cry that rose unbidden to her lips. It was as if his future, dark as a cannibal king, had smiled, and revealed a golden tooth. Vascal declared unequivocally that a handsome fortune was coming to this young man on the death of someone very near to him.

"Have you any relations?" she asked. "Any near relations, I mean, who are well off?"

"No," said he. "Not unless Uncle Joe soaked anything away before they got him."

"That must be it," she thought. "Well," she said aloud, "it doesn't matter much. There's no sign of any uncle leaving you anything. This card means money troubles. This means you're doublecrossed by a blonde. Looks like you're beaten up, too. I don't know what these two men in uniform are doing."

She continued prattling and laying out the cards, her mind working meanwhile like a three-ring circus. One ring was taken up with the story she was telling to her visitor, the second in reading the real future as it unfolded itself, and the third in wondering what she was going to do about it.

She stole another glance at her unattractive client. The fortune, as far as she could judge, appeared to be rather more than a million. Her visitor, on the other hand, seemed a good deal less than human. Myra had not expected romance, but there are things which make a nice girl hesitate, and he was one of them.

While she pondered she was still automatically laying out the cards. Suddenly her eyes brightened. She looked again. It was true. All her troubles were ended. The cards indicated, beyond the shadow of a doubt, that her client would die of a sudden, violent shock within a few months of inheriting the money. This made quite an eligible bachelor of him.

Myra at once began her manoeuvres. "You seem," said

she, "to be at the parting of the ways. One road leads to misery, poverty, sickness, despair, prison..."

"I'll take the other," said the young man.

"You show great powers of judgment," said Myra. "But I can tell you it is not as easy as all that. The other road, which leads to riches and happiness, can only be travelled hand in hand with a good woman. Do you know a good woman?"

"Oh, phooey!" said her client in dismay.

"What a pity!" said Myra. "Because if you did, and if she was dark, and not bad-looking, and wore a number-five shoe, all you'd have to do would be to marry her, and you'd be rich for life. Very rich. Look—here it is. Money, money, money—coming to you from someone very near to you. If you marry that girl, that is. Look—this card means you at the Waldorf. Look—this is you at Palm Beach. Here you are at Saratoga. Gosh! You've backed a big winner!"

"Say, lady," said her client. "What size shoe do *you* wear?"

"Well," said Myra with a smile, "I *can* squeeze into a four. But usually..."

"Look, baby," said he, taking her hand. "It's you and me. Like that. See?" With that he extended his other hand with two fingers crossed, as an emblem of connubial bliss.

Myra controlled a shudder. "When he's dead," thought she, "I'll have a million, and get me one of these young film stars, in order to forget!"

Soon afterwards they were married, and took a small shack in an unprepossessing part of Long Island. Lew appeared to have strong reasons for living in inconspicuous retirement. Myra commuted, and drudged harder than ever with her greasy pack of cards, in order to keep them both until death should them part, leaving her a rich widow.

As time went on, and the fortune still failed to materialize, she was bitterly reproached by her hulking husband, whose

stunted mind was as impatient as a child's, and who began to fear he had been married under false pretenses.
He was also a little sadistic.

"Maybe you ain't the right dame after all," said he,
pinching her black and blue. "Maybe you don't wear a
five. Maybe you wear a six. Gimme a divorce and let me
marry another dark dame. The money don't come along,
and you're black and blue anyway. I don't like a black and
blue dame. Come on, gimme a divorce."

"I won't," said she. "I believe marriages are made in
Heaven."

This would lead to an argument, for he claimed to have
evidence to the contrary. In the end his brutish wits would
be baffled; he would fling her to the ground with a curse,
and go into the back yard, where he would dig an enormously deep hole, into which he would gaze for a long
time, and then fill it in again.

This continued for some months, and Myra herself began to wonder if the Vascal System could possibly have
let her down. "Supposing he doesn't come into the money.
Here I am— Mrs. King Kong, and working for it! Maybe
I'd better get that divorce after all."

These defeatist notions came to a head one gloomy
winter evening as she trudged home from the ferry. Crossing the dark yard of the shack, she stumbled into another
of the enormous holes dug by her simple-minded husband.
"That settles it," thought she.

When she entered the squalid kitchen, Lew greeted her
with an unusual smile. "Hello, sweetie," said he. "How's
my darling wifie tonight?"

"Cut the sweetie stuff out," said she tersely. "And the
wifie stuff, too. I don't know what's bit you, you big gorilla,
but my mind's made up. You can have that divorce after
all."

"Don't talk like that, honey," said he. "I was only

joking. I wouldn't divorce you, not for all the world."

"No, but I'll divorce you," said she. "And quick."

"You gotta have grounds for that," observed her husband, with a frown.

"I've got 'em," said she. "When I show that judge where I'm black and blue, I'll get my divorce pronto. I'm sitting pretty."

"Listen," said he. "Have a look at this letter that came for you. Maybe you'll change your mind."

"Why did you open my letter?" said Myra.

"To see what was inside," said he with the utmost candor. "Go on, read it."

"Uncle Ezra," cried Myra, staring at the letter. "Left a million and a half dollars! All to me! Gee, the old geezer must have made good! But, say, the cards must have slipped up, then. It was supposed to come to you."

"Never mind," said Lew, stroking the back of her neck. "Man and wife are one, ain't they?"

"Not for long," cried Myra in triumph. "I'm rich! I'm free! Or I will be."

"And what shall *I* do?" asked her husband.

"Go climb a tree," said Myra. "You ought to be good at it."

"I thought you might say that," said he, clasping her firmly around the throat. "Gypped me a dollar for that fortune too, didn't you? Well, if you won't do right by me, the cards must. Death of someone very near to me—that's what they said, didn't they? So they was right after all!"

Myra had no breath left to pay testimony to the Vascal System, or to warn him of the sudden, violent shock that awaited him.

Youth from Vienna

oung men with open faces, red cheeks, and brown hair all behave in the same way, and nothing in the world could be more reasonable. They fall into a job or in love with the utmost readiness and enthusiasm. If oil and Lucille let them down, they pretty soon console themselves with steel and Estelle.

Other young men seem born for one passion only, or maybe two, one job and one woman. If both passions are there they run together, like railway lines; they are strong as steel, and as devoid of romantic colouring. They go on forever, and if one or other fails the results are apt to be serious. Young men of this sort are sometimes very tall, lean to emaciation, with skull-like faces, deep-set and rather burning eyes, and mouths either terribly sensitive or terribly cruel, it is hard to say which. If they are poor they look like nothing on earth; if they are rich they look like Lincoln in the rail-splitting period.

Such young men frequently devote themselves to science; sometimes to medicine. The research side appeals to them. If they are brilliant enough, and have money enough, they study under the world's greatest authorities. If they are interested in certain functions of the glands, this takes them to Lilley's or the Ford Foundation, but in the old days, in the days of our youth, it took them to Vienna.

Before going to Vienna, Humphrey Baxter went to dine with a married couple of his acquaintance. These, not having a word to say about glands, had provided themselves and him with tickets for the theatre. The play turned out to be a light romantic comedy which was also only very indirectly concerned with the glands. Humphrey sat regarding it with forebearance until, at a well-chosen moment early in the first act, Caroline Coates walked on to the stage. Humphrey leaned forward in his seat. The movement passed unnoticed because everyone else in the theatre also leaned forward.

It may well be asked why this considerable expenditure of human energy was exerted on account of a girl who only escaped being the worst actress in the world by being so very obviously not an actress at all. The fact is, Caroline Coates was a goddess. I think it was Alexander Woollcott who wrote: "To enquire as to her capacity as a mummer would be like asking, of a real actress, what is her prowess in trapeze work. Talent in this young woman would be a mere dilution, like soda in a highball; the less of it the better. When the divine Aphrodite walks on the stage, we do not wish her to perform like the divine Sarah."

Caroline had been put into a play by some fantastic mistake in the very year she left Bennington. It was at once apparent that she was one of those girls—there is only one in each generation—whose fortune it is to stand for something greater than talent and greater than beauty, and hence to be universally adored. The essential quality in

Caroline was her youth. It aroused in the beholder the
keenest, liveliest, and most exquisite sensation of pure
joy, which is the rarest and finest of all sensations. Besides
this, as I happen to know from private sources, this Caroline was a good-natured, well-bred, truthful, simple, kind,
merry, and unaffected girl, and she smelled like a florist's
shop, which is not always the case with goddesses.

Humphrey observed this phenomenon with a concentration he had hitherto reserved for sections of the obscurer
glands mounted on microscope slides. As they left the theatre he turned to his host and hostess. "Do you by any
chance happen to know that girl?" He saw the question
surprised them, so he continued without waiting for an
answer. "Or do you know anyone who knows her?"

"No, Humphrey. She lives in the great world. She's altogether beyond our class. She lives with people with the
names of buildings and breakfast foods. And when she's
not on the stage she's on yachts and polo fields and such
like, and we wouldn't know even this if we didn't read
the Sunday papers."

Humphrey was in no way dismayed by this answer. He
knew very well it needs only two or three introductions to
bridge the gap between oneself and anyone anywhere in
the world. He therefore asked everyone he knew, stating
his purpose very clearly, and before many weeks had
passed he found himself on a certain terrace, looking over
Long Island Sound, being curiously regarded by the name-
sakes of buildings and breakfast foods, and talking to Caroline Coates. He found her amazingly ignorant of the immense importance of recent researches into the functions
of the ductless glands, and it was a keen pleasure to him
to tell her of the great strides in human health and happiness and longevity that were promised by the new knowledge. You may imagine the effect of this gaunt, gauche,
hollow-cheeked young man, in altogether the wrong sort

of jacket, sitting among the well-groomed crowd, lecturing a popular idol of twenty-three on the effects of certain unsavoury juices upon horrible insane little girls, who wallowed in their own dung. Of course, she fell wildly, madly, head-over-heels in love with him, and before the month was out it was announced they were engaged to be married.

Certain buildings rocked a little; certain breakfast foods popped and crackled even more snappishly than usual. But in the main people felt that it showed what a fine girl Caroline was, and yet it was in no way a threat, because it couldn't possibly last. For example, what would happen when Humphrey went to Vienna, to work under the celebrated Vingleberg?

"I shall be there," said Humphrey, "for three years straight. And if I get out of that lab for forty-eight consecutive hours any time in those three years, it'll be because the place has burned down. I can't get back here to see you."

"Maybe I'll come over between shows."

"I wish you'd change your mind."

"Darling, I'd like to get married now, just as much as you would. But I simply *cannot* walk out on a new show and leave everyone flat. Besides . . ."

"You want just one more."

"Yes, I do. Maybe I could come when it's over."

"They say the damned thing'll run for years."

"It may fold up in six months. Humphrey, I know you think I'm just greedy to have a fuss made over me . . ."

"I've never suggested such a thing."

"But you think so. And if you didn't you'd be crazy. Because I am, just a bit. But if ever I feel it getting a *real* hold on me . . ."

"And what do you think a real hold feels like? Like this?"

This terminated the conversation just as they were on an important point, which was rather a pity. Humphrey's boat sailed; Caroline's play opened; she was more idolized than ever, and everyone expected her to fall in love with someone else. But the first year passed, and the second year passed, and the third year wore on, and Caroline was still faithful. There were two excellent reasons for this. She was so extremely fond of Humphrey, and she was so extremely fond of herself.

When the three years were over, Humphrey Baxter was on the boat, and the boat was docking. For some weeks he had had a picture in his mind of how Caroline would look when she greeted him, and this picture was so much with him that when he was reading the right-hand page of his book, it hovered like an illustration on the left. Because this was the 1920's, he had costumed her in silver fox and violets. He looked down on the landing stage, and saw plenty of fur and flowers, but he saw no sign of Caroline.

He went down the gangway and through the barrier. Two people came up and grasped his either hand. They were Dick and Stella Archer, the very people who had introduced him to Caroline in the first place, and thus established squatter's rights in the relationship. They held his hands and looked at him, and uttered the pleasantest and friendliest of greetings. Humphrey looked this way and that. "Where's Caroline?" said he.

The greetings were gone like a burst bubble. Three altogether greyer people stood, in an east wind, in the giant cheerlessness of the landing shed.

"Carrie couldn't come," said Stella.

There was no doubt at all that Humphrey's mouth was sensitive, extremely sensitive. "Is she ill?" he asked.

"Well . . ." said Dick.

"She's not ill," said Stella. "But she couldn't come.

Humphrey, get your things through, and we'll go to lunch at the Revestel, and we'll tell you about it."

"Very well," said Humphrey.

They went to the Revestel, where they had eaten so often in the old days. They ordered lunch. "I think it's about time you told me what it is," said Humphrey.

"Humphrey," said Stella, "you've got to understand."

It was perhaps, after all, rather difficult to decide whether Humphrey's mouth was very sensitive or a little cruel. "Go on," he said.

"We're old friends," said Dick. "we've known you and Carrie the hell of a long time, you know." Humphrey looked at Stella.

"Carrie's fallen in love," said Stella.

Humphrey closed his eyes. He might have been asleep, or dead. These skull-faced men can look astonishingly dead at times.

However, after a few long seconds he opened them again. Dick was saying something.

"When?" asked Humphrey of Stella.

"Last month, Humphrey. And almost at once it was too late to write."

"With whom?"

"He's quite a decent sort," said Dick. "In fact, it's Brodie."

"Alan Brodie the tennis champion," said Stella.

"National Singles eight times," said Dick. "The last six years in succession."

"He talks like that because he is scared and miserable," said Stella.

"Alan Brodie toured Europe the first year I was there," said Humphrey. "He came to Vienna. There was some kind of fuss at his hotel. A mob of women scuffling. It doesn't often happen over there."

"He's a popular idol," said Stella.

"Do you mean like Carrie?"

"He's a beautiful creature, Humphrey. He gives people the same sort of thrill that Carrie does. And the two of them together. . .!"

"She must have changed a great deal."

"Not really, Humphrey. I think she's realized what she's meant for."

"She's not meant for that sort of thing at all," said Humphrey, not loudly or emphatically, but with complete finality.

"Humphrey, you'll just have to wait till you see them together."

"I can wait," said Humphrey.

In New York it is seldom necessary to wait very long. Humphrey had a book to publish, and therefore a publisher, and therefore an invitation to lunch, and at a certain restaurant frequented by the people who are known to each other and to the gossip columnists. A woman for whose glands he would have paid a small fortune was sitting at the next table. Suddenly she uttered a sort of squeal. Then Humphrey, with a sensation that made of him a life-long opponent of electrocution, heard her utter the following words: "Oh, look! The lovers!"

Humphrey had no reason to turn his head. He saw other people looking in the direction of the door. He had time enough to observe, on faces horribly besmeared with success, a look of simple pleasure such as made even those faces seem quite attractive. Humphrey not only observed this, but reflected on it. "It must be a good thing," he thought, "that can so transfigure faces like these."

All this time the faces in question were turning, like searchlights converging on an unseen objective, as they followed Caroline and her Alan Brodie. Suddenly Humphrey found himself caught as it were in the full blaze, which meant she was close behind him. He turned, and they met.

Everything was very pleasant, good-humoured and gay. Caroline and Brodie sat down with Humphrey and his publisher; other people came to greet them and were induced to sit down also. Everyone talked a great deal except Humphrey, who was not expected to talk a great deal.

The truth is, Humphrey had a decision to make. He was prepared to believe this new impression of his, that Caroline's approaching marriage was a good thing. He wanted to believe it, as far at least as a man nearly insane with jealousy could be expected to. Indeed, as far as is consistent with that very human weakness, and with knowing deep down that the whole business was nothing but an imbecile, narcissistic delusion, it may be said he *did* believe it was a good thing, and that his impulse to kick it to pieces and drag Caroline out of it was barbarous, atavistic, and on no account to be indulged in.

Caroline helped him in this noble endeavour. Her every word and every look was exactly right for the occasion. She made no bones about asking the publisher to move so that she could sit next to Humphrey. She spoke to him with the utmost tenderness and concern. Her look appealed to him to understand. Her smile, and the glow about her, proclaimed that, even if he didn't understand, there are values and glories in life that must be held paramount. And when she looked at her lover it was perfectly plain what those glories were. "So be it!" thought Humphrey. "It's a good thing." And he joined with the rest of the circle in watching the happy pair, and the light that was reflected on the faces of the others was reflected on his own, though no doubt in a broken sort of way.

There then ensued a *divertissement* such as often happens in restaurants frequented by celebrities. Sallow young men arrived with cameras and flash bulbs; Caroline and Alan were required to get together and to take first this pose and then that. The process was more elaborate than the usual snapping of pictures in a restaurant, partly because an important magazine was involved, partly because there was a great deal of by-play with the manager and with people at other tables. It was the sort of thing that would be an awful pain in the neck unless you like that sort of thing, in which case of course it could be very gratifying.

Caroline was flushed, smiling, and immensely gratified when she sat down again beside Humphrey. It is in such states of happy excitement that words pop out that are utterly different from what one really means, words that anyone but a cold-blooded scientist would have the decency to ignore. "Well?" said Caroline. "What do you think of us?" She stopped herself suddenly, and looked at Humphrey in blushing embarrassment, for such words are not fit to be heard by a psychoanalyst, much less by a forsaken lover.

"I think," said Humphrey, "You're both charming, and I hope we'll be friends. Why not bring your young man around to see me?"

"We go off on Friday, you know," said Caroline, still confused. "There's not a chance in the world before then."

"But you will when you get back?"

"Of course. We'd love to. But it won't be for two months at least."

"I can wait," said Humphrey.

About a week before Alan and Caroline were due back from their honeymoon, Humphrey, who had been thinking a great deal while he waited, called up a man named Morgan. This was Albert Morgan, whose vocation it is to take the ambiguous and uncertain mutterings of scientists and transform them into clear, downright, and extremely thrilling articles for the weekly magazines. "Morgan," said Humphrey, "It's now three months since you last pestered me to give you some private information about Vingleberg's experiments."

Morgan explained why he had abandoned the attempt to get Humphrey to talk.

"If you think clams do that sort of thing," said Humphrey, "I can understand why your articles are so extremely inaccurate. But, anyway, I'm not a clam, and to prove it I'm calling you to say I've just had a letter from Vingleberg. It concerns some tests we started just before I left. Now, listen; I shall tell you nothing that's in the least confidential, because I know damned well I'll see it in all the headlines tomorrow morning. But if you want to hear about twenty very carefully chosen words . . ."

"Hold it!" said Morgan. "I'll be right over."

It was really remarkable what Morgan could do with twenty carefully chosen words. Or possibly Humphrey, being a guileless scientist, had been cozened into uttering twenty-five or even thirty. At all events the news broke, not in the headlines, it's true, but in very impressive articles on important pages, to the effect that stocky, balding, Viennese endocrinologist Vingleberg and Johns Hopkins' Humphrey Baxter had succeeded in isolating V.B. 282. And V.B. 282, it appeared, was neither more nor less than the glandular secretion that controls the aging of the tissues. And since we all have tissues, all aging, the promise in these paragraphs was seized on with avidity by all who read.

Meanwhile Caroline and Alan returned, and soon—very soon—they came round to Humphrey's apartment for a drink. He received them with the utmost cordiality, and asked them a thousand questions about themselves, all of which they answered fully and frankly, like people who had nothing to conceal. They were so anxious to give him all the information that might be of interest to him that neither of them observed his reactions very closely. Had they done so, they might have noticed that at certain answers, particularly from Caroline, his cruel and sensitive mouth tightened itself with that painful satisfaction with which a pathologist might regard the slide which tells him that his difficult diagnosis was right in every particular, and his best friend needs immediate surgery.

I do not wish to convey that the conversation of the newly married pair was entirely egotistical. Before a single hour had passed Caroline herself broached a new subject. "Humphrey, dear," she said, "we hear you've become famous. Is it true?"

"It's true if you've heard it," he replied. "That's what fame is."

"But is it true about eternal youth and all that?"

"My dear girl," said he, "I think you've got all the scientists beaten as far as eternal youth is concerned. You looked eighteen when I met you, and you were twenty-three. Now you're twenty-six . . ."

"Twenty-seven last week, Humphrey."

"And you still look eighteen."

"But I shan't always."

"I can't say I've noticed myself slowing up any," said Brodie. "But some of these youngsters from the West Coast . . ." He shook his head with the melancholy always induced in tennis players by a mention of the West Coast.

Humphrey ignored this interjection. His eyes were fixed on Caroline. "Of course you won't be young always," said he. "I imagine you'd hardly want to. Those people you see around, who never seem to mature, they belong to a particular frigid, inhibited, narcissistic type—they're in love with themselves; they can't love anyone else; therefore they don't really live; therefore they don't get any older."

"Yes, yes. But this stuff you've discovered . . .?"

"Oh!" said Humphrey. And smiling, he shook his head.

"It's not true then?" cried Caroline. Her disappointment would have moved a heart of stone.

"I told you it was all a lot of hooey," said Brodie.

"These journalists always omit to mention the snags," said Humphrey.

"And they wrote as if you'd really truly discovered it," lamented Caroline.

"It's completely untrue," said Humphrey. "It was Vingleberg, almost entirely."

"You mean it *has* been found," said Caroline, her face lighting up again.

"I didn't say so, to the newspaper men," said Humphrey. "However, they chose to take it that way." His tone suddenly became very cold and hard. "Now I want both of you to understand this. This is something no one in the world must know about."

"Oh, yes! Yes!"

"Do you understand that, Brodie?"

"You can rely on me."

"Very well," said Humphrey. He sat very still for a moment, as if conquering some final reluctance. Then he rose abruptly and went out of the room.

Caroline and Alan didn't even glance at each other. They sat there looking at the door through which Humphrey had disappeared, expecting him to return with a crucible or an alembic at the very least. Instead, he came back almost immediately, dangling a piece of very ordinary string.

He smiled at his guests. He gave the string a jerk or two, and in through the door, leaping, frisking, clapping its paws in hot pursuit, came a kitten. Humphrey enticed it right over to where Caroline was sitting, made it jump once or twice. Then he picked it up and handed it to her.

"It's sweet," said Caroline. "But . . ."

"It had a birthday last week," said Humphrey. "Five years old."

Caroline dropped the kitten as if it were hot. "I hope people will be able to overcome that sort of instinctive prejudice," said Humphrey, picking it up again and handing it back to her. "Before very long the world will have to get used to this sort of thing."

"But, Humphrey," said Caroline, quite agitated, "it's a dwarf or a midget or something."

"I assure you," said Humphrey, "that kitten is as normal as any kitten you've ever seen in your life."

"But what will happen to it? Will it go on forever?" And, as Humphrey shook his head: "Will it go off bang, or crumble into dust or something?"

"Almost surely heart failure," said Humphrey. "But only after forty years of glorious youth. That's two hundred for a human being. But remember this, both of you . . ." He paused impressively.

"Yes? Yes?"

"I went to Vienna," said Humphrey very slowly and clearly, "exactly three years and four months ago. This kitten is five years old. So you see it's Vingleberg's discovery."

"Oh, yes. Yes, of course. But they said in the papers it was human beings," said Caroline.

"I was helping Vingleberg adapt it to human beings."

"And you succeeded?"

"Remember you have promised not to mention this to a living soul. Yes, we succeeded. To a limited extent, that is."

Alan spoke in a voice at once impatient and business-like. "Mr. Baxter, you said before very long the world . . ."

"Humphrey," said Humphrey with a friendly smile.

"Yes—Humphrey. But . . . but *when?*"

"It's a question of finding a new source for the extract," said Humphrey. "Or possibly making it synthetically, though I doubt we'll ever do that. I should say thirty years. With luck—twenty."

"Ah!" said Caroline. "I thought you meant now."

"To get this stuff," cried Humphrey, "we have to perform an extremely delicate operation, which unfortunately is fatal to the animal we get it from. So it's terribly difficult."

"What animal?" asked Alan.

"It's quite a common one," said Humphrey. "Man."

"Oh!"

"I think we've discovered another source, but it'll take years to test, and more years to manufacture an adequate supply. That's the point. That's why I swore you to secrecy. All merry hell would break loose on this planet if people knew there was just *some* in existence, being kept for the privileged few."

"There *is* some then?" said Caroline.

"The extract has been made," said Humphrey, "in very odd circumstances, about which I'll tell you exactly nothing—it has been made three times."

"Three!" exclaimed Alan, as if impressed by the coincidence, because there were three people right there in the room.

"I took one," said Humphrey with a smile.

"And the others?" cried Caroline.

"Fortunately one dose is enough," continued Humphrey. "I don't want to bore you with technicalities, but this is extremely interesting. This secretion actually changes the functions of two distinct glands, neither of them the gland from which we originally extracted it. Now . . ."

"But, Humphrey dear, what happened to the other two doses?"

"Vingleberg took one of them. He's sixty-eight and as

ugly as a monkey. He'll stay sixty-eight, and stay ugly, for the next two hundred years."

"For God's sake!" said Alan bitterly.

"And the third?" asked Caroline.

"Caroline, my dear," said Humphrey, "I brought that back with me. I needn't tell you why." As he spoke he unlocked a little drawer in his desk. "Here it is," he said, holding an ordinary phial full of a colourless liquid. "Life, youth, love, for nearly two hundred years! Probably more, because in that time we'll have found out all sorts of things. I nearly poured this away, the day I landed."

"Oh, Humphrey, I . . . what can I say?"

"I don't feel that way any longer," said Humphrey. "In fact, I didn't from the very first moment I met you both. So I'd like you to have this, if you'd care for it. Call it a sort of belated wedding present. Here you are. To both of you."

He held out the phial and, finding two hands extended to receive it, he brought them together. "But you do solemnly swear never to say a word?" he asked.

"I do," said Caroline.

"I do," said Alan.

"It sounds quite like the wedding service," said Humphrey with a smile. He laid the phial in their joined hands. "But, of course, it isn't. Well, there it is, for both of you."

"We shall take half each," said Caroline.

"A hundred years apiece!" said Alan.

"Here! Wait a minute! Hold on!" said Humphrey. "I'm afraid I've misled you. I suppose one works on a subject for years, and gets so close to it, one forgets other people don't know the first thing. There was an interesting example of that . . ."

"*Why* can't we take half each?" said Caroline rather loudly.

"Because, my dear, glands don't understand arithmetic.

A half-changed gland won't give you half two hundred years of youth and beauty. Oh, no! Caroline, I remember the very first time I met you I told you what people were like when certain glands were deranged."

"You mean those awful idiots?"

"Exactly. This is one dose here, and one dose only. It can be drunk in one gulp; it's got a little flavour, but hardly unpleasant. It's simple, but it's dangerous if you fool with it—like dynamite. Keep it as a curiosity. It's no use; it isn't pretty; it's a wedding present. At least it's unique."

"Well, thank you, Humphrey. Thank you very, very much."

Thereupon Caroline and Alan went home, where they set this interesting little bottle on the mantelpiece. They then took a long look at it, and a long look at each other. Had it been possible they might have taken a long look in that enormous mirror, the public eye, before which— almost in which—their lives were lived, and in which they were the perfect lovers.

"You must take it right away," said Alan. "I'll get you a glass of water to drink afterwards."

"I shall do no such thing. Alan, I want you to drink it."

"Darling, come here and look in the glass. Do you see? I'm being perfectly selfish. I want you to be like that for-ever "

"I can see you, too, Alan. And that's how you've got to be."

Some compliments were exchanged. They were sincere and enthusiastic, and became more so. In the end the lit-tle bottle was entirely forgotten. But the next morning it was still there.

Alan and Caroline were as determined as ever, each that the other should drink the precious potion. It is im-possible to say exactly what it was in their protestations that suggested that each of them may have thought a little about it during the night.

"We can't spend the rest of our lives doing a sort of 'After you, Alphonse,'" said Caroline. "I swear to you; I cross my heart and hope to die—I *want* you to take it. Now please do."

"Get this straight once and for all," said Alan. "You're going to take it, and I'm not. I'm going to be like that fellow what's his name who fell in love with—you know—the goddess."

"But darling, think of your overhead smash!"

"What's wrong with it? Are you trying to tell me it's not holding up?"

"Of course not. It's wonderful how it holds up. Everyone says so. But you'll be up against that awful boy from California in August, you know."

"I can take care of that pip-squeak without any monkey gland," said Alan. "I must say I'm rather suprised you think I can't."

"I don't think you can't," said Caroline. "But . . ."

"Oh, there's a 'but' to it!"

"But you *are* six years older than I am."

"Oh, listen! A man's got ten years at least on a woman."

"Not every woman. It's true some women like going around with men old enough to be their fathers." She studied him thoughtfully. "I think you'll look awfully distinguished with grey hair."

Alan looked unhappily into the mirror. Then he looked at Caroline. "I can't imagine *you* with grey hair. So, you see, if I *did* drink it, just to please you . . ."

"I wish you would," cried Caroline, whose basic goodness and kindness are a matter of record. "Alan, I *won't* see you get old, and ugly, and ill . . . and die. I'd rather it was me. Truly I would. Rather than have you die and be left without you."

"And that goes for me," said Alan, with just as much emphasis, but yet in a way that caused her to look at him searchingly.

"But you'd love me?" she asked, "even if I did get old? Wouldn't you?" Then, giving him no time at all: "Or would you?"

"Carrie, you know I would."

"No, you wouldn't. But I would you."

"If that's what you think," said Alan, "you'd better take it yourself. It's obvious. Go on—take it. And let *me* get old."

"I wish Humphrey had never given us the wretched stuff!" cried Caroline. "Let's pour it down the sink. Come on! Right now!"

"Are you crazy?" cried Alan, snatching the phial from her hand. "The only bottle in the whole world! From what Baxter said, a man died for the sake of what's in that bottle."

"And he'd be awfully hurt if we threw it away," murmured Caroline.

"To hell with *him*," said Alan. "But after all it's a wedding present."

So they left it right there on the mantelpiece, which is a good place for a wedding present, and their wonderful life went on.

The only trouble was, they were both becoming age-conscious to a degree which gradually amounted to an obsession. Caroline became extremely exacting at the beauty parlour. It was pathetic to see Alan hovering in front of the mirror, trying to decide if that was only a sun-bleached hair on his temple, or a grey one. Caroline watched him, and in the mirror he saw her watching him. They looked at themselves, and they looked at each other, and whoever looks in that way can always find something. I shall not describe the afternoon when Alan's birthday cake was brought in with the wrong number of candles on it.

However, they both tried desperately to be brave about it, and Caroline might have succeeded.

"It won't be so bad," she said. "After all, we can grow old together."

"A nice old couple!" said Alan. "Silver hair, plastic dentures . . .!"

"Even so, if we still love each other," maintained Caroline.

"Sure! On a porch! With roses!"

It was that very night, in the middle of the night, Alan was suddenly awakened. Caroline had turned the light on, and was bending over him, looking at him.

"What is it? What's the matter? What are you looking at me for?"

"Oh, I was just looking at you."

Most men, if they woke up in the middle of the night and found Caroline bending over them, would think they must have died and gone to Heaven, but Alan took it very peevishly. He seemed to think that she was examining him for enlarged pores, deepening wrinkles, sagging tissues, blurring lines, and other signs of incipient decay, and she found it hard to make a convincing denial, because she had been doing exactly that.

"I've a good mind to take that stuff and swallow it down right now," said Alan in a rage.

"Yes, it's just the sort of thing you *would* do," retorted Caroline.

It will be seen that a situation had developed in which almost anything that either of them did would be certain to offend the other.

Things went on like this until the last day of the tournament at Forest Hills. It was on this day that Alan encountered the boy-wonder from California. He saw, as he had seen before, that the stripling had a game very noticeably lacking in finesse. He had tremendous force and a great deal of speed, but no finesse at all. His reflexes were uncanny; it was impossible to fool him by a change of pace. But reflexes are one thing; finesse is quite another. "Why the hell do I keep thinking about finesse?" said Alan to himself before the first set was over. When the last set was done, the answer was there as big as the scoreboard. The stringy boy from California put his hand on Alan's shoulder as they walked off the court together. To a man who has been played to a stand-still, the hand of the victor is a heavy load to carry.

Nevertheless Alan took his defeat very well. All through the evening he firmly discounted the alibis that his friends invented for him. "The son of a bitch just plain battered me off the court," said he with a rueful grin. Even when Caroline explained to everyone how tense and nervous he'd been lately, he showed no slightest sign of the rage and desolation which howled within him.

That night, in spite of his aching weariness, he lay awake long after Caroline was sound asleep. At last he got up and crept with infinite caution into the living-room. He took up the little phial, unscrewed the top, and drained the contents at a single gulp. He went to the little faucet behind the bar, and refilled the phial with water. He was about to replace the cap when a thought struck him, and he looked about among the bottles until he settled on some bitters. He added several drops to the water in the phial, and then put it back on the mantelpiece. Over the mantelpiece was a mirror; Alan took a long look in this mirror, and he smiled.

Now it happened that at this time Caroline was playing the part of a girl who was encumbered with an amiable fool of a younger sister. The girl who played this sister walked out in a fit of temper, and a new girl had to be found in a hurry. One of the producers, without even the excuse of a villainous motive, but out of sheer sottish good nature, nominated the niece of a friend of his. The girl had to be sent for and looked at, and at once everyone saw that she was the crazy kid sister in person, for she was nothing more or less than a long-limbed, wide-mouthed, dazzle-eyed version of Caroline in slang, so to speak, with a grin instead of a smile, and a stumble instead of Caroline's wonderful walk; and instead of that look of spring morning joy that beamed from Caroline's face the newcomer had an expression of slap-happy bewilderment, as if the world was playing a succession of highly diverting tricks on her.

Everyone thought she was charming, and everyone approved the choice, Caroline included. The first time she went on, Caroline stood in the wings to see how she took to it. She could see just by looking at her back that the girl lit up as she stepped into view of the audience. It hardly amounted to a premonition, but she stepped forward and watched attentively as the girl blundered through the agreeable little routine that the part called for. It was a scene that always drew a pleasant round of applause. This time, as the girl came off the stage: "My God!" thought Caroline, "that's *my* applause."

She was perfectly right. The sound that was mounting out front was of a timbre discernibly more feverish, and with more of the humming undertone of the human voice in it, than the applause that rewards a good piece of acting. This was the sound made by an audience that has fallen in love. Caroline knew it well. She had heard it every night for a good many years, and she heard it that same night when, a few minutes later, she made her own entrance. But, rightly or wrongly, it now seemed to her that a certain amount was missing, and to Caroline's ear that amount was exactly equal to what had been bestowed on the gangling youngster.

In the passage outside her dressing room a small group was listening with new respect to the producer who had found the girl. "What do you think of her, Carrie?" he asked amiably as Caroline approached.

"I think she's a darling," replied Caroline.

"Carrie," said he, "she's the biggest discovery since you walked on that night in Newport."

Caroline smiled and entered her dressing room. Through the half-open door she heard someone say, "But do you think she'll make an actress?"

"Let me tell you, my boy," returned the fortunate discoverer. "I was out front all through the second act. Now, when you're talking to that kid the way I'm talking to you, what is she? Just a kid. But, my boy, when she walks on the stage—she's YOUTH. The crazy, lovely, dizzy, unlucky, stumble-bum youth of this day and age, my boy! And she tears your goddam heart out. So I don't give a hoot in hell if she ever learns to act. In fact I hope to God she never will. I've put on as many good shows as anyone else over the last fifteen years, and I remember what Wolcott Gibbs said about some dame quite a time ago. 'When youth and beauty walk on the stage,' he said, 'to hell with Sarah Bernhardt.'"

Caroline closed her door.

That night she couldn't get home fast enough. She felt she needed Alan. She felt like a wounded animal that instinctively seeks some bitter herb, the one thing that will cure it. She knew, as it were, the flavour of what she needed from him: harsh, astringent, healing to the bruised ego; the acrid emanation of . . . which of his qualities. "Anyway, it's there," she thought in the elevator. "It's there in his ugly smile; in the way he . . ." Here she stopped short. "Alan's smile? Ugly? I'm certainly good and mixed up. Never mind! At least I'm home."

She went in, and the place was empty. The emptiness of one's own home at midnight, when one has fled there for comfort, is an abomination and an injury, and Caroline took it as such, though it was the most ordinary thing in the world for Alan to go out while she was at the theatre, and to get home after she did. Recently, he had done so almost every night, and she hadn't given it a thought. But tonight she was injured and angry.

She walked from one room to another, looked at the largest photograph of Alan, and felt dissatisfied with his smile. "It's not mature," she said. She looked in the glass and tried, with considerable difficulty, a smile of her own. This she found even more unsatisfactory, but for the opposite reason. "I may as well face it," said this valetudinarian of twenty-seven, "I'm old." She stood there watching her reflection as she drew down the corners of her mouth, and in the stillness and silence of the apartment she could feel and almost hear the remorseless erosion of time. Moment after moment particles of skin wore away; hair follicles broke, splintered, and decayed like the roots of dead trees. All those little tubes and miles of thread-like channels in the inner organs were silting up like doomed rivers. And the glands, the all-important glands, were choking, clogging, abrading, falling apart. And she felt her marriage was falling apart, and Alan would be gone, and life would be gone.

Her eyes were already on the little phial. She took it up, she unscrewed the top, and she drank the contents. She was very calm and controlled as she went to the bathroom and refilled the phial with water, and added a little quinine to give it the bitter taste. She put the phial back in its place, eyed her reflection again as she did so, and called herself by a name so extremely coarse and offensive that it is almost unbelievable that so charming a girl as Caroline could have uttered the word.

When Alan returned that night, she did not ask him where he had been, but overwhelmed him with tenderness, feeling of course as if she had unspeakably betrayed him, and was going to desert him, and go away into an endless springtime, where he could never follow her.

This mood continued over the weeks that followed, and should, one would say, have been matched by an equal remorseful tenderness in Alan, but things are not always as they should be. The fact is, the only inconvenience he suffered from his little secret concerning the phial, was the thought of being married to an aging woman, which makes a man feel like a gigolo.

So time, which was the cause of all this trouble, went on, and both Caroline and Alan, secure in imperishable youth, saw in the other, as through a magnifying glass, more and more of the hastening signs of decay. Alan began to feel very much ill-used. He felt that Caroline at the very least should have provided herself with a younger sister. One night he dropped into the theatre and discovered that, in a manner of speaking, she had done so.

Soon after this Alan began to win his matches again, and by the same comfortable margin as before. The experts all noted that he had entirely regained his old fire and aggressiveness, and they confidently expected him to win back the championship the following year.

All this time, Humphrey, being trained to await patiently the outcome of his experiments, waited patiently. It may be asked how he knew that both of them would take the potion. The answer is, he was completely indifferent as to whether both of them took it, or one of them, or neither. It was his opinion that a good marriage would survive the

phial, and a bad one would be wrecked by it, whichever
way it happened.

Very late one evening his doorbell rang three or four
times in rapid succession. He raised his eyebrows, and hurried to open it. There stood Caroline. Her hat, hair, dress,
and all the rest of it looked just as usual; yet she gave the
impression of having run all the way. Humphrey gave her
his ugly smile, and, saying never a word, he led her through
into the living-room, where she sat down, got up, walked
about a little, and at last turned to him. "I've left Alan,"
she said.

"These things happen," said Humphrey.

"It's your fault," she said. "Not really yours, perhaps,
but it was that horrible stuff you gave us. Humphrey, I'm
the lowest, the most despicable rat; I'm such a hypocrite
and traitor as you can't ever imagine."

"I very much doubt it," said Humphrey. "I suppose this
means you drank the stuff."

"Yes, behind his back,"

"And what did he say when you told him?"

"I haven't told him, Humphrey. I wouldn't dare. No.
I filled the thing up with water and put some quinine in
it, and..."

"Tell me why you put quinine in it."

"To give it that bitter taste."

"I see. Go on."

"Oh, I felt so horrible afterwards. I can't tell you how
awful I felt. I tried, I tried so hard to love him more than
ever to make up for it. But you can't make up for a thing
like that. Besides..."

"Yes?"

"Oh, it just ruined everything, in all sorts of ways. I
suppose I've been watching him—you can't help watching
a person who's aging in front of your eyes. And when you

watch anyone like that you see all sorts of things wrong
with them. And I know he's felt it because he . . . well, he
hasn't been very nice lately. But it's my fault, because I
don't love him any more. Maybe I never did." With that
she began to weep, which showed a very proper feeling.
"Don't tell me," said Humphrey, "that you don't want to
be young forever."

"Not if I can't ever love anyone again."

"There's always yourself, you know."

"It's cruel of you to say that. It's cruel even if it's true."

"It's lonely being like this," said Humphrey. "But that's
the price we pay for our little immortality. You, and me,
and of course old Vingleberg. We're animals of a new species. There's us"—his hand swept a little circle around
them—"and the rest of the world." They sat for quite a
long time in silence, alone together in this imaginary circle. The sensation was not at all unpleasant. "Of course,"
added Humphrey, "I used to think we were like that for
quite a different reason."

"If it could . . . Oh, but I'm so worthless! I let you
down. Now I've let him down."

"The first was a mistake. It can be put right."

"But not the second. That we can't live with."

"Yes, I think so. You say the stuff tasted bitter? There's
no mistake about *that*, I suppose?"

"No, oh, no, it was very bitter."

"You see, that has far-reaching implications. *I* used
nothing but ordinary salt in the water."

lan Austen, as nervous as a kitten, went up certain dark and creaky stairs in the neighbourhood of Pell Street, and peered about for a long time on the dim landing before he found the name he wanted written obscurely on one of the doors.

He pushed open this door, as he had been told to do, and found himself in a tiny room, which contained no furniture but a plain kitchen table, rocking chair, and an ordinary chair. On one of the dirty buff-coloured walls were a couple of shelves, containing in all perhaps a dozen bottles and jars.

An old man sat in the rocking chair, reading a newspaper. Alan, without a word, handed him the card he had been given. "Sit down, Mr. Austen," said the old man very politely. "I am glad to make your acquaintance."

"Is it true," asked Alan, "that you have a certain mixture that has——er——quite extraordinary effects?"

"My dear sir," replied the old man, "my stock in trade

is not very large—I don't deal in laxatives and teething mixtures—but such as it is, it is varied. I think nothing I sell has effects which could be precisely described as ordinary."

"Well, the fact is——" began Alan.

"Here, for example," interrupted the old man reaching for a bottle from the shelf. "Here is a liquid as colourless as water, almost tasteless, quite imperceptible in coffee, milk, wine, or any other beverage. It is also quite imperceptible to any known method of autopsy."

"Do you mean it is a poison?" cried Alan, very much horrified.

"Call it cleaning fluid if you like," said the old man indifferently. "Lives need cleaning. Call it a spot-remover. 'Out, damned spot!' Eh? 'Out, brief candle!'"

"I want nothing of that sort," said Alan.

"Probably it is just as well," said the old man. "Do you know the price of this? For one teaspoonful, which is sufficient, I ask five thousand dollars. Never less. Not a penny less."

"I hope all your mixtures are not as expensive," said Alan apprehensively.

"Oh, dear, no," said the old man. "It would be no good charging that sort of price for a love potion, for example. Young people who need a love potion very seldom have five thousand dollars. Otherwise they would not need a love potion."

"I'm glad to hear you say so," said Alan.

"I look at it like this," said the old man. "Please a customer with one article, and he will come back when he needs another. Even if it *is* more costly. He will save up for it, if necessary."

"So," said Alan, "you really do sell love potions?"

"If I did not sell love potions," said the old man, reaching for another bottle, "I should not have mentioned the other matter to you. It is only when one is in a position to oblige that one can afford to be so confidential."

"And these potions," said Alan. "They are not just—just—er——"

"Oh, no," said the old man. "Their effects are permanent, and extend far beyond the mere casual impulse. But they include it. Oh, yes, they include it. Bountifully. Insistently. Everlastingly."

"Dear me!" said Alan, attempting a look of scientific detachment. "How very interesting!"

"But consider the spiritual side," said the old man.

"I do, indeed," said Alan.

"For indifference," said the old man, "they substitute devotion. For scorn, adoration. Give one tiny measure of this to the young lady—its flavour is imperceptible in orange juice, soup, or cocktails—and however gay and giddy she is, she will change altogether. She'll want nothing but solitude, and you."

"I can hardly believe it," said Alan. "She is so fond of parties."

"She will not like them any more," said the old man. "She'll be afraid of the pretty girls you may meet."

"She'll actually be jealous?" cried Alan in a rapture. "Of me?"

"Yes, she will want to be everything to you."

"She is, already. Only she doesn't care about it."

"She will, when she has taken this. She will care intensely. You'll be her sole interest in life."

"Wonderful!" cried Alan.

"She'll want to know all you do," said the old man. "All that has happened to you during the day. Every word of it. She'll want to know what you are thinking about, why you smile suddenly, why you are looking sad."

"That is love!" cried Alan.

"Yes," said the old man. "How carefully she'll look after

you! She'll never allow you to be tired, to sit in a draught, to neglect your food. If you are an hour late, she'll be terrified. She'll think you are killed, or that some siren has caught you."

"I can hardly imagine Diana like that!" cried Alan.

"You will not have to use your imagination," said the old man. "And by the way, since there are always sirens, if by any chance you *should*, later on, slip a little, you need not worry. She will forgive you, in the end. She'll be terribly hurt, of course, but she'll forgive you—in the end."

"That will not happen," said Alan fervently.

"Of course not," said the old man. "But, if it does, you need not worry. She'll never divorce you. Oh, no! And, of course, she herself will never give you the least grounds for —not divorce, of course—but even uneasiness."

"And how much," said Alan, "how much is this wonderful mixture?"

"It is not so dear," said the old man, "as the spot remover, as I think we agreed to call it. No. That is five thousand dollars; never a penny less. One has to be older than you are, to indulge in that sort of thing. One has to save up for it."

"But the love potion?" said Alan.

"Oh, that," said the old man, opening the drawer in the kitchen table, and taking out a tiny, rather dirty-looking phial. "That is just a dollar."

"I can't tell you how grateful I am," said Alan, watching him fill it.

"I like to oblige," said the old man. "Then customers come back, later in life, when they are rather better off, and want more expensive things. Here you are. You will find it very effective."

"Thank you again," said Alan. "Goodbye."

"*Au revoir*," said the old man.